IMPETUS

A NOVEL

IMPETUS

A NOVEL

S.J. LEONE

proving press

Book Design & Production:
Columbus Publishing Lab
www.ColumbusPublishingLab.com

Paperback ISBN: 978-1-63337-959-6
Hardcover ISBN: 978-1-63337-966-4
E-book ISBN: 978-1-63337-960-2

Printed in the United States of America
1 3 5 7 9 10 8 6 4 2

For Cheryl:
I loved you before I knew you
I love you more every day

And for Willow:
The cat saved my life

AUTHOR'S NOTE

Inserted between most of this book's chapters, following Chapter 9, are headlines reporting actual shootings. They are taken from various media all over the United States.

PROLOGUE

JIMMY STILL CAME HERE OFTEN, especially, as now, in the very early morning. He had left his house when dawn was peering over the horizon, grabbing his hydration pack and a bag of granola on his way out. He hated the smell and taste of coffee and was always glad that morning ritual didn't slow him down. The screen door slammed as he left, but he paid no attention. There was no one in the house to be awakened by the noise, no neighbor near enough to be disturbed.

By the time he arrived at the trailhead, the morning light showed the way into the woods, but the woods still hid their secrets in the shadows. But he knew the secrets. Knew where the muskrats burrowed into the muddy stream banks, where the eagle pair nested year-round, and the nearby river where they fished.

Jimmy had been coming here since he was a child. Sometimes with his father, when they hunted these woods. Always now with Hank, his rescued mutt, his constant companion. First as a pup, now full grown, spry and anxious to get on the trail.

They set off, Hank trotting ahead, Jimmy setting a steady pace, stabbing the ground with the walking stick he held in his right hand. He didn't need it, but he loved its smooth, wooden texture. The recent light rains had left the trail slightly soft, and the fall leaf drop had just begun. He breathed in the dank, mucky smell—perfume to him.

They came to the first rise. Jimmy strode easily, his tall, lanky frame eating up the slope. His long brown hair reaching his shoulders and flowing behind him, his boots gripping the dark earth, rustling the fallen leaves, kicking them up where they were the thickest.

This morning, he wore his briar pants—he never knew when he and Hank might veer off trail in search of adventure—and a quilted sweatshirt underneath his color-block anorak. They would be out here for hours this morning, and he could peel layers as he went. He reveled in these chill mornings that made their way into bright, warming afternoons.

Jimmy and Hank descended into a narrow glade, then started up the next rise. Here it was all pine and fir and spruce trees, their dropped needles padding the trail, the evergreens' scents filling the air. It was "trail quiet" this morning, the way he loved it, and, now, needed it. He heard no other people on the trail, no other dogs. Instead, the trail symphony was performed by singing morning birds, rustling rodents, deer slipping parallel to the trail.

In the past, he had been convinced by Alice to bring his guitar when they walked the trail together. It would be slung awkwardly over his back and slap against his butt as they moved, but it pleased her and so it pleased him. They would stop where there was a favorite vista and, although he almost felt that it was blasphemous to disturb the woods, he would play for her, and she would accompany him with her honey-sweet voice. Then they would gaze over the valley below, watch the eagles dive and strike and splash up with their dinner. Jimmy longed for those days. Would he ever feel that way again?

He no longer brought the guitar along; it carried too many memories that he tried to avoid.

Hank had gone off the trail ahead, snuffling in the undergrowth for some irresistible treasure, causing ground thrushes to burst and flap to safety and squirrels to race deeper into the woods. Passing by Hank, he quickened his pace.

"Come on, boy," he called. "Hank, let's go."

Hank fell dutifully in beside him and they attacked the next incline. His joy in the woods in the past had always been to inhale the peace and luxuriate in the scents and sounds. Now, his need was to exhaust himself, leave himself panting and empty of energy, too tired to allow his mind to ruminate.

Alice would not be with him again. She was gone.

And she would never be coming back.

PART ONE
(SIX YEARS EARLIER)

1.

JIMMY

ON A TYPICAL SATURDAY NIGHT, they sat at the corner table at Pietro's Pizzeria. Red-and-white checked tablecloths, Chianti bottle candles, dripping with white wax rivulets. The waiter weaved through the crowded dining area, set the pizza stand down, and placed the extra-large pizza with extra cheese and extra pepperoni in the middle of their table. Jimmy sat next to his longtime girlfriend Alice and across from his twin sister Jenna and her right-now-steady but frequently on-again, off-again boyfriend Mike.

Jimmy topped off everyone's beer glass from the pitcher they were sharing. He tilted the glasses just so, finishing the golden ale with a thin white head. "A thing of beauty," he announced when he had finished.

Three of them grabbed a slice, folded it haphazardly, and went to work. Jimmy cut his slice with a knife and then used a fork to eat each piece.

"Man," Mike laughed, "you have to stop doing that. It's embarrassing!"

The clinking glasses, the banter at the other tables, the owner joking with the diners nearby made it hard for them to hear each other. Jimmy leaned into the table and said, "This is the *sophisticated* way to eat pizza."

"Oh, like you would know," said Mike, and they all laughed at the ribbing as comfortable friends do.

"Forget *how* to eat pizza," Jenna said, then looked straight at Alice: "All right, you, out with it."

"What?" responded Alice, her mouth half-full of pizza. She covered her mouth with a hand, but she couldn't keep a straight face.

"You've been hiding something all night," said Jenna. "I know that look. Lay it on us."

"Okay, okay, here it is," said Alice. "A friend from work offered me four free tickets to a concert at Dawn River!"

"Cool," said Jenna. "Please tell me it's country."

"It's not country."

"That's okay, I've been wanting to introduce you to a Broadway review."

"Jenna, you have the weirdest taste in music of anyone I've ever met," said Alice. "It's…wait for it…it's Dani Blue!"

"Oh my God!" the other three said in unison. "That's teenybopper music."

"No way," said Jenna, "no way. I could never stand that stuff."

"Did I mention to you three struggling twentysomethings that it's free?" asked Alice. "And come on, going to a teener concert will be retro for us. Hey! You can wear your poodle skirt!"

"Very funny," said Jenna. "No thanks, not for me."

"Come on," Alice continued. "You'll see me screaming and throwing my scarf."

Despite herself, Jenna started to laugh.

"Jimmy?" asked Alice.

"Whatever you want, babe." At that they all broke up.

"Mike?"

"Up to Jenna."

"Jen! Pleeease," said Alice as she batted her eyes.

Jenna smirked and surrendered. "Free, huh? Oh, all right, I'm in."

The night of the concert, Jenna and Alice sat together, Jimmy and Mike across from them, on the swaying subway. The beige seats were worn, the fabric smelling faintly of the sandwiches and drinks that thousands of riders had dropped or spilled. Like old times, the four reminisced: Before any of them could afford a car, the subway was where they met up on their way to the park or the city pool or to just hang downtown. Sometimes with Jenna and whomever she was dating, but always Jimmy and Alice were together. With school loans and rent to pay now, they still looked for the cheapest way to get around.

"I…uh…think you may have your generations mixed up, Alice," observed Jenna.

Alice smirked, then turned sideways in her seat to show off the long-sleeved, multi-colored tie-dye shirt and bellbottoms and the big hemp shoulder bag that she carried, a bright yellow bandanna around her head.

"Thrift stores rock," said Alice. "Besides, you're just jealous I found this retro swag before you did!"

They arrived downtown, exited the subway car, ascended the stairs, and headed toward the Dawn River Concert Center. Alice and Jenna walked ahead, arm-in-arm, babbling and laughing like schoolgirls.

Jenna will make a wonderful sister-in-law and aunt, thought Jimmy, as he and Mike followed behind. He had not asked Alice yet, but he was just waiting for the right time. Even though they had been talking about making a life together, he still wanted to ask the question in a romantic setting and style. He had practiced three different proposals on Jenna, who played the part of Alice. Jenna/Alice had loudly turned him down every time, prompting a series of creative curses from Jimmy, followed by raucous laughter from them both.

They continued toward the arena entrance, Jenna and Alice, long blonde hair flowing, athletic bodies prancing, enjoying the envious glances from the girls and the lingering stares from the teenage boys.

"Eat your hearts out, boys," Jimmy said just loud enough for Mike to hear. "Those two are with us." He laughed at himself as he threw an arm around Mike's shoulders, and they strutted toward the venue's gates. Jimmy high-fived several of the outside vendors hawking t-shirts and posters of singers he didn't recognize, drawing puzzled looks from them as he passed.

Jimmy was glad that he had moved beyond his teenage years. He may have been a little nervous about making the proposal special, but he knew that Alice would say yes. *God, I'm living a good life*, he thought.

Jimmy and Mike caught up to Alice and Jenna, and they all blended into the crowd moving into the arena. Alice had already distributed the tickets, and they passed through the turnstiles. The security guard stationed there raised his eyebrows and smiled at the four of them, almost ten years older than most of the crowd.

"Reliving your not-so-distant youth?" he asked them.

"Just gettin' our groove on, dude," replied Alice as she bumped fists with him, and they laughed together.

Turning to Jimmy as she held his hand she said, "Babe, I'm hungry already."

"All right," said Jimmy with a smile and an exaggerated sigh. "Everybody give me ten bucks and I'll get us drinks and snacks."

Jimmy left them and headed toward the line at the closest food station, while the other three went to the seating section, showed their tickets, and were escorted down to the second row from the stage.

Jimmy rushed forward. Still filled with images of Alice, a smile on his face, he bumped right into a young woman headed in the other direction.

"Oh my God," sputtered Jimmy. "I'm so sorry."

The young woman gathered herself enough to say "no worries" as the younger girl with her took her elbow and steered them toward their seats.

2.

ARIEL

"ARIEL, YOU ARE SUCH A KLUTZ! You ran right into that guy!"

"Patty, I did not! He ran into me."

"Well, I wouldn't blame you if you did it on purpose. He's kind of cute."

"Patty!" said Ariel, with a smile. "You're my little sister. You should show some respect." Neither of them could keep from laughing. "And remember, I'm your ride home."

Ariel shook her head as she found her seat and sat down. Patty was jumping up and down in hers. How had she let Patty talk her into this? A Dani Blue concert at the Dawn River Concert Center? Ugh. This certainly wasn't her style.

Dani Blue? Every time she saw him or heard that screeching voice when Patty played one of his videos, her skin crawled. And those tight blue halter jumpers? As skinny as he was? Looked like a neon-blue string bean. She would much rather be practicing with her high school string quartet. She didn't care what others thought; the violin was cool and melodic and beautiful, with no klieg lights or break-your-ears speakers.

But Patty loved him.

So here she was, twenty years old, in college, chaperoning sixteen-year-old Patty and her equally excited friends.

Patty was in her glory. Dressed in different shades of pink: hot pink sequin hat, light pink blouse, dark pink jeans. And those boots? Who knew leather could be made with that many colors? Ariel glanced at her sister and couldn't hide a smile. This was Patty, bouncy, boisterous, happy all the time. Ariel did not envy her one bit, but she loved their differences.

It was a shame, she thought, that her parents didn't know what they were getting when they chose their daughters' names. "Patty" was simple and common, right? Ariel? How could she disappear into the back of the class when she was named after a Disney character?

Ariel had refused Patty's insistent advice on what she would wear. Instead, she proudly went with her plain jeans and simple white shirt, feeling under attack by all the surrounding color. Still, Patty was her younger sister, her sidekick when they were growing up, her cute little partner. Now, their four-year age difference felt like a decade, but Ariel loved her just the same.

Dawn River was cavernous, holding some twenty thousand people. Blue and red championship banners for the sports teams that played there hung high in the rafters, mostly for the hockey team. The upper tier of seats seemed to her to be angled precariously, but Ariel had to admit that the plush seats on the lower level where they sat were comfortable, and they were only ten rows back from the stage. It was heaven for Patty, though Ariel wished she had brought earplugs.

She was thankful that the seats reclined. *Maybe it won't be so bad*, she figured. As she leaned back, her eyes traveled up to the menagerie of rafters in the ceiling. She squinted to see better and noticed a worker up there, mixed into the mess of conduits and catwalks, fussing with something, too far away for her to see what it was.

Must be a tough job to put something like this together, she thought, *and still working at the last minute, plus it looks like nobody's helping him.*

At least he probably has the best seat in the house. He can see everything from up there.

3.

ALFRED DUNKEL

ALFRED DUNKEL MOVED ALONG the catwalk, high in the Dawn River roof's support structure, with a clear view of the stage and the growing crowd of concertgoers. This was always a chaotic time: patrons rushing to their seats, ushers in bright vests with the white Dawn River logo on the chest calling after them to keep them on track. Food and drinks being dropped or spilled, laughter and shouts. There were times when he thought the din would drive him crazy. That's why he usually popped a ketamine or Xanax before a special night. Thank God his mother's medicine cabinet was overstocked with just what he needed.

Dunkel had worked part-time at Dawn River for nine months. He had arrived with the other workers about two hours ago. Dressed in his standard Carhartt jumper and hat, and carrying a six-foot aluminum ladder, he was just one of the guys. They were all thankful that Dawn River deactivated the metal detectors when the techs and electricians and laborers arrived. Otherwise, the detectors would be performing their own obnoxious concert, with constant beeps and warning bells.

He had the tools he needed for tonight in a black zippered case that he had nestled inside the closed ladder. He set the ladder and case down and unzipped the case to double-check its contents, but he didn't pull anything out. He was distant from the crowd but still didn't want to risk a reflection from his tools that would bother the concertgoers. At least not yet.

One of his jobs was to make sure that the catwalks were clear of debris before an event began. Sometimes the electricians dropped bits of wire or conduit as they did their work or even left a screwdriver behind. The lighting techs could make a mess when they checked and oriented the floodlights. Those slobs left half-filled coffee cups and sandwich wrappers everywhere. The older laborers didn't want to make the strenuous climb into the rigging. Dunkel volunteered for it. There was something about looking down, literally and figuratively, on all those people below.

4.
BARRATT

AFTER MONTHS OF PLEADING, Elijah Barratt's daughter, Gabrielle—he loved calling her Gabby—had finally convinced him that seeing Dani Blue live in concert was the most important, meaningful, life-changing thing that would ever happen in her entire life. Dani Blue. Every teenage girl's heartthrob and every parent's aggravation. He held out as long as he could, but they both knew that he would eventually give in. So, Barratt overcame his safety concerns about dangerous venues, filled with fights and drugs, and said okay.

He had just transported five constantly chattering fourteen-year-olds, crammed into the family van, to the Dawn River concert center. When he parked, they spilled out of the van and started hugging and jumping in place, squealing all the time. They might have stayed there all night, stuck in excitement, if he hadn't moved them along. Once inside, they became even more animated, though almost unnoticeable in the sea of like-minded girls, the waves of noise breaking on the parent chaperones dotted among the crowd.

His wife, Lucy, had taken Gabby to the mall to find just the right outfit for her first live concert. He couldn't believe that something called Uggs could cost that much or that jeans with holes in them were actually new, but his daughter was in her glory. He had to admit that for Gabby, this really was, in her mind, the most important night of her young life. And nothing made him happier than seeing her beaming and caught up with her friends. Turning in his direction, Gabby smiled a smile of pure joy. His heart melted, as it always did for her. Lucy and Barratt had tried for years to conceive. They had all but given up hope when the home pregnancy test showed two beautiful dark pink lines. Barratt was a well-known attorney, on the partner track at one of Charleston's most respected firms. He had ambitions, and the talent and focus to achieve them, but Gabrielle was now the center of his life.

5.

JIMMY

JIMMY WAS NOW FIFTH IN LINE at the concession stand, but it was moving quickly, fans wanting to reach their seats before the show started. He was next after a woman with two young girls by her side. The woman was encouraging the girls to choose from among popcorn, pretzels, and nachos.

"Okay, girls," she said to them. "Take your time and get what you want."

The arena lights blinked, warning people to get to their seats.

"I don't know," said one of the girls, twirling her hair. "'Cause, I like popcorn, but we had that at the movies yesterday. What do you think?" she asked, turning to the other girl.

Jimmy checked the time on his phone and pursed his lips as he saw most of the crowd heading for their seats. The girls went back and forth over their choices. Jimmy shifted his weight from one foot to the other, swaying from side to side. The woman and the girls finally made their selections and moved away. Jimmy rushed the counter.

"Four Cokes, four pretzels, and a large popcorn!" he blurted, then added a quick "thank you." Gathering everything up, he hurried through the concourse toward the seating. He wasn't rushing to see Dani Blue; he actually couldn't care less. But he loved watching Alice get excited, as she often wonderfully did. It was infectious. Dancing in the aisles at concerts; playing cutthroat Scrabble with his mother, the two of them giggling at each other's competitiveness; screaming a *Braveheart* yell after scoring a goal when she had played high school soccer. She shared with him her excitement with the PR job she had started; there, she fast became the go-to for creative problem solving.

The concourse crowd slowed as it funneled into the seating aisle. Then Jimmy saw the lights go low and heard the crowd erupt with applause and whistles, screams and shouts of "We love you, Blue!" He could see the stage over the heads of those in front of him as Dani Blue rose up out of the middle of it, dressed in shades of electric blue. Sequined jumper, sparkling shirt, mid-thigh boots with rhinestone buckles. Four different colored floodlights hit him, reflecting off his bling, as if fireworks were trumpeting his entrance. He blew kisses to the balcony, then to the back of the house, then to those sitting closest to the stage, including Alice and Jenna, who swooned dramatically and laughed in response.

6.

ALFRED DUNKEL

ALFRED DUNKEL GAZED THROUGH the small binoculars he had brought with him, looking at the crowd, below him where they belonged. He loved to bring the binoculars and spy on those people, most having no idea that he was up in the rafters. All those smug guys with their fawning girlfriends. The guys with their arms wrapped around the girls' waists, letting their hands slide down a little lower, the girls feigning offense.

Those girls. How long had he fantasized about having one of them curled up against him, being the one who made them moan with delight. There was a time when he wanted to be one of those smug guys. But that time had passed. He saw the guys for the shallow, simple-minded pricks that they were. And the girls for the cruel teasers they were, not worthy of his time.

Everyone else was focused on the stage, waiting for that idiot Dani Blue.

After the Army, where he truly belonged, didn't want him, he got stuck with this job. It sucked. But hey, he was getting paid to be here—they were blowing all their cash on that faggot.

7.
BARRATT

BARRATT LOOKED AROUND THE CONCERT HALL, a cauldron of noise, constant chatter from the audience, warm-up music blasting from speakers the size of small trucks, announcements calling for parents to come retrieve their already lost kids, the mostly teen girls in the crowd wearing a kaleidoscope of colors. He saw one young girl racing down the aisle to the stage front dressed entirely—head to toe—in pink. It made his khakis and light blue dress shirt actually stand out. Most of all, there were smiles and laughter, though he did see more than one adult with a look of bored, resentful resignation.

Then his gaze locked with someone that he recognized. A lawyer, some twenty years older than Barratt, who also practiced in Charleston. Chad? Charles? Something like that. But this guy was grinning ear to ear. The man saw Barratt as well and spread his arms out, palms up, in a what-are-you-going-to-do gesture. When he turned away, he reached out and smoothed the hair of the little girl, maybe twelve, beside him, obviously his granddaughter.

Barratt had hesitated when Gabby asked if she and her friends could go down to the front of the stage and join what seemed like a million other screaming fans. *But I can't let my daddy paranoia ruin this night for her*, he thought, and grudgingly said, "Go ahead." Gabby and her posse rushed out of their row and raced to the pit of the stage.

8.

ALFRED DUNKEL

DUNKEL FINALLY PULLED HIS TOOLS from the black zippered case: an AK-15, a scope, and a barrel rest. He placed the rest on the lowest rail of the catwalk and settled the gun barrel there as he sat cross-legged behind it and sighted in. He had worried over the sequence of his targets, but now felt comfortable with his plan: take the silly girls who had rushed to the stage first. When he had everyone's attention and could see the panic in the slightly older girls and their dates, he would make them part of the show. He didn't really need to be selective, he thought; there were plenty of flopping fish in this sea.

"They didn't know it when they arrived tonight," he said out loud, "but they're here to see me."

BARRATT

Barratt's reverie was interrupted by a discordant sound, some sound that didn't belong but was somehow loud enough to break through the din in the concert hall. Then another boom. "Are you kidding me?" Barratt mumbled. "Someone brought firecrackers in here? That's just what I was afraid of." Then he heard a series of blasts as people turned to locate the sound, but not everyone. Some of the kids who had rushed the stage were on the floor and not moving. Then, a series of rapid thumps. Red spots bloomed on the floored girls' torsos.

ALICE

Jimmy heard distinctive loud pops coming from somewhere above the balcony, and he saw Alice with a stunned look on her face. Red splotches bloomed in the middle of her chest, mixing with the blue and green circles on her shirt. She descended in slow motion until she was kneeling on the floor between the seats, then fell face down.

Jimmy froze for an instant, then threw away the pretzels and Cokes and smashed into the screaming people in front of him, fighting the panicked wave washing against him, slipping on spilled soda and stomping empty red plastic cups.

"No!" he shouted. "No no no no!"

Shoving people out of the way, he struggled to where he saw Jenna frozen in place, tears streaming down her face. He reached for Alice and gently turned her, then his throat caught as he saw her eyes open in a vacant stare. Sobs burst and tears flooded his face as he hugged Alice to him, her blood turning his shirt crimson, the floodlights still strobing, reflecting from the blood, the lights doing a macabre dance on his chest. He started rocking back and forth as Jen knelt beside him, crying and cursing.

"Don't go, Alice," Jimmy said softly. "Don't go."

BARRATT

"Oh my God! Someone's shooting!" Barratt screamed as he leaped out of his seat, but his words were lost in the madness.

Gabby had turned from where she stood at the stage, and they looked at each other wide-eyed. Barratt screamed: "Gabby! Get down! Behind the seats!" She was frozen in place. Waving his arms to direct her, he burst from his row and charged into the aisle. He struggled against the panicked tide. "Gabby!" He couldn't hear his own words. "Baby! Down!"

But she was paralyzed, mouth open, tears streaming. He pushed through, around, over the mass of stumbling, crying, screaming. He lost sight of his daughter. He screamed again, gibberish and panic and terror. He got closer, closer.

Then he saw her and spread his arms wide to cover her. Just as he was about to reach and enfold her, he felt an impossibly heavy thud in his back. It lifted him and flung him forward on top of Gabby. They crashed to the floor in one indistinguishable heap. She lay beneath him. He pushed himself up and saw she was bloody: her blouse, her neck, her hair. He tried to wipe the blood away but there was more pooling.

"Gabby! Baby!"

"Daddy!" she cried. "Daddy!"

"Gabby! Where are you hit?"

"I... I'm...not."

Why, Barratt thought to himself as he looked down, *that's because it's my blood*. Then he fell into darkness.

ARIEL

On stage, Dani Blue was spangled and glittering, in as many shades of blue as Patty wore pink. He stepped off the platform that had risen and danced to the mic stand in front of him. He grabbed the mic and started to belt out what must have been the crowd's favorite. Then he stopped abruptly and looked down at the girls who had rushed to the stage, and his face contorted.

Ariel stood up at her seat. Something was wrong. She looked around as people started to scream, not with excitement but with panic. The musicians behind Dani Blue could not see what was happening in front of the stage and continued to play, a morbid imitation of the *Titanic* as the concert hall sank into the depths of terror. The crowd was starting to move and turn and run. Ariel looked for Patty in the madness in front of the stage. She saw her, then screamed in agony as Patty was involuntarily lifted up and flung onto her back at the same instant Ariel perceived a sound like every movie gunshot she had ever heard.

"Patty! Patty!" Ariel screamed. She raced to her sister, reached under her arms, pulled her to her. Patty's blood covered Ariel's hands and face and started to turn Patty's happy pink outfit a disgusting burnt red.

Patty's mouth was open; her eyes were unfocused. Ariel started to rock her. She pressed her mouth to Patty's ear and kept repeating: "You'll be all right, you'll be all right."

ALFRED DUNKEL

Dunkel had emptied the first magazine, removed it, inserted another one, and emptied that clip too.

"That should do it," he said out loud. He placed the AK-15 back in the case and zipped it closed.

Then he sat back and marveled at the chaos he had wrought.

9.
BARRATT

THREE DAYS AFTER DAWN RIVER, Barratt swam out of an intense, dark gray fog and surfaced into consciousness. With obvious effort, he slowly opened his sand-caked eyes. What he saw startled him further awake. It was a grapevine of cords and tubes growing out of his arms and attached to his chest, a cannula in his nose. The steady beat of the surrounding equipment reached his ears. He was in a private hospital room; the light from the unshaded windows made him squint against its glare. He turned his head to the left, just far enough to see Lucy slumped in a chair, her head resting on her chest, breathing in shallow sleep.

"Luce." He had barely made a sound, his throat like sandpaper, burning when he spoke. He reached for the energy to raise his voice. "Babe." It was now a loud whisper.

Lucy slowly opened her eyes. For a moment she seemed startled by the strange surroundings, then she raised her head and saw Barratt's face.

"Oh," she exclaimed. "Eli," more softly. "Eli, honey." Rising from the chair, she stepped forward and slowly, softly reached her hand through the nest of cords and tubes and took his hand in hers. "Welcome back," she smiled.

"Gabby. Our little girl." He struggled to voice the words but forced them out.

"Gabby's okay. She's still frightened, but more than anything, she's been worried about you. She was here with me for two days, and I finally sent her home. Emma's been staying over."

"Two days?"

"Yeah," Lucy said. "You're in Jefferson General. You've had a three-day siesta."

Barratt squeezed Lucy's hand. His grip was weak, but he wasn't letting go.

"Lucy, what happened?"

Lucy released Barratt's hand, retrieved the visitor's chair, moved it next to the bed, and sat down, hunched forward.

"Eli," she started. "Eli, it was horrible. A twenty-something guy, worked at Dawn River. They say he kept to himself, seemed a little odd, but was never violent. They said he was fascinated with guns; he bought the one he used at a gun show. They still don't know how he got the weapon into the concert."

"Gabby?" he said her name again.

"Really, Eli, she wasn't hurt. You're her hero now even more than you were before."

"How…how many?" he asked.

Lucy drew in a breath. She rose and sat on the side of the hospital bed, gathered herself, and took his hand again. "Eight dead, they think ten more injured, some critical."

Tears formed in Barratt's eyes.

Lucy pursed her lips. "Eli, do you know an attorney named Chandler Bosworth?"

Barratt swallowed painfully. "*That's* his name. I saw him there and thought I knew him. Is he…"

"No," Lucy said. "But his granddaughter, ten years old… she's…oh, Eli, she's gone. I can't stop thinking that it could've been our Gabby." Now tears formed in Lucy's eyes. Leaning forward, she lay her head on Barratt's chest, ignoring the nest of connected lines there.

"Do they know why?" Barratt asked.

"Oh, Eli, do they ever know why?"

DADEVILLE BIRTHDAY PARTY SHOOTING: 20 PEOPLE REPORTEDLY INJURED, AT LEAST ONE KILLED

Montgomery Real Time News
The Alexander City Outlook
(Alabama)

10.
JIMMY

AS THEY LEFT THE CEMETERY after Alice's funeral, Jenna drove. Jimmy sat stone-faced in the passenger seat.

The crisp weather had turned the trees lining the street into brilliant orange and red and yellow fireworks. Families in front yards were raking the leaves that had fallen, children leaping onto leaf piles and scattering them with leaf angels. Dog walkers were out in abundance, luxuriating in the bright fall sunshine. Jimmy saw none of it as he kept his eyes straight ahead.

Jenna pulled over to the curb and parked in front of a modest but meticulously maintained Craftsman home, the home where Alice grew up. They walked up the three steps to the front door, which was flanked by flower boxes, the hardy geraniums still vibrant. When Jimmy was dating Alice, he saw the flowers as a prelude to the beautiful, spirited girl he would find inside. Now, their bright red petals were obnoxious and taunting.

The after-funeral luncheon was crowded with family, friends, and some people Jimmy had never met. He made his way through the swirling sea of mourners to Alice's parents. They hugged long and tearfully but silently, as none of them could speak, then Jimmy separated.

People were gathered in small clutches, precariously holding plates piled high with cheeses and grapes, fancy chips and red salsa. Some guests were dressed in suits or black dresses, others in jeans and loud sweaters. There was a constant din of indecipherable conversation, some laughter and loud greetings as more guests entered.

Jimmy's skin pinged with the noise, a thousand tiny pricks traveling up his chest and onto his neck. He struggled to breathe. The small room became smaller. The people turned into a gray mass that grew bigger and bigger. Without a word, he pushed through the crowd, threw open the front door, flew down the steps, and started to run. Out to the sidewalk, across the street, onto the other side, then down the street, running as fast as he could—his black dress shoes painfully slapping the pavement, his necktie ripped off, then tossed away.

2 ARRESTED, 1 DEAD, 14 INJURED IN MASS SHOOTING AT SOUTHWEST OKC HALLOWEEN PARTY

KOCO NEWS
Oklahoma City

11.
JIMMY

FOUR WEEKS LATER, Jimmy sat and stared at the shaded front windows of his apartment, daring the light to enter. A dusty pallor filled the front room. The walls to either side of him held selfies of Alice and him, mugging for the camera, with his guitar hanging from his neck; the two of them in Myrtle Beach; the laughing couple at the outdoor concert by the Waylon Jennings cover band. There were several pics of Jimmy and Jenna blowing out the candles on their twenty-first birthday cake, decorated half with pink icing, half with blue. Jimmy held a sign that read: "We're twins, but I'm the younger one!" Jenna's sign said: "And I'm the cute one!"

A sandwich, missing only two bites, and a half-empty bottle of beer sat on the end table next to his chair. On the other side, Hank, his mixed-breed rescue dog, sat on the floor, his head resting on Jimmy's knee. Jimmy scratched Hank on the top of his head and behind his ears. A car passed by outside, and Hank raised his head and perked his ears, then returned to Jimmy's knee when the sound receded.

Jimmy's cell phone rang. He had changed all the ringtones. Jenna's used to be "The Two of Us," Mike's was "You've Got a Friend in Me." Alice's was Taylor Swift's "Lover." Now every call sounded with the same innocuous smartphone default. It rang until it went to voicemail.

A moment later, Hank rose and wagged his way across the living room and stopped at the front door. There was a knock, then a key entered the lock and the door opened. Jenna stepped in, bent to greet Hank, who smiled and shimmied in response, then she looked up at Jimmy.

Jenna spoke softly. “Hey. I haven’t talked to you in a week. You haven’t been at work. I just called but you’re not answering. I only see you when I come here.”

“What’s the point?” Jimmy mumbled.

Jenna advanced toward the chair and placed the large bag that she was carrying onto the floor. She knelt in front of Jimmy’s chair.

“I brought your favorite soup, some fresh bread. Clementines and those Pink Lady apples you like.”

“What’s the point?” Jimmy repeated.

“Jimmy, the point is that it’s been more than a month. You’re disappearing—you need to come back. *I* need you to come back.”

From where she was kneeling, she could see the kitchen table. It was covered with cardboard boxes wrapped with packing tape.

“You’re really moving out?” she asked.

Jimmy nodded.

“Where are you going to go?”

“I’ve got a place. Out of town, lots of room, no neighbors.”

“I’ll help you move.”

“Don’t need help.”

“What about work?”

“Got a construction job lined up.”

Jenna sat back on her haunches. “Jimmy, come with me tonight.”

“Don’t need it.”

“We all need it. The group helps. They’re good people. We’ve all lost someone. They know how it feels.”

Jimmy raised his eyes and looked at her with a steely glare.

Jenna carried the bag into the kitchen, put the bread on the counter and the soup into a nearly empty refrigerator. “I’ll come by tonight and pick you up. 7:30.”

When she came back that night and Jimmy didn’t answer the door, Jenna let herself in. The boxes were gone; the photos were off the walls.

The apartment was empty.

FOUR PEOPLE KILLED, TWO CHILDREN INJURED IN KINGSESSING MASS SHOOTING; SUSPECT IN CUSTODY

Philadelphia Inquirer

12.
ARIEL

THE BEEPING WAS INSISTENT.

Ariel's home was a typical shotgun affair in the working-class neighborhood. The front door opened into the living room, then there followed in order a dining room, kitchen, the one bathroom, and the rear exit. Doors opened from the dining room and the living room into the three bedrooms, one of which Ariel and Patty shared. Ariel stood in their bedroom doorway, aching for her little sister and sad about how their home had changed.

The living room was usually a comfortable, homey place with overstuffed furniture and hardwood floors covered with yellow, red, and blue Oriental rugs. The fireplace mantel held photos of Ariel in her green and gold band uniform, playing clarinet, Ariel dressed all in black, performing on the high school stage, playing violin with her string quartet. Alongside those photos were pictures of Patty laughing in wild Halloween outfits—one year casting against type as Cruella de Vil—in her cheerleader uniform, in her frilly party dresses. Ariel's favorites were of the two of them mugging for the camera.

When Patty was released from the hospital, the living room chairs and coffee table were pushed back against the walls, the rug rolled up. A hospital bed was positioned in the middle of the room, its side rails raised. Patty had slept most of each day since returning home, the doctors assuring them that this was part of the recovery process. Monitors hung from poles, their wires and cables attached to Patty's body, checking blood pressure and heart rate and oxygen levels. *She looks so small,* Ariel thought, as if she were slowly sinking into that awful, ugly bed. Ariel wanted to leap in and pull her out of the quick-sand nightmare.

Their mother, Tessa, delicately washed Patty's hair several times a week and brushed it every day. Patty's friends came by after school, and she tried to laugh and chat with them. The three of them took their meals on tray tables in the living room so that Patty was never alone.

But now, in the early mornings, with Patty asleep, all was quiet. Except for the damnable beeping of the monitors.

Ariel fought against the sound that pushed her to replay that terrible night. She fought in the way that she knew best: She sat by Patty's bed with her polished maple violin settled between her knees, her shoulders relaxed, and she played. When Patty was asleep, Ariel played soft sonatas. When Patty was awake, she played Vivaldi, up-tempo.

Ariel, voluntarily or not, slept very little. Her performances for Patty started around 4:00 a.m. and continued until their mother shepherded Ariel into the kitchen for a quick breakfast and then pushed her to leave for classes at State College, located in the city, bus and subway rides away. Ariel's teachers had let her postpone completing some assignments, but that could only last so long. She had to get back in the classroom or lose the whole semester.

"Ariel," said Tessa, "you've done everything you can. There's never been a better big sister." She wrapped her arms around Ariel and spoke softly into her ear. "But you have to get back to your life."

"I know, Mom, I know. I will." But Ariel knew that her life had changed too, and that there was some compulsion deep within her that demanded more.

These family moments would be shattered at 7:00 a.m. That's when the media arrived. Patty had survived the mass shooting at Dawn River; that was enough to bring a horde of cameras and reporters and satellite trucks to their front door on a regular basis. The reporters jostled each other on the front lawn, wounding the manicured grass with their boots or high heels or camera stands, all hoping to get video of a sobbing mother, a grieving sister, the cute victim.

The fenced yard prevented the media from invading from the back of the house, allowing Ariel to escape most mornings in that direction. This morning, just before she left, Ariel narrowly parted the living room drapes and eyed the chaos outside. It was not her nature to confront, but this intrusion, this smashing of their privacy, this violation at this time in their lives, made her stomach churn, her face flush, and her hands form into clenched fists. Wasn't what had happened to Patty horrible enough without this constant attack?

"Mom? …Mom! When are they going to stop?"

Tessa was busying herself in the kitchen, getting ready to leave for her job as soon as the home health aide arrived.

"Honey, I don't think that there's anything we can do about it. I know that I'm not going out there, and I don't want you to either."

"But they're awful. Now they're in your flower beds! Your impatiens are being crushed!"

"I don't like it either, but for now we're just going to have to put up with it."

Maybe for now, Ariel mouthed to herself, *but not for much longer.*

THERE WERE SEVEN MASS SHOOTINGS ON SATURDAY, THE MOST OF ANY DAY THIS YEAR

CNN

13.
BARRATT

LIFE-CHANGING EVENTS COME IN all shapes and sizes, and the responses to them are just as diverse. The birth of a child can lead to maturation and celebration or can be the cause of abandonment and neglect. An illness can cause depression and bitterness or generate a new spirit and love of life.

How about getting shot?

Barratt had only partially recovered from his injuries. The bullets that entered his back and passed through him had broken ribs and damaged a lung, and the shock waves generated by the speed and mass of the bullets caused internal injuries. While he had not been in danger of exsanguination, his blood loss was significant. Although he was hospitalized for many days, he was never thought by his doctors to be in danger of death. He did have residual pain and limited movement, but was expected to regain significant strength and range of motion. In common parlance, he was "lucky."

But the steady, solid good guy with the wry sense of humor, everyone's friend, had become morose, consumed, unsure of how to respond to what had happened to him and his daughter.

Was he feeling anger? At the shooter? At himself for not seeing what was happening sooner? Did he want vengeance? Justice? Did he want to turn away and not have to see what had been done to him? Was he experiencing survivor's guilt? In quiet times, alone in the morning, up before anyone else, as he struggled against the pain on walks, just as the dawn was breaking, he would ruminate, constantly replaying the events of that night over and over. If he had not given in to Gabrielle's plea to attend, none of this would have happened, would it?

Tonight, he sat in what used to be his favorite chair, a swivel/rocker club chair with rolled arms. He used to throw his left leg over the left arm and rest a good book against his left thigh. The chair was in his study, agreed by the rest of the house to be off-limits to everyone else. He would lose himself in that good book or close his eyes and lean back and, perhaps, comfortably doze.

But tonight, the chair couldn't help him. No matter how he shifted, the pain would find a way to aggravate. That aggravation was usually the trigger for his mind's steady demand: What are you willing to do? He wanted, *needed*, to act. He would never heal, he thought, if he did not assert some sort of control over the consequences, the painful vestiges of the shooting. He needed to know what one man could do to disrupt the constant reminders. He formed plenty of ideas, but rejected each one as impractical or impossible or simply ridiculous.

On his next morning walk, completely unbidden, there moved over him a sense of peace, like the most comfortable blanket or the most loving hug. Breathing deeply, he felt his spirit shift and rise within him. It was not happiness. It was not contentment. It was commitment. It was when The Plan suddenly took form: complete, resolute. And unstoppable.

LAS VEGAS POLICE: THREE DEAD, ONE INJURED AFTER WEDNESDAY SHOOTING AT UNLV

Fox5vegas.com

14.
ARIEL

THE LAST DULCET NOTES of Ariel's selection from Vivaldi's *Four Seasons* lingered in the living room. The drapes still covered the front windows, but now the morning entered through the open slatted blinds and fed soft light throughout the rest of the house.

"I love that one," said Patty.

"You have me play it over and over," replied Ariel.

"I know," said Patty, "but you have to. I'm the one in the wheelchair. You *have* to do everything I say!" Patty started to giggle.

"Hey, little girl. This is getting old. Starting tomorrow you're going to take care of me."

"Nuh-uh."

"Oh yeah," said Ariel. "Let's see: I can get the ironing board set up and you can iron all my jeans. Hey, you can clean my hairbrushes. There is just no end to the possibilities!"

"No one irons jeans!"

Now both sisters were giggling.

Four weeks after Dawn River, the hospital bed had been removed, taking with it the monitors and the cords. Patty sat in her wheelchair. The wound to her back had damaged her spinal cord and made her a paraplegic. Tessa usually wrapped her legs in a green fleece blanket, or a cream-colored sheet as the weather warmed. Neither she nor Ariel wanted Patty to constantly see how her legs and feet were starting to atrophy, since she was unable to put weight on them and there would be no new bone formation. Phantom sensations in her calves raised Patty's spirits and made her think that her paralysis was temporary. Ariel didn't tell her otherwise.

Each morning still started with Ariel serenading Patty. Sometimes, especially earlier in Patty's convalescence, Ariel played slower, softer pieces. Little by little, she had increased the tempo. It was no longer necessary to mask the noise of the medical equipment, but neither one of them wanted to start their day without these intimate moments. Ariel saw that Patty was in denial of what lay ahead for her, of the ways in which her life had totally changed. She hoped to help Patty ease into recognition of her fate, at least until she was further along in her therapy, and these mornings helped. Chronic depression could be caused by paraplegia, and Ariel saw it as her job to make sure that Patty didn't fall into that dark place.

Patty was due to return to school next week. The school had provided a video tutor, but it was not the same as classroom socialization.

There was noise from the front yard, some chatter and the sound of equipment being set up. The TV trucks and the national reporters had moved on to the tragedy du jour, but there were still two or three die-hards who showed up periodically, mostly independents hoping for the "money shot" and a quote. They were outside today. Try as she might, Ariel was incapable of blocking out their chattering, their laughter, their mostly vulgar repartee. She set down her violin and bow and gritted her teeth.

"Let it go," said Patty, "there's nothing we can do about it."

Ariel left her chair and stepped quickly to the front windows and slightly parted the drapes. As many times as she had seen the chaotic deployment of the invaders on the front lawn, even this reduced intrusion still rankled. The lawn was now, in fact, no longer a lawn. The legs of the lighting stands and the trampling by the photographers, together with the intermittent rains, had turned it into a quagmire. Ariel enjoyed watching their disgust when the mud clung to their shoes. She grieved for the few remaining patches of green that were under attack.

"Why do they still come here?" asked Patty, her voice tinged partly with confusion, partly with apprehension.

Ariel knew the answer, but she didn't share that knowledge with her sister. Patty, at the insistence of Ariel and their mother, never watched the news coverage of Dawn River, but Ariel did. She saw the photos of Patty in her cheerleader uniform and the pictures apparently obtained from one of Patty's friends showing Patty dancing in her too-short skirts. To Ariel, it was perverted, as if the media had some sort of prurient interest in this cute young girl. The stubborn few who still congregated outside were desperate for what they hoped would be an image of Patty's tragic transformation into a helpless little waif.

Ariel couldn't care less about what they wanted, but she knew her sister. Patty's spirit seemed unbroken, her outlook still rose-colored, deluded or not. But if the media had their way, even upbeat Patty could be beaten down by the appropriation of her image. Ariel was not about to let anything derail her sister's journey to whatever improvement she could reach.

Despite Patty's protest, Ariel closed the drapes and walked to the front door. She took a deep breath, opened it, and stepped outside onto the porch landing. Cameras clicked. Questions exploded.

"Where's Patty?"

"Will she ever walk again?"

"Bring Patty out!"

"Can we come inside?"

"Is Patty crying all the time?"

"Did she have a boyfriend?"

She eyed each of them in turn, assessing their de facto uniform: khaki-colored army jackets with a dozen pockets, three or four cameras around their necks, backward caps and dangling cigarettes. The staccato questioning only abated when it became clear that Ariel was not about to answer. She took one step forward and spoke a single word: "Soon."

Questions were fired again.

"Soon?"

"What does that mean?"

"When is 'soon'?"

"Where? Where should we be? Here?"

Ariel simply turned and walked back inside.

Ariel hadn't planned her spontaneous, opaque, one-word message to the few stubborn paparazzi, but it triggered what she was about to do. She had played enthusiastically before high school assemblies and now, as a music major in college, in front of more sophisticated audiences. Speaking in front of strangers was not something she was used to or sought. But when her mother said there was nothing they could do to fight back against the devasting blow to their lives, it felt like a call to arms.

Several days later she was back in her old high school, now Patty's school. She was happy that the school still had a morning homeroom period, a time when students could center themselves before classes started, say hello to several friends, ask about special events, relax.

Not today.

Ariel figured that Patty's homeroom was a good place to start a journey she never imagined she would have to travel. She had reached out to Patty's homeroom teacher, Ms. Zamel, and asked to address the class. It was quickly cleared with the principal, and here she was.

The late spring morning was still dim, and little light slipped through the windows that lined the outside wall. Two boys were playing paper football; kids were turned in their seats, laughing and gossiping. Ariel wore her plain denim jumper and a man's long-sleeve cotton shirt, but she had drawn stares as she entered the room by wearing Patty's signature pink hat, with its purple piping and rhinestones.

The homeroom teacher frequently came up with short, funny projects to settle the kids before they were released into the rest of the building. The week before, she had asked the students to reproduce the first drawing they remembered making in first grade. A bunch of handprint turkeys still hung on the message board, bracketed by cute amateurish pictures of the sun and huge flowers. Patty had sent hers in and it was tacked to the board. It showed two pigtailed stick figures with triangular skirts, holding hands. She and Patty, tiny in the drawing, smiles so wide that they spilled beyond the sides of their heads. It caught Ariel's eye as she entered and she looked at it wistfully, seeing such a different, innocent time, a time they no longer lived in, a time that had morphed into this scary, living, voracious thing that threatened to consume her.

The students' chatter lessened as she walked to the front of the room and smiled hello to the teacher, but the class went silent when she reached up and muted the loudspeaker that was droning with the morning's announcements. Ms. Zamel returned the smile, and Ariel began.

"My name is Ariel. Most of you know my sister, Patty, and you know her story. She survived Dawn River, but she'll never cheer again. She'll never dance again. She can't run, so I will run for her. She can't walk, so I will walk for her." Ariel's voice caught in her throat, but she cleared it and continued. "This weekend I will stand in front of Dawn River. I will point my finger at every person who was elected to protect us. I will demand that they tell me how many Pattys they'll turn away from before they act." All eyes were on her now. "And if they don't respond, I will knock on their doors, I will confront them at their meetings.

"You are her friends. I hope you live long, healthy lives, but the same thing could happen to you. You are young, you are energetic, and you can do something about it. I want you, and every person you know, and every person you don't know but will tell, to walk and run with me. I will keep doing it and keep doing it until the people who can change things change things."

Ariel finished speaking, stood quietly for a moment, nodded a thank you to Miss Zamel, then strode toward the classroom door, her shoulders back, her head high, as everyone in the class stood and erupted with applause.

SHOOTING AT PADDOCK MALL LEAVES MULTIPLE INJURED, ONE DEAD

Ocala Gazette

Florida After 10

15.
LONE WOLF

HE APPARENTLY WAS NO LONGER a member of the pack; he once thought that he was. Listened to the ribbing and sports talk around the water cooler. So what if he never joined in? It was all so puerile. Attended those lame office birthday parties. Even went out for drinks once after work, but they never asked him again.

He was the best thing that had ever happened to Pensaid Engineering. He should have been the leader of the pack. His work was so much better than the rest. After all, he had his engineering degree, and some of them were still draftsmen. Yeah, some were design engineers like he was, but their work was frequently sloppy. He had tried to help them, point out their mistakes. Instead of thanking him, the more he tried to help, the more they resented it. "All I did was demand the respect they should have given me," he many times mused, and they thought that was "offensive." Pussies.

And now they had called him into the office. Make that *she* had called him into *her* office. It wasn't the first time. He had an "attitude" problem, she had told him in the past. His "constant criticism" of his coworkers was "creating problems with office morale." Hey, he told her, the problem wasn't office morale; it was office incompetence. Starting with her.

She had given him verbal warnings, then she'd had the nerve to give him a written warning *AND PUT IT IN HIS FILE! BITCH!*

Now, she "called him in" again, like some mangy dog called to his master to be punished. He walked in, expecting more of the same. But this time, something was different. Eddie, that moronic oaf from security, and Deborah, head of HR, were standing there. He took his usual seat in front of her; he hadn't asked if he could. Best to take the upper hand—the lead—right away, show her that he wasn't going to be intimidated.

"Ralph..." How he hated his name. "We've talked about these issues before, and we've given you every opportunity to solve them. But there hasn't been the progress we had hoped for."

He didn't say a word. He stared straight at her until she averted her eyes. Just like he knew a frightened little girl would.

"Ralph, we have to let you go."

What! She was firing him? He was the best thing this office had ever seen! And *she* was firing *him*?

He shot up out of his chair. She recoiled, and Deborah slunk away. He smiled, more of a sneer.

Eddie shifted toward him.

Turning, he walked out of the office and then the building. He didn't say a word to any of them. To himself he said, "They will regret this day."

Ralph spent a lot of time with his younger cousin Nicky. Nicky idolized Ralph, wanted to be just like him. Ralph loved that. He especially loved shooting with Nicky. Ralph didn't own any guns, but Nicky did. Nicky had a bunch. Ralph's favorite was that Bullpup with the sixteen-round capacity. That thing was a beast. Nicky and Ralph would go down to the junkyard after it had closed for the day and light things up. Blowing out windshields was fun, especially the ones on those big trucks. But his favorite was blasting old toilets. The toilets just exploded when he shot them, sending ceramic shrapnel raining down.

Ralph had a key to Nicky's house. Nicky didn't have a gun safe; he liked looking at his weapons too much to lock them out of sight. When he knew that Nicky would be out with his buddies, he let himself in and borrowed the Bullpup and a 9mm pistol and as many rounds as he could stuff into his cargo pants.

Now he stood outside of his old office. The anger had been building in him since his last day at work. Looking at the building heated that anger until it reached the boiling point. "Morale problem? Difficult attitude?" That was the last time that he would suffer these fools, he promised himself. Today was the day he would make them understand who the alpha dog was, who the rightful leader of the pack was. *He* was the Lone Wolf who would discipline the pack. This would be as good for them as it would be for him.

When he stepped to the front door it automatically opened for him.

He walked into the lobby. The receptionist lifted her head from her cell phone. When she saw him, she reflexively shot to her feet, opened her eyes wide and promptly fainted, collapsing onto her chair, her head landing on the desk in front of her. She had not uttered a sound: no scream, no cry for help. Thus, no warning to anyone else in the building. This was her lucky day, he thought. He didn't bother killing her. She was just a dunce and not someone who deserved his attention.

Moving forward, he pushed open the door to the big workroom. The cad operators, draftsmen and engineers, were bent over their tables and desks, eyes fixed on the screens in front of them. No one had noticed him enter. He paused and took in the scene. The light-green-painted walls—supposed to help everyone relax and stay calm—disgusted him.

He looked deeper into the room. This really was *his* lucky day: his manager, that bitch who had fired him, and Eddie and Deborah and one of the dolt engineers were standing around a workstation, all peering down at something.

Wait—this wasn't just lucky. This was confirmation. This was *meant* to be.

Ralph's plan was to shoot all sixteen rounds from the Bullpup, then use the pistol on himself. This world, *their* piece-of-shit world, didn't deserve him. He cleared his throat loudly and they all looked up. When recognition dawned, their confused faces turned to terrified looks. That was more like it, he thought.

Tucking the shotgun against his shoulder, he started firing.

When he was finished, he put the pistol under his chin and pulled the trigger.

MULTIPLE DEAD, WOUNDED IN LEWISTON SHOOTINGS; POLICE GIVE FEW DETAILS ON OVERNIGHT SEARCH FOR GUNMAN

Sun Journal
(Maine)

16.

ARIEL/JIMMY

THE CONCERT HALL LOOMED BEHIND HER, all steel and glass and angles. She had been there through rain and cold and wind. Today, the sun promised to make the heat oppressive; it reflected from the concert hall facade and backlit Ariel and her modest set-up.

For the last eighteen months, Ariel had held rallies in front of Dawn River every month. She set up some three hundred feet in front of the main entrance, so as not to interfere with deliveries and employees, and because she was more visible somewhat closer to the street. A gray folding table was set up, holding a mic, a small amp, and pamphlets from Everytown for Gun Safety, Sandy Hook Promise, and The Violence Policy Center, plus handouts with contact information for senators and representatives and the White House.

Ariel sometimes timed her rallies to coincide with Dawn River events, but this morning she had an early day. She would be home this afternoon to celebrate Patty's birthday, with friends and cake and one of those horrible reality shows—egocentric kids thrown together in a beach house, wealthy "housewives" bemoaning their complicated lives, one guy choosing from among fifteen or so unreasonably desperate women—that Patty loved so much.

At 11:00 a.m., the rally drew only her fifteen or so most faithful supporters from among her usual thirty-five. Jake and Emma had lost their son to a shooting outside of a club. Robert and Linda had seen Natalie and Eliza, their seven-year-old twin daughters, board the school bus one morning and never saw them alive again. Eddie and his mother were drawn to any drama, rubbing up against it, hoping to be a part of it themselves. There were Betty and Howard, an elderly homeless couple; Ariel always brought bottled water for them. There was one sketchy guy, wearing an old navy peacoat and worn boots, a watch cap pulled tight on his head even on warm days. He never clapped or cheered, but he stared at Ariel and glared at the others. She kept a wary eye on him, constantly cautious since Dawn River.

Ariel figured they had all heard her presentation so often that they could present it on their own. On small-crowd days, the rally was frequently more of a support group, but today Ariel had something she needed to say. Congress had just passed, and sent to President Charlotte Bostic's desk, legislation which the president promised to sign forthwith. It repealed the last few limitations on the ownership of semi-automatic weapons. Ariel keyed her mic and began to castigate the sponsors of the bill for cowering before the gun lobby.

Jimmy had never been back inside Dawn River and vowed that he never would be. But he had seen this girl and her followers outside of the concert hall several times when he came into the city. She was usually dressed in jeans and t-shirts or a plain sweater, rarely wore any makeup. As he walked by today, for some reason he paused to listen. The streets were busy with morning traffic moving slowly, horns beeping. The sidewalk he was on was crowded. Workers were unloading cases of soda and water and boxes of corn chips and Slim Jims and candy, then piling them onto hand trucks and wheeling them to a nearby deli. Office workers, some in athletic shoes, rushed to their buildings, some holding their dress shoes as they did. Chatter, street noise, workers barking to each other; Jimmy moved closer so that he could hear what the girl was saying.

"They think," said Ariel, "that we will eventually tire, that we'll wear out and give up. They don't know us, do they?" All but the sketchy guy applauded and cheered. "They think that we have stopped watching. But we won't stop watching until we bring this to an end."

Jimmy had heard it all before, from cable "news" shows with pontificating commentators:

"We need to come together as a society." *Yeah*, thought Jimmy, *how's that been working so far?*

"This is not who we are." *Really? Look at the stats. More mass shootings than days in the year, year after year after year. This*, thought Jimmy, *is exactly who we are.*

"Put your trust in God." *Where was God when Alice was shot down at Dawn River?*

And candidates running against incumbents. Documentary after documentary. Late-night entertainment shows. Everybody had an answer, but nobody had a solution. This girl sounded like everybody else.

"I have another handout," said Ariel. "It's the email addresses and the phone numbers of the specific sponsors of this bill. And I have President Bostic's chief of staff's contact information." She handed the handouts to Jack and Emma to pass out. "Please reach out to them, please tell them your stories, again, and tell them what a dangerous idea this is." She paused and spread her hands. "Look, I know that Bostic has not been a friend to us in the past, but she can't ignore us forever."

Yeah, she can, thought Jimmy. *What a fool. Maybe well-meaning, but so naive.* To Bostic and the rest of them, what this girl was saying was just so much background noise, drowned out by the drumbeat of their selfish intentions, muted like the street noise muting that girl's words. Jimmy turned away from the gathering and moved along the sidewalk, weaving through the crowd. *There is a solution*, Jimmy thought. *Retribution. Fire with fire.* Enough blather. Somebody needed to *do* something.

3 DEAD, 4 INJURED IN "GUN BATTLE" IN UPSCALE BEVERLY CREST

Pasadena Star News

17.
JIMMY

JIMMY SHOOK HIS HEAD as he walked away from that naive girl and her silly rally. Her approach was never going to change anything. He had a different idea.

He was finally doing something, not just begging for overtime to keep his mind busy when he had a job, not sitting in the dark, ruminating about what he *wasn't* able to do on the night of Dawn River. Wallowing so long in the mire of his grief, feeling his legs sucked back when he tried to lift them from the mud, feeling the putrefactive slime slowly consuming him, he feared he would never be able to pull himself out. Or that he would stop trying. When the idea of vengeance gradually formed in his mind, he felt release, he felt alive, he felt that he had a chance for redemption.

His idea was to target the parents of the shooters, no matter where they were.

The Supreme Court had overturned a previous ruling that, under certain circumstances, held parents responsible for the violence of their children, now protecting them from legal liability.

Well, if the law won't punish them, then I will, vowed Jimmy.

After Dawn River, he felt compelled to ask: What drove these people to commit such atrocious, devastating crimes? The answer was still elusive, but he did educate himself. He learned that a high percentage of the shooters were in their late teens or early twenties, and almost all were male. They had experienced a disturbed adolescence, been bullied, the bullying ignored. They were hotheaded and sullen, and frightened their teachers and the other students. And they showed clear signs of being suicidal. Many of the shooters stole weapons from their parents' home or stole cash to buy a gun.

So let me get this straight, he thought. *Your son is angry and withdrawn and the school has told you that he is scaring students and teachers with his dark, brooding, dead-eyed demeanor. You told him to just toughen up when he was bullied in grammar school. When he complains about how horrible his life is and whether it's worth living, you don't notice? You don't see the signs?*

And because you don't, people die.

Such was the case with Randy Borrelli, nineteen years old, isolated, taking alcohol from his parents' cabinet and money from his mother's wallet, harassed by bullies who shoved him into lockers, constantly ruminating on movie scenes of shootings and suicides. All of this came to light *after* Randy went on a rampage. Mr. and Mrs. Thomas Borrelli, interviewed on TV, sobbed and insisted that they had no idea that Randy would do such a thing

Bullshit! thought Jimmy. How could they not?

Randy took the shotgun out of his father's unlocked closet. This frail, awkward kid, his thin face with the protruding nose topped by disheveled dirty-blond hair, wearing jeans and a t-shirt and barefooted, walked into the Wellington, Missouri, shopping mall food court.

Senior shoppers, resting tired feet, had piled their bags on the floor and leaned wearily over tables, sipping coffee. Young girls dominated the crowd, wearing yoga pants and long-sleeved shirts. Most of them hadn't purchased anything. Theirs was just a day out for giggling and gossip and shyly glancing at the cute boys. The boys were less shy about looking their way. There were scattered businesspeople in suits and loosened ties or business-casual dress, taking a break for a quick lunch. The din of conversation and counter service formed a bubble of distraction over the diners. Unaware, people relaxed and chatted, taking a little time to decompress.

For a determined shooter like Randy Borrelli, it was a shooting gallery.

Four killed, six wounded.

So, Jimmy set his sights on Lamplighter Bank. Lamplighter was a mid-sized bank, trying to compete with the big boys. It looked for any edge—slightly higher interest rates, friendlier service, more aggressive lending practices—and, most importantly, assiduously avoided even a hint of the scandals that plagued the local branches of its competition.

Jimmy had used the city library and painstakingly searched online through years of back editions of the Missouri Daily Business website and, posing as a journalist and promising anonymity, spoken by phone with some disgruntled former employees of Central Bank, located on the other side of the state. He knew that Thomas Borrelli had previously worked at Central Bank, during which time it had quietly released several unnamed mid-managers suspected of embezzlement. Borrelli wasn't let go then and was never publicly accused of any wrongdoing. He left on his own some months later and relocated to Wellington. That was all irrelevant to Jimmy.

He drafted a single-sheet letter addressed to *Bank President Kimberly Long/for her eyes only.* He typed on a library computer and mailed it from a town about an hour away in a different state.

When the bank clerk sorted the mail, he noted the specific addressee. Probably another complaint by some customer who didn't understand where his money went, he figured, even after the bank pointed to his overdrawn account. Nevertheless, bank policy was that if it was addressed to the president, that's where it went. He walked it up to the president's office and presented it to the secretary.

Kimberly Long rolled her eyes when the envelope reached her. She followed her typical practice of slicing the envelope open while holding it over a wastebasket in case any white powder floated out. When nothing did, she removed and opened the one folded page. The entire message read:

> *HAVE YOU ASKED THOMAS BORRELLI ABOUT THE HISTORY OF EMBEZZLEMENT AT CENTRAL BANK? HOW CAN ANYONE TRUST YOUR BANK NOW?*

She didn't care that the letter did not accuse Thomas Borrelli of embezzlement or state that Borrelli could not be trusted. In fact, it made no defamatory statement of any kind, and the bank had vetted Borrelli before quietly hiring him. No matter.

Long summoned her secretary and curtly stated, "Get Judy from HR up here. Then find Thomas Borrelli and tell him to wait in the conference room for us."

Two weeks later, Jimmy found a small blip on the Daily Business site. It indicated that Lamplighter Bank, while thanking Thomas Borrelli for his work as an account manager, had announced Borrelli's departure from the company.

ST. LOUIS CANCELS YOUTH FOOTBALL TEAM'S SEASON AFTER PARENT ALLEGEDLY SHOT THE COACH

CNN

18.
ARIEL

THE SECOND HOME ELDER CARE FACILITY dominated its landscape. Five stories of red brick, columned portico entry, expansive landscaping. There was a high trellised wall providing privacy for the swimming pool beyond it. Bocce ball and croquet courts roofed with sun tents. Many of the residents could not make use of the amenities because of their physical infirmities, but the peaceful setting, and the chance to recount days when they could, was part of the design.

Ariel tried to visit once a month. When she did, she left behind her go-to denim jumpers and canvas jackets. Today, she wore a dark blue dress with a subtle flower print and a flattering, just-above-the-knee hemline, along with her mother's pearl necklace and a small pearl ring, one of the few pieces of jewelry she had ever purchased for herself. As usual, she had applied just a hint of makeup.

Ariel passed through the entry doors and entered an airy lobby festooned with potted ornamental grasses and ficus trees.

"Ariel!" Maggie, the receptionist, greeted her. "It's always good to see you. And you brought your violin. I'll sign you in, honey, but don't you start playing until I have my break, you hear?" Pointing down the main hall, she said, "She's in the farthest sunroom. She's waiting for you."

Ariel moved into the hallway and headed toward the back of the first floor. The space was immaculate. The hardwood hallway was waxed bright, the walls painted subtle shades of green with darker green accents. Her shoes—no sneaks today—clacked her progress. She exchanged greetings with the familiar residents she passed, then arrived at the wide archway of the sunroom and peered inside. Near the window to her left sat a woman in a wheelchair. Her hair was silver but styled and becoming. She wore a delicate lapis lazuli necklace and a matching bracelet, her hands folded and lying on her lap, her chin resting on her chest as she dozed in the warmth of the sun's Rembrandt lighting.

Ariel approached quietly, knelt by the side of the wheelchair, and lay her hand on the woman's arm. She spoke softly, "Aunt Birdie? It's Ariel."

Ariel's Great-Aunt Bernadette raised her chin and slowly opened her eyes. "Hi, sweetie." She placed her hand over Ariel's. Ariel had followed that hand's journey from strong and smooth with brightly painted nails, to arthritic but still gifted with a strong grip, to the delicate, spotted, thin fingers that graced it now. "Look how you brighten the day."

"Aunt Birdie, there's sunshine all through this room."

Birdie's smile widened. "Perhaps, but it's not as bright as you."

Second Home had independent suites, assisted living apartments, and nursing care units. Birdie may have used a wheelchair, but she was whip-smart, a good cook, and the very definition of "independent." Ariel often joked that she would need assistance with living before Birdie did.

They talked about Ariel's plans for college, Birdie's friends at Second Home and the "mean girl" clique that none of them liked, how the food here was better than Birdie had expected. Birdie was Ariel's go-to sounding board. Her years as a college professor had made her an empathetic but realistic listener. Ariel had spoken with her during past visits about her rallies outside of Dawn River and everything that had led up to them. Birdie had taught women's studies and several advanced sociology courses and had become a well-known women's rights activist.

Eventually, other residents started filing into the room, some with walkers, others in wheelchairs, some spry; Maggie followed behind. They all looked expectantly in Ariel's direction. "You're a celebrity here, Ariel," Birdie said. "Time to play for your audience."

Ariel serenaded the residents when she visited, and they had come to expect it. She turned and met the waves and hellos directed to her with a smile of her own.

"Hi, everybody," she said. "What would you like to hear today?"

She fielded several requests and played each one. Up-tempo, a little bit of country, but most of them enjoyed the classical pieces the best. Birdie smiled her approval, but her eyes were asking questions. After about twenty-five minutes, Ariel bowed and waved her bow, acknowledging the applause, and her audience started to drift out. She went back to Birdie's side and re-cased her violin.

"That was beautiful," said Birdie. "Honey, it's such a nice day outside. Let's go for a walk." Birdie reached down and unlocked her wheelchair. Ariel stepped behind her, gripped the handles, and they moved through the automatic sliding doors and out into the open areas. Gardens lined the paved walkways, where flowers of the season bloomed on a regular basis and were tended with care. The crocuses—blue and white and pink—had already surfaced; now the daffodils were flourishing, and the tulips were just pushing through. They moved in silence for several minutes until they reached a bench under a flowering pear tree, its delicate white petals not yet descending. Ariel placed the wheelchair next to the bench and sat down.

"Tell me, Ariel, what is bothering you today?"

"Nothing, Aunt Birdie. Why?" Ariel had not met Birdie's eyes as she spoke but had turned her face as if to study the flowers lining the walkway.

"Honey, this is your Aunt Birdie. I've known you since before you were born. Your playing today was elegant as always, but you were holding back. Talk to me."

Ariel had never really known her father. After he left, her mother worked two jobs to care for her and Patty, asking for extra shifts and always accepting overtime. There were days when dinner was hurried and days when there was no time to prepare. As the girls grew older, their mother was there for them as often as she could be, but after-school clubs and weekday summer play dates presented problems. Ariel's maternal Great-Aunt Birdie filled the void. She was a cook, chauffeur, story reader, and co-conspirator in practical jokes. In her nineties now, Birdie could look back on a career that not only included teaching but also serving as a faculty union shop steward and a leader of protests for gender equality. But she always made time for the girls. To Ariel, she was a second mother, and Ariel knew that Birdie would support her without judging.

Ariel turned to face her aunt. "Aunt Birdie, I've started something, but I'm not sure what to do now."

Birdie took Ariel's hand in hers. "What you said in your classroom was courageous and powerful," she said. "You're on the right track."

"But how do I keep it going?" Ariel asked. "Already some of my friends are getting bored with me. I don't blame them. I start talking about this stuff and I can get carried away." She sighed and shrugged her shoulders. "I'm making it up as I go. I've never done anything like this before." She shook her head and lowered her eyes. "Am I an imposter? I didn't get hurt. Shouldn't somebody else be doing this? It's like I just barged in."

Birdie patted Ariel's hand, then reached and brushed a wisp of hair from Ariel's forehead.

"I know how difficult it is. I've been there. Most people can't march with the same enthusiasm as the one leading the parade. That doesn't mean that you stop marching. Some of them will drop out, but others will join in." Birdie reached down and snapped the stem of one of the daffodils—a definite no-no at Second Home—and handed it to Ariel. "Such a rebel I am," she laughed.

"You're gonna get us in trouble." Ariel laughed with her.

"Honey, I know you think you're doing this for Patty, because some part of you feels guilty, which you shouldn't. You did everything you could. And partly you're doing this for me and your mother and everyone who struggles with the unfairness that life can bring." Birdie took both of Ariel's hands in hers. "You may not have chosen this, but it has chosen you. You're the right person for the job."

Birdie gently caressed Ariel's face.

"You come from a line of women who take on the hard jobs. Your mother and, yeah, me. And your great-grandmother."

"I don't know much about her."

"She was the first one of our family to come to this country. She went from working in an ugly, steaming, unbearably hot laundry to owning her own dress shop—and fighting all the male merchants who didn't think she belonged. You're doing this because of who you are and where you come from.

"Just remember this, young girl, there's a warrior inside of you."

DON'T FISH WITH A GUN IN KANSAS, GAME WARDENS SAY

ksn.com

19.
SURVIVOR'S LAMENT

THE FLOWERS LEFT OUTSIDE the Communion River Church had withered. Well-meaning people had left them there, together with prayer cards and votive candles. Rebecca had stopped there every afternoon for the last two weeks. The sleepless bed she lay in every night restrained her with its mussed sheets and pillows, holding her prisoner until she struggled her way up, frequently after noon. The weight of loss that paralyzed her and the weight she had lost over the last two weeks would have startled her if she had not been drained of all emotion.

Her husband, Sebastian, had been shot in the church three Sundays previously. Rebecca was just getting over a horrible cold that day; Sebastian insisted that she stay home, out of the frigid weather, to rest. She reluctantly agreed. They had been walking the short distance from their home to the church together for all thirty years of their marriage. They had exchanged their vows there. It was the place of their children's christenings.

The church itself was a solid, stately, inviting oasis. Constructed decades ago by immigrant Italian masons, it consisted of blocks of gray granite, perfectly joined and mortared. Its steeple, topped by a polished wooden cross, was the highest structure in their small town. Rebecca and Sebastian were typically among the first to arrive for mass. They sat halfway up on the left side, on the aisle, near the confessional, so that Sebastian could unobtrusively step out of the pew and stretch his arthritic knees. While seated, they would hold hands and solemnly gaze at the stained-glass windows.

The windows depicted Saint Francis tending to the birds that flocked to him, Moses descending the Mount with the Ten Commandments, Mary at the foot of the cross. Rebecca had always been infatuated with the brilliant red and blue and gold and green of the glass, brought alive by the morning sun shining from behind. This was, she frequently thought, her place of comfort, of sweet memories, her safe place.

That Sunday morning Sebastian took his regular seat, nodded to the other early arrivals, and whispered to them an explanation for Rebecca's absence. The congregants' attention was drawn to the altar as Reverend Martin and the acolytes entered. The fragrance of fresh flowers rose from the altar and floated over the nave. Despite the cold weather the pews were almost full.

The church was an ecumenical one; it had been at the forefront of welcoming refugees from the violence in Colombia and, more recently, in Argentina, and assisting them with assimilation. The church's position was not popular in the wider region, but the church members agreed that providing ESL classes, assisting the new arrivals in a search for housing, and donating food baskets were part of their mission. They had received letters and emails from those who disagreed with the church, some threatening and referred to the police. There was talk in the parish council of having security on Sundays, but the church lacked the budget to provide it.

With his arms spread wide during the celebration, Reverend Martin appeared distracted as he looked up and toward the back of the church. Some of the parishioners turned in their pews to gaze down the aisle toward the church doors. A man whom they had never seen before, appearing to be in his twenties, conservatively dressed, stood there with a calm look on his face. Reverend Martin returned to his task, but quickly looked up again when a collective gasp went up from the congregates. That's when the young man started shooting.

When Rebecca received the phone call from the police that day, telling her only that there had been a shooting and that she should come to the church, she threw off the blanket she was lying under, bolted from the couch, and raced out the door in her white flannel robe, the door hanging open behind her. She ran toward the church, wheezing and struggling to breathe, her slippers slapping the pavement. The crowd outside the church was hugging and crying, some sitting on the curb, their heads in their hands. Rebecca searched the crowd for Sebastian, trying to see his face on every man but not finding him there.

Rebecca saw her friend Mickey and called out, "Mickey! Mickey! What happened? Where's Sebastian?"

"Oh, Becky," her friend said. "Oh, Becky, it's horrible."

Rebecca grabbed her friend by the shoulders and shook her.

"Mickey. Mickey, talk to me." Her friend's eyes widened and she went mute. Rebecca turned and raced up the church stairs, stumbling halfway along, regaining her balance, then tripping on the last step and falling into the arms of a uniformed officer.

"Ma'am, you can't go in there."

"You called me! My husband might be in there!" Rebecca started to sob. "I have to see. I have to... I have to find my husband, my Sebastian." Her legs weakened and the officer held her upright.

The doors to the church were opened by two other police officers to allow the EMTs to roll out a gurney. The body on the gurney was covered by a tightly secured sheet, but the left arm and hand were exposed. She saw his favorite striped shirt and the watch their son Jacob had given him one Father's Day. When she saw the wedding band she had placed on Sebastian's hand thirty years earlier, Rebecca slumped to the concrete and cried uncontrollably.

Three weeks later, Rebecca stood before the impromptu memorial. In addition to the flowers and the candles, photographs of the five people who died that day were propped on the pavement. When she was asked for a photograph of Sebastian, Rebecca chose one of the two of them mugging for the camera on their vacation the previous year; she didn't want Sebastian to be alone outside the church, mixed with the flowers, passersby gawking. The photo showed Sebastian and Rebecca sitting on garish green and orange beach chairs, feet in the sand, laughter in their eyes, palm trees behind them. She tenderly removed some of the dead flowers that had fallen in front of the photo. The flowers had collapsed in on themselves; what had been vibrant red and yellow petals were now curled and brown.

The next day, Rebecca walked toward the church in midafternoon. The sun was out and the wind was down, but she still wore her heaviest coat, a scarf, and a knit hat. The chill that consumed her as she hugged her knees on the pavement that day had afflicted her every day and night since. When she neared the church entrance, she saw workers with shovels and bags and refuse totes. She quickened her pace and arrived just after the workers had closed the totes and were wheeling them away.

Her Sebastian gone forever.

AT LEAST FIVE MASS SHOOTINGS TOOK PLACE AROUND THE COUNTRY OVER THE WEEKEND

Fox 10 Phoenix

20.
BARRATT

BARRATT COULD NOT TURN AWAY from any news report of a mass shooting. Having been in such a hellish scape himself, his stomach churned, his face flushed, and he could feel the pain of every victim, every family. Even sometimes the shooter's family. Did they know that their son or cousin or brother-in-law had a volcano inside that would erupt in violence? Did they look the other way? Or try to help? Think of telling someone what could happen? Or were they completely oblivious and now dumbfounded and ashamed?

Each death, each suicide formed ghastly apparitions that chased him in his dreams and followed him every day.

One horrible but, for his purposes, helpful aspect of this madness was that the stories provided an endless inventory of potential allies.

Barratt knew that to be successful, The Plan needed people who would understand what he was trying to do. And the truth was that most of these allies had to be people of means to support what would become a wildly controversial plan.

Barratt had closely monitored cable news, online newspapers, witness lists for the lawsuits that inevitably followed a shooting, and the Everytown for Gun Safety and Gun Violence Archive websites. He learned the identities of shooting victims who survived, of families of those who died, of businesses that lost key people and shut down, of teachers who tried too hard with troubled students, of officers shot in the line of duty, and on and on. Young, old, black, white, Asian, Latino, all religions and nonbelievers. Barratt saw that violence did not discriminate. The murderers included spouses, young people, older people, parents, the deranged, the highly intellectual, the failed, and the successful.

Barratt called ahead, then met in person with whoever agreed to see him, then tried his best to recruit them. He shared with them as much of The Plan as he thought prudent, but explained that there was an endgame that was still taking shape.

John Amarillo owned one of the biggest architectural firms in the city. His wife, Sheila, worked at Pensaid Engineering, the site of the horrific shooting several months earlier. Barratt started his introduction, as he did with each person, by saying, "You and I have something horrible in common." Amarillo recognized that he needed some way to vent his consuming anger and ended their conversation by simply saying, "I'm in."

Benjamin Monroe's brother-in-law and best friend was Sebastian, another person in the right place at the wrong time. He was one of the victims of the Communion River Church mass murder. But he wanted nothing to do with politics or with the intense conflict surrounding gun rights.

Asa Tucker's son was on the campus of Bethel University and died in the shooting there. Tucker refused to revisit that time and told Barratt to never call him again.

Maria Dominguez, the majority owner and CEO of one of the largest grocery store chains in the Southeast, lost her sister, Isabel, when Isabel took Maria's daughter to the Dani Blue concert at Dawn River. She embraced Barratt's Plan and promised to help.

Barratt's efforts were grueling and intrusive but, he felt, necessary. He was used to persuading judges in the courtroom but felt that in some ways trying to persuade the people he approached would dishonor their loss. He respectfully accepted whatever their response was. Some people just hung up on him. Barratt didn't know if they thought he was scamming or if they refused to reopen the wound caused by the worst moment in their lives.

In the end, Barratt felt that he had assembled a team of supporters who could not only provide the means for him to pursue his goal but also wanted to be a part of what he was doing.

And, thus, Dawn River Associates was formed.

MAN SHOT DEAD ON THE SAME WILMINGTON BLOCK WHERE HIS BROTHER WAS KILLED IN 2021

delawareonline.com

21.
BARRATT

BARRATT WAS UNSURE HOW TO reach out to Chandler Bosworth, but he felt compelled to do so. Chandler's loss was monumentally greater than his. Barratt struggled to imagine how devastated Chandler must be, given his own emotional struggles.

Barratt's recovery was slow. It was still difficult to draw a deep breath. Three cracked ribs, shattered right shoulder blade. His range of motion was almost comically limited. He had to turn his body to turn his head, he gasped for oxygen after just a few stairs, and raising his arms above his head was a challenge he sometimes couldn't meet. He was grateful the rounds didn't tumble as they passed through, or his internal organs would have been eviscerated. The doctors assured him his recovery would be significant, but not total. They didn't need to tell him that the journey would be a long one.

Barratt shuddered when he flashed back to the shooting, as he did constantly, but it wasn't only because of the physical pain. The nightmares weren't as frequent now, but they were still horrific. In them, Barratt ran and ran and ran toward Gabrielle, but he was running in quicksand. He never reached her. He stretched and dove, but he was always too late. He would awaken an instant before Gabrielle would have been shot. If she was hit, he didn't know if he would ever wake up.

How must Chandler feel? Barratt wondered. Regret for taking his granddaughter to Dawn River? Cursing himself for letting her go to the front of the stage? Guilty for not saving her? There was absolutely nothing Chandler could have done. He was too far away, and she was one of the first to fall, but Barratt knew that would not assuage Chandler's feelings of failure. Was he consumed with anger? Was he paralyzed by depression? Did his daughter blame him?

Barratt did not know Chandler well and wasn't sure how he would be received, but when he called Chandler's office he was put through so quickly it was as if the call was expected. Barratt had practiced what he would say, but when Chandler answered, his mind went blank.

"I know," said Chandler softly, "I know."

"Chandler, I thought about what to say, but now I realize how impotent any words would be. I am literally convulsed with sorrow at your loss."

"I keep seeing your face when we glanced at each other before... everything..." said Chandler. "I remember we both smiled." He paused, and for a moment neither man spoke. "I have not smiled since that day... I can't speak to my daughter about it. Neither one of us can force a word through our sobs. No one who hasn't been there can understand. Friends want to talk about it, but that only makes it worse. But I think now I need to hear myself speak about it, I need to hear myself say my granddaughter's name, I need to speak it to someone who will listen and not judge or cover me with cloying sympathy. I need to talk to someone who knows."

"That's why I'm calling," said Barratt. "Would you want to...get together?"

"Yes," Chandler said immediately.

"When would be good for you?" Barratt asked.

"Now."

About halfway between Chandler's and Barratt's offices sat Melody's Meltables. It was a popular sandwich shop/bakery. The sandwiches were steamed, and the baked goods would melt in your mouth. In the past, when Barratt needed a break from the pressure of his practice, he would walk to Melody's, order a coffee and anything with buttery crumbs on top, take an empty table in the window, and enjoy humanity's parade. He hadn't been back since Dawn River.

Today, the bakery was between morning rush and lunch, but still busy, with an undertone of chatter. The scent of cinnamon and brown butter seemed to tempt the patrons, but Barratt was oblivious to the tease. A middle-aged man in a striped business suit sat alone, nursing a steaming mug and grinning at something he must have seen on the iPad he was holding. A mother and her two young children stood before the baked goods display, eyeing the sweets and giggling at the endless choices. An older couple sat at a table against the wall, silently holding hands. She had sunken cheeks and an ill-fitting turban that didn't successfully cover her balding head. Barratt was offended at the normalcy of the whole scene, the view of life going on as if nothing had happened. Didn't they know what devastation Dawn River had wrought?

Barratt arrived first. Chandler walked in a moment later. They nodded a silent hello, made for the table farthest from the windows and the register, and sat down heavily.

Barratt had lost significant weight during his recovery but had started to regain some muscle tone by taking long walks with Lucy. He tried not to stare at Chandler's face, which was gaunt and pallid, his skin stretched so taut that he appeared skeletal. Barratt folded his hands and set them on the table in front of him. A perky young waitress arrived and broke the silence. Her chipper "Hi, boys. What can I get for you today?" was met with muttered orders for two coffees. She encouraged them with a description of today's bakery special, but they declined. Appetite was a friend that visited rarely now.

"Thank you for meeting me," Barratt started.

"Of course," Chandler said.

The waitress returned with their coffee and set it before them. Despite the pleasantness of the late summer day and the warm air wafting through the bakery's open door, they each wrapped their hands tightly around the porcelain coffee mugs. Barratt was almost always cold during his recovery; Chandler looked as if he needed the heat to keep his blood flowing. They started to speak at the same time, then they both stopped and smiled sardonically.

Barratt waited a beat, then spoke. "They say that survivors suffer as much as the victims. I'm both, and I don't know which is worse."

"I'm one, but I wish with all my heart that I, not Tanya, was the other," Chandler said.

"I'm sorry," said Barratt. "Tanya...that's such a beautiful name."

"A family name," said Chandler. "Amazingly, both of her grandmothers were named Tanya. When it came time for my daughter to choose, she just couldn't resist."

The conversation quickly became intimate. They shared their experience with counseling and the mixed results. Chandler said he had started to drink, but it didn't last; he couldn't stand the taste. Barratt shared that the only thing he had any appetite for was pizza; not the Chicken Cordon Bleu he used to enjoy at Le Papillon on date nights with Lucy, not the medium rare filet at the Roadhouse. Chandler described nibbling at whatever was placed before him, causing his wife to annoyingly urge him to eat. They both lowered their eyes and admitted that they hadn't made love to their wives since Dawn River, each acknowledging how insensitive that was. Barratt described moving from anger to depression; Chandler's track consisted of stultifying guilt.

"You know you couldn't have stopped it," said Barratt.

Chandler dropped his eyes and gently spun his mug back and forth. "That doesn't help," he muttered. "You saved your daughter's life. I saw Tanya die. I...I...don't know if I can handle this."

Barratt was silent for a moment, then asked, "If you could do something, act, make something happen in response to Dawn River, what would it be?"

Chandler looked up, confused. "I've been buried so deep I haven't thought about that. I know the trial against Dawn River told us who this...shooter...this *kid* was. I'd want to know how he came to that point in his life. What the hell was happening that he thought this was going to fix it? How was killing my Tanya going to fix his life? What would you do?"

"I wanted revenge at first. But I've lived long enough to know it would be unsatisfying, a pyrrhic victory; it would make things worse. I think now I would want to stop the next one, and the one after that."

"You know that's impossible, Elijah."

"Yeah, that's what everyone says, but we could make it a lot harder."

Chandler raised an eyebrow. "We?"

"Chandler, I've talked to a number of the families who lost someone or suddenly became caregivers, not only because of Dawn River but because of this scourge of violence. I've put together a group that is hurting the same way you and I are. And they all want to turn their pain into power."

"How did you find them?"

"I read the police reports, searched the web, looked at Everytown and some of the other sites that track shootings, talked to some of the prosecutors, and got the contact info for the plaintiffs and the witness list."

"Gun violence is entrenched in this country, Elijah. It's a way of life. For some it's a badge of honor. And, no offense, but I'm not in a state of mind to join a victims' club. Anyway, how do you, no matter how many of you there are, how do you deal with *that*?"

"I'm not asking you to join that group. There's something else I hope you will want to do.

"I have a plan. It won't be easy, and it will take years. But it *will* work, and it will answer your questions." He paused, and his gaze turned to steel.

"And you, Chandler, you are the key."

AT LEAST 10 WOUNDED IN DENVER SHOOTING AFTER NUGGETS WIN NBA TITLE

ESPN

22.
JIMMY

ALFRED DUNKEL'S CRIMINAL TRIAL was set in the historic courthouse—its cornerstone dated 1827—located in the county seat. The building wasn't designed to accommodate the volume of business that it had to handle in the present day. In the 1800s, murder trials were infrequent but sensational. Now, if not necessarily commonplace, they were at most a passing curiosity unless a celebrity was involved or the murder was particularly gruesome. Or, as in Dunkel's case, it was a mass shooting.

The undersized layout provided no private spaces for the attorneys, clients, or witnesses to wait for their turn in the proceedings. Potential witnesses were not permitted in the courtroom during jury selection or during argument of pretrial motions anyway, so they didn't need to be present.

Jimmy wasn't scheduled to testify for several days, but he had vowed to be at the courthouse every day. So had Alice's parents, Frank and Carole. They were present each day anything involving Alfred Dunkel was taking place, even though they were stuck outside the courtroom. The three of them were seated on a high-back wooden bench just outside the courtroom door. They sat mostly in silence, their grief enhanced by the presence of Alfred Dunkel mere feet away. The old building had worn tile floors and weary walls painted an institutional pale green. If the wall color was intended to be soothing, it wasn't working. As in so many older spaces, the HVAC struggled to keep it cool on this summer day.

"This place's life should be over," Jimmy mused aloud, "just like mine is."

"Don't talk like that," said Frank, "you have a lot of life left to live."

Jimmy just pursed his lips and shook his head.

Frank pulled an envelope from inside his jacket pocket and handed it to Jimmy.

"We want you to have this," he said.

"What is it?"

"Open it, please."

The envelope was not sealed. Jimmy opened the flap and pulled out a blank paper that had been folded in three. Inside of the fold was a very large check, payable to Jimmy.

"Frank, what… What is this?"

"Jimmy, I haven't slept more than three hours a night since…since the concert. I'm using up my sick and vacation time, but I don't know if I'll be able to go back to work. I know you received a small settlement from Dawn River. What did they call it… 'Intentional infliction of emotional distress.' But it wasn't that much. Our settlement was much larger. Together with taking my pension early, we're going to be okay.

"But you're suffering as much as we are. I don't know exactly how you're handling it, but this will help while you're figuring it out. We've stayed in touch with Jen, and she told us you're having a hard time keeping a job right now. I can sure understand that."

Jimmy looked at the check again.

"I can't accept this, Frank. This is yours and Carole's."

"The settlement of the wrongful death"—Frank's voice caught with the words, and he stifled a sob—"from the...lawsuit...was very significant. Dawn River wanted to get this out of the news as quickly as they could, although this trial puts it back in.

"You take this, son. You're part of the family. Helping you feels like I'm still helping my little girl."

Jimmy looked at the check again. He had actually been living hand-to-mouth for months and struggled emotionally to make it through the next day, let alone the next year.

"I don't know what to say."

"Nothing needs to be said."

"Then thank you, Frank...Carole. This means...a lot to me."

Jimmy left his seat and knelt in front of Alice's parents and the three of them hugged and quietly wept together.

Jimmy had become familiar with some of the sheriff's officers rotating in and out of the courtroom, securing the premises. They kept Jimmy informed about what was going on inside. Officer Steve Howard had just exited the courtroom and reported to Jimmy and Alice's parents that jury selection had been paused while the lawyers were conferencing with the judge.

Just then the doors opened and dozens of men and women wearing big white jury badges left the courtroom and marched upstairs to the jury assembly room.

"I'll head back in and see if I can see what's going on," said Howard. He returned about ten minutes later. Lowering his voice, he said, "The defense attorneys are telling the judge that Dunkel had a tough time growing up, that he has a learning disability that should be taken into account."

"Into account for what?" asked Frank. "They didn't plead insanity."

"I don't know," said Howard, as he opened the door and went back in.

Fifteen, then twenty minutes passed.

"This doesn't feel right," said Jimmy. "Something's going on."

When a half hour had passed, Howard came back and stepped to the three of them.

"Look," he said, his voice low, "two other officers are bringing Dunkel out. You know by now that there's no other exit. They'll walk by here and take him downstairs to the holding cell.

"And...you need to know this. Dunkel's pleading guilty and the... the death penalty is off the table."

"What!" said Frank and Carole in unison. "He gets to live while our baby's in a grave?"

Jimmy stood up quickly. "And I don't get to look this son-of-a-bitch in the eye! He killed my life!"

"You've got to keep it together," said Howard. "I don't want to make you leave but stay cool."

Howard turned his back to Jimmy; another officer came over to stand next to him, creating something of a barrier. The courtroom doors opened. Dunkel was shackled, his cuffed hands secured to the leather belt around his waist, his feet only able to move inches at a time. Officers held him by the elbow on either side. Jimmy glared. Dunkel shuffled and stumbled. The officers tried to hold him upright, but as he pitched forward his eyes locked with Jimmy's. Jimmy saw no recognition, no sympathy, no remorse, just two dead eyes. The two officers in front of Jimmy had taken a half step forward as Dunkel tripped, creating a space between them.

Jimmy burst through it.

"You fucker! You fuckin' piece of shit!" he yelled as he lunged for Dunkel, swinging wildly. Howard grabbed a handful of Jimmy's shirt and tried to pull him back, but Jimmy's rage propelled him closer. The officers escorting Dunkel turned to block his way, lost their balance, and the three of them tumbled to the floor. Jimmy raised a foot and went to smash it into Dunkel's head, but Howard finally yanked him away, spun him, and pushed him toward Frank and Carole, who reached for him as Jimmy landed butt-first on the floor, screaming, "You don't deserve to live! You don't deserve to live!"

Officers rushed Dunkel down the steps toward the basement and the holding cell.

Jimmy sat on the floor, angry tears burning his eyes. Now his voice was barely audible.

"He doesn't deserve a life," he whispered. "He killed mine...he killed mine."

2 KILLED, 28 WOUNDED IN MASS SHOOTING AT BALTIMORE BLOCK PARTY EARLY SUNDAY: 'THEY WERE RUNNING FOR THEIR LIVES'

The Baltimore Sun

23.
BARRATT

THE RIDE WAS LONG, but no one seemed to mind. Elijah driving, Lucy in the front passenger seat, Gabrielle in back. This was the family's third "trying to decide on Gabrielle's college" trip. Elijah and Lucy tried to make each one a fun visit to a college town. Gabrielle had made clear that she wasn't interested in a big-city university. She wanted a simple setting where she could study and make new friends. Seizing on a lull in the conversation, Elijah pushed play and Neil Diamond's greatest hits filled the SUV.

"OMG," Gabrielle said, as she rolled her eyes. "Do you think we could have something from, like, this century?" She had nested in the back seat, pillow on one side, soft blanket on the other, lounging in yoga pants and an oversized top.

"Hey," Elijah responded, "this has been our soundtrack on each trip. I'm not gonna jinx us now." "Sweet Caroline" rolled into "Coming to America."

"Let me know when you play something on the list I gave you," Gabrielle said with a grin as she inserted her earbuds and disappeared into her own music.

Elijah and Lucy smiled at each other, reached over and held hands. Three years ago, they wondered if these days would ever come, worried over Gabrielle's return to school after the summer of Dawn River. After their daughter would leave the dinner table, Elijah and Lucy would lower their voices and exchange concerns. Would she always be known as "that girl who almost got shot?" They huffed about the obsequiousness of the school principal when they met with her in August to pave the way for Gabrielle's return. They raved about her new homeroom teacher's comfortable sensitivity. "How would Gabrielle like to be addressed?" the teacher had asked. And would she want him to deal with the Dawn River history on the first day of class, or, as he suggested, let the kids all find their way?

The night before the first day of the school year they revisited the litany of questions they had been working through. Should they drive her or let her take the bus? What would she like to wear? Would they urge her to have her friends meet her at the school entrance? What were their own schedules, and which one would be available if they got a panicked call from her during the day? And was college looking too far ahead? Was Gabrielle's preference for a remote campus a frightened search for a safe place? They tried to joke about it being like her first day of kindergarten, but the jokes fell flat.

The tension had been semisweet all those years ago when five-year-old "Gabby" approached the first day of kindergarten. She tightly gripped Lucy's hand and her tiny body pressed against Lucy's leg. The morning was filled with competing emotions: excitement at this rite of passage, teary-eyed pride and joy, and mutual separation anxiety, but a pervasive sense of optimism.

Gabrielle's return to school now was completely different.

They recalled that Gabrielle was only slightly subdued as, at her insistence, she took the school bus. Elijah and Lucy both left work early and waited anxiously at home for her to return. At the end of the school day, she stepped off the bus, cell phone in hand to complete a call that obviously couldn't wait another minute, then chatted with them about the girl in her class who was *actually from Paris* and somehow loved the same music that she did! Their concerns were somewhat lessened, but they remained cautious. Their counselor had advised them she was likely experiencing denial, that her upbeat affect could be a defense, and that *she* was ironically feeling guilt at abandoning *Elijah*. He had saved her life, and the counselor suspected that Gabrielle felt ungrateful with every age milestone, moving farther away from him. Still, Elijah could sense a gradual peeling away of her layers of tentativeness, slowly revealing more and more of the girl she had been.

Elijah and Lucy knew that the "old normal" was gone, and that they needed to stay vigilant. But these days when Gabrielle left the dinner table to do homework and Elijah loaded the dishwasher while Lucy worked on the pans, it was more likely that Elijah would wrap his arms around Lucy's waist and lean into her at the sink. His whispered question now was: "Is Gabrielle going to Jane's to study tonight?"

The night before this road trip, Elijah and Lucy lay next to each other. Elijah had hoped for a restful night, but the anxiety about his daughter, his only child, soon being away from him would not yield. He turned and gazed at his wife and saw that she couldn't sleep, either. He touched her arm, and she smiled softly back.

The bedroom windows were open, the nights still not cold, but rather cool and comforting as they lay under fleecy blankets. They murmured to each other now in that soft way that lovers do. They talked about how they had dealt with Elijah's depression, how Lucy's helicoptering over Gabrielle after Dawn River had slowly lifted until now it just hovered on the side, how day by day Gabrielle's spirit was being resurrected. The tender conversation finally exhausted them. Elijah took Lucy's hand and gently kissed it.

"Good night, babe," he whispered, and they both drifted off to sleep.

As Elijah continued the drive toward the university, he was comforted by the remembered intimacy of that conversation. He glanced at the car's GPS screen. "About an hour left," he announced.

"Good," said Lucy. "That will give you plenty of time to answer my question."

Elijah gave her a puzzled look. "And what question is that?"

Lucy turned her head and looked directly at him. "When were you going to tell me?"

UPDATE: 9 INJURED IN TARGETED SAN FRANCISCO MASS SHOOTING: SUSPECT AT LARGE

CBS NEWS Bay Area

24.
BARRATT

"TELL... TELL YOU WHAT?"

Barratt's hands gripped the steering wheel tighter. He didn't glance at Lucy in the passenger seat. He wasn't ready to have this conversation. And once he told her, he knew he would be committed, that there was no going back.

"Hey, I'm your wife," Lucy said. "I know when you're holding something back."

"Let's see," she said, rubbing her chin as she feigned a quizzical look. "You could be having an affair."

"What!" Barratt blurted.

"Oh, right," said Lucy. "You have neither the time nor the energy. And why *would* you, when you have a hottie like me sitting next to you?" She laughed at Barratt's discomfort.

"You think this is funny, huh?"

"I do!" Lucy laughed again, then stopped, and her voice turned soft. "I know you're struggling with something, and I'm guessing it has to do with Dawn River. Talk to me."

"I am thinking about something, but I was trying to figure out how to share this, because I don't want to give you something else to worry about. And I'm not sure myself how...or if...I can handle it."

"Eli, we're partners. We share the important things. You can tell me anything."

Barratt relaxed slightly, Lucy's tenderness providing comfort. He knew that he couldn't go down this path until he did tell her, and felt a sense of relief as he began to speak.

"When I read about these mass shootings now, I feel it differently. It's no longer 'one more,' what a shame, and move on. I guess I was like everybody else: It was too much to take in, so I left it out. TMI."

Lucy touched his arm and left her hand there.

"But when I read about those shootings now, about the Communion River Church, about the guy who attacked that engineering firm, it gets inside me. I ache; it burns. I know what it's like to be in those places. The fear, the panic, the helplessness. And it doesn't stop. It's one after another and another and another. It just doesn't end. It's like a fucking epidemic."

"Eli, I know you always want to fix things, you always want to make things better, but how do you fix this?" Lucy squeezed his arm. "You're a wonderful man, but you...none of us...have the power to stop this by ourselves."

"Not yet," said Barratt, to a questioning look from Lucy.

"And..." said Lucy, "and we know...how dangerous it is out there. I want you to live with me for a long, long time."

"Yeah, Luce, but if I don't try, how do I live with myself?"

Barratt took a deep breath and, for the next hour, explained passionately and in great detail the elements of The Plan.

15 HURT, 2 CRITICALLY, IN MASS SHOOTING AT HALLOWEEN PARTY ON WEST SIDE

CBS News Chicago

25.
PATTY

PATTY WADDED UP ANOTHER TISSUE and tossed it toward the wastebasket under her desk. She would have to ask her mom to get a new box of Kleenex. They kept the tissue, TP, and paper towels in the only place where there was room to store them, on the wire shelving above the washer and dryer, and Patty couldn't reach that high anymore. The tissue slid off the overflowing basket and floated to the floor. Her mom would have to pick it up, since she could not get in and out of the wheelchair by herself.

Couldn't pick up the tissue. And couldn't mow the grass, couldn't run to the store, couldn't wash the car—all things she used to do as her chores, her part. Maybe she resented them sometimes, but now she longed for the mundane and the silly: squirting Ariel with the hose, racing her to the 7-Eleven at the corner, singing along with something on Spotify when she cut the grass. *What good am I now?* she asked herself.

Fingering the high school yearbook on her lap, she sat in front of her computer, reading about her friends' updated lives, although her teary eyes made it hard to focus on the screen. She did her best. Darla texted that she was following her boyfriend to Arizona State. Cindy was taking a year off to travel, then starting a job with the city tourism department.

She read, then reread, her best friend Tasha's long email. Tasha was going to UCLA on a volleyball scholarship.

Patty had concentrated on cheer her whole high school career and had scored one of the precious University of Southern California cheerleading scholarships. She had taken the USC commitment letter to school and opened it with a flourish when she showed it to Tasha. They whooped and hollered and danced and were tossed out of the library, laughing through the halls. USC and UCLA were practically next door to each other, and they would be best friends forever.

"Our lives," Tasha told Patty, "are about to change. We're going big-time!"

Patty wiped her eyes. When she was alone in her room these days, there were times when she just couldn't hold back the sobs. She didn't want anyone to hear and rush in to "pity Patty"—she had had enough of that. She gazed around her bedroom, hers since she'd left the crib. Her childhood toys and stuffed animals were boxed and in the closet. The posters of her teenage crushes—actors and singers—were packed away as well. She couldn't stand to look at the Dani Blue Big Head and had torn it to shreds after ripping it off the wall. They had all been replaced by a USC pennant and a big poster showing California beaches. *But I should get rid of this USC stuff too*, she thought. *I won't be going there now.*

She couldn't help but look again at the last USC letter, the one she'd received two months after the concert, the one she read and reread, ruminated about, the one that made her face flush and stomach churn. The school had reached out for a routine update and learned about Patty's horrible change in circumstances. USC now regretted to inform her that, given her condition, it was withdrawing her scholarship. She knew that had to be, that she couldn't perform, but it still cut deep. She thought about her conversation with Tasha when she got the first scholarship letter, all their plans. *Yeah, my life has changed, all right.* Her friends were moving on, while she was still here, in the same town, the same home, the same bedroom. Left behind.

Patty heard the front door open and realized that she hadn't shut her bedroom door. Ariel breezed in, walked up behind her, and started massaging her shoulders. "Hey, Pats, what's… Patty, what's wrong?" Patty saw Ariel looking in the mirror over the desk, where she could see Patty's red-rimmed eyes reflected.

"Nothing's wrong," said Patty.

"But your eyes are all red. Were you crying?"

"I *said* nothing's wrong."

"Jeez, don't bite my head off." Ariel moved to the edge of the bed and sat down as she turned the wheelchair so the sisters were looking at each other. "C'mon. Talk to me. Maybe I can help."

"Really, Ariel? What're you gonna do?" Patty snapped. "You're always gonna fix everything, huh? Well…" Patty spread her arms and glared at her lifeless legs. "How are you gonna fix this?!"

Ariel recoiled. "I...I don't know. I just want to...to help." She paused a beat. "Let's get out of the house. You said you wanted to go shopping. I can drive you to the mall."

Patty picked up the yearbook and slammed it onto the floor. "I don't want you to *drive* me to the mall!" She spread her fingers, tensed her hands, and stared at her sister.

"Well, *Jesus*, Patty, tell me what you do want."

"I want to drive *myself* to the mall!" Patty slumped her shoulders. "I want to drive to the mall and then walk into the mall with my friends when we're on break from college. I want to walk by the shops and look at the new running shoes, and I want to *need* new running shoes. I want other shoppers not to turn and run into me because their eye level is two feet higher than my head. I don't want them to give me those startled looks and lame apologies."

Ariel reached out and placed a hand on Patty's knee, but Patty brushed it away.

"Patty, where is this coming from?"

"*Where is it coming from*? *Where*? Gee, let's see. It's coming from my friends telling me what they're doing next in their lives. Good for them, but what's next in my life?" Patty abruptly turned her chair so she faced the desk, picked up the tissue box, turned back to Ariel, and flung the box against the wall behind the bed. It exploded. Fluffed tissues swam above them, drifting snow in a room that was icy with anger. "What's next for poor Patty?"

"Patty," she said, "you're starting college in the fall, too, right?"

"Yeah, I'm going to be four miles away. USC, California, was my *dream*. No, I'll still be living at home, and while I'm on campus I'll be the one everybody stares at, then they cover their mouth and turn and whisper to their friends, 'That's the girl that got shot.'"

"Maybe you need to give people more credit," Ariel said. "You'll make friends."

But Patty was on a roll.

"What do I *want*?" she said. "I want to cheer again. Not from a wheelchair. I want to do cartwheels and handstands and be the one on top of the pyramid." Now her voice, riding its roller coaster, softened. "I want to dance. I *loved* to dance. I want to dance standing up and have a cute guy pull me against him while I look in his eyes." Her voice fell to a whisper. "And...I don't wanna get shot again. God, Ariel, I am so afraid I'm gonna get shot again wherever I go."

Patty shook her head. "Ariel, what's going to happen to me?"

Ariel wiped her own eyes. "I...I don't know... I wish I did. But, look, you've handled everything so far, and you're really smart. You're still young. And you want to dance?" asked Ariel. "We'll get you one of those elevating wheelchairs, the ones where you push a button and you rise up. Those cute boys will have to look up at *you* and they'll be lined up to do it."

Despite herself, a slight smile tickled Patty's lips.

Ariel slipped to her knees next to the wheelchair. She hugged Patty, and as the tears flowed, she said: "You're still my annoying, amazing little sister. You can still make a life."

Patty wanted to believe her.

KANSAS CITY SHOOTING: ONE DEAD AND 21 INJURED NEAR SUPER BOWL PARADE

BBC.com/news

26.
THE DEDICATED RETURN ADVISORS

THE DEDICATED RETURN ADVISORS had its headquarters in the office of Roland Turret. Its perceived purpose was financial investment calculated to deliver above-average, low-risk returns. A total of twelve men and women made up its board of directors. They sat that morning around the twenty-foot-long table in Turret's private conference room. By meticulous design, the room managed to be richly elegant without being ostentatious. The table was fashioned out of solid mahogany; the sideboards, holding crystal and china serving pieces, were dark stained oak. The directors' seats were plush leather, with each person in attendance having before him or her a computer screen that rose up with a touch of the table surface. The artwork was eclectic, including an original Miro and Mary Cassatt. Floor-to-ceiling windows offered a thirty-fourth-floor view of the city's business district. Turret's patrician mien was the perfect fit for the room.

After staff members had set out fruit, croissants and scones, an array of juices, and still and sparkling water, Turret began the business of the day by rapping on the table.

"I call this so-called meeting to order," he said with a smile. In return he received some light laughter.

He gazed at the faces arrayed around him. They constituted a who's who of the national and international elite from the worlds of law, finance, academia, business, technology, and entertainment. Some of their names and faces would be immediately known to the public if spoken or seen; others managed to personally stay out of the public glare, but their work was likely known to everyone.

The agenda included reports by each of the members concerning their individual financial and public relations projects designed to advance the group's goals. There were, however, no shareholder reports, no officers' presentations, no budget questions. Their ersatz business's name may have been the Dedicated Return Advisors, but they referred to themselves internally as the Dawn River Associates, so-called because of their support of Barratt and out of deference to their leader, Roland Turret. They had no clients. The company's only goal was to shepherd Elijah Barratt into the White House so that he could effectuate The Plan.

These were the people Barratt had named when he first told Lucy that he was going to run.

When Barratt did run, the press, pundits, and public puzzled over the support he received from these titans. They were, however, members of an unfortunate community, of which Barratt was also a part. Barratt had lobbied each of them because all of them had suffered injury or loss by a gunman, random victims of indiscriminate shootings.

Anna Appleton was an artificial intelligence startup star, creating and then selling three of the leading companies in the field, becoming a billionaire in her fifties. Her partner was the CEO of a huge management firm whose clients included the stars of a professional soccer team. Her partner was one of eight murder victims when Ben Tabor shot up a rally before the team's playoff game.

Maria Dominguez was the CEO and principal shareholder in a chain of grocery stores. Her sister took Maria's daughter to the Dani Blue concert as her birthday gift. Only the daughter came home.

Morris Jackson was a Wall Street broker with three million followers of his podcast. His wife was shopping on Rodeo Drive when she and five others were shot down outside a jewelry store that was targeted in a daylight armed robbery.

Hatha Mandu came to the United States with $90 and a promise of work at his uncle's neighborhood pharmacy. Mandu now owned the largest chain of pharmacies in the Southwest. His son and two of his son's friends were killed in a shooting during a college rave.

The board was bound together by tragedy, by blood, in the most literal way.

The DRA did not solicit donations. They were each wealthy enough to fund an election on his or her own, if need be. Instead, they used their wealth and specialized backgrounds to publish their own ads, command op-ed space, and use their prodigious influence to persuade many opinion-makers and political aspirants to see the value of a Barratt ascendancy. The members of the DRA were sufficiently powerful that the media gave them attention and airtime. Since they did not operate as a PAC, did not coordinate with any other entity, and were not aligned with any campaign, they were not required to report their operations. Technically and legally, they were simply twelve interested citizens who each, in their own way, advocated a position.

They each had all the notoriety they wanted. Their goal was closure. They were problem-solvers, they were big thinkers, they were used to leading people and moving mountains. But they couldn't move past their grief, couldn't find their way out of the muddy morass of their loss.

Barratt gave them a way.

When Barratt ran for city council, they moved slowly, searching for the most effective way to proceed: a phone call here, Barratt's name dropped during a business show appearance there. By the time he ran for the United States Congress they had honed their methods: prime-time

TV ads, business conference sidebars, acting individually but coordinating through the Dawn River Associates. By the time Barratt ran for president, they were a force to be reckoned with, but the details of their coordination were known to few outside the boardroom.

Roland Turret was their acknowledged captain. He was a self-made conglomerate, with interests in precious minerals, wind and solar energy, gemstone mining, real estate investment, and a myriad of other businesses.

He had taken his twin fourteen-year-old daughters to the Dani Blue concert. One of the girls suffered a collapsed lung and a ruptured spleen; the other escaped with only a flesh wound. Turret's left arm was so mangled by several rounds that it had to be amputated above the elbow. He eschewed a prosthetic, instead having his dress shirts and suits custom-made to accommodate his half-length arm. His thick black hair, square-jawed visage, athletic body, and piercing black eyes, juxtaposed with his damaged body, caused those who met him for the first time to be taken aback. He had used their responses to his advantage, stunning them with his confidence and shunning any pity.

"I'm the same man I was," he would tell them. "There's just a little less of me."

He knew that wasn't true, that he was missing more than pieces of flesh and bone. He was missing his sense of indestructibility.

I'll never get that back, he acknowledged to himself, *but I can fight back, and if Barratt is my weapon, then let's go to war.*

10 PEOPLE KILLED, 10 INJURED IN MASS SHOOTING AT MONTEREY PARK DANCE STUDIO

Los Angeles Times

27.
BARRATT

AND NOW, GOD HELP ME, thought Barratt, *I'm a politician.*

When Barratt had explained to Lucy that the next step in The Plan was running for office, she looked at him doubtfully. When he told her that he had already secured support from Dawn River survivors and families of the victims, she seemed somewhat reassured. When he said that Bobby was going to be by his side, she broke out a smile. When he described an ad hoc group of people damaged by the gun violence, and named some of its members, she was excited.

Bobby Gennaro—just Bobby or Bobby G to Barratt and Lucy—was Barratt's best friend, college roommate, and confidant. They didn't see each other as often after graduation, but following the night of Dawn River, Bobby was there at the hospital, there during Barratt's rehab. Barratt considered him one of the smartest people he knew, and Bobby proved it when he became Barratt's campaign manager.

Barratt now sat in his car outside of the Second Home Senior Complex. The facility was elegantly appointed and meticulously maintained. Bobby G sat patiently next to him. Barratt had breezed through the primary and general elections for his seat on the county board of supervisors. His personal story was compelling, and Dawn River had become notorious as the worst mass shooting in the state's history.

Barratt had neared the end of his three-year term on the county board and was now running for an open congressional seat.

"This is a very different ballgame," Barratt said as he turned to Bobby. "This district has five times the population of the county. We have our work cut out for us."

"And there's a new long list of people who don't want you to succeed. The gun rights organizations are right at the top."

"Hey, right now I'm less concerned about that than about standing in front of some well-informed senior citizens."

Bobby smiled. "Well-informed and opinionated and ready to tell you what to do."

Barratt had stood in front of juries, he had addressed conferences, he had argued before panels of appellate judges. This was different, he thought. In most of those cases, he was arguing for someone else, but this was his cause, this was his claim, this was personal. This was the next step in The Plan. His supporters were indeed powerful, but he didn't just want to win elections; he wanted to prepare people for what was to come so that, when the time *did* come, they would support—they would understand—what he was doing and why.

"You know, Bobby, for all the bluster and polling and pontificating we do, no one really knows what makes up a voter's mind. Everybody's unique. Everyone sees the facts from their own perspective. If I want them to understand, to *embrace,* what I'm saying, I need to move them out of their preconception, out of their safe place."

"What was it you always told your witnesses?" asked Bobby. "Just tell the truth. Now *that* will be something different for a politician."

They exited the car, and Barratt stopped on the portico. He took a deep breath. Sometimes the journey he was on seemed as if it went on forever. One foot in front of the other, he told himself, and they stepped into the building.

They met their host inside and were escorted to the commons room. It was filled with round tables each set with six chairs. Wheelchairs were dotted throughout. A podium stood against a bank of tall windows with the sun bright behind them. The home's policy was to have one candidate at a time meet with their residents. No debates, just remarks and then questions and answers. The candidate was expected to provide food and drinks, and Barratt had catered an impressive array: cold cuts, potato and chicken salads, bowls of fresh fruit, chocolate chip cookies. Vegetarian and low-salt dishes. He could see that most of the residents had already filled their plates and were busy eating and chatting.

Six women sat at one table, looking to be dressed for a night out. Two wore pantsuits—one green, one bright yellow—and the others wore dresses with busy patterns. Some wore bright yellow or red earrings and matching necklaces. Men at another table were somewhat more casual, but they still wore dress pants and buttoned shirts. Barratt knew from his county supervisor campaign that they all expected to be entertained and were likely to be a tough audience. Barratt told Lucy when he started practicing law that he quickly learned that every client had a story, had a dignity that he respected. He recognized that in front of him at Second Home were men and women who had lived life, succeeded and failed and mostly risen up again, who had lost people close to them and knew that it wouldn't be long before they joined them. *These are no fools*, Barratt thought. If I want them on my side, with what I will one day propose, there can't be any BS.

Barratt had considered having Bobby introduce him, but he rejected that as being too self-important. As Barratt approached the podium now, a voice called out from the back of the room.

"You're already doing better than the last one, young fella," a man said. "This food is a lot better." This brought a laugh from the crowd and a smile from Barratt, thankful that someone had broken the ice for him.

"I'm glad you like it," he said.

He noticed that many in the audience were squinting because of the sun glare behind him, and that he was probably backlit to the point of being indistinct. The podium was on wheels; he unlocked them and rolled the podium to the side of the room where no one was affected by the sun.

"Now that's what I call a problem-solver," said a woman seated near him, and the seniors laughed again.

"Oh, Birdie," another woman at the table said. "You always have something to say."

Bobby remained in the back of the room, raised his eyebrows, and smiled at Barratt as if to say, *off to a good start.*

"First," said Barratt, "I'm going to tell you things you already know, because I would like you to understand that I know them too."

He spoke for several minutes about protecting Social Security, reducing Medicare deductibles, and securing funding for better handicapped access to several local parks.

"Every candidate that comes in here is likely to tell you the same thing, and I suspect that most of us will do our best to fulfill those promises. But I want to talk to you today about quality of life, about you and your kids and their kids."

Barratt recounted what happened at Dawn River, with many in the audience nodding in recognition, sitting in respectful silence. He asked them to understand that the victims weren't limited to those who were shot, but included those caught in the exploding, expanding, foul cloud of suffering that rose up out of such shootings.

"Your grandchild's teacher might never come back. Right here in your town, A-1 Automotive lost two key employees at Dawn River. Children are left without a parent. In the next town over, you know that great little diner, Matt's Place? After one of their cooks brought a gun to work and shot up the oven, customers never came back. They went out of business. People lost their jobs. Distraught survivors take their own lives. Bottom line: we're killing ourselves, and we're condemning so many to unendurable pain.

"If you give me the chance, I'm going to do something about it."

"A lot of people have tried, Mr. Barratt," said a patrician-looking, gray-haired, bespectacled man from one of the tables. "What makes you think that you can keep that effort heading in the right direction?"

"If I don't," said Barratt, "I'm counting on the ol…the *experienced* men and women in this room to steer me straight."

He received a loud ovation.

Five months later, Barratt won his seat in the US House. His secret supporters made sure that his every vote, every bill sponsorship, every university address had maximum exposure.

Then lightning struck.

The state's long-serving senior United States senator dropped dead of a massive heart attack on the Senate floor. Governor Harman, no fan of Barratt, whom he considered a Johnny-come-lately who hadn't paid his dues, had designs on the seat but didn't want to make a move until his gubernatorial term was over. Bobby, with a heads-up from his contacts in the State House, told Barratt about the governor's intentions: Harman would appoint Barratt to complete the unexpired term, then move Barratt aside when it expired and clear the way for Harman to run for the seat. Barratt would become irrelevant.

"Let him," said Barratt. "We'll get our foot in the door, then shove it open. We'll start running against Harman the minute I'm confirmed. This moves The Plan's timeline up by two years."

When the unexpired term ended, Barratt was still the fair-haired boy, and a seething Governor Harman was the curmudgeon who was slammed for trying to stand in his way.

After winning the full Senate term, Barratt launched the final phase of The Plan's Part One.

"I'll be damned," Bobby told him. "This might actually work."

Five years later, Barratt was sworn in as the president of the United States.

GUNMAN RIDING SCOOTER IN QUEENS KILLS ONE PERSON AND INJURES THREE OTHERS IN BACK-TO-BACK 'RANDOM' SHOOTINGS, NEW YORK POLICE SAY

CNN

PART TWO

28.
JIMMY

JIMMY WAS, RELUCTANTLY, back in the city. It seemed to be where most of his targets lay. As usual, he parked remotely and rode the MetroTransit high-speed line and exited downtown. He was headed for the headquarters of Priority Health Systems and once more would have to pass by Dawn River. Why was it that every time he came into the city he wound up near it? Was it coincidence? Or was it pulling him back, holding him back, never letting go?

As he made his way along the crowded sidewalk, he once again felt the looming presence of the concert hall to his right. All these years later and Dawn River kept stalking him. His muscles tightened, his breathing became rapid. He turned his eyes down and away and bumped into a couple coming toward him. Bouncing off them he reflexively stepped into the street. Horns blared and tires screeched as a car stopped a foot from his knees.

The driver lowered the passenger window and yelled, "Hey, asshole? Watch where you're goin'!"

"Yeah, fuck you!" Jimmy shot back.

Jimmy wobbled away from the car as the driver moved off, his heart racing, adrenaline coursing, his face hot as he stumbled the next hundred feet in the gutter before stepping back on the sidewalk, leaving Dawn River behind, at least physically.

"What's wrong with me?" he muttered. "Why won't this pain stop?"

His intent today was to go after Helen Martin, who had worked at Millville Memorial Hospital when it was investigated for the suspicious death of elderly patients, some in her care. No charges, but a cloud of suspicion. She now worked at Priority Health Systems. Her son, Shawn, was a high school wrestling star whose world had suddenly crashed. He had lost his scholarship to Colford College when it canceled its wrestling program; he had caught his impossibly cute girlfriend, Tessa, making out with his teammate Frank, and his coach called him out in front of the team for losing focus.

Shawn took the 9mm Smith & Wesson pistol, which his father had purchased in his own name and then gifted to his son, to school. He shot the coach, Frank, and Tessa, in that order.

Then he shot himself.

Jimmy had anonymously attacked parent targets almost ten times now, seven successfully. Helen Martin was next.

He hadn't completely gained his equilibrium after stepping back onto the sidewalk, swaying and stumbling. His face was still hot; his mind was still racing.

Jimmy stopped abruptly in the middle of the sidewalk, people bumping into him from behind. Standing stock still, he leaned his head back and looked at the sky. The morning drizzle had stopped, but the clouds would not surrender. The air had that dank, musty smell that a littered city street emits when summoned by the rain. Passersby stared at this rumpled, scruffy man staring at the sky, his mouth half open.

"Don't stare at him," a mother cautioned her young child as they neared Jimmy.

"What's wrong with him, Mommy?"

"I don't know, honey. He's probably sick."

Before she could stop him, the little boy reached out and touched Jimmy's arm. Jimmy recoiled and looked at the child, his eyes wide and wild. The child started to scream and the mother rushed him away.

Jimmy looked around him, as if seeing the people on the sidewalk for the first time. He panicked and started to run, brushing people aside, banging into a light post, then a street sign. Pulling out the envelope he had planned to deliver to Priority, he crumpled it and dunked it in a trash can.

"What's the point?" he shouted. "Nothing changes! None of this matters! None of this changes anything!"

He kept repeating it, louder each time, screaming it now. The stream of people who had swirled around him gave him a wide berth. Then his voice lowered as he shuffled to the curb and sat down on it, his feet in the gutter that was cluttered with wet paper cups and food wrappers.

"Nothing helps," he said one last time, then quieted and slumped.

Finally, an older man approached him and gently touched his shoulder. He didn't react, oblivious.

"Son," said the man, "you look like you're having a rough time. Can I call someone for you?"

Jimmy turned his head to face him.

"There's only one person who can help," he said, "but she can't answer."

SHOOTING IN YELLOWSTONE NATIONAL PARK LEAVES ONE DEAD, RANGER INJURED

Oil City News

Wyoming

29.
DEREK

DEREK WAS A BIG FAN of those who used bell towers, but he deserved something more creative, he thought.

The Washington Monument? At 555 feet tall, it was too high; the angles would be too difficult. The Empire State Building? *Yeah, right,* he thought. What was it, about 1,300 feet? Deal-breaker. The Statue of Liberty was only 305 feet tall, but the difficulty of getting his gear onto Liberty Island was likely prohibitive.

All right, he mused. He needed something that at first would seem mundane but would become unique. After looking throughout the mid-South, he actually found it close to home: the Midtown Parking Garage. The typical height of a parking garage floor was between ten and twelve feet. This one was nine stories, close to one hundred feet. Perfect.

And he had the perfect occasion: this ridiculous parade. Some aging B-movie actor, born and raised right here in this dump, was getting the keys to the city. Big deal. And in a spasm of what Derek thought was typical overreach, the brilliant city council decided to shut down the main road and put this has-been on a float. They expected hundreds to line the street.

More targets for me, Derek thought.

The weather was cooperating as well. There was no rain in the forecast, and the skies were mostly cloudy, limiting the chance of significant reflection. The temperature was still quite warm, predicted highs in the eighties, so he expected most people to stay in place once they found a spot, fanning themselves and not expending too much energy.

Derek had figured that the parking garage would be the first stop for paradegoers and they would rush to the uncovered top floor, a prime viewing spot, but he had come prepared. He made sure that he was the first to arrive, before the sun was up, and immediately drove his pickup to the eighth floor. Once there, he removed from the enclosed cab a pair of sawhorse barricades. On each of them he had affixed official-looking signs declaring: *Top Floor Under Repair. No Access.* To make sure that everyone got the point, he laid a nail strip just in front of the signs. Then he quickly returned to his truck and drove to the top.

I am so good at this, Derek praised himself, but he expected to be. He was, after all, a professional. Over six feet tall, classic square Eastern European face, shock of unruly dark hair, thick body, stern visage. He knew he looked the part. Chechen by birth, ten years in the Russian army had honed his sniper skills. He considered himself the best they had, even if he didn't receive the medals and acknowledgements *he* deserved but that were given to others. Eventually he grew tired of the disrespect, and those arrogant Russians grew tired of what they considered his insubordination. He left, but not without surreptitiously taking his best friend with him: his Chukavin sniper rifle, or SVC.

Introduced in 2017, it replaced what he thought of as a relic, the Dragunov SVD. The Chukavin had a max range of over 1,600 yards; he was unlikely to need that today, but he loved knowing that it was there. He shook his head at the US's fascination with the semi-automatic Kalashnikovs. *What a joke*, he thought. They were notoriously inaccurate for the untrained, good only in close quarters for shooters who didn't know what they were doing.

Derek parked his truck in the middle of the top floor so that it wouldn't be seen from ground level, then walked to the edge. He assessed the crowd gathering below him. He saw city workers directing people to keep out of the roadway itself, the workers laughing with them as the parade watchers struggled to hold on to their vantage points. Street vendors hawked balloons and noisemakers, cotton candy and Day-Glo necklaces, while children danced around the carts, giggling and holding out crumpled dollar bills. Groups of young men gathered in fours and fives behind the crowded sidewalk, laughing and jostling, hiding beers in paper bags, slapping each other's backs. The crowd noise rose as its numbers filled out and the start time approached.

Derek turned back to the task at hand. He deployed the rest of his equipment. He had brought three eighteen-foot-tall sky dancers or air dancers or tube men—whatever they called those crazy dancing figures that all the car lots displayed to attract attention. He fitted them to their related generators and set them for a low airspeed, which would produce the kinks and bends in the body that made the inflated goofballs wave maniacally. Just for his own amusement, he brought one each in red, white, and blue. He planned for them to draw the attention of people on the ground.

One hundred feet west of the air dancers, he assembled and set up his sniper gear, attaching the tripod and dialing in the scope. He had already changed his clothes, donning all gray to blend in with the concrete parapet that ran along the border of the top floor. The parapet was wide enough that he could use his small sandbags along with the fitted tripod to rest the Chukavin. He felt the perspiration that the heat and his exertion produced forming on his body, his corded muscles rippling and glistening. At the same time, he breathed steadily, his pulse calm, his throat clear, as he spoke his mantra: "I was born for this." He was ready, but he would wait until shortly before the actor's float came into view.

He was good at waiting.

The crowd was indeed large, but it was compressed because the parade route was relatively short. Many had brought their folding chairs, some with umbrellas attached, some with cupholders filled with beer or soda bottles, the different colored chairs forming a festive rainbow. People were mostly in shorts and sandals. Some wore bright Hawaiian shirts; others wore caps with logos that looked to Derek to proclaim loyalty to some sports team. There was a mix of older folks—gray hair and sunglasses and wide-brimmed hats. The younger contingent wore t-shirts and halter tops. There were plenty of kids, all ages represented, including toddlers nestled on a mother's or father's lap. The rhythm-challenged high school band marched by. The mayor and council moved slowly along, sitting with their spouses on the top of the back seats of red or white convertibles, magnetic signs on the doors announcing who they were, tossing candies that set the children scrambling.

What a wonderful day for a parade, Derek smirked.

He knew, from the order of the parade participants, which had been posted online, that there were perhaps five minutes left before the guest of honor arrived. Many people had noticed the air dancers and pointed them out to those around them, but Derek wanted their full attention. He sounded the high-decibel air horn that he had brought. People turned toward the garage's top floor, likely expecting some further entertainment to come from there.

He didn't want to disappoint them.

Age was not a consideration as he selected his targets. First, he killed a mother and the toddler she was holding with one shot through the child's chest. Then he acquired an older couple as they sat there holding hands. He shot them both through the forehead.

His rifle was suppressed, and the distance was sufficient that no one on the ground could hear any noise from his firing. People near to those who had fallen now noticed what had happened and stood in shock.

Their shock was eliminated when they were next.

Now he aimed at the other side of the street—he didn't want to play favorites—and took out three teenagers sitting on the curb.

He continued to fire along that side of the street, but now, with so many bodies dropping, there was an explosion of chaos. Some rushed to render aid, a pointless exercise. Most had started to run, in all different directions, screaming and tripping and falling. He panned their track and brought down two more, plus one who had stopped to help them up. He moved quickly to another vantage point, set up there, and started firing again. Several police officers who had deduced where the shots were coming from pulled their sidearms and began shooting at the garage roof. Given their pistols' notorious lack of accuracy at distance and their inability to actually see him, they were no threat. Since they were uniformed officers, Derek had no desire to fire on them.

The street below was emptying quickly. Whoever was driving the actor's float had apparently seen the chaos and diverted, so Derek would not have the satisfaction of adding the actor to his count. No matter, he thought; this had been a complete success. He would finally get the recognition he was due.

He knew that as part of the ensuing investigation everyone would ask: Why did he do it? What was his motivation? They would propose all sorts of explanations: what they thought was his humiliating departure from the Russian army; his abusive father and distant mother; his acting out in response to being jilted by a lover.

Fools, he thought. They'd never understand. For him, it was the rush, the control, the high of being the arbiter of who would live and who would die. With his rifle in his hands, he was a god!

Whatever answer they were looking for, it wouldn't be coming from him.

Holding his beloved sniper rifle at port arms, he climbed up onto the parapet, stepped forward, and became a literal air dancer as he dove into infamy.

WHAT WE KNOW: MOTORCYCLE GANG SHOOTING KILLS 3 AND INJURES 5

KOAT Action News
(New Mexico)

30.
PARADATION ONE

PARADATION RESTS BETWEEN Mount Yolke and Mount Bounty in the Upper Midwest. They can only generously be called mountains. Neither is over eight hundred feet, but they are part of a series of large hills that ring the city. With a population of about 18,000, the city supports several pharmacies, four grocery stores, two high schools, one medical clinic, three churches, various retail shops along the main street, and seven bars. Its claim to fame, however, of which the local populace is somewhat alarmingly proud, is that it has more firearms per capita than any other municipality in the United States. Its residents learned early: six-year-olds shooting targets with BB guns, ten-year-olds hunting with shotguns. The conversations before school are less about the mediocre football team and more about who has what in the gun safe. The same conversations can be heard not only in the bars but also outside the churches on Sunday.

My kind of place, figured Tommy Estes, President of Guns Are Us, one of the more prominent and aggressive gun rights organizations. That's why he chose Paradation as the site for its rally. The city had no problem granting the permits for their march through town, and he was assured that open carry was not only permitted but encouraged. Thus, on a sultry Saturday night, close to three hundred Guns Are Us members assembled in Paradation City Park in preparation for the march. GAU brought two flatbed trucks with floodlights; the marchers had flashlights with orange hoods to suggest torches. The group had used actual torches in the past, but after several members inadvertently set each other on fire, they switched. They were scheduled to kick off at 9:00 p.m. MST.

Estes stood on the back of another flatbed truck that would lead the parade. It was adorned with American flags, *Don't Tread on US* banners, and the band that would accompany the march. He was of average height, but rail thin, with a hank of unruly brown hair. In his early fifties, his weathered face gave him the appearance of a much older man. His jeans sagged, but his USA hat stood high on his head. He approached the microphone connected to the band's speakers, stumbling sightly as he did. His whole affect was that of a frumpy old man, but when he began to speak that image fell away. *Showtime*, he whispered to himself, and was transformed. Now he was the man his followers called "Tommy Thunder." His voice boomed across the assembled crowd and compelled their immediate attention.

"We are here today to celebrate the Second Amendment," he said. "We are here today not because our rights were given to us by the Founding Fathers. No, these rights were given to us by God. And they are ours to use in the way God intended." Estes paused as the crowd cheered. With a sweep of his hand he directed his audience to the posters attached to the sides of the flatbed. The ALL YOUR AMMO ad depicted a ripped young white man in camo holding his AR-15 at port arms, with a long-haired blonde woman in a camo bikini draped admiringly on his shoulder. "And y'all know that the guy with the gun gets the girl," he said to enthusiastic laughter.

He paused again, affected a more serious tone, and continued: "And the reason God granted us our Second Amendment rights is because we are the guardians. We are responsible for protecting that girl and all the women and all the children and all the families!" The crowd roared and waved the American flags that had been distributed. "We are here today to march, to demonstrate, to *testify* that we are ready, willing, and able to do our job, safeguard our country, and protect our heritage!" The response was raucous, with whistling, clapping, cheers, and chants.

These are my people, Estes thought. *This is my family.*

"At my signal," he said, "we will move out. We will follow this truck. We will march peacefully." There were some snickers from the crowd that he squelched quickly with an upraised hand. "But we will be prepared; we will march proudly and we won't be intimidated by any intruders. You know how they like to follow us around." Laughter and hoots from the faithful. "We will march for our families, ourselves, and for all of America!" Now the crowd was a roaring torrent, a crashing wave of shouts and whistles, rolling inexorably forward.

Estes stepped to the truck cab and slapped the roof. The driver fired up the engine and pulled slowly out of the park and onto the roadway. Estes gave the signal to begin, and the Guns Are Us members fell into a random line behind. They marched four or five or six abreast, rifles—mostly AR-15s—held loosely or slung over their backs. They chatted and joked with each other. Some punched each other playfully in the arm, or bumped fists or high-fived. There was an air of guy fun, the testosterone level rivaling that of a football locker room.

Residents lined the parade route. The older ones were seated in lawn chairs, coolers open in front of them. Mothers held children in their arms or were seated on the benches that bordered the street. Everyone stood as the flags went by, hands over hearts or saluting, and then, as the truck passed, they began to clap in rhythm with the band. Many in the crowd waved their phones with the flashlight engaged. Most of the shops stayed open late, hoping that they might do a little business, their signs illuminated, some with American flags in their windows.

Benny and his friend Dude had ridden their bikes to the parade route. They had decorated them with red, white, and blue crepe paper. Eleven years old, born during the same month, they had been best friends forever. Both beanpoles, with mops of blond, scarecrow hair, the color of the corn silk in the nearby farm fields. They rocked back and forth on their bikes, arms draped over the handlebars, bodies languid, seemingly almost liquid as only young, flexible kids can be. They bantered and laughed and from time to time raised a can of pop to their lips and swigged deeply. This was the most exciting thing that had ever happened to Paradation, and they were going to revel in every minute of it.

The people who lived in Paradation had noticed that others from all over the surrounding area, judging by their out-of-state tags, had flooded into the small city over the last several days. The visitors carried holstered pistols or slung long guns, nothing unusual in Paradation. The locals could sense the outsiders, but they mostly looked and acted just like they did. They didn't see a threat.

They should have.

1 DEAD, AT LEAST 22 HURT IN SHOOTING DURING JUNETEENTH CELEBRATION NEAR WILLOWBROOK

Daily Herald
CHICAGO

31.

PARADATION TWO

THE VISITORS TO PARADATION did look different in one consistent but rather innocuous way. While they were mostly in plain jeans, some in overalls, some with Timberland boots and some with Caterpillar, they all wore black shirts and had a red bandanna around their necks. They were not gathered in one place but rather spread along the streets or standing in front of Resnick's Pharmacy, the Ante Up Bar, and some of the other storefronts. As Guns Are Us started to march, the Bandanna Men started to coalesce. They moved slowly but steadily until suddenly there were twenty, then fifty, then one hundred gathered in the roadway, about two hundred feet short of where the parade route would end. As they did so, they pulled the bandannas up on their faces to just below the eye line. Some broke off, unfurled banners, and joined those positioned at the storefronts, where they stapled the banners across the doorways: *Fascism Ends Here*, *You Are Your Own Government*, *Welcome To Perdition.* Those who stood in the street unfurled their own banner: *Right Wing; Wrong Way* and *Fuck You, Racists.*

When the Bandanna Men first started to smash the store windows with the butts of their long guns, the sound of the band and the cheering of the crowd drowned out the explosion of broken glass. But as they worked their way along the street and closer to the front of the parade, more and more of the spectators heard and saw what was happening. It took several moments to sink in. When it did, spectators stood and ran and scrambled away, leaving chairs and umbrellas and cups and bottles in their wake. Mothers clasped their children and hurried from the roiling wave of men and guns and glass and now the chanting: "Right Wing—Wrong Way! Right Wing—Wrong Way!"

The distance between the two street groups started to narrow. From his perch on the truck, Estes saw them strung across the street. At first he thought it could be some of his men arriving late, but realized that there were too many and the body language was all wrong. He moved along the flatbed toward the cab and stood on one of the railings to get a better view, raising his binoculars to his eyes. He saw the firearms and the bandannas and knew exactly what was happening. He banged on the cab roof and yelled for the driver to stop. Then he quieted the band, rushed to the back of the truck, picked up the mic, and shouted to his followers.

"We have company, boys! They're some of our old friends. Let's tell them they're not invited to our party!" He hopped down from the flatbed, strode around the truck, and started to march up the street. His men fell in step behind him.

Benny and Dude heard the commotion, but they couldn't see what was causing it. The crush of people prevented them from riding down the sidewalk, but they knew every little shortcut in town. They wheeled their bikes around and darted down a side street to an alley that ran parallel with the main road. They hit the alley, pedaled hard, then leaned into another turn and headed up another side street toward where they heard chanting. "Let's see what's goin' on," shouted Dude. "Must be somethin' pretty cool!"

They hit the main street at warp speed and raced into the intersection. As they did so, they looked right and saw the Guns Are Us crowd approaching with their long guns unslung and held at the ready. They looked left and saw a different group, gunned up as well. This group had hats pulled down tight, with red bandannas pulled up, so only their eyes showed. The front line of eyes was intense and dark and malevolent. "Oh shit," they said in unison. They hit their brakes, tires squealing and fishtailing, lost control, and smashed together, a tangle of boys and bikes. They lay in a heap in the middle of the street, looking furtively left and right, their heads on swivels.

Everything stopped.

Both groups facing the boys went quiet, momentarily hesitant to move forward. It was an inflection moment. Either side, or both, could have taken a step back, could have lowered their guns, their point made, their "integrity" intact. There was total silence: no one spoke, no music played, no feet shuffled, no birds sang, no squirrels scurried.

Then two women who had seen the boys crash and stopped their own flight ran toward them. They wrestled the boys apart, grabbed the bikes, and shepherded the mess out of the street. "Come on, boys," they yelled, "we have to get out of here." They kept their voices calm as their hearts beat wildly. The motley group reached the sidewalk and rushed down the side street. Guns Are Us and the red Bandanna Men stood transfixed, staring each other down.

Then a shot rang out.

THREE DEAD, 11 INJURED IN MASS SHOOTING AT SOUTH ARKANSAS GROCERY

Arkansas Advocate

32.
MOJO

DARKNESS, AS IT DID EVERY NIGHT, enveloped the city. Just after 10:00 p.m., the roads were still busy with traffic, the sidewalks thick with those coming in or going out. Headlights, taillights, the glow of open cell phones, the beckoning, illuminated restaurant signs all fought against the end of the day. They always lost.

Inside the Oval Office, Barratt sat alone. Rereading a paragraph of the report before him, he stifled a yawn and worked to comprehend the wording. The soft classical music playing from the hidden speakers was too seductive, and he struggled to keep his eyes open, Vivaldi's *Four Seasons* too enervating. It was a melancholy regret of his that he never learned to play a musical instrument, but he enjoyed an eclectic playlist. Perhaps he should have chosen something more upbeat tonight, some of the old stuff—Joan Jett, Jude Cole—so he could borrow its energy. He rose every morning at 5:30, which meant that, especially given the burden he carried every day, his stamina waned as the next morning got ever closer. Still, he pushed to finish the document.

Then Mojo entered the office. She could be as quiet as a whisper or as loud as a stampede. Padding softly across the multicolored woolen rug, stopping to scratch enthusiastically at her favorite corner, she effortlessly leaped onto Barratt's desk, settling atop the report and looking at him rather sympathetically. Barratt reached out a hand for her to sniff, then scratched the cat's head and behind her ears.

"Thank you," he said. He talked to her constantly whenever they were together. "I didn't realize it was getting late."

He continued smoothing the soft fur around her neck and under her chin. As he did so, his eyes glazed over.

After the shooting at Dawn River, after he had left the hospital, Barratt struggled to get out of his own bed. His physical recovery was proceeding, albeit slowly, but emotionally he was buried. He would lie there hour after hour, in the same gray sweatpants and sweatshirt, day after day. The sheet would become bunched and mussed with his turnings, would become ripe with his anxious scent. Lucy had to insist they change the bedding and that he submit to a shower. He would endlessly ruminate: Should he have said no when Gabrielle begged to go to the concert? Should he have anticipated that the times were too dangerous to risk her safety? Should he have kept his head on a swivel and seen the shooter before the carnage? Should he have stopped her before she moved to the front of the stage?

Lucy struggled to help, then gave in to helping herself and brought home Mojo, a rescued shorthair calico tabby kitten, all orange and gray and white and black and brown, to bring a spirit into the house. Mojo ignored Barratt's protestations, and from the first day climbed into bed with him. She didn't judge. She didn't scold, just curled up between his chest and his arm and used her softness and innocence to heal him. Barratt absorbed her spirit and gradually, painstakingly—she never grew impatient—he started to live again.

Mojo uncurled herself from the report on Barratt's desk and rose from the scrunched paper. She preened, stretched, and sat on her haunches. Looking at him, she mewed, then made sounds that only a cat makes. Barratt smiled every time he looked at her, no matter what she was doing. He smiled now.

"All right," he said, "let's go."

Barratt rose from behind the desk, raised his arms above his head, and did his own stretch. As the Presidential day would end, he sometimes struggled to leave the chaotic world of his job and simply become a person again. Mojo came to get him every night that he was in the White House and led him upstairs to the private quarters. They left the Oval Office and walked down the hallway leading to the stairs, receiving knowing nods and goodnight wishes from the Secret Service officers. Mojo disdained the elevators. Barratt deferred to her, and they climbed to the second floor.

Upstairs, Mojo trotted and Barratt shuffled to Lucy's bedroom.

"Hey, babe," Barratt grinned as he entered. Lucy was propped up in bed, a mountain of pillows behind her back, one of the cable news shows muted on the TV as she messed with her phone. They kissed lightly and said good night.

Lucy smiled down at Mojo: "Are you sleeping with Daddy tonight?" she asked the cat, then answered before Mojo could reply: "Of course you are."

Barratt reentered the hallway, at the other end of which was his bedroom, but detoured to the kitchen, where he filled Mojo's food bowls and checked her water fountain. He grabbed some treats that he would leave for her on the floor at the foot of his bed. He was the leader of the most powerful country in the world, but he loved being Princess Mojo's attendant.

Barratt and Mojo returned to the hallway and moved toward his bedroom. Long ago, he and Lucy had let go of the fiction that a married couple should always sleep in the same bed. Better to get a good night's sleep: Lucy would be up until 1:00 a.m. with the TV droning on; Barratt would pick up the book he was currently reading and be asleep before he finished a page. Besides, he sometimes thought, one of the things you sacrificed when you were elected president was a robust—that is, frequent—sex life. They both understood that. When they were able to slip out to a favorite restaurant and enjoy a private romantic meal, they considered it foreplay. When either one of them quietly stepped through the hallway and crawled into bed with the other, they felt they had challenged a taboo and were young again.

Barratt made his way into bed now, said his simple nighttime prayers, and picked up one of the apocalyptic novels he could get lost in. The more zombies, the better. Mojo glided up onto the bed, made her way to his side, kneaded the covers there, then settled in for the night. Barratt's cell phone was off; he would be awakened by his aides if needed. It was quiet; even the outside nighttime noises could not intrude here. Tomorrow would bring another crisis that was his responsibility to resolve, but in this moment, he relaxed into being just another working man at the end of the day. As he closed his eyes, the book slipped from his hands. Mojo started to delicately snore, and Barratt fell into a deep, dreamless sleep.

Barratt felt the bed shaking, his body moving. Half-asleep, he mumbled to himself: "An earthquake? In DC?"

"No, sir, just me," his aide said as he removed his hand from Barratt's arm. "I'm sorry to disturb you, but we felt that you would want to hear about this one immediately."

SIX PEOPLE DEAD AFTER SHOOTING SPREE IN AUSTIN, DOUBLE HOMICIDE IN BEXAR COUNTY

KXAN
Austin

33.
BARRATT

AS MUCH AS BARRATT REVERED the Oval Office, it was not a place where he could rest. The presidential trappings, the reminders of the crises confronted in that room, cloaked him, pressed him down with the weight of his responsibility. Even sitting at the Resolute Desk, as powerful as it was for him, as much as it filled his spirit and fed his energy, it was not a route to an escape.

He had moved down the hallway to the small conference room near the Oval Office and took his usual seat with his back to the windows to await Bobby G's arrival. *There is no room in this house where I am not the president, where I am not dragging the weight of the country, and the world, wherever I go.* But any change of location could bring a momentary respite. Sometimes it was a walk along the veranda outside his office, sometimes a visit to the Rose Garden, frequently accompanied by Bobby or Lucy or one of his advisors.

Barratt had been briefed about the late-night shooting in Paradation when he was awakened earlier, and was expecting further information plus the detailed report on the massacre by the former Chechen named Derek. "Hate to think that an earthquake might have been easier to deal with," he mused.

Bobby knocked lightly on the door, then entered the room.

"I have the early report on Paradation and the details on the parade shooting," Bobby said. "It's worse than we thought. In Paradation, preliminary numbers are nine dead and six wounded, and two of them may not make it. At the parade, ten were killed and two survivors died yesterday in the hospital. The oldest were a couple in their early eighties."

Bobby stopped speaking, but Barratt could sense that he had more to say.

Barratt raised his eyebrows and spread his hands. "And?"

"The youngest was, uh, was an infant, six months old, sitting on his mother's lap. One shot went through the baby and killed them both."

"Jesus," Barratt said in a low, tortured voice. "I still just don't understand. What moves a person to shoot a stranger? And an infant. What makes them think that it will change their lives, make things better?"

"They're all nuts," said Bobby.

"It's not that simple," said Barratt.

"Okay, then, what's the answer?"

"ASPD."

"Which is..."

"Antisocial Personality Disorder."

"Like I said, they're all crazy."

"And like *I* said, it's not that simple. I've read the psychological profiles of mass shooters. There are different opinions about psychopaths and sociopaths. They all have ASPD, whether they're born or made. Some experts believe that it's at least partly genetic, others that it's the consequence of childhood abuse or trauma, loss. Some think they just come out of the womb fully formed like that. Either way, it's a mental disorder.

"But what, *what,* do they want?" Barratt shook his head, pursed his lips, wrinkled his brow. Then his face suddenly relaxed. "Wait, maybe I'm asking the wrong question. Maybe I should be asking if they *know* what they want."

Barratt stood and walked back to the windows, feeling that he might actually be getting a bit of a grip on something.

"They usually have lousy self-esteem. Does killing give them power, does it cover up their self-loathing? Does this in some bizarre way make them feel better about themselves? 'Look what I can do?' Or do some of them, God help us, just...like it, just do it for the rush, for the thrill." Barratt paused before saying: "That's almost too monstrous to conceive of."

"Are you really looking for a rational explanation? There isn't one," said Bobby.

"Then how the hell do you get to the root of all this? Get to the bottom of the well and stop this from bubbling up, stop this volcano from spewing?"

"I thought you already had the solution."

"But you know that The Plan should be the last resort. What if we could change things before we get there?"

"Isn't that what we're trying to do?" Bobby asked. "Not that we have a snowball's chance in hell of doing it."

Bobby softened his tone. "Sorry, Mr. President. Do you want me to go back to the leaders in the House and Senate, see if after Paradation they've come to their senses?"

"Yes. I want to give them every chance before we would launch The Plan."

Neither man spoke for several moments, then Bobby said: "You made a statement right after both shootings, and they weren't that far apart. Do you want to make a further statement?"

"Yeah," said Barratt, "and get me the phone numbers."

"Eli, that's almost thirty phone calls. I know you've been calling each family so far but—"

Barratt glared at his chief of staff.

"Yes, Sir, I'll get the contact information."

Barratt had returned to the Oval Office when Bobby entered an hour later, carrying a packet of papers that he laid on Barratt's desk.

"We're still working on getting a couple of phone numbers, but these are almost all of them, and I thought you would like to have them now."

"Thanks," said Barratt.

As Bobby left the office and closed the door, Barratt took a deep breath. This was one of the worst parts of the job, but he had campaigned on the promise to fix this. He had to tell the survivors and the families that he wouldn't quit, that he was sorry that a solution was too late for them. Some would understand, would actually commiserate. Some would curse him and wish it had happened to him. They wouldn't say anything he hadn't said to himself already.

He heaved against that lead weight.

Then he picked up the phone.

2 KILLED, 8 INJURED IN SHOOTING AT UNDERGROUND NEW YEAR'S EVE PARTY IN DOWNTOWN LA

EYEWITNESS NEWS 7
Los Angeles

34.
CHRISTINE GRAMMAR

CHRISTINE BRIGHTLING-GRAMMAR paused outside her Senate office.

"Christine Grammar, Senator." She read the gold-leaf words emblazoned on the door. It never got old. She had just escaped from the cacophony of congressional staff and other senators rushing through the hallways and lobbies, speaking into phones, some dodging reporters, others seeking a TV camera to get in front of. About to enter her domain, she lingered. It was not a sense of accomplishment that she felt; she believed she was entitled to this status. Rather, it fed her sense of herself: sophisticated, important, more worthy than other people.

Every morning, she stood before her full-length dressing room mirror and gloried in her appearance. *You've still got it, girl,* she would muse. Standing five-foot-ten with perfectly coiffed silver hair; a jawline that cost her dearly, paid to the country's most sought-after plastic surgeon, who knew how to keep a confidence; $3,000 fitted suit; black Manolos on her feet. Born into the powerful Brightling financial services empire, she married into the equally powerful Grammar pharmaceutical empire, but she never felt out of place. The marriage didn't last; she quickly discovered that her husband was not up to her standards of erudition and aggressiveness. While she rued taking his last name, she accepted it because she knew it would serve her well. Besides, she thought, it gave her an intimidating three-part name:

Christine Brightling-Grammar, which pushed open doors in business and political circles.

"I married well," she shared with close friends, "just not for love."

She maintained good relations with her former mother- and father-in-law and didn't hesitate to call on them when it was advantageous. Her father-in-law once laughingly confided to her that *she* was the son he had always wanted.

Undergraduate from Vassar. Postgraduate work at Radcliffe. Juris Doctor from Yale. She knew that she could have had any position she wanted at Brightling Financial, but she had no interest living in the carefully guarded private world of the business elite. Her desire was for people to know who she was, what she had, where she was heading. And that she would do whatever it took to get there.

Given her connections and family names, her entry into politics was smoothed and even encouraged. Funding was not an issue, and she knew that she could help her father from the inside. She had bypassed the more typical route of running for the House before reaching for the Senate. *Waste of time*, she told advisors. *I have places to go.* She won her Senate seat easily. Now she exercised her imposing will as a member of both the judiciary and finance committees.

Before her she saw a path to the ultimate confirmation of her importance, not just to the country, but to the world. Grammar considered herself a political savant, carefully cultivating the loyalty of her party's most influential players. It was, she knew, all about the money in her transactional world. She delivered when they asked her to, but always required that she be paid back with a commitment to her plans. They knew that very important people had her back; their promises had best not be broken.

She couldn't very well run against President Eileen Caldwell when the first woman ever elected president ran for reelection, but she was sure that she would be next in line.

Then Elijah Barratt happened. And he was sending his minion, that Bobby G, to "negotiate" with her.

"Who the hell does he think he is?" she asked of anyone who would listen. Jumping over the veterans of his party, audacious enough to think that he could be president. And then, unbelievably, he was! He was such a common man. He didn't belong in Washington, *her* Washington. She was confident that he would implode, and she would help that happen. Then, the door to her office would read differently:

Christine Grammar, President of the United States of America.

2 DEAD, AT LEAST 16 INJURED IN WEEKEND YBOR CITY SHOOTING

Tampa Bay Times

35.
BOBBY

BOBBY SAT IN SENATOR CHRISTINE GRAMMAR'S waiting area. The room was almost unnaturally clean. He couldn't see a speck of dust or a mote; nothing was out of place. Her secretary was a handsome young man who wore a look of caution, maybe slightly frightened, as if he would jump six feet if someone tapped him on the shoulder. He wondered if Grammar's office persona was a take on *Mommy Dearest*, à la Joan Crawford. It would certainly fit with her reputation.

His appointment was for 3:00 p.m. It was now 3:40. He was getting more and more tired of the DC pecking order game.

He was surprised, after being named chief of staff, at just how deferential, obsequious, even cloying most of the members of Barratt's party and the junior legislators were to him. It was, he knew, all transactional. They needed something, and they had to go through him to get it. He had handled it well, he thought, but it was frequently awkward and often tedious.

Bobby was less surprised by how arrogant and condescending the opposition leaders were. They looked at Barratt as an interloper. *What the hell does that make me?* Bobby would laugh.

The Queen Offender: Senator Christine Brightling-Grammar. He had no issue with the idea of hyphenated last names, most an effort to respect both sides of a family or maintain an identity. With Grammar it seemed to be one more cudgel she used to beat down her perceived enemies: two heavy-hitter legacy surnames. Each as imposing as the other.

Plus, Bobby saw Grammar constantly practicing gamesmanship. She told the press she marveled at Barratt's story: overcoming personal tragedy. Privately, she called him a "three-hit wonder," a really bad joke referencing the three shots that struck him at Dawn River. The only reason, she insisted, he was ever elected to anything. She waxed collegial when she said that it was great working with Bobby. Behind closed doors it was a different story: she was dismissive and vulgarly critical. The "made you wait" game was one of her favorite ways to diminish whoever asked for an audience.

At 4:00 p.m. he couldn't take it any longer. None of the phone lines on her aide's desk had been lit the whole time, and he doubted that Grammar had granted anyone an hour with her. He stood to leave, then the aide raised his hand, signaling Bobby to stop. The aide's intercom had not buzzed, but he punched a button and spoke into his mic as if it had.

"Yes, Senator. Yes, I'll send him right in," he said. He clicked off and smiled at Bobby as he said, "Mr. Gennaro, you can go in now."

"Oh, thank you so much for your gracious hospitality," responded Bobby. He didn't try to hide the sarcasm, but he needed to let it out. He didn't want it to creep in when he spoke with Grammar. Today, *he* needed something from *her*, or at least he had to ask.

"Bobby, so good to see you," Grammar said in greeting as he entered her office.

Yeah, thought Bobby, *it would have been even better if you saw me an hour ago.*

"Thank you for making the time," he said. *Careful, Bobby, careful!* he thought. Sarcasm: Danger, Bobby G, danger!

Bobby had to give her credit. Her office, which she had completely remodeled when she was elected, was impressive, if somewhat pretentious. Her desk was huge but totally uncluttered. It had cream-colored alabaster inlays on the corners, one Tiffany lamp hanging over it and another on the desk. In contrast, the credenza had stacks of bound documents, but they were all neatly arrayed. And she fit in perfectly. *Or perhaps*, Bobby thought, *the office fits perfectly around her*. Tall, lean-muscled, styled silver hair, a severe black suit, a diamond necklace, a small American flag lapel pin encrusted with rubies, pearls, and lapis.

Bobby couldn't recall anyone referring to Grammar as beautiful, but rather as "powerful, commanding, imposing." He knew that she imposed her will on her caucus and in her committees.

Grammar directed him to one of the chairs in front of her desk. He had been here twice before, so he knew what to expect. The chairs were made so that his butt was lower than his knees and he was forced to look up at her while she peered down at him.

"Senator, I know you like to get right to the heart of the matter. The president has asked me to inform you as a courtesy that he is preparing gun-reform legislation to send to the Hill. We think it's something we can all get behind. One of the key elements is restoration of the assault weapons ban."

Grammar shot her shirt cuffs, extending them beyond her suit sleeves.

"What else is in it?"

"Universal background checks. These are two things that the people clearly want."

"Exactly whose people, Bobby? I go by what my constituents tell me, and they're fine with the laws just the way they are."

Bobby controlled the urge to rise up out of his chair and stand in front of Grammar to add more stature to his response. Settling for moving forward in his seat, he perched uncomfortably on its front edge.

"Senator, you've seen the reports on Paradation, on the church, the massacre at the parade. Some of the carnage may have been avoided if these laws were in place."

Grammar did stand up and looked down at Bobby, diminishing him even further.

"You don't know that," she said.

Bobby started to recite statistics and paraphrased studies supporting the president's position. Grammar waved him off.

"I read the same data you do, but my question is: How does that benefit the people who sent me here?"

You mean how does it benefit you, Bobby thought, but didn't say it. Instead, he hoped to appeal to her ego.

"You could be the senator who saved lives," he said.

"Don't be flip with me," Grammar shot back. "You know that I would have a revolt on my hands in the caucus."

"But, Senator, this could hel—"

Grammar cut him off again. "And don't tell me that Elijah Barratt would share the credit."

"Senator, that's not—"

She clipped him again: "Thanks for coming by. Tell the president I said hello."

With that, she sat back in her chair, swiveled to the credenza, and picked up a binder.

Bobby wanted badly to sit there until she realized that he hadn't left and she turned back around, but that would only make things worse. He knew that Grammar would destroy any chance of Barratt's proposal passing. Grammar not only had great influence in the Senate, but she pulled the strings of enough representatives that she also held sway in the House. She couldn't let Barratt have a victory; that would only make her effort to put herself in the Oval Office even harder.

Well, it looks like I've been told by the queen to leave her court. And it looks like if we submit this omnibus bill it will be dead on arrival.

When Grammar heard the door click closed, she slammed shut the binder she had opened.

Really, now Barratt thinks he can charm Congress into passing a laundry list of gun reform laws?

Barratt made her blood run cold. *Okay,* she thought, *he was shot. That's horrible.* But it was also eleven years ago. She gave him credit for parlaying that into his rapid political rise, but there was an expiration date on sympathy. His had already passed.

And, she mused, he was making a neophyte mistake. He wasn't bargaining for one law now and one law later in exchange for the support of some senator's or representative's pet project. Apparently, he thought that good policy was enough to win the day. In truth, some of what he had proposed was workable and helpful and certainly popular, but that's not the way it worked in her town.

Grammar did not want to be the majority leader in the Senate. She didn't want the hassle. Just a couple of nuts could make a leader's or speaker's life miserable; there was history to prove that. But with her committee chairmanships and fundraising prowess, she dominated her conference and had become the real power in Congress. She could operate in a less fettered way, with fewer procedural leashes on her. Is that why some of her "colleagues" called her a bulldog? She did demand loyalty from her caucus, loyalty she had bought and paid for both with PAC contributions and backroom arm twisting. This was a transactional town, she knew, and she had become the Transaction Queen.

She buzzed for her aides. It was time to give Elijah Barratt an education in Washington, DC.

CHICAGO REELS FROM VIOLENT HOLIDAY WEEKEND: MORE THAN 100 SHOT, 19 FATALLY

WPDS Local 6
KENTUCKY

36.
BARRATT

ELIJAH BARRATT DIMMED THE LIGHTS as he stepped into the Oval Office. He removed the jacket of his gray sharkskin suit, hung it up, and loosened his dark blue tie. It was almost midnight, the city smothered by a heavy mist beyond the office windows.

He moved to his chair and sat down. He gently ran his right hand over the gleaming wood of the Resolute Desk. When he was still practicing law, his office desk was typically cluttered. He kept this desk clear, in deference to its history. The Resolute Desk had been a gift from Queen Victoria to President Hayes in 1880. It was made of wood salvaged from the remains of the HMS *Resolute*, which had been abandoned during an Arctic expedition.

Legend had it that the desk contained secret compartments. He facetiously searched for them from time to time, hoping to find a blueprint to help him handle the challenges he constantly faced. The desk was an anchor for him. As he sat behind it, he felt the ghosts of presidents past, and from time to time he called upon them.

Bobby rapped lightly on the open office door as he entered. "Long day, Mr. President?" his chief of staff asked. His subtly striped navy suit was still unwrinkled. His tightly knotted, black-and-red-striped tie contrasted with his starched white shirt. He shot his sleeves, revealing the gold presidential cufflinks that Barratt had given him.

"They're all long, aren't they?" the president responded.

"You're right about that. But then, we knew what we were getting into."

Barratt sighed as he reached a hand behind himself and rubbed the back of his neck. "I can't believe," said Barratt, "that anyone really knows what this job is until they're sitting here. But I will tell you this: I'm glad you're sitting here with me."

"Always, Mr. President," said Bobby, as he took a chair across from Barratt.

Barratt and Bobby had known each other only casually in college, until they realized that they had each dated the same girl—and that she had dumped them both. They laughed too hard about it not to become friends. Bobby was in Barratt's wedding when he married Lucy twenty years ago; Barratt in Bobby's two years later when Bobby married Zoey. After Dawn River, when Lucy had to care for Gabrielle, it was Bobby who stayed by Barratt's hospital bed. Then, when Barratt made his first foray into politics as he ran for city council, it was Bobby who knocked on doors with him. They had been beating down doors together ever since.

They began their nightly debrief and decompress, reviewing the next day's schedule and anticipating the problems that would arise. When there was a lull in the conversation, the president eyed his long-time friend and advisor.

"Bobby, I know that look. I've seen it before. You've got something to say."

Bobby hesitated, then spoke: "Mr. President, tomorrow's press conference..."

"Yes?"

"You know it's not going to be well received."

"And?"

"And...do you really need to get everything at once? The omnibus bill is going to go nowhere."

Barratt leaned forward, rested his elbows on the desk, and tented his fingers. He had been pushing this boulder up the mountain for over ten years. He didn't need to be challenged now, especially by his best friend. He waited a beat, then said, "Bobby, we've talked this to death."

"I know, but five of our own senators haven't committed, and the House is...well, anything can happen in the House. And Senator Grammar is on the warpath. I told you when I spoke with her that it was clear. She's never going to agree to anything you propose."

Barratt rose abruptly from his chair, stepped away from it, and turned to stare through the windows. The lights of the city tried their best, but the night remain shrouded. He turned back around and grabbed the back of his chair in a death grip. "Screw Grammar. She's always on the warpath," said the president. "We can't let that slow us down."

"But if we run too fast," said Bobby, "we might run ourselves right out of bounds."

"Bobby—"

"I'm just saying that half a loaf—"

"Enough with the damn clichés. Say what you mean."

Neither man spoke for almost a minute.

"You're gonna blow it," Bobby finally said. "You've got to eat this one bite at a time. You're asking for five new gun laws all at once, from a Congress that can't find its balls with a magnifying glass. Let's just go for the universal background checks first. It's got the best chance. Why push it all at once?"

Barratt released his grip on the chair and spun it in front of him. "Why? Because someone in this country gets shot every fourteen minutes—every fourteen goddamn minutes, Bobby—of every goddamn day. That's why!"

"I know the stats, but—"

"But nothing. I keep seeing their faces, Bobby. I see them on TV. I see them when I try to sleep. Then I go to their funerals and speak some platitudes that don't mean shit."

"Eli, you can't do this all at once, not in one term, and Lord knows if you keep pushing there won't be a second term."

"A second term?! Do you really think I care about a second term?! I'm here in this office for a reason. I was sent here to stop this."

"Eli, you're not making sense."

"Bobby, they repealed the bump stocks, the semi-autos, laws that could have made a difference. And what happened when we introduced the safety-lock bill?"

"I know—" started Bobby.

"Yeah, you do know. They lied to you and it went down."

"But Eli. Listen, for once in your life. You *can't* do it this way."

Barratt regained his seat. He now leaned forward and pressed his palms on the desk in front of him and pulled its power into his words. He glared at his chief of staff. "Bobby, I'm going to hold their feet to the fire," Barratt said. "Let them keep explaining why they care more about their re-elections than about the bodies piling up." Barratt clenched his teeth and formed a fist with his right hand. He raised it as if to hammer it on the desk, then instead lightly touched it down. His voice was steel. "We are doing this, Bobby. And we're doing it my fuckin' way."

They both went quiet. Bobby stared at the ornate rug below him. Barratt relaxed his jaws and looked to the side, away from his friend.

Then, after several moments of silence, Barratt looked back, pulled his hands off the desk, and asked: "Are you hungry? I'm goin' to the kitchen. I'll make us some cheesesteaks."

"I could eat," said Bobby. "But hey, this time not so many hot peppers."

"Bobby G—what a wuss."

"Yeah, and you're not much of a chef. Can we get some fries?"

They both rose from their chairs and headed out of the office.

"No, too late," said Barratt.

"Too late? Some president *you* are. Can't even get midnight fries. I shoulda voted for the other guy."

Three months later, Barratt's omnibus bill died in Grammar's committee.

1 TEEN KILLED, 4 PEOPLE INJURED FOLLOWING SHOOTING AT OKLAHOMA HIGH FOOTBALL GAME, AUTHORITIES SAY

CNN

37.
STANLEY KNIGHT

STANLEY KNIGHT LEANED BACK against the top of the wooden picnic table, sitting in the middle of a dirt clearing. Wearing a satisfied smile, he held his prized possession, the only thing of any real value that he could call his own: his Steyer Scout sniper rifle. He had just cleaned it, again, and now caressed the textured grip and stroked the smooth black muzzle. Stanley was stunned when he realized that he could order it online. His job at the auto parts store didn't pay much, but every available dollar—for over four years—went toward the Steyer's purchase. His anticipation of its delivery was agonizing. When he cradled it in his hands for the first time, he was filled with a sense of joy, power, validation. As he held it at port arms in front of a mirror, he saw someone different than everyone else did; he saw himself as he wanted to be seen, a newly minted, rugged man, a man capable of great things.

The home behind him was a small two-bedroom house in need of paint, care, and caulk, the faded green shutters hanging loosely by just a few rusted hinges. It sat back off a long dusty road in thick woods, dense trees providing camouflage. He lived there alone. His mother had left when he was six years old; his father was gone and not missed. He had essentially been on his own since he was sixteen.

Knight had struggled in school. His school counselor had told him and his father that his stammer, facial tics, and Tourette's might be signs that he was on something called the "spectrum," but neither of them understood what that meant so they never followed up.

He was bullied by some of the other students, who called him "Slow Stanley." He cried to his dad, who thought the nickname was hilarious and laughed derisively. Knight was glad that his father couldn't laugh at him anymore. When he somehow summoned the courage to approach one of the pretty girls in his class and stammered "hello," she was petrified and ran away. Mortified, he ran home. Every day in school was renewed trauma; he quit school at fourteen and then home-schooled himself in sniper craft, and, he proudly proclaimed, he was the best student in *that* class.

He knew the Steyer's specs by heart: a muzzle velocity of about 2,300 feet per second and an effective range of 900 meters (870 yards). Knight was slightly built, about five foot eight and 145 pounds. Given its lightweight aluminum housing and use of polymers, the Scout weighed in at only 6.6 pounds, perfect for him.

He had consumed the videos detailing the Marine Corps Sniper Training Course, read everything he could get his hands on, constantly played the awesomely realistic sniper video games. He read the cautions that without rigorous military training no one could ever become proficient. He vowed to prove them wrong.

He had set up his own training site, deep in the backwoods, reached by trails that only he knew. In the forest, his incessant eye tic stopped, his breathing slowed, his stride lengthened, his Tourette's quieted. The leaf canopy was his shelter, his womb, where he sometimes slept on the forest floor, curled in a fetal position. He had spent hours training: shooting at targets, then at distant trees, and finally at the animals that were plentiful in his woods. He picked the small ones, because they made harder targets. First foxes and raccoons. Then rabbits and squirrels. His Scout's 7.62 NATO round (.308 Winchester) obliterated them every time.

He wore camo, blackened his face with anti-glare, used netting over the nest that he had fashioned, preened in his outfit. He bought a bipod, field glasses, and other optics; he splurged on a Leupold sight. He made his own rifle rest, feathered his nest with a camo blanket, and set water and food inside. He became a sniper savant, and reveled in knowing that he had, indeed, found what he was born to do.

UPDATE: 9 KILLED IN SHOOTING AT ALLEN PREMIUM OUTLETS ON SATURDAY

Dallas Observer

38.
WILLIAM JAMES PERCY IV

WILLIAM JAMES PERCY IV paused as he entered the long driveway leading to the Second Home Retirement and Nursing community. The drive was bordered by stately oaks, at the base of which were well-tended rings of white and red impatiens. Percy gazed through twilight at the edifice itself. High red-brick walls extended from either side of the imposing four-story building, graced by the roundabout at the end of the driveway. He had been inside years ago when he brought his mother here. He knew that those walls masked the opulence behind them: pools and cabanas; manicured gardens with paved walkways; lawn bowling courts; trellises and arbors; vegetable beds used by the two chefs who oversaw the upscale meals served to the residents. Never mind, thought Percy, that some of the people living there were physically incapable of using the amenities and likely couldn't taste half the food that was served.

Percy thought about the eight generations of his family that had brought him to this. His forbears had fought in every US conflict beginning with the War of 1812. He himself was a US Army veteran deployed along with NATO forces in the last Balkan conflict. Over the earlier decades, the family's tobacco and cotton businesses, multilevel real estate holdings, sharecroppers, indentured servants, and slaves had made the family wealthy. Percy had marveled at the photos of his great-great-grandfathers and grandmothers, especially on the Percy side. Wearing the finest tailored suits and couture gowns, attended by servants, presiding over feasts served to the region's most important people, elegant southern soirées with orchestral performances.

The depression had changed all of that.

That economic disaster devastated the Percy empire. Percy cursed that damn socialist FDR; he may have been considered a savior by many, but none of the New Deal programs saved *his* family. His people had started over and worked their way back when the second government whammy hit. Percy could still hear his grandfather railing against the new labor laws and the civil rights laws and the cultural revolution that threatened to cut the feet out from under the family again. He, and they, had been reduced to work-a-day people, fighting to stay above water.

The arrow-straight driveway of Second Home focused his sight on the looming entrance of the building. He knew that inside lived many of the self-important nouveau riche. Percy's family had shed blood for this country for two centuries; what had these come-latelys done? As far as Percy was concerned, if your family hadn't lived here for at least 150 years you were a pretender, an invader.

And perhaps the most ignominious cut of all: When Percy's own mother, suffering from dementia, needed a place of care and comfort, he had brought her here, but there was no room for her at Second Home. His family didn't know the right people anymore, the cost was too expensive, their arguments that the family history entitled them to some deference were disdainfully rejected.

But that wasn't the only insult. His ancestors had helped create a booming economy in the southern states, with a quality of life to be envied. The children were educated at the finest southern schools; the women were invited to the best parties; the men were elected to positions of power. Later, his family was vilified by self-righteous do-gooders and haughty academics as antebellum slave owners, although Percy had heard stories from his oldest relatives about how well the slaves were treated and how they weren't capable of caring for themselves if given the responsibility to do so. In many circles of so-called polite society, the Percys were avoided, their presence "inconvenient." People like those who lived behind the Second Home walls had contributed to that. He was mystified that not just elite Whites but somehow wealthy Catholics and Jews and Blacks were welcomed while his mother—a veritable saint during her lifetime—was rejected.

The family, history, his lineage had been denigrated. When a petition was circulated to change the name of his hometown from Percyville, named after his third great-grandfather, to Central City, that was the final ignominy. He could no longer tolerate the disrespect. He and his cousin Henry believed that it was necessary, that it was their *obligation*, to make a statement, to make a point, to show that the fight had not gone out of the Percy descendants.

Percy had chosen the dinner hour, a peaceful time of respite and socializing for the residents. A peace that he was about to shatter. Almost all of the residents would be in the dining hall. Gathered as they were, and as quickly as Percy planned to act, surprise would be guaranteed, and the chance for a successful call for help would be minimal. Percy had created the True Americans, a paramilitary cadre formed up first with twenty men, then fifty, and now over two hundred. Some harbored the same resentment that Percy did, others because of inbred racial hatred, some because of their penchant for violence for violence's sake. Given the availability of military surplus following each United States armed conflict, the True Americans easily created an arsenal of semi-automatic weapons, tear gas, flash bangs, and even two RPGs, plus surplus military Humvees.

Percy had brought just Henry, his second in command, and eight other men with him, enough for this operation, all in one camo

Humvee. He held halfway along the access drive as he glared at Second Home, a physical manifestation of the injustice that had crushed his family and defiled his heritage. Though the times and intentions were far different, he fancied himself the second coming of Revolutionary War General Francis Marion, nicknamed the "Swamp Fox" by British officers and revered as a hero of South Carolina. And just as Marion did, Percy had made his camps on islands deep in the dismal swamps of the coastal Carolinas, where small bands of his troops could secrete themselves. When they finished this job, they would disappear into the cypress gums and cedars and dark shadows, gone before any emergency vehicles arrived.

Percy waved his troops forward, and they headed toward Second Home. The Humvee pulled into the roundabout fronting the building. They immediately exited the vehicle and formed up in front of the main entrance, outfitted in camo, boots, and ammo belts. Percy knew that the camo was hardly necessary for this op, but it was all part of his "presentation." His own uniform was accentuated with a general's star on his epaulets, a rank he had proudly conferred upon himself. He was the Resurrector, the embodiment of his legacy, the instrument of his forefathers' revenge.

He knew that the entry doors were unlocked, but he had planned to noisily announce his arrival. He nodded to Henry, who aimed his AK-15 at the entrance and obliterated the double glass doors, shards exploding in a blizzard of transparent shrapnel, the echoing rifle fire destroying the quiet that preceded it. Percy led his people into the building. A middle-aged woman at a reception desk just inside the entrance stood up, her mouth agape, her eyes wide with fear. She knocked over a vase of yellow flowers that had been in front of her, sending it crashing to the floor. She still held a pen in one hand and a sheaf of papers in the other.

"I'm just a fill-in!" she shouted.

"Then it's just not your lucky day, is it?" Percy responded.

He fired a short burst from his rifle, and she was flung up and over her chair and crashed with a thud behind the desk.

Percy strode forward and took in the scene: Residents who could stand were by the tables in the crowded dining room; those who needed walkers were struggling to get up from their chairs; those in wheelchairs were frantically trying to turn away from the tables. A silver-haired woman had fallen to the floor; one wrinkled hand reaching up for help was ignored. With her other hand she tried to cover the diamond necklace hanging from her neck. *Really?* thought Percy. *She thinks I'm here to rob her?* Several of the more capable residents had rushed to the elevators situated in the lobby and were banging on the Up buttons in a panic. Percy sneered at them, finding it laughable that they thought that was a means of escape.

Directing his men forward, they proceeded to cut down everyone they encountered. Screams and moans mixed with blood sprays turned the dining room into a surreal scene of butchery. Plates and table centerpieces were obliterated. Mashed potatoes and brown gravy and vanilla pudding littered the floor, the ambulatory slipping on the mess, the wheelchairs unable to gain traction. Several of Percy's people had moved through the lobby and the dining area to a rear exit. Several residents had rushed to that exit, only to be hit with a fusillade of gunfire.

One of the wait staff, a young woman no more than twenty years old, stood frozen in the middle of the dining room, in shock as she gaped at the carnage around her, holding in two extended hands a tray of red velvet cake slices and small bowls of strawberry ice cream. Percy told Henry to bring her to him; he did so and presented her face to face.

"You're still alive because you are the witness to me avenging my family. Go. Tell the police, tell the press, tell everybody that the True Americans are taking back what is rightfully ours," Percy told her. She stood paralyzed before him, still holding the serving tray.

"Go now," Percy said, "before I change my mind."

Henry pushed her away from Percy and toward the front door. She took a hesitant step, flung the tray down—a kaleidoscope of colored crumbs and melting ice cream cascading to the floor—then stumbled forward, away from him, and raced through the shattered door, running for her life.

THERE ARE TOO MANY MASS SHOOTINGS FOR THE US MEDIA TO COVER

The Washington Post

39.
ARIEL

"PATTY," YELLED ARIEL, "call her again!"

"I just called her!"

Without realizing how shrill her voice was, Ariel demanded, "I don't care! Try her phone again!"

Ariel pushed the old minivan harder: ten miles, fifteen, now twenty miles over the speed limit. Second Home had been attacked! Aunt Birdie's home had been attacked! Patty was in the passenger seat. She had insisted on coming along. Ariel had quickly used the lift to stow the wheelchair in the back after helping Patty into the van.

Patty put the phone on speaker and redialed Birdie's number. It went to voicemail. The repetition of that frustrating invitation to "leave a message," mixed with the sound of Patty's wheelchair bouncing in the back of the van, hammered at Ariel.

"Dammit!" Ariel shouted as she banged her fist against the steering wheel. Then, in a lower, plaintive voice, she mouthed: "Please God, let her be okay."

She had seen the breaking news on TV. Now the car radio was tuned to a twenty-four-hour news station. The reporter on scene described one ambulance after another pulling up to the nursing home portico, EMTs and detectives and crime scene inspectors, all wearing hair coverings and booties, entering through the shattered main door.

Ariel pictured them all clomping through the lobby, like so many awkward aliens. *This has to be science fiction, right?* she thought. *Because this can't be happening to us again.* The reporter continued the macabre description, waiting for word on the number of casualties and for information about survivors.

Ariel pushed the minivan even harder, close to its limit, and it started to fishtail. She saw Patty's frightened glance at the speedometer as Patty gripped Ariel's shoulder. Ariel shuddered at the touch, then exhaled deeply and tried vainly to expel some of the tension from her body.

"Ariel!"

"Okay, okay," said Ariel, as she slightly slowed her speed, but still pushed aggressively forward.

"Finally," she muttered as they reached the access road that led to Second Home, but they could go no further. Police vehicles blocked the roadway. Media trucks, their extended telescoping poles topped by communication arrays, formed a forest of cold metal trees with limbs of antennae. Ariel pulled to the side of the road and stopped.

"Patty, I'm going to see what I can find out."

"Go, go!" Patty replied, but Ariel was already out of the van.

She weaved through a crowd of what she thought must be other relatives mixed with reporters challenging the police barricades, photographers pushing for position. Unseen by Ariel, Ace Gerund, one of the paparazzi who had harassed Ariel's family and was the last to leave them alone, eyed her with a confused hint of recognition on his face, then looked at the van she had exited.

The scene was chaotic. People were yelling at the police, calling out their loved ones' names, crying, shoving. She saw some in housecoats, others in work clothes; one was barefoot. All, she figured, had dropped everything and raced here in a panic, as she had. The entire scene was strobed by squad car overhead lights and emergency vehicle flashers, a pulsating, consuming laser show, like something you'd see—she couldn't help but go there—at a rock concert. She made her way to the police barricades and faced an officer with hands out telling her to stop.

"My aunt..." she gasped, "my Aunt Bernadette, she lives here!" Ariel cried.

"I'm sorry, we're not letting anyone through," the officer said.

Ariel pleaded her case. "But I have to know!" Then Ariel heard her name being called from beyond the yellow sawhorses. She looked up and saw Maggie coming toward her.

"Maggie! Maggie!" Ariel shouted and waved her hands.

Maggie walked quickly up to the police line. "Ariel, honey, she's okay. Birdie's okay."

Ariel closed her eyes and let out a breath she didn't realize she was holding. Then she opened her eyes and looked at Maggie. "Thank God. But how..."

Maggie reached across the barrier and took both of Ariel's hands in her own. "She was up in her room. She didn't come down for dinner. Said that she was full from lunch, that she was just going to read for a while, so she turned off her cell phone. When the shooting started she locked her door and hoped for help. I was with the police when they went room to room, and I saw her. Ariel, really, she's okay. She's the most 'alive' ninety-year-old I know."

"Can I get in there?" asked Ariel. "Can I see her?"

Before the officer listening to the conversation could speak, Maggie answered, "Sorry, sweetie, they're not letting anybody in. Look, I need to get back inside, but I'll let you know what's going on."

"Oh, Maggie, thank you so much," said Ariel as they hugged. "We'll stay here. Patty's with me. I'm going back to the car to let her know."

Ariel turned, her arms and legs almost limp as her adrenaline abated, and walked back toward where she had left Patty. She pulled up short as she approached the van. A gaggle of reporters surrounded it, microphones extended, questions shouted, photographers clicking cameras with their flashes firing.

"Hey!" she shouted. "Hey! What are you doing?" she shouted as she started to run. "Get away from there!"

As she moved closer, she heard the waves of reporters' questions crashing against Patty's window. She saw her nemesis Gerund leading the charge.

"I thought that was you," Gerund said as Ariel approached. "I never forget a face. And that's your sister, right? How come you guys are here."

"Get out of here!" she yelled at him. "Just leave us alone." She pushed past him and entered the scrum of other photographers who were peppering the car with flashes and shouted demands.

"Hey, aren't you that girl who was shot at Dawn River? Your name's Penny, right?"

"No, it's Patty, isn't it! Patty! Look over here!"

"Do you know someone who lives here? Was he shot? Is he dead?"

"Patty, roll down the window! Hey, is that your wheelchair back there?"

Patty had turned away from the window and was cowering in the space between the front seats. The camera flashes strafed the inside of the car. Ariel ran to the driver's door, pushing reporters out of the way as she did so, leaping inside. She slammed the door shut and wrapped Patty in her arms.

"It's okay, Patty. It's okay. Aunt Birdie is okay. She's fine."

Patty looked up at her sister, her eyes and face wet with tears. "Ariel," she pleaded, "get us out of here. Please, get us out of here."

Ariel started the van and hit the horn. She started to pull away from the roadside. She had intended to stay as long as it took to get in and see Aunt Birdie, but Patty, sobbing beside her, moved her to change her mind. She kept pushing forward as some of the reporters backed reluctantly out of the way, while others kept pace alongside, knocking on the windows, extended microphones hitting the van, digital cameras shotgunning images.

Dawn River was still haunting them, she thought, the screams, the chaos, the crushing crowd, the unbearable noise—Patty frightened and in pain.

"Damn you, Dawn River," she mouthed, "when are you going to leave us alone?"

METRO DETROIT MASS SHOOTINGS: ONE DEAD, 19 HURT AT 3 LOCATIONS ACROSS SOUTHEAST MICHIGAN

Fox 2 Detroit

40.
BARRATT

BARRATT LOVED THE EARLY MORNING.

He stood at the window in the small conference room near the Oval Office, files spread on the table behind him. The daily briefing. He liked to review it before he met with agency aides. The media reports of Grammar's speech at Liberty University where she couldn't help taking shots at him. The vicious electioneering in Belarus and Israel.

And the latest stats on gun violence.

He had stepped away from these issues when he walked to the window. *How different the world is out there*, he thought. Morning bird songs, music to his ears; screeching squirrels always complaining about something. Even the sound of the mowers and the smell of freshly cut grass that was blocked from him now, but always a good memory scent that he could conjure.

Underneath it all was the imp that constantly danced like a dervish, teasing his mind day and night and demanding that he answer the seminal question:

What the hell's going on out there?

Barratt was sometimes given to using football analogies and related quotes. One of his favorites was Green Bay Packers Coach Vince Lombardi's shouted question from the sidelines, whenever he couldn't understand the chaos his team was creating on the field. "What the hell's going on out there?" he would yell.

"What the hell's going on *here*?" Barratt asked himself. He had all the statistics, was conversant with all the societal and psychological analyses and all the opinion writers' takes on the issue.

But why?

Why? Barratt asked himself. He knew the problem. He knew The Plan wasn't a perfect solution, but he believed in his heart that it was necessary if the carnage was going to be stopped, or even slowed.

Americans owned over 400 million guns, a larger number than the entire population of the country, and about 50 percent of the civilian firearms owned worldwide. *Why so many?* Barratt questioned over and over. Why were guns such a part of the American zeitgeist?

The first settlers understandably needed firearms for hunting, protection against attack, for law enforcement—although they actually had, he knew, far fewer guns than one would expect. The American Revolution necessitated the arming of fighting forces. The intrusion into Native American territory and the horrific, almost complete, genocide of the First Americans was made possible when the army's firepower overcame the Native American's superior strategy.

The Second Amendment, as he learned on his own because he was never taught it in school, was a compromise to enable southern slave owners to put down the slave rebellions they always feared and which sometimes came close to succeeding. The slave owners insisted on maintaining their arms in exchange for continuing to support a Union, and the desperate founding fathers grudgingly agreed, resulting in the tortured language of the amendment. All these exploits, no matter how noble or abominable, explained the need or desire—in those circumstances—for firearms.

But why, now, halfway through the twenty-first century, did the civilian population of America need all these guns? Barratt had watched plenty of TV westerns and shoot-'em-up movies when he was a child, but was the cowboy myth still believed by the adult population? Did the macho image of James Bond and graphic novel super soldiers and grassroots Americans fighting an alien invasion make people want to arm themselves? Was their fear of assault, kidnapping, home invasion so profound that it offered a rationalization for preparing a defense? Was there *any* legitimate reason for a suburban homeowner or an urban apartment dweller to own an AK-15?

"What the hell's going on out there?" It was becoming Barratt's mantra.

What on earth, Barratt pondered, really motivated William Percy's so-called "True Americans"? Was irrational, racist hatred really the simple answer? Was fear of being confronted with the changing world so terrifying that violence was rationalized, and murder and terrorism acceptable?

If the main reason for owning a gun was protection, was that gun just needed to protect one from all the other people who owned guns?

We are, Barratt realized, *in an arms race with ourselves.*

NOTES: SEVEN PEOPLE WERE SHOT AND ONE DIED AFTER MULTIPLE SHOOTERS EXITED A SILVER LEXUS HATCHBACK AND OPENED FIRE ON A GROUP OF MEN HANGING OUT NEAR THE INTERSECTION, POLICE SAID

The Baltimore Sun

41.
ARIEL

IN THE FORTY-EIGHT HOURS FOLLOWING the assault on Second Home, five morning shows, four newspapers, several bloggers, and two TV magazines had called Patty's house, including the most watched, the *Start Your Day Show*. The producers couldn't resist a promo that would trumpet: "CHEERLEADER VICTIM OF DAWN RIVER MASSACRE ALMOST LOSES AUNT IN SECOND HOME ATTACK."

Ariel's mother was intimidated by the badgering; Patty wanted nothing to do with the attention. Ariel had her own apartment now, but she visited most days, her school-counselor hours flexible enough to permit it. She was there now and still upset by the reporters' actions outside of Second Home.

Ariel sat silently in the front room. The room looked much like it had before Dawn River. The old photos sat in their old spots, the furniture—some of it replaced—was where it belonged. The walls were freshly painted a version of the same color, her mother hanging on to a different time. But everything in Ariel's life had changed, and everything she was doing now was about seeking change. Her mind went to next week's rally in front of Dawn River. She would preach to some of the same people, to some newcomers, and they would have the same supportive response. But no one else would even know she was there. Except for a short bit on one local TV show after the first two rallies, there was no attention at all. It was as if she was becoming the crazy cat lady of protests. More than once she felt like giving up, and held the rallies less frequently now.

"I am as one crying out in the desert," she had sardonically described herself.

But then the attack on Second Home happened.

Could she ignore this horrible gift that the press was offering? The *Morning Show* producers had expressed little interest in her message, but was this an opportunity to get that message out? She was committed to her rallies. She would continue to speak to anyone who would listen. But how many people would really hear her if she remained just a crazy girl with a microphone in a parking lot? She rose from her chair and went into Patty's room.

"Hey, Patty, what's up?" she asked her sister.

Patty was at her computer, in a specialized computing chair. Playing against type, she had earned a degree in computer programming, working most of the time from home. The walls in her room were painted pink, and the comforter was still ruffled; she would always be a frilly girl. But the photos of Patty's high school graduation and of her shooting foul shots in a wheelchair basketball game were joined by photos of her college graduation, of Patty and the inventor of the *Corky's Wild Ride* video game, which had become the new hottest thing. She turned her chair when Ariel came into the room.

"Patty, I need to talk to you," Ariel started. "You know all these reporters who've been calling?"

"Yeah, and I don't want to talk to any of them."

"I know you don't," said Ariel, "but…I…I do."

Patty gave her a confused look. "You're kidding. Why?"

"Because at the rallies I'm talking to the same few people about the same few things. I feel like I'm running in place. I want...I need... to move this forward."

"Yeah, well, I've moved away from it, and I don't have any intention of going back."

Ariel sat down on Patty's bed. Patty turned in her chair again so that the sisters faced each other.

"I don't want to do this unless you're okay with it. I...I'm not...the one who was...shot. I didn't get hurt. I don't want you—or anybody else—to think I'm, you know, *using* you. But I...I may have a chance here." Ariel's voice was barely above a whisper. "I might be able to do something, make a real difference, if I can reach more people. You know me. You know I never really wanted to be out front. That was your thing, and that was fine."

Ariel lowered her head.

"When I talked to Aunt Birdie, we talked about how she felt compelled to do the hard things, compelled to be a part of something bigger than herself." Ariel raised her head, reached out and took both of Patty's hands in hers. "I read a quote the other day, in a book that somebody gave me at a rally. It was by an old Supreme Court justice. He said, 'A man should participate in the action and the passion of his time at risk of being judged not to have lived at all.' Now, you need to substitute 'woman" for 'man' to make it sound right." She smiled. "But it, you know, it got to me. I've found something out about myself through all of this. *I* feel that way. But right now I'm running in place."

Patty's eyes began to moisten.

"Ariel, you've been there for me through all these years. All that sweet music, I think it saved my life, gave me something beautiful to hold onto. I'm finding my way, and I wanted you to find peace, too. I even—don't hate me—hoped you would give it up by now. But you haven't, and that must mean that you can't.

"And I can't do what you're doing. I don't want to. I don't want to let them make me a spectacle, be a victim my whole life. With you it's different. You can handle it. If this is what you feel you need to do... then...you should do it. Use it, for both of us."

Patty removed her hands. "I'll be all right with it, but I do have one condition."

Ariel tilted her head and looked at her sister questioningly. "What's that?"

A smile formed on Patty's face. "Let me do your makeup before you put yourself further out there."

"What?" Ariel laughed. "Why?"

"If you're going to be a star, you have to look the part."

"Come on, I wear makeup."

"Yeah, but I'm the only one that knows you have it on. You're so pretty. I've been trying to get you to wear a little more makeup forever. So, that's the deal. Take it or leave it."

Ariel faked a frown and looked at her younger sister.

"All right, if that's what it takes," she said, laughing. "You know what, Patty? You're a little pain in the ass."

FLORIDA MAN, 78, FATALLY SHOOTS NEIGHBOR WHO WAS TRIMMING TREES OVER PROPERTY LINE

News Channel 8
Tampa Bay

42.
JOINT CHIEFS OF STAFF

GENERAL SAMSON, chairman of the Joint Chiefs of Staff and one of only fourteen four-stars in the army, sat in the cabinet meeting room, the first one there. He knew that he was at least twenty minutes early; he hated to be late for anything. Late was the equivalent of disrespectful, and he had no intention of disrespecting the recently elected president of the United States.

He had not expected much from Barratt, whom he had considered a neophyte and in over his head. He was surprised that he now saw a lot to like in Barratt: whip-smart but not arrogant; aware of how fortuitous his political rise had been, despite the tragedy that was its launching pad; no change in demeanor when addressing men or women; loved and apparently faithful to his wife. He listened in meetings and gave everyone a chance to provide their opinion, but there was no question that he was the man in charge.

And most importantly, the kid—Samson smilingly acknowledged to himself that most of this new administration was substantially younger than he—seemed to be tough as nails and wise beyond his years. Samson was a student of military history. He recalled that Uriah Galusha Pennypacker was a US Civil War brigadier general at twenty, the only general too young to vote for the president who appointed him. Samson himself was on the cusp of retirement. *Youth will be served*, he thought.

Samson recognized that Barratt had no military service on his resume, but he did not hold that against him. The previous six presidents, and now Barratt, had come of age at a different time. Samson himself was a proud lifer: West Point; battle-tested in Iraq, Afghanistan, Belarus, and Iran; loved, respected, and followed by his troops in each conflict. He embraced the responsibility of leading soldiers. An expert at the military politics necessary to keep advancing, he assiduously avoided any *party* politics and for that reason did not vote, refusing to appear partisan in any way. Barratt, he thought, was someone he could have voted for.

He knew that the president always sat with his back to the windows looking out on the Rose Garden; Samson's position was directly across from that. Even alone in the room—the president's chief of staff had made it clear that no aides were invited—Samson sat ramrod straight. The insignia on his uniform was perfectly aligned, his shoes shined to a mirror finish, his fingernails perfectly trimmed, his face close-shaven.

Samson had been advised only that the president was to meet with just the Joint Chiefs about a national dilemma. *Vagueness*, thought Samson, *always a dangerous sign*. His contacts were as good as anybody's, but he had not been able to learn anything else about the agenda, which in his world was very unusual. As he mused about what could be in the offing, Air Force General Abigail Meadows entered the cabinet room.

"General," she said and nodded hello.

"General," he replied, and they laughed lightly. Samson had known Meadows for over twenty years. He depended on her as a sounding board and as someone whose insider connections were almost as good as his.

"Abby," he said, "I take it you haven't heard anything more about this meeting either."

"Nothing," she responded. "I know that practically everything we do is confidential, but I don't appreciate this mystery."

They both turned as General Patrician, the commandant of the Marine Corps, and Admiral Simpson entered the room. They were followed by the chief of the National Guard Bureau and the chief of Space Operations.

Samson was proud that the Joint Chiefs were a diverse group in terms of color, gender, and ethnicity.

They did have one thing in common. He shouldn't have been, but he was stunned, after Admiral Simpson was elevated to the Joint Chiefs and he realized that now every single one of the chiefs had been affected in some way by gun violence. Relatives, though sometimes distant, shot or assaulted at gunpoint; off-duty shootings by or even between the enlisted; active and retired soldiers' suicides. The tidal wave of incidents had smashed into society, especially in the last four years. Samson thought that the congressional rollback of firearms safety laws was reckless. Barratt had run on a promise to do something about this epidemic.

Wait, he thought, *could this meeting be related to that?*

Samson knew that something needed to be done, but not by the military. That was off-limits, right? There were certain exceptions, but they were very rarely used and based on arcane laws. These times were extraordinary, but invoking those laws would be beyond extraordinary.

Samson's mind went back to his own experience with non-combat gun violence. Two of his men committed suicide in Afghanistan by shooting themselves. He was devastated. He had embraced the need for mental health assessments of men and women in the theater of war and made counseling available, but in those two cases it wasn't enough.

Then there was his nephew, Wyatt. He had always been rebellious, despite being raised in a good home by Samson's sister and brother-in-law. They tried their best. Samson had tried to reach the boy as well.

Nothing worked. At eighteen, with a gun he had purchased on the street, he walked into a convenience store, wounded the cashier, and left with all of $41. He was still behind bars.

The impact on so many personal connections by so many people with similar stories was horrendous. The damage to society of one mass shooting after another, with the states apparently unable to stop it, couldn't continue. It would, Samson thought, bring the country down. If Barratt had an idea that had a chance of working, he would listen, out of the box or not.

Samson started to talk shop with the other officers, but before any further conversation could ensue, President Barratt entered the room, followed by his chief of staff.

Barratt acknowledged the group and exchanged pleasantries. Samson saw Barratt take a deep breath and look at every member in turn. Barratt pointedly advised them that what he was about to reveal was confidential and that, as their commander-in-chief, he was ordering them to maintain complete secrecy, even when making preparations for the operation they would implement.

Then Barratt explained, in great detail and with obvious emotion, The Plan.

TIMELINE OF EVENTS: JULY 18 HOUSE FIRE, SHOOTINGS LEAVE 4 DEAD, INCLUDING GUNMAN, AND OTHERS INJURED IN TUCSON

tucson.com

43.
ARIEL

ARIEL SHIFTED AGAIN, this time leaning more onto the arm of the sofa. Then she crossed her ankles and put her hand to her chin. She was in the green room of the *Start Your Day Show*, the most-watched morning show on national TV.

She had googled the other guests in the room: Nathan Mercanti had gone viral with his self-help podcasts, a guru of sorts to the millions he referred to as "those who are searching"; Ben Comet was a heartthrob rom-com actor; Janis Painter was a journalist who had written a bestselling book about the Chicago dating scene.

Ariel had been quiet after initial "good mornings" were exchanged, but in her mind a question ran on a continuous loop: What am I doing here? *Start Your Day* was considered a friendly platform for celebrities pushing a movie or a book, usually something innocuous and upbeat. She uncrossed her ankles, but her left knee started bouncing, so she crossed them again to stop it.

The green room's walls were a pale green; the sofa and the club chairs the others sat in were plush and inviting. The producers had made sure that there were fresh flowers on the end tables, a glass-front refrigerator stocked with water and juices and sodas, soft lighting from floor lamps, and a TV showing the day's program with the volume turned almost completely down. Everything was designed to relax the guests.

It wasn't working for Ariel.

When the show's assistant producer had called after the assault on Second Home, he wanted Patty, the cute cheerleader with the sad story, but Patty said no. Patty had made it clear that she didn't want to be an object of curiosity, someone to be pitied, and had no interest in appearing on the show. When the AP defaulted to her, Ariel, comfortable with Patty's okay, accepted the invite, seeing an opportunity to reach a greater audience. When he called again to prep her over the phone, he seemed to know a little something about the Dawn River shooting but very little about what she was trying to do. She couldn't avoid asking herself: *Are Patty and I just another flavor of the month? Will people still take me seriously if I look like one more self-promoter? Have I made a mistake coming here?*

One by one an assistant producer opened the green room's door and summoned the next guest. Comet, the actor, left without a backward glance. Mercanti looked over his shoulder as he departed and said, "Make yourself better today and every day." *Yuck*, thought Ariel. She watched Comet's segment on the green room TV screen. It was all laughter and false humility. *Nothing wrong with that for him*, she thought, but *that's not what I'm here for.*

Why am I here? This is the real question, she thought. *Patty and all those other people were hurt, but I'm the one on TV. Their tragedy has become my notoriety. If this goes the way I hope it does, this will be just the start. As sweet as Patty is, will she feel the same if I become the face of Dawn River? Am I the right one? And am I really capable of doing this, of making a change in people's lives?*

An assistant producer opened the door and nodded toward Painter. "Five minutes, Ms. Painter." As he left, he looked at Ariel and said, "Ariel, you'll be last on. Seth will come and fetch you."

Fetch me?

As she continued to ruminate, an old clichéd mantra jumped into Ariel's mind: "If not me, who? If not now, when?" Trite, for sure, and she didn't know who said it first, but it came unsummoned at difficult or complicated times in her life. She sat more upright on the couch. Her knee no longer tried to bounce.

Her internal conversation resumed.

Well, why not me? Do I believe in what I'm doing?

Absolutely.

Am I capable of doing it?

Yes, I am.

Is this the right program to do it on?

Uh-oh.

Painter looked across the room at her. "Are you OK?" she asked.

"Yeah, I think so," said Ariel.

"You know, I saw the video of your early rallies. You have something to say."

Ariel sighed. "But I feel like I might be blowing it. I said yes to the invite because of its high profile. I just don't know if I've made a mistake agreeing to *this* show."

"It's not the show, it's the message," said Painter. "This is your shot. You never know if you're going to get another one. Your message is going to be heard by millions of people this morning. You control your message. Don't let the host dumb it down."

They both heard the door open and the assistant call Painter's name.

"You can make this about the message, not the medium," she said as she moved toward the door. "I'm going to go sell my book. You go save the world."

Sooner than she had expected, the door opened again.

"Hi, Ariel. I'm Seth. I'll walk you up now." Seth escorted her toward the stage wing and pointed her toward the set.

Ariel walked onto the stage, said a friendly hello, and shook the host's hand. Someone miked her up and offered a seat. She sat down and formed a confident smile.

Then the red light came on.

Later that day, Patty greeted her in the living room.

"You were great! I told you I'd make you a star!"

GUNMAN LIVESTREAMED MASS SHOOTING AT LOUISVILLE BANK THAT LEFT FIVE DEAD AND EIGHT INJURED, POLICE SAY

CNN

Louisville, Kentucky

44.
ARIEL

ARIEL DIDN'T HAVE A public relations department. She didn't have an agent or any PR know-how. So, she picked up her cell phone and started to make calls to all those press reps who had reached out to Patty. She began with the first voicemail and called Chris Jacobs, from one of the cable news shows.

"Mr. Jacobs, this is Ariel," she started. "I just wanted to let you know that I'm inviting you all to my next rally at Dawn River." She gave him the date and time. "And I wonder if you could do me a favor. Could you let the rest of the reporters know so I don't have to call them all?"

Jacobs laughed lightly. "Oh, honey, that's not the way it works," and he chuckled again.

"Honey"? thought Ariel.

"Look, if I'm the only one there, I get the scoop. Anyway, thanks for the invite. We'll be there."

"Well, I just wanted to give you the courtesy of letting you know." Ariel ended the call. Maybe "courtesy" wasn't the way it worked.

Her next call was to Margaret Pennies from one of the national newspapers. She repeated the information about the rally, speaking in a slightly deflated voice.

"Thank you, Ariel," Pennies responded. "I think what you're doing is courageous. Not every young woman could pull this off. I wish you all the best."

After her interaction with Jacobs, Ariel was slightly surprised at the sensitive words. Before she could stop herself, she related to Pennies what Jacobs had said.

"Oh, honey, don't worry about him. That's just the way he is. Trust me, you make a few more phone calls and everybody's going to know."

"Honey" again, thought Ariel. Somehow, "honey" didn't sound so condescending this time.

Ariel spent the rest of the morning on the phone. She figured that Pennies was correct, that the word would get out, but she didn't want to take any chances. When she finished, she suddenly had a vision of having more press there than rally-goers. She needn't have worried. The chyrons tracking across television screens did the job for her:

**DAWN RIVER SURVIVOR TO SPEAK AT RALLY*

**SITE OF MASS SHOOTING TO BE SITE OF MASSACRE PROTEST*

**HUGE CROWD EXPECTED AT RALLY*

**ARIEL TO SPEAK ABOUT MASS SHOOTING*

**PARALYZED CHEERLEADER'S SISTER TO LEAD RALLY*

Still, Ariel was unsure what to expect. Her efforts to date had received so little traction that she didn't want to get ahead of herself.

She had stayed in the family home the previous night, as she often did, and rose early on the day of the rally. In her old bedroom were arrayed some of her PDR—pre-Dawn River—favorite things. "PDR." That's what she sometimes called it to avoid conjuring the pain that using the venue's full name could bring. The stack of books she longed to read but couldn't get to. Her throwback black-and-white Casio keyboard, covered in dust, on its stand against one wall. Her clarinet, which she had not been practicing as often as she knew she should, rested in its case.

Her violin, however, was resting on a red upholstered chair, waiting for her. It remained her comfort instrument, which she played as often as she could. And her pre- and post-PDR lives came together on her bureau. Photos of her mother, Patty, and her on the shore at Myrtle Beach, a rainbow of bathing suit colors, frothing water tickling their ankles. Ariel on stage at one of her quartet performances, photo by Patty. Patty cheering on the high school basketball team, photo by Ariel. Next to them: pictures that some supporters had taken at one of her Dawn River rallies; Patty racing across court in a wheelchair basketball game, leading her Flaming Wheels team to victory. Her musings were interrupted by a voice from across the hall.

"All right," called Patty. "Get in here. It's time to get your star face on."

‘HE WAS SO INNOCENT’: FAMILY MOURNS 12 YEAR OLD KILLED IN DRIVE-BY SHOOTING IN LONG BEACH

Long Beach Post
CALIFORNIA

45.
ARIEL

ARIEL DROVE TOWARD DAWN RIVER on the afternoon of the press conference. She was alone in the car, but with her makeup done by Patty and wearing her mother's cashmere sweater, she felt as if all three of them were heading toward something unknown, some destiny she couldn't avoid, important in a way she had never experienced. Something different that could make a difference in people's lives. She was nervous, exhilarated, fearful of failing, and energized all at the same time. She had the sense of racing on white water, trying to control the bucking raft, but wholly unable to do so.

About a half mile from Dawn River, the traffic slowed almost to a stop.

"What's going on," she asked herself. "I can't be late. Not today." The traffic moved in fits and starts. She was in the right-hand lane to be able to enter the venue parking lot, but so were most of the other cars. As she moved closer, she glanced into the lot; there were cars everywhere. She knew that there was nothing on Dawn River's schedule for today, and none of their weekday events started this early anyway. The press had asked her to schedule for the early afternoon so that they could film in daylight and get their reports on their evening shows. She reached the parking lot entrance and pulled in. If there was something going on here, why wasn't anyone charging for parking?

Ariel pulled into the first spot she found, grabbed her gear, jumped out of the car, and weaved her way through the parked vehicles. As she lifted her head to make sure that she was heading to her spot, she saw a huge crowd milling about where she would set up. Wait…were all these people here for her press conference? She stopped abruptly. *What am I going to say to them?* The plan was to speak extemporaneously, as she always had. Would they want more from her? Just then, Aunt Birdie rolled into her mind and she felt her spirit. Her shoulder muscles relaxed; her taut face softened as she started moving quickly. She would speak from her heart as she always had. Her message was the right one; now there were just a lot more people to hear it.

The late spring afternoon was pleasantly warm, though the sun had dipped below the multi-floored concert center. Instead of its glass facade reflecting the morning light, it was now backlit and loomed like a dark, brooding behemoth. Ariel walked through the crowd, most of whom didn't recognize her in person. The street noise was blocked by the chatter of the crowd, which ebbed and flowed. Finally, she reached the front line of the gathering. As Penny told her there would be, a podium was set up with a nest of microphones perched on the front edge. When she stepped behind it the crowd noise started to abate, then lowered to a murmur.

Not so for the press. They launched a staccato barrage of questions, as the cameramen brought their equipment to their shoulders and started to film. The questions kept flying, but Ariel, feeling Aunt Birdie behind her, stood silently, then raised both her arms, palms out. She held that position until the questions stopped.

Ariel took a deep breath. She didn't tremble, her throat didn't clench, she didn't hesitate. Looking through the crowd, she made eye contact with Jake and Emma, two of her regulars. They smiled back and nodded. She began.

"My sister Patty was the victim of a mass shooting. My Aunt Birdie almost was. But my aunt is the strongest person I know. Patty refuses to live the life of a victim. They have a relentless support system. But what about the hundreds of victims who have died, and the thousands who have been injured, some paralyzed, all damaged? Those who are left to struggle on their own, those who are left to mourn."

She paused, hoping that would sink in.

"Many have been diagnosed with PTSD. It's like they've been in a war zone. Uninjured survivors struggle with guilt. Even those who weren't there are now fearful. Scared to go to school, to church or a synagogue, afraid to go to work."

The crowd was still respectful, but she could see the reporters struggling to hold back.

"It all comes back to this: too many guns in the hands of too many people. Layered on top of that is the failure of places"—she turned and pointed at Dawn River—"like the one behind me to take the few steps necessary to help keep us safe."

The reporters could control themselves no longer. The thin dam of respect holding back their questions burst.

"Ariel, what would you say to the president?"

13-YEAR-OLD CHARGED AFTER ALLEGEDLY PLANNING MASS SHOOTING AT CANTON

Cleveland 19 News

46.
ARIEL

"ARIEL, WHAT WOULD YOU SAY to President Barratt if you could talk to him?" The reporter repeated her question, shouting over the din of the crowd and the rest of the press. Ariel was prepared.

"I *have* tried to talk to him, sent emails and phone messages," Ariel responded, "but I've only gotten his aides telling me to be patient, that he wants to meet me. *If* and when he does, I'll make him understand that we are real people out here, not statistics. We are not numbers on a report. We are not lines on a graph."

The reporter followed up: "Don't you think he knows that?"

"Of course he does. He was there. He knows the pain firsthand. But since he was elected, nothing has changed. Nothing. I expected more from him. This country *needs* more from him."

"Do you blame Congress as well?"

"They're all responsible, because each one of them could do something about this epidemic. But I don't want this to be about singling someone out for blame, and it shouldn't be a political football or an empty can being kicked down the road. It's about who can fix it. Everyone who sits in Washington has the power to do something. I can't. You all"—she waved her hand across the crowd—"can't. They *won't*. Are their egos and their so-called status and their temporary power more important than our lives?"

"Ariel," came the next question, "why isn't Patty here?"

Ariel looked at the reporter, then out over the crowd. "Patty is doing her best to go on with her life. She has her whole life in front of her. She worked too hard to get back to herself after the shooting. My sister is not a victim, and she's not going to act like one."

The questions now came fast and furious. What will you be doing next? Are you going to speak somewhere else? Who is funding you? Do you own a gun yourself? Has anyone been threatening you? Have you gotten any frightening phone calls? Ariel answered, as calmly as she could, one question after the other. She relaxed into it and even smiled at one of the questions.

As she was responding to a network news reporter, she noticed those in the front of the crowd focusing on something behind her. She turned and saw George Porter walking with a Dawn River employee who was pushing a cart in her direction. He had never come out during a rally before. The cart was loaded with water bottles, cases of pop, Dawn River logo towels and logo cups, boxes of snacks. Despite the pleasant temperature, his shirt front and underarms were dark with perspiration.

Porter was the facilities manager at Dawn River. He had calmed and deferred to the divas who performed there, met the quirky demands of the boy bands. But he didn't know what to do about this girl, Ariel.

Her rallies had been small and hadn't inconvenienced the concert-goers. There *was* the unending stream of emails from Ariel calling for increased security and some unwanted attention, but none of that had had any real impact. So far, he had ignored her and her motley crew of hangers-on. He *had* asked her to find another place for her rallies; she refused. He hadn't stopped her for fear of a publicity nightmare.

But when he looked out of his office windows at this rally he saw a swelling crowd. Ariel's TV appearance had attracted the masses—some curious, some true believers—who had effectively taken over the parking lot and frustrated the vendors trying to make deliveries. His boss must have been watching the news and called to chastise him. The message was simple: turn this constant reminder of the shooting into something positive or "get rid of it."

This time the press was here in force, swarming the girl's podium like buzzing wasps, their camera stands and truck masts like so many quivering fishing lines, trying to hook the story. If this turnout was a harbinger of things to come, that could be a real problem. He had to get out in front of this. He decided to try to kill this mess with kindness, show the press how gracious he was, then manipulate Ariel into toning it down, or, he could only hope, moving her rallies to someplace else. She might be a celebrity now, he thought, but he was a public relations pro. He could handle her.

Ariel gave him a "What are you doing here?" look as Porter reached the microphones and leaned in.

"Please know," he said, breathing heavily, "Dawn River management respects and supports what Ariel is doing and everyone's efforts to make our lives safer." He reached as if to put an arm around her as he waved the other arm over the cart, but Ariel subtly increased the distance between them. The crowd rewarded Porter with the applause he had hoped for, and he thanked them with a smile and a salute.

"Thank you, Mr. Porter," Ariel said, recovering. "It's nice to finally see you out here." *If he wants to suddenly be a part of this, he's going to have to pay for it*, she figured. She regained the mic and gave voice to the question that had suddenly come to her: "Does this mean that Dawn River will upgrade the metal detectors, as we had requested?"

The smile slid off his face as the crowd applauded again. Ariel could see that this *wasn't* exactly what he was hoping for. The applause was dying down as the people awaited his answer.

"Well..." There was an air of expectancy. "Well...uh...yes...yes we will, and thank you for your suggestion." Porter turned and walked away quickly, as if he wanted to escape before he gave anything else away.

Damn, thought Ariel, *I might be getting the hang of this.*

ARREST MADE IN KILLING OF THREE HOMELESS PEOPLE, LAPD SAYS; SUSPECT ALSO TIED TO SAN DIMAS MURDER

Eyewitness News, ABC7
Los Angeles

47.
JIMMY AND ARIEL

ARIEL COMPLETED HER REMARKS, which were followed by loud cheering and applause. As she continued to take the reporters' questions, the people gathered before her kept their places, her longtime supporters reveling in the turnout. God, how she loved them, drew energy from them, was lifted by their validation.

Pedestrians passing on the street in front of Dawn River slowed and looked. Ariel expected them to be a little confused. The concert center rarely had outdoor events, and she had no music, no stage, just some modest sound equipment and a phalanx of the media's microphones.

Jimmy was one of the people passing by. He walked through the foot traffic and noticed people looking at the crowd in the center's parking lot and glanced that way himself. He had vowed never to step foot onto Dawn River property again, and certainly did not plan to do so today, but he hoped whatever was happening was something negative for Dawn River. That would make his day. He repositioned himself so that he could see what was going on in front of the audience.

I'll be damned, it's that same girl. Jimmy had not been in this part of the city for about three months. What were the odds of her holding another rally today, the next time he was here? The last time he saw her there may have been twenty people listening to her naive ramblings; now there were hundreds. What changed?

There *was* something different about whatever was going on here. She was the only one speaking, and she certainly didn't have the appearance of a politician or a celebrity, and he couldn't see anyone in a Dawn River security uniform. He felt a sudden compulsion to learn more, but this building accosted him with the memory of the worst day of his life, and he was loath to get any nearer to it. But what if DR was getting its comeuppance, a goes-around-comes-around, a little well-deserved retribution?

He stepped gingerly off the sidewalk and moved onto the parking lot. As soon as his feet touched the blacktop, he felt a shudder race through his body, an electrical charge. He was frozen in place, his heartbeat quickened, and his breath came in short, panting swallows. Dawn River rose behind the crowd, dark and foreboding, seeming to grow before his eyes. But the crowd was upbeat, applauding spontaneously and loudly every few moments. He had not heard or read anything about something else happening here, but was there something he had missed? He willed his breathing to slow and his pulse to settle. He didn't want to be here—he wanted to be anywhere but here, but something compelled him to know—impelled him to move forward.

Now he was close enough to hear the back-and-forth of the reporters' questions and the girl's replies, punctuated by reactions from the crowd. As he moved nearer he could make out the dialogue. Someone she knew was almost killed in a nursing home, and someone—her sister?—was shot? Here? *The same night as Alice!* Who *was* this girl?

They were calling her Ariel. His body involuntarily moved him even closer. Now this Ariel turned while she was speaking and looked directly at him. Dawn River, shooting, Dani Blue. Jimmy's heart started to race again. He broke contact with the girl's gaze and walked as fast as he could back to the sidewalk, into the stream of pedestrians, melting into them, wrapping himself in them, defending himself with them, as the Dawn River banshees wailed and gnashed and chased him down the street.

ONE TEEN DEAD, TWO OTHERS INJURED IN LAUREL SHOOTING SUNDAY, SCHOOLS CLOSED MONDAY

The News Journal
DELAWARE

48.

IN THE YELLOW ROOM

"PATTY, CAN YOU BELIEVE WHERE WE ARE?" Ariel asked her sister. "We're actually in the White House! Not only that, we're in the private residence."

"You know I'm not into the 'Pity Patty' thing, but this is pretty cool," said Patty.

They had been shown into the room by the White House butler and directed to chairs placed at a small dining table, but Ariel couldn't sit still. Stepping to the windows set in the oval projection in the west-facing wall, she could see the South Lawn and all the way to the Ellipse. When she turned back, she took in the pale-yellow walls and period furniture; she expected it to be pretentious and overbearing, but instead it was comfortable and welcoming.

Barratt was taken aback when he read the details of the attack on Second Home. Not because there was an attack; he had been dealing with domestic terrorist attacks since he took office. But he was surprised by the Dawn River connections. Ariel was the woman holding those ever-larger rallies; her sister Patty was one of the Dawn River victims, paralyzed and confined to a wheelchair; their Aunt Birdie had hidden in her room from the shooters at Second Home. He was struck again by how mass shootings caused devastating ripples that formed massive waves and flooded people's lives, washed away their dreams, left them struggling to keep their heads above water. But here was this Ariel leading the charge for gun control. He felt compelled to reach out and bring her and her sister to the White House.

He had chosen the Yellow Room for its welcoming atmosphere and its distinctly feminine history. Barratt knew that Abigail Fillmore, Laura Bush, and other first ladies had influenced the decor to match their own style. Jackie Kennedy had hired the American interior designer Sister Parish, who created the ambience of the room with soft yellow walls and a pale oval carpet. Jackie designated it the Yellow Oval Room.

"What do you think he's like?" asked Patty.

"I don't know," said Ariel. "Remember how when we were kids we believed that the singers we loved were exactly the same on stage and off?"

"Yeah, we wised up after all this, huh? Why do you think he wants to see us?"

"I'm not sure," said Ariel. "His people agreed pretty quickly that we wouldn't do photo ops or anything, so I don't know. I do know why *I* want to see *him*."

"Behave yourself," said Patty. "He *is* the president."

"And that means he can do a lot more than he's doing. At this point, he's not much better than that two-faced witch he took over from."

Barratt entered the room with Lucy, the butler, and several servers. He greeted Ariel with a firm handshake and a pleasant welcome. Lucy said her hellos and took a seat across from Ariel. Then Barratt sat down next to Patty's wheelchair to be on her same level and took her hands in his.

"You and I have something horrible in common," he said to her. "You are a remarkable woman to come as far as you have."

"Tha... Thank you," Patty stammered, then seemed to gather herself as she said: "You've done pretty good yourself."

There was laughter all around. The staff took their brunch orders while serving coffee and tea in delicate china cups, the cups softly clinking as they were set on the saucers.

"I'm so glad you agreed to meet with me," Barratt said.

Keep your guard up, Ariel said to herself. So many of the politicians she had met were obsequious, phony. Why should she expect Barratt to be any different? Yet, he had seemed sincere when he just spoke with Patty, and he certainly had his own Dawn River history. If he was the real thing, she couldn't pass up this opportunity. If she wanted to make an impact, get the guns off the street, protect the children, keep the lost and depressed from taking their own lives, didn't she have an obligation to use this chance to her best advantage?

"It's certainly our pleasure, Mr. President," Ariel said, "though I was surprised that you wanted to see *me*."

"I've been really impressed by your performances at the rallies," said Barratt.

"*It's not a performance*," Ariel said in a knee-jerk response and a stern voice, then immediately regretted it, as Patty did a quick inhale.

There was a moment of awkward silence before the president smoothly said: "Poor choice of words, but you're doing a great job.

You've got people thinking. And, you may not think so, but it helps me with what I'm trying to do."

"Mr. President, I know I'm a very small fish in a huge pond out there, but I'm just trying to get the attention of people who can change things. With all due respect, your legislation has gone nowhere in this Congress, and thoughts and prayers are just not enough."

"You really don't know what a big fish you've become," said Barratt. "And in the pond you're swimming in now, you're making some waves."

"Well, thank you, but what's next?"

Barratt wasn't going to give her all the details yet, but he did want her to know that there was hope. He leaned back in his chair at the same time as the staff entered with their omelets, plates of French toast, and bowls of fresh fruit. He waited until they left, then looked at her with a steady, reassuring gaze. He held back the end game from almost everyone he discussed The Plan with; he would do the same with Ariel. But he wanted to give her hope, so he said:

"Ariel, I have a plan."

MORE THAN 390,000 STUDENTS HAVE EXPERIENCED GUN VIOLENCE AT SCHOOL SINCE COLUMBINE. THERE HAVE BEEN 426 SCHOOL SHOOTINGS SINCE 1999, ACCORDING TO POST DATA

The Washington Post

49.
BARRATT

THE STAFF HAD ALL LEFT, the West Wing empty except for security. As Barratt liked to do, he kept the Oval Office drapes open. He could see the South Lawn delicately illuminated by landscape lighting, and the aerial warning lights made the Washington Monument look wonderfully mysterious. The view would momentarily let him flee the office and fly, President Peter Pan looking down on the dazzling city. But as soon as he turned back inside, Neverland was left far behind, and he asked himself the seminal question that haunted him during the quiet nights: "What do I want?"

The obvious answer was the most simplistic one: He wanted to reduce the horrible incidence of gun violence. But he would never have accepted such a clichéd answer from any of his aides. He couldn't accept it from himself.

Things were moving forward: General Samson and the other military officers he needed were on board, and he was confident that Chief Justice Chandler would ultimately secure the Supreme Court's imprimatur for The Plan. He knew, however, that The Plan was not going to move in a straight line. And no matter how hard he tried to keep every aspect of the operation secret, he was becoming paranoid about leaks. Christine Grammar had her spies everywhere. She was one of the most transactional, self-absorbed, and—he had to admit—effective politicians he had ever met. She wanted his job and would do anything to get it.

But these were side trails. What did he want? What did he *need*?

Closing his eyes, he leaned back in his chair, the one he had moved to the Oval Office as soon as he moved in. Lucy had bought it for him when he was first elected to Congress. It was a security blanket, soft brown leather shaped by long days to fit him perfectly. He breathed deeply, centered himself. This was not a policy question; this was an introspective demand that had to be met if the policy was to succeed.

What did he want?

He opened his eyes and gazed around the room, at the busts of Washington and Jefferson, at the paintings of Teddy and Franklin Roosevelt, presidents who had prevailed against doubt and fear. He felt the power of his office and the almost unbearable weight of his responsibility. His mind went back to the concert and the terrible sound of the shots being fired, to his relief when he knew that Gabrielle was safe, to the hundreds—an awful number—of people whom he now met with and tried to comfort when nothing would make their loss any less crushing.

What did he want?

Not personal aggrandizement. He didn't care if he got reelected. Didn't care if he was popular at the end of his term. What did he want? He wanted to lead his country to a place where gun violence was curtailed, and then for it to be seen as a horrible, unacceptable aberration. He wanted the idea of someone killing another human being over a parking space, or the last toy in a store, or because they knocked on the wrong door, to be seen as ludicrous, to be met with thundering outrage by people on both sides of the aisle, on both sides of the religious divide. He didn't want to have to tell *one more* sobbing parent that all he could do was send her the country's impotent thoughts and prayers.

But there was more.

Why did he *need* to do this? Deep down, he knew that he couldn't have done more at Dawn River; he couldn't have saved them all. But deeper down, where all was visceral, where logic had no purchase, where rank emotion ruled, where self-worth was challenged and dignity could sink into the mire, he judged himself and found himself wanting. As ridiculously unreasonable as it was, he felt he owed the world; he was still upright, and Gabrielle was still alive. He didn't want to leave this life with the debt unpaid. Yes, he had saved Gabby, but he couldn't save Chandler's granddaughter or all those other kids who just wanted to see Dani Blue sing.

Okay, he thought, *if I couldn't do that, I might as well just save the whole damn country.*

4 INJURED BY GUNFIRE IN 2ND NC CENTRAL ACTIVE SHOOTER ALERT DURING HOMECOMING IN DURHAM, OFFICIALS SAY

CBS17.com

Raleigh-Durham-Fayetteville

50.
GRAMMAR

SENATOR CHRISTINE GRAMMAR had purposely kept William Williams waiting in the outer office.

Williams was the executive director of Gun Rights Unlimited (with the apparently oblivious and certainly unfortunate acronym of "GRU"). Unlike the unpredictable American Firearms Confederacy, the GRU maintained a public respectability, styling itself as a gun safety and education organization. Its dues-paying members came from all walks of life: engineers, truckers, doctors, waitresses—a wide spectrum of Americans and hundreds of elected officials or wannabes, who had their own agendas.

Williams was the perfect director for the GRU, Grammar thought, a classic poser. He was well-educated and articulate, wore expensive, tailored suits, and peppered his remarks with references to obscure historical events. By design, he presented himself as the antithesis of the stereotypical gun advocate. *You won't hide from me*, Grammar mused. Like everyone else with whom she dealt, she knew that Williams had his secrets.

Her "research assistants," the ones she only met with outside the office, were experts at finding the person behind the pose, at digging up the dark dirt. Her "miners," she called them. Grammar didn't need to know the details or their methods, just the results. They had, indeed, drilled down to the hidden Williams mother lode.

Before rising to the top of the GRU, he was an unimpressive insurance broker, a modestly successful Wall Street trader, and—most relevant for her purposes—a suspect executive at another nonprofit entity. "Suspect" because despite his middle-class income he lived a very upper-class lifestyle. His separation from those companies was "mutual." Grammar knew what that meant: get out or get fired, don't tell anyone how you conned us, keep quiet or get charged. He kept landing on his feet, primarily because, while the guilt was all but certain, the proof was difficult, and a public airing damaging. Williams always left with an agreement that his former employer would tell any inquiring company that they no longer gave recommendations on former employees.

Williams needed the money he "allegedly" siphoned. Grammar's miners found that he had some pricey tastes: the enviable wine cellar, the big Mercedes and the little BMW, a collection of—this was her favorite—athletic shoes, including unworn Air Jordan Retros and the Jordan High Dior. More importantly for today's meeting, the miners reported that some of Williams's worst and closet friends were unpaid Las Vegas bookies.

Grammar leaned forward at her desk and pressed the button on her phone.

"Rachel, show Mr. Williams in."

The office door opened, and Williams entered. He had never been in her office before. She stifled a smile as Williams, a man given to ostentation, cast an envious eye around her office: at the massive wooden desk inlaid with alabaster and displaying polished bronze accents, the Tiffany lamps, the photographs of her with the Washington power elite at the Correspondents' Dinner, at the State of the Union address, near the stage at President Barratt's inauguration.

"Senator Grammar, it's a pleasure to see you again," Williams said.

"Mr. Williams," Grammar replied, "it's good to see you as well."

"May I ask how your father and the rest of the family is?"

"All fine. It's good of you to ask," Grammar said. *I couldn't care less about your crew,* she thought, but she asked anyway. "How are Melissa and the kids?"

"All well, thank you."

Grammar feigned collegiality. She had long understood that different people needed to be approached differently. And it was, even after the election of the first female president, still mostly men whom she had to manipulate to get what she wanted. Some needed egos massaged, some needed to be bullied, and some, like Williams, needed to feel the fear of God.

"Mr. Williams," Grammar said, "I summoned you here for a purpose."

"Summoned?"

"Okay, let's say that I made you an invitation that you couldn't refuse." Grammar felt herself struggling not to laugh out loud. She had been waiting to use that line. *I am, after all, the powerful Godmother, but I'd never let you actually kiss my ring. Ugh.*

Grammar leaned forward. "However we phrase it, let me tell you why you're here. I understand that fool Barratt is planning to announce some gun control proposal. My sources tell me that it may be more than the typical word salad that makes a point but spoils over time. Whatever it is, it gives us an opportunity."

"And what would that be, Senator?"

"When he makes the announcement, I will, of course, respond in a dignified way. Your role will be to rally your membership in outrage. I will argue the sanctity of the Second Amendment, but it would be unseemly for me to revisit all the self-defense arguments and the home-intrusion stories. Instead, your membership will do that. I expect continuing and boisterous complaints and accusations of unconstitutional action."

"Senator, I appreciate what you're saying, but we've had some rough PR lately. I'll have to run this past the board and get their direction."

"We both know that you run the GRU show."

"Senator Grammar, I'm only one voice. And our advertising budget is stretched right now."

"Don't play hard to get, Mr. Williams. I know exactly what your budget is. I know exactly how much you need to keep your operation going, and you know that my family, through several unconnected companies, funds 10 percent of your budget, although that's not obvious to anyone who audits. That number can change, of course, depending on the economy. Who knows? It could go to 15 percent, or it could drop to zero."

Williams' face started to pale. Grammar lowered her voice and said: "And it certainly seems fair that, if that funding did increase, some of it would be well-spent on certain gambling debts to protect its CEO's reputation."

Williams's face was now completely colorless. "I...I don't know what you're talking about, Senator. We, uh, we run a clean ship."

"But loose casino chips do sink ships, don't they, Mr. Williams?"

Williams sighed heavily and sat back in his chair. "Yes, Senator, they have been known to do that."

Grammar rose from her seat, signaling that the meeting was over. "I'm so glad that we could get together and work this out. Be sure to give my best to Melissa."

Williams rose from his seat and walked unsteadily toward the door. When he closed the door behind him, Grammar stood and stepped to the office windows. Looking out at the most powerful city in the world, she smiled as she recalled her father's mantra, which had become her own: "When money is on the table, saints will sin and devils will grin."

TWO JUVENILES, ONE ADULT SHOT IN FRAYSER

News 3
Memphis

51.
BARRATT

BARRATT NEVER LIKED having makeup applied. A finger or brush coming close to his eyes always made him cringe. He marveled at Lucy's patience with foundation and eyeliner and under-eye cream. Now he sat in the press prep room as Theresa, his longtime makeup artist, urged him to stop fidgeting.

Over his years of campaigning, he had studied other candidates' speeches as he prepared for his own. He not only listened to the substance and the cadence, but he also noted their gestures, their body language, their appearance. With one look at Richard Nixon's dark five o'clock shadow and deeply lined skin, contrasted with JFK's Hollywood presence—the perfect tan, the dazzling white teeth, the hair—he overcame his reluctance to use cosmetics to deal with the harsh lights and unforgiving cameras. He looked for any advantage now as he anticipated his address to the nation, just twenty minutes away.

He and Theresa typically enjoyed a light banter when she prepared him for the cameras. They had been through this so often that she would dismiss his protestations and joke her way through the job. This time, Barratt noticed that her movements weren't as fluid. She had knocked several things off her table, dropped one of her brushes. There were no respectful digs, no grinning jokes. He knew why: The tension he radiated dominated the room.

Barratt had cleared his schedule for two days, unusual for him. He devoted the entirety of that first day to preparation for the address. With his experience in jury trials and before appellate courts, he knew the danger of over-preparing, that the presentation could become flat and stilted. But with what hung in the balance with this address, he knew that committing himself to the goal of perfection could release some of his anxiety.

He had practiced two days ago in the study near the Oval Office. Lucy and Gabrielle and Bobby were his audience. Bobby was up and down, in and out of his chair, pacing behind it and destroying his concentration, until Barratt stared him back into his seat. Lucy had her eyes closed and her head slightly bowed, fully focused; he knew that she would give him her unvarnished critique. Gabrielle sat quietly, her hands folded and resting in her lap, giving him her total attention.

The following day, Barratt practiced his presentation in the Oval Office, with full klieg lights and the teleprompter scrolling. The producer and the technicians, typically lighthearted, exchanging comments and advice, went about their business in almost complete silence. There was a literal electronic buzz from some of the equipment and an ineffable one pervading the room. Four run-throughs, after each of which Barratt would study the video and make subtle changes to his anticipated gestures and inflection. When they were finished, Barratt thanked them all for their work and especially for understanding that they would surrender their phones and be isolated in the White House until after the address. He was disturbed that the circle of people who now knew the content of his remarks was widening, but it was unavoidable.

After that session, he decided to decompress in the pool. Waiting for twilight, he kicked off the side and glided through the soft, waning light, his strokes precise, his kicks hardly making a ripple. He didn't do flip turns anymore; Dawn River made that movement awkward and painful. Falling into the rhythm of the swim, he turned his head to breathe on every third stroke, enveloped by the water, concentrating on his technique, pulling away from rumination, becoming one with the water as it flowed over him and he flowed into it.

When he finished, he stood for a moment in the shallow end, bent at the waist and breathing hard, embracing exhaustion. He completed his after-swim stretches and stepped out of the pool. Lucy had been sitting on the pool apron, waiting for him. He turned now to see her approaching him, holding a towel open. Barratt smiled, enjoying the sensual memory of when, after showering together, he would prolong the intimacy by softly drying Lucy's back and arms and breasts, caressing her dry. Standing alongside the pool, he closed his eyes and welcomed Lucy, wrapping the towel and her arms around him and gently kissing his neck. He could feel the last of the tension draining from his body; he could feel her strength intertwined with his, a strength he welcomed.

Theresa finished and gently removed the blue plastic drape from his shoulders, the swishing movement the only sound in the room. Holding the drape in one hand, she stepped back to check her work, then reached and smoothed an undisciplined hair.

"You look very handsome, Mr. President."

"You tell me that every time, Theresa," Barratt said, as he gave her a slight smile.

Theresa left the room, and for a moment he was alone. He was about to engage the country in a seminal, existential moment. He knew that he hadn't just been preparing for this over the last two days, but, in a way, for every day since the concert. Dawn River was the impetus for a change that would transform the country, and it had chosen him to make that happen. Looking in the mirror, which was ringed by the makeup lights and positioned over the counter, he saw a face that had been weathered by the recurring, visceral memories of racing toward the stage at Dawn River and diving to cover Gabrielle. Of climbing through his rehab to reach a plateau from which he could launch The Plan. Of confounding the "experts" by connecting with the millions who were begging for the killing to stop. He had been impelled to this place, this time, by every moment of his life since those shots rang out. Barratt took a deep breath and nodded to the man in the mirror.

He was ready.

LAS VEGAS SHOOTING: 59 KILLED AND MORE THAN 500 HURT NEAR MANDALAY BAY

NBC News/US News

52.
MEDIA

THE MEDIA HAD BEEN UNIMPRESSED when a White House press release indicated that President Barratt would be addressing the nation and making a major announcement concerning gun violence in America. On its 9:00 p.m. edition, the Your News Now (YNN) network's "Posse" was in its usual bombastic form.

Randy Trisscup led the way. He played the role of the intellectual, which he was well suited to do. Harvard and Cambridge educated, centrist family background, his patrician appearance promised a careful, respectful perspective—until, that is, he discovered that obnoxious sold better.

"What does he think he's going to do? His feckless administration is no match for this issue. This is just going to be more ineffective posturing." This was Trisscup at his pontificating best. "Any effective effort at controlling the problem needs to be led by someone who has the trust of America. He hasn't done anything to demonstrate that he has the force of personality to accomplish what needs to be done."

The token opposition on the choreographed panel responded: "Well, he did win his election comfortably, so he does have something of a mandate," Nathaniel Jeffries said. Jeffries was frequently the whipping boy but was so enthralled with being a regular on the show that he suffered willingly.

The Posse's set consisted of five club chairs in a semicircle, a low coffee table before them with plastic flowers at both ends. The camera showed the newsroom behind it, reporters and researchers sprinkled at the desks. They half-watched, half-listened to the Posse; most had become jaded, having heard the outrage and seen the drama with too many minor stories to be excited now.

"And he's done nothing with that mandate," Trisscup said. "Read my lips: He's already a lame duck."

"Calling him lame is an insult to all ducks everywhere!" blurted Alton Edwards, who filled the role of attack dog. Edwards was famous as a professional wrestler, going by the name "Ultra Alton." On set, he wore bicep-hugging shirts with a loosened tie and no jacket. He was imposing: still ripped, six foot two, 225 pounds of muscle. He was also a closet intellectual, a graduate of Stanford, but that wasn't his role on the show. "He's laughable! He's wasted our time with his time in office."

Betty Bobic, all blonde and lean and leggy, nicknamed "Betty Boop" by the wags on rival cable news stations, sat in the middle of the five-person array, the presumptive moderator. On many other outlets she could have been the lead economic reporter; here, she had very little to say but was paid twice what she was offered elsewhere.

"But," offered Jeffries, "he's had some foreign policy successes."

"Oh, we're not going to talk about that again!" countered Edwards. "We need help right here in this country! And if he lets any more lice-ridden immigrants across the border, we're going to be known as the United States of Latin America."

"America needs strong leadership," Trisscup said. "Men in this country are losing their courage and their understanding of the way to take charge. Barratt is the poster child for risk-averse posturing. I will go on record right now as saying that this 'major announcement' will be nothing more than a political move to appease the radical faction of his party."

Edwards guffawed as he joined in. "You are exactly right. This will be one more laughable joke of a policy."

CLINTON AREA PARTY IS SCENE OF SHOOTINGS THAT INJURED FOUR

Beloit Daily News
Wisconsin

53.
BARRATT

BARRATT HAD LABORED OVER the greeting he would use to start his address to the nation.

He joked with Bobby that he would begin with Walter Winchell's famous line: "Good evening, Mr. and Mrs. America, from border to border and coast to coast and all the ships at sea." It was an effort to ease the tension. It didn't work.

With five minutes to go, he sat in the Oval Office. One of the joyous surprises he had experienced was his practically spiritual relationship with the Resolute Desk and the strength that he drew from its lineage. FDR addressed the country from the desk during World War II, JFK dealt with the Cuban missile crisis, Barack Obama made history the first time he simply sat down at the desk. There was no place in the West Wing where Barratt felt more comfortable. He wasn't hiding behind it, wasn't using it to protect himself. Rather, when he rested his elbows or hands on it, he could feel its power; there was nothing that he could not overcome.

Three minutes. He had been moving inexorably toward this day for almost fifteen years. From the groundwork he had laid to create the Dependable Return Advisors, to his campaigns for local office, then the Senate, then the presidency, to his doomed efforts at gun control. If, in all that time, anything—*anything*—had been done, any law passed, any honest effort made, he would have celebrated it, and, he thought, not be sitting here. Instead, the country had gone backward, wallowing in a Wild West mentality. After Dawn River, as he lay first in the hospital, then in the recliner at home, pursuing the torturous path toward recovery, The Plan had come to him—audacious, ridiculous, madly presumptuous, and fully formed. When he became president, he had prayed that it was *not* inevitable, that he would never have to use it. But now, now it was the only alternative.

One minute. Barratt took several deep breaths and worked his jaws.

Thirty seconds. His producer looked at him and raised an open hand. He counted down from four by closing fingers: three, two—red light on. At one he pointed at President Elijah Barratt. Barratt looked directly into the camera lens and began.

"My fellow Americans, since January first of this year there have been 173 mass shootings, more than one a day. The synagogue and the grocery store massacres, the attack on Second Home. Over eight hundred—*eight hundred*—people have been victims of gun violence in fewer than six months."

Barratt had purposely cut to the chase, hoping the numbers would shock the conscience.

"There are so many shootings that news outlets are selective about the ones they report, because they have neither the space nor the manpower to cover them all. We have, tragically, become numb to the stories."

Bobby was pacing behind the cameraman, the production crew silently doing their jobs. Barratt didn't look at them, but he felt their presence. *They all know what I intend to do*, he thought, *but some of them probably think that nobody would ever really do it.*

"But we should not be numb.

"These people were just trying to live their lives. Rabbi Horowitz and the elders reciting the Torah in temple, Frank Wilson just released from prison after his conviction was overturned, five children at the Time for Tots preschool."

A photo of Barratt, Lucy, and Gabrielle, taken when he first ran for office, rested on the credenza behind him. He could not see it, but he could *feel* it, could picture it clearly. It usually sustained him, but now the image threatened to take him back to Dawn River, the start of the journey that had brought him here. The fright, fear, shock, and anger of that day was a tide rising within him, threatening to wash away his focus. He swam hard through it, swam toward Lucy and Gabrielle, reached them and renewed his focus.

"This scourge of shootings does not discriminate. Some are targeted; many others are random, spontaneous. Whether they are motivated by rage or religious fervor or racist hatred or the compulsions of the mentally ill, there is no justification."

Barratt increased his pace, pushing, pulsing toward the finish. He detailed the fourteen bills he had presented to Congress and how they were all shot down. How the Second Amendment had been drafted to appease the southern states and now was co-opted to rationalize doing nothing.

Barratt was hardly glancing at the words on the teleprompter as they scrolled by. He felt his spirit lift out of him, that he had become incorporeal. It was as if he had slipped through the camera and the cables and the airwaves and alighted in people's homes and workplaces and offices. Through the screen on a security guard's desk, the radio in a Lyft driver's car, the headphones of those on an overnight shift, through the big-screen TVs in living rooms everywhere. He was no longer in the Oval Office. He was in the ether, dispersing his energy, desperately reaching out to touch the people he was responsible for protecting.

"Gun ownership in this country has reached bizarre levels. We have more guns than we have people. We have more shootings annually in this country than we have days in a year. Other countries are issuing travel warnings about *us.*"

"So, my fellow Americans, this horror ends now."

Barratt moved a sheaf of papers that had been sitting beside him on the desk, placing it before him. Picking up the fountain pen that had rested there, he signed two documents, then regained direct contact with the camera lens.

"By signing these documents, I am this day declaring a national state of emergency and invoking the Insurrection Act. Using the powers conferred upon the president pursuant to that Act, I am announcing that, effective immediately, private gun ownership in the United States of America is absolutely forbidden."

LAS VEGAS SHOOTING: 59 KILLED AND MORE THAN 500 HURT NEAR MANDALAY BAY

NBC News/ U.S. news

Note: This headline is purposely repeated. The shooting was considered the worst mass shooting by a civilian in the history of the United States. The shooter used a bump stock to convert his semi-automatic rifle into what was essentially a machine gun, then strafed concert goers at an outdoor performance.

54.
MEDIA

WHEN BARRATT, DURING THE SECOND HOUR of the *Posse's Show*, with the gravitas required, from the Oval Office, announced the Gun Ban Executive Order, the YNN newsroom was apoplectic.

Trisscup, Edwards, and the rest of the crew sat stunned into silence as producers shouted into their earpieces. Trisscup was the first to regain his balance.

"I knew that Barratt's announcement was going to be something earth-shaking. This is exactly what I expected. He's obviously gone too far. The American people will not stand for this." He spoke in what he considered his most serious tone.

Edwards said: "This is unconstitutional! This is a violation of basic American values!"

The newsroom crew behind them was riveted to the big screens carrying the broadcast; the stunning action by the president getting even *their* attention.

Trisscup continued: "It is difficult to conceive of just what Barratt is trying to accomplish here. The American people won't stand for it. And there is no doubt—and you're hearing it right now from me—that the United States Supreme Court will declare this action unconstitutional. And then, I predict, Barratt will be quickly impeached."

When they were off the air and off camera, they all leaned in closer to each other and, in quiet, subdued, voices, shared their shock.

"What in God's name did he just do?" Trisscup asked.

Bobic turned to Jeffries. "Nate, you have great sources inside the White House. Did you see this coming?"

"No way," Jeffries responded. "I knew there was an announcement coming, but nobody had any details."

"This is surreal," said Edwards. "He has the Senate but not the House. Where does he think this could go?"

"Randy," Jeffries said, "your son's a police officer. This could go south real fast; give him my best and tell him to be careful."

"Thanks, Nate, I will." Trisscup shook his head. "No good can come of this," he said. "I know I wouldn't want to be out on the streets tonight."

No one spoke for two minutes. Then Bobic said out loud what they were all thinking, "Buckle up, boys. Things are about to get medieval."

RETIRED POLICE SERGEANT WHO KILLED 3 AT CALIFORNIA BAR SHOT HIS ESTRANGED WIFE FIRST, OFFICIALS SAY

KTLA 5

LA's very own

55.
BARRATT

BARRATT MAINTAINED HIS STEADY GAZE as he continued his address.

"As we speak, the United States military has been directed to seize each and every firearm in the hands of civilians wherever they may be found. I urge every patriotic American to freely surrender their weapons and cooperate fully with law enforcement.

"For the next thirty days, any gun owner may voluntarily turn their firearms in to the task force without any penalty. You will be compensated. From and after that day, any civilian who possesses a firearm will be considered in violation of the Insurrection Act and will be dealt with accordingly."

Barratt and his aides had anticipated a tidal wave of responses to the address. He tried to short-circuit one of those now.

"Do not expect to be able to hide your weapons in the ceiling of your garage or in the woods or under the ground. In days to come, my administration will be further explaining the details of this operation. That explanation will include a description of the enhanced magnetometers that have been developed and deployed, and which will pinpoint firearms wherever they are."

Barratt took another pause and softened his countenance.

"I know that these steps are extraordinary, totally unprecedented, the stuff of dystopian novels. But we are losing our people, we are draining our treasury, we are filling our jails. We are condemning families to never-ending grieving. Our very existence as a nation is under threat."

He had refolded his hands; he now unfolded them and spread them in front of him.

"I understand now why presidents who addressed the nation ended their remarks by asking for God's blessing, and I do so tonight. But I also believe that God helps those who help themselves. And that is precisely what we must do.

"Thank you. Please know that my goal is to make you safer tomorrow than you are today."

When the address concluded, Barratt moved from the Oval Office to the small conference room down the hall. The room was crowded: Bobby, the president's communications director, the deputy chief of staff, Barratt's secretary, the vice president, several other staff. Lucy and Gabrielle. Several cabinet officers.

Bobby's cell phone was ringing constantly, his cathedral chimes ringtone resounding through the room.

"That sounds like a celebration...or a death knell," said Barratt.

"Some of both," said Bobby as he scrolled through the texts. "And some very creative curses thrown in."

It was now 10:00 p.m., and after long days of preparation and practice, exhaustion was showing on Barratt's face. His shoulders sagged slightly, he had loosened his tie, he sipped continuously at the water bottle he held. He knew that not everyone in the room had been privy to what he had just announced. Those who weren't wore looks of surprise or thinly veiled disapproval. Vice President Jackson was struggling to disguise her angry visage. Barratt would have to explain to her privately why she was left out of the loop, to protect her from the backlash, to avoid destroying her political future the way he had probably destroyed his. But this was neither the time nor the place.

He also figured that many were incredulous at the rest of the address, after he had told the country that he was taking their guns away. His description of the enhanced magnetometers must have sounded like science fiction, or that he had lost his mind. He wondered if anyone was looking up the Twenty-Fifth Amendment.

"I'm going to ask you all to understand," Barratt said to those gathered, "that the circle of people who knew the details of The Plan had to be kept very small. It had nothing to do with my trust in you, but I wanted you to be able to distance yourselves from this if it doesn't go as planned."

Barratt could sense the tension in the room abate, but only slightly. It still hung in the air like a shroud, one he would have to shrug off quickly.

Over the next several days, responses to the address were swift, vociferous, and heartfelt; they ran an extraordinary gamut of emotions.

"Let's have the latest, Bobby."

They sat in the Oval Office at 6:00 a.m., three days after the address to the nation. Barratt had the curtains open and all the lights on. He remembered the *Doonesbury* comic that followed weeks depicting the Nixon Watergate White House surrounded by barbed wire on top of high fences, patrolled by armed guards. When Nixon resigned, the next day's panels showed the fence coming down and the wire removed, with the guards gone and birds flitting and singing over the White House portico. He wanted to feel that the light was shining into his White House now that the polls showed that most of the country felt phenomenal relief, which was a great relief to him.

"It is quite a mixed bag, Mr. President."

"Mix the good in with the bad," said Barratt. "It might make it easier to digest."

"Okay, the GRU—how the hell didn't they know what the acronym would be? Oh, well—continues to hold protests. So far, they've been essentially peaceful. At the same time, Stop the Violence and Save Our Children are singing your praises. They've had marches in support. The SOC chairwoman described herself as being stunned, then euphoric. She told the press that the gift they had been hoping for had finally arrived. You saw the videos of them taking to the streets the night of the address, banging pots and pans. As usual, they had some very creative signs.

"We're up to three cabinet resignations. You've seen all three of the letters: Transportation, Interior, HUD."

"Only HUD surprised me," said Barratt. "I thought that she would welcome removing guns from housing. But I know she was born and raised in Wyoming, so we probably should have expected it. What are you seeing on cable news?"

"Dueling experts," said Bobby. "The conservative ones think that The Plan is totally unconstitutional, will die a quick death in the courts, and that you should be immediately impeached, if not taken out and, ironically, shot. The liberal experts cited the Insurrection Act and thought that The Plan was totally defensible.

"And you'll get a kick out of this one," said Bobby. "A movie theater in Dallas is showing a nonstop Clint Eastwood movie marathon. The audience is standing and cheering every time Dirty Harry shoots somebody."

"Well," said Barratt, "at least they're getting some exercise."

"Oh," said Bobby, "and thirty more death threats today."

"I wonder what the record is?" asked Barratt.

The longtime friends laughed together, but Barratt knew it was gallows humor.

"Whatever it is, Mr. President, you're going to break it."

THREE DEAD, FOUR INJURED IN NEW YEAR'S EVE SHOOTING IN GULFPORT

WXXV 25

Gulfport-Biloxi-Pascagoula

PART THREE

56.
STANLEY KNIGHT

WHEN BARRATT ANNOUNCED that he was taking everybody's guns away, Knight went ballistic, literally. He spent the entire next day shooting anything that moved in the backwoods, tears clouding his eyes as he sighted in. He trembled and his heart raced as he contemplated life without his gun, his partner, the one thing that made him feel normal, that shoved Slow Stanley aside and let Mr. Knight move on. And now some politician was going to steal it away. As he held it against his chest that day, he comforted himself with the promise that he would never let it go. The news reported on the equipment that would be used to find any hidden weapons; Knight knew that he had to find a way to protect the one thing he treasured above all others.

He fantasized about how he would show them all that he could outsmart them, because he knew something they did not: that when he focused all his energy and emotion and anger, he could not be stopped. When he balanced his competing feelings of rage and self-pity and applied the power they morphed into, he could be truly "special," he thought, in a way that none of them ever could. He would be famous for something that they would never dare think of.

Now he celebrated the solution to his dilemma. He had figured it out all by himself, he mused proudly, had figured out how to keep his best friend alive.

After lovingly cleaning his rifle, stealing what he could from his workplace, and adapting things he found around the house, he had solved his problem. Wrapping the Steyr in layers of heavy plastic sheeting, he secured that with duct tape, placed it in a waterproof sleeve, and finally enclosed it in a ceramic case. There was a handle on the finished package, and he tied a length of jute rope to it.

The next morning he rose long before dawn—and lucked out with a dark, moonless sky. He moved quickly, almost slipping on the dew-wet grass as he delicately placed his rifle onto the passenger seat of his truck, secured it with the seat belt, and headed for the town's remote water tower. He drove without headlights and clicked off the dome light.

Parking in the shadows behind the tower, he grabbed his Steyr, went to the tower ladder, and scrambled up 135 feet, exhilarated as he ascended to the catwalk. He climbed the secondary ladder to the portal at the top of the dome, opened it, and carefully lowered the package into the water. His final innovation was the float that he had attached halfway along the length of rope. He tied the rope around a large, heavy magnet, reached into the portal, and stuck the magnet on the inside of the tower bowl, where it could not be seen by any worker coming to inspect.

He had reasoned, accurately it turned out, that the tower's metal signature would be ignored by Barratt's henchmen and that his carefully packaged rifle would not register on the scanners. His Steyr would be there when he needed it.

He knew he would need it soon.

MAN FATALLY SHOT, SEVERAL HURT WHEN CONFRONTATION IN SPRING LAKE PARK PARKING LOT ESCALATES

Minnesota Star Tribune

57.
THE MAGEE FARM

LIEUTENANT COLONEL PAPPAS was the battalion commander, and Captain Scott was the company CO. Scott had ordered Second Lieutenant Baxter, fresh out of Basic Officer Leaders Course, to lead the platoon that was deployed to the Magee farm. The need for troops was great because of the scope of the president's national address. The Super Mags had lived up to their billing, and he was proud to be at the forefront of the operation.

Baxter assessed the farmhouse. It was old, but he could see that it was well maintained. Only a few chips on the painted clapboard, a solid roof, clean windows. The steps were strong, and the porch looked recently swept. He approached the front door and knocked loudly, expecting an older and likely respectable man to answer. Travis Magee opened the door and fit the description.

"Mr. Magee?" asked Baxter.

"Yes, sir."

"I'm Lieutenant Baxter of the United States Army. We have reason to believe that there are firearms stored on this property. Consistent with the executive orders issued by the president, I am asking you to voluntarily surrender them."

Magee scratched his thick beard with one hand and removed a worn, red Wilton Feed hat, revealing a classic farmer's tan.

With a friendly smile, he said, "I don't know how that can be. As soon as I heard about it, I turned my shotguns in to the police station. You young boys have a tough enough job without some old geezer like me making it harder on ya by hiding stuff."

Baxter did not return the smile. "Nevertheless, the magnetometers pinged on your farm."

"Oh, now, son, you know how some machines play games with you. I've got an old John Deere that has a mind of its own."

"Sir, just the same, I'd like my men to search the house."

"Of course. Believe me, I have nothing but respect for you boys."

Magee moved aside as Lieutenant Baxter called to Sargeant Matthews.

"Sargeant, search the farmhouse."

Matthews led three men into the house. Two moved through the first floor and then the basement, while he and the other trooper went upstairs.

Baxter and Magee stood silently on the porch until Magee asked, "So, where are you from, Lieutenant?"

Baxter's reserve softened slightly. "Out of state. We're not supposed to give out more information than that."

"Well, youse are probably a long way from home and a good meal. I served. I know what army chow is like. I've got some leftover fried chicken if you want some."

Baxter gave a small laugh. "Thank you, Mr. Magee, I'm good, but I appreciate the offer." *This guy's not so bad*, Baxter thought.

Sergeant Matthews came back outside and said, "Lieutenant, we found nothing inside. It's clean."

"All right," said Baxter, "let's check the outbuildings."

"Now, that's not really necessary," Magee said immediately. "That's just a bunch of farm equipment, fertilizer, and some of my animals that get nervous when they're disturbed."

Baxter noticed the immediate change in Magee's demeanor. "Is there something else that you want to tell us?"

"Uh...uh, no...no, it's just that there is, uh"—he raised his voice and shouted—"no reason for ya to waste ya time lookin' in them old barns." He cast a nervous eye toward the nearest building.

"Sergeant," said Baxter, "you're with me. Williams, Miller, you too. Simmons, Walters, post here, and don't let Mr. Magee leave this spot. The rest of you spread out and check out those other buildings."

Baxter, Matthews, and the two soldiers moved toward the nearest building. It was a very small red structure, more like an oversized shed. Baxter approached the doors and fingered the hasp, which held a rusted lock that hung loose. The building had two hinged doors, touching in the middle.

"Do you know, Sergeant," asked Baxter, "why barns are so often painted red?"

Matthews was already used to humoring Baxter when he shared irrelevant expertise. He started to respond but stopped as Baxter grabbed both door handles and started to pull them open.

"Lieutenant, might be better if you stood to the side until we open those doors and—"

Matthew's words were cut off as Baxter spread the doors and a deafening fusillade roared out of the barn. Baxter was struck in the chest, lifting him off the ground, flinging him backward and bouncing him along the hard-packed dirt yard. Matthews yelled to his two men, "Get down! Return fire! Return fire!" Then, "Medic! Medic!" though this was drowned out by the blistering blast of the troopers' fire. The doors burst into splinters of wooden shrapnel. The firing from inside the building stopped.

Finally, he said, "Hold your fire."

Matthews sidled along the building and used the end of his rifle barrel to pull one of the doors farther open, then peered cautiously inside. Even for a combat veteran, the sight was gruesome. Two men he figured to be maybe in their forties lay partly on the wooden floor, in pieces. One was riddled through the chest. The other had been sliced in half across his torso, eyes open, dead staring at the shed roof. His upper half was flat on its back, the lower half astonishingly standing upright, booted feet solidly on the floor. Arranged along the interior walls were numerous firearms, shotguns, rifles, dozens of boxes of ammo. Near the casualties on the floor were two AR-15s.

Matthews moved to where Baxter lay on the ground, dead eyes staring at the clear blue sky. The medic kneeling next to the body looked up and just shook his head.

Matthews walked toward the middle of the yard and gave orders to the rest of the platoon to carefully complete the search of the other outbuildings, collect the cache of weapons, and secure them in their truck. He turned back toward the farmhouse and heard Magee screaming.

"My sons!" Magee cried. "You killed my sons!"

Matthews looked at him without sympathy.

"Your sons murdered my lieutenant. And you, you fuckin' idiot, you're the reason your sons are dead. If you had followed the law no one would have died here today."

"You bastard!" yelled Magee. "I served in Iraq. I'm a United States citizen. I have a right to bear arms! You, and that prick president of yours, you did this!"

Matthews clenched his fists and wanted nothing more than to lay the old man out but held his fire. Instead, he calmly ordered Magee placed under arrest and taken to one of the Humvees for transport. He walked somberly to his Humvee as well and sat down heavily in the passenger seat. He knew that ambulances would soon arrive to remove the bodies, and three identical black zippered bags would be placed inside. MPs would follow up the action and report on the incident. He sighed as a thought rolled into his mind: What just happened here was likely being repeated in other states, right here in the United States, confrontations that would lead to more dead.

His country, goddamn it, was at war.

3 TEENS DEAD, ONE CRITICAL IN SHOOTING AT TEXAS GAS STATION

Associated Press
(REPORT REGARDING GARLAND, TEXAS)

58.
BOBBY

BOBBY KNEW IT WAS going to be bad. Immediately after the president announced The Plan, emails and texts started to bombard the White House. Everything went to the Secret Service, but Bobby had established a protocol with his staff for filtering what he and the president should see. The emails and texts from the regulars, the ones who commented and complained about everything, were retained but not sent to Barratt; those people had been vetted before. New entries that made garden variety threats were set aside for follow-up by the Secret Service. The ones that were novel or threatening or particularly rage-filled were investigated by the Secret Service and passed on to Bobby. He determined which ones should be brought to the president's attention.

To be sure, there were fewer but still many positive ones:

From a grandmother living in Philadelphia: *Thank you, thank you! For the first time in many years, I feel I can safely take my grandchildren to the park.*

From a father in Milwaukee: *I have lost both of my sons to drive-by crossfire. They were just walking to school. This won't bring them back, and I mourn them every day, but finally, FINALLY!, somebody is doing something.*

Bobby now sat back in his chair. He had always liked, and was known for, an uncluttered desktop. Today, however, his workspace was covered with early reports of The Plan's enforcement teams; summary briefs submitted by Homeland Security, the army commanders, and the press officers who were monitoring the reactions of the different state governments; and a pile of printed emails. He styled himself a modern man, but the emails that were filtered through to him were printed so that he could easily mark them up and make marginal notes.

Kimberly, his chief administrative assistant, walked in with another batch. She had been with Bobby from the beginning. In every office there is the go-to person, the one who knows the rules better than the rulemakers, who leads the team, who keeps the trains running. Kimberly was Bobby's go-to. Tall and lean and no-nonsense with the staff but given to happy talk with Bobby. He smiled at her.

"No more, please," he joked. "I'm going to have to get a new room just to store this stuff." His smile disappeared when he noted her serious look.

"Bobby," she said, "you need to see the one on top. It's personal, and it's chilling."

Bobby took the stack from her, separated the one on top, and read it aloud:

"Hey Bobby, how do you like your new BMW? It's a shame you're not going to get to drive it too much longer. See you soon."

"When...when did this come in?" Bobby asked.

"Just now," Kimberly replied.

Bobby stared at the printed copy of the text. His mind raced: Somebody was...stalking *him*? How did they know about his new car? How close had the guy gotten? Did he see his *family* in the car with him? Did he see his kids?

"Kim, have we gotten anything with this style before? Personalized this way?"

"I don't think so, but I'll run a search right now."

As she left his office, Bobby realized that the page was shaking in his hands; he was gripping it so tightly that his knuckles were turning white. He and the president had been the target of verbal attacks and threats in the past, and the attacks on Barratt had frequently been specific and personal. But this was the first time that one targeted Bobby personally. An electric buzz coursed through him. He forgot to breathe. *This must be how Elijah feels every day*, he thought. He forced himself to take several deep breaths, then got back to being the chief of staff. He called in his Secret Service detail, debated whether to tell the president. He decided that if he did not tell Barratt, Barratt would be upset, as *he* would be if the situation were reversed.

Later that night, Bobby attended his son's high school basketball game. He was so proud that Teddy was a senior and a starter on the team, with an outside chance of playing in college. Basketball was big at Teddy's school and the gym was packed and raucous. Bobby listened to a cacophony of cheerleaders and cheering parents, a few assailing the refs.

His eyes roamed through the crowd. Was his stalker here? His Secret Service detail had been increased and its presence purposely obvious: black suits and earbuds, serious demeanors and taut body language. He paused his search of the crowd on anyone who looked out of place, suspicious. All he saw were parents and uncles and aunts and grandparents enjoying the night, leading peaceful lives, siblings dealing with boredom and disappearing into their cell phones. Zoey was home with their daughter, who had successfully begged off attending one more of her brother's games. A police cruiser was parked outside his house. Bobby was keeping Zoey updated on Teddy's performance when his cell phone signaled an incoming text. *We're okay*, he thought.

Hey Bobby, enjoying the game? Your kid's not much of a player.

Bobby clutched the phone and instantly forwarded the text to his detail. He felt another buzz course through his body. How the hell did this guy get his cell phone number? His fatherly instinct treated the text as a call to action, a command to protect. He scanned the gym again. Was this guy really here? His eyes opened wide as he practically x-rayed the crowd. He rejected anyone who was focused on the game or shouting some kid's name. His intense gaze stopped on a security guard whose hair was sloppy under his uniform hat and his stance awkward, standing near the northeast exit, but moved on when the guard was slapped on the back by the school resource officer, and Bobby noted that the man didn't have a phone in his hands, as another text came in.

Pretty soon poor Teddy will have an excuse for poor play. Gonna be tough going through life without a father, and with a bullet in his leg.

Bobby stood abruptly and searched the gym again, his Secret Service detail doing the same. *Where are you, you bastard? Messin' with my son!* Looking, looking. He saw a man in a dark hoodie backed into the corner made by the bleachers and the short wall near an exit door. Bobby had practically the only angle that let anyone see the man. Their eyes locked and the man rushed toward the exit. Bobby shouted into his own mic to alert his detail.

"Black hoodie! Just went through the southwest exit!"

Agents inside the gym raced through the door. The agent designated to stay close to Teddy remained in the gym. Bobby froze as he fought panic: Should he grab Teddy off the floor? He didn't have to. The agent assigned to Teddy had gone onto the floor, grabbed him, and pulled him from the court. The agent stationed outside the southwest exit came on: "Saw him. Ran into the parking lot. In pursuit." Teddy's agent radioed to them all: "Go. I've got Teddy."

Bobby bolted from his seat and ran out of the stands. As Bobby exited the gym, he saw agents race toward opposite sides of the parking lot and another run up the middle. Bobby headed toward the cars. Two agents by the door stepped into his path.

"Sir, stay here with us."

"Bullshit! That bastard—"

"Sir, for your safety, stay here with *us*," one of the agents commanded, as they stepped between Bobby and the lot.

Damn it, he's right, thought Bobby, as tried to slow his breath and complied.

Bobby rocked back and forth on his feet, clenched and unclenched his fists, exhaled his frustration, his breath condensing in the cool night air. The school had had so many problems with vandalism in the lot that it had erected bright lighting standards that illuminated the tops of the cars but left dark areas between them. Thank God, Bobby thought, the completely fenced lot appeared clear of students and the only gate had apparently been locked after the lot was full. The stalker should be trapped in, but what if he had cut an opening in the back fence? Could he get out?

"We can't let him get out," Bobby said softly, then much louder: "We have to get him." He was terrified that his kids would become prisoners in their house until this guy was taken down.

"We'll get him, sir," one of the agents with him said calmly.

Over that agent's radio, Bobby could hear the reports from the chasing agents as they searched the parking lot.

"West first row clear."

"East first clear."

"Moving your way."

"Holding in the center."

Bobby didn't realize that he had started to stamp his left foot, not from the night's chill, but to burn off his churning anxiety. *How did this guy know that Teddy played and was playing tonight?* he asked himself. He had laid down an ironclad family rule prohibiting personal content and pre-event schedules from going on any social media. *Hell, it was probably no one's fault*, he thought. *This is the post-Internet age. Anyone can find anything about anybody.*

"East second clear."

"West second clear."

"C'mon, c'mon," Bobby whispered.

"Suspect moving west toward you! Suspect is armed! Repeat. Suspect is armed!"

Oh my God! Bobby thought. *He was armed! He could have shot Teddy!*

Then he heard a concussive report at the same instant that an agent barked through the radio: "Shots fired! Shots fired!" The agents near him moved Bobby back toward the school doors.

Bobby resisted. "I have to see this guy!"

"Suspect down. Suspect restrained," came the next radio communication.

The agent standing next to him stopped the push. He calmly reported to his superiors and called for an ambulance. Two city police cruisers, lights flashing, rolled through the now-opened gate and into the parking lot, followed by a Secret Service SUV, officers and agents pouring out before the vehicles came to a stop. Bobby heard doors slam, orders shouted, was buffeted by the power unleashed.

The agents who had gone in among the parked cars now emerged from the lot; two of them held the man between them, his hands cuffed behind him. He was bleeding from his left arm. His pants were torn, the hood of his sweatshirt had been ripped mostly off, his face was scraped where it must have come into contact with the pavement. One of the agents held a semi-automatic pistol by the barrel and away from his body. It was obviously the stalker's gun. They half-walked, half-dragged the man toward the police cruisers, keeping him one hundred feet away from Bobby, one on either side, but as they did so the man turned and spat in Bobby's direction.

"You prick!" he shouted. "You and that asshole Barratt!"

He spat toward Bobby again and tried to break toward him, but he was firmly held in check. "You can't take our guns! This is the Second Amendment you're fuckin' with."

The ambulance had arrived, and the agents were escorting the man toward the EMTs. As they did so, the man twisted and screamed out, "You've opened the gates of hell!"

As Bobby struggled to slow his heart rate and to process the hate that was spewing, a thought entered unbidden into his mind: Maybe that's exactly what we've done.

5 LAKE CITY TEENS SHOT MONDAY

Main Street Daily News
Gainesville, Florida

59.
GRAMMAR

THIS WAS NOT WHAT Senator Christine Grammar had expected.

When Barratt signed his draconian gun control executive orders on national TV, she thought that he was simultaneously signing his reelection death warrant. This was a country whose zeitgeist had for centuries been built around the image of the Revolutionary War Minutemen, the western marshal, all those cowboys riding to the rescue while shooting the bad guys on TV, and John Wayne winning the war with a gun and a prayer. There was every reason to believe that the response would be overwhelming outrage. Add to that the gun-rights crowd's tortured but popular reading of the Second Amendment. Even those who supported gun safety legislation should have been calling out Barratt's obviously unconstitutional action. That's not, Grammar grieved, what had happened.

Instead, Barratt's approval rating had actually increased. There was a sense of relief among many in the country that something was finally being done to stem the violent tide. For Grammar, who was ready to announce her own presidential campaign, the executive order had looked like a heaven-sent gift. Her staff had started calling her "Madame President." She had cautioned them not to get ahead of themselves but did so with tongue in cheek.

Now, before her, in her senatorial office, sat Douglas Boxer, the chairman of her political party. It had been weeks since Barratt had announced the new regulations, and she considered her party's response to be scattershot and ineffective.

"This is a shit show," said Grammar.

"Senator," responded Boxer, "we knew there could be a short-lived bump."

"Bump?" rejoined Grammar. "He moved five points. That's not a bump; that looks more like a goddamn rocket lifting off!"

Grammar stood and started to pace behind her desk. She shot the sleeves on her Armani jacket, making sure that she didn't cover the ruby rings on her left hand. She always paired them with the diamond and ruby necklace that graced her neck. At five foot ten and impeccably dressed, she was regal and intimidating when she towered over whoever sat before her. By design, the windows behind her desk accosted any sitting visitor with the morning sun. Boxer started to rise as well.

"Sit down," she commanded, not wanting to lose her advantage.

Boxer quickly did so.

"Senator," Boxer said, "we just have to be patient. Yes, he's up five points, but he's still slightly underwater. The backlash is going to grow. The opposition is just getting start—"

"We *are* the opposition, Douglas. We should have been blasting away immediately."

Boxer leaned forward. "This is going to blow up on him, no pun intended. We're going to sell the idea—"

"Your *job* is to sell *me*."

"We need to play the long game here," Boxer said. "This is a complicated prob—"

"There is no 'long game' in a presidential campaign! My God, you're the chairman of our party—even you should know that."

"Now wait a minute, Christine. Yes, I *was* elected the chairman of this party. And if you would stop interrupting me long enough—"

"You were elected, Douglas, only because *I* endorsed you. You've never been elected to anything else. You don't—"

Boxer jumped out of his chair. "Damn it, Christine! We're on the same side here."

"There's only one side, Douglas, *my* side. I'm the one who's running. I've gone after him on all the cable shows, but at some point I'm going to look like some whiney old bitch."

Grammar's legislative aide opened the office door and walked in with a small packet of papers.

"Senator," he said, "you wanted this report as soon as it came—"

"Stop!" she directed. "Turn around." As the aide did so, she grabbed the documents then put her hand on his back and pushed him toward the door. "Get out!"

"Well," said Boxer, as the aide hurried away, "we certainly can't sell your soft and fuzzy side."

"I don't have a soft and fuzzy side," said Grammar. Returning to the desk, she sat down, tossing the papers in front of her. The frown on her face slid off as she folded her arms and sat back in the chair. "Never have," she said. "Never have," she repeated, more wistfully.

"I still don't get this guy Barratt," she said more loudly. "I don't think he's for real. How do you come up that fast? I mean, what, some ten years ago he was on some Podunk town council. Now he's the president?" She shook her head but stopped as she eyed the photos over the office fireplace. She saw herself with three different presidents, with the pope when he came to DC, with the queen when Grammar visited England. "I'm the one who pushed through the federal open carry law, who quashed the ethics complaint against Senator Enos. I've had the backs of the last two presidents. *I* should be the next one sitting in the Oval Office."

"Christine," said Boxer. "I'll craft another response to the executive order. The party and I—"

Grammar shot forward and banged two closed fists on her desk. "I am the party," she said. "I *am* the party. Without me there is no party."

"I know what I'm doing!" said Boxer.

"Look, *Dougie*," Grammar responded. "I know *exactly* what you're doing. You're trying to be the star. It's not working for you." Standing again, she looked down on Boxer. "But I'm your best chance to look like one." She refolded her arms and drew herself up. "Here's what you're going to do," she said, pointing a finger at him. "You're going to go after Barratt with guns blazing, and that pun *is* intended. You're going to call him out as a dictator; you're going to get those dolts in Congress who owe their seats to me to go after him too. I'm going to pick my spots and jump elegantly in when the time is right."

She sat quickly down again, as if she couldn't decide which posture to take, which way to vent her anger.

"And," she continued, "you're going to make damn sure I don't have any competition in this primary. When I'm the president, you'll get some bit of the credit, and you can twinkle away." She buzzed for her aide, and the previously chastened man crept in.

"*Chairman* Boxer is leaving. Please show him out."

Boxer started to speak, then abruptly closed his mouth. With a small shake of his head, he followed the aide through the door.

MAN WANTED IN SHOOTING THAT LEFT 2 DEAD, 2 WOUNDED

9NEWS+
Denver

60.
SANCHEZ

GENERAL SANCHEZ HAD SEEN war up close. He had served in the Iraq wars and had led soldiers in Iran and Afghanistan. He had participated in traditional military operations and been close to the devastating bloodshed and destruction of morale wrought by terrorist actions.

But I never thought I would be leading troops in my own country against other Americans, he thought as he sat in his command Humvee, deep in the Appalachian forest. His driver, Sergeant Richie Sorrento, sat next to him.

President Barratt had convinced Sanchez and the other generals that the cadres and those who gave them aid and comfort were violently undermining democracy, that they threatened the very existence of the United States. He had to admit that when one mass shooting followed another and another, he had been appalled. When politicians of every persuasion offered thoughts and prayers but refused to deal with the underlying issues, he was disgusted. When those same politicians encouraged violence with their inflammatory, partisan rhetoric, he feared for his country.

Sanchez was respected by his peers and admired by his subordinates. At six feet two inches tall and trim, with only the hint of a paunch, he was the quintessential commanding officer. But he was just under three years from mandatory retirement, and the years had taken their toll. His hair was now gray, crow's feet nested next to his eyes, and his square jaw was becoming slightly elliptical. He was, however, as energetic and imposing as ever.

He had earned Purple Hearts in both Iraq and Afghanistan and a chest full of combat and service medals and ribbons. He had trained young men and women, some just teenagers, fresh-faced and eager to protect the US and their comrades in arms. He grieved every casualty and celebrated every time he was invited to one of his soldiers' weddings. He was proud of his service and humbled by his responsibility as a leader in the world's most powerful military.

Was his country now to be surrendered to civilian groups who declared themselves "protectors" but clearly pursued their own agendas? Their stated goals were not always the same. Some swore to "defend their land," which was actually federal land where they illegally grazed their livestock. Others convinced themselves that their state really *was* being invaded by immigrants. There were those who craved chaos as an end in itself, designed to destabilize the government, and those who believed that starting a race war would "cleanse" their homeland. But their actions all had two core motivations: fear and hate.

Fear and hate.

Sanchez had studied the history of warfare at the US Army War College, where he started his own search for the historical reasons for conflict. *Why did millennia of war seem inevitable?* Sanchez asked himself.

He kept coming back to fear and hate. Hannibal, Alexander the Great, Napoleon were all famous for conquest, but each of them was a troubled man with a fragile ego. Crusaders hated the Moors and considered them defiling nonbelievers. The Moors considered the European invaders to be barbaric infidels. Prehistoric tribes fought each other for food and shelter and mates. Sanchez came to understand that if one could reduce his antagonist to an unworthy subhuman entitled only to hate, then he could justify any atrocity.

The AWC's goal was to produce graduates who "are intellectually prepared to preserve peace, deter aggression, [and] compete below the threshold of armed conflict..." For Sanchez, this was a mantra that guided him throughout his military career, but the homegrown cadres, whom he considered terrorists who attacked the country's institutions and beliefs, denied him the opportunity to fully employ that approach. The conundrum robbed him of sleep and abused his desire for peaceful resolution.

Even when he had the chance to visit his lake house, there were too many nights when he had lain awake, finally giving up and slipping out to the dock, careful not to disturb his wife. The air would always be quiet at first, until the night critters accepted his invasion, and the loons and chittering insects and night herons resumed their haunting songs. He would find solace in their natural music, but on many nights even their symphony could not drown out his dismay. He had found the professed reasons for the sickness of fear and hate, but not the cure.

Fear and hate.

There were times, Sanchez despaired, when he felt that centuries of blood had been spilled with no progress at all.

"So," Sanchez said to no one in particular, "here we are."

"What was that, sir?" asked Sergeant Sorrento.

"Centuries later," said Sanchez, "it's still the same."

"What is, General?"

"Nothing. Nothing, Sergeant. Let's keep moving."

MAN GETS LIFE SENTENCE FOR KILLING 5 IN FAR SOUTH SIDE HOME INVASION

Fox 32

Chicago

61.
GENERAL SANCHEZ

THE FLYOVERS WITH THE enhanced magnetometers had identified the cache of weapons that the Powers Patriots had in their camp deep in these woods. Intelligence indicated that the cadre had between eighty and ninety men present in their hideout. Once William Percy and his group had become the dominant force resisting Barratt's edict, most of the other cadres had ingratiated themselves and allied with Percy, benefitting from his money and ability to secure arms. Sanchez therefore expected the so-called "Patriots" to be well supplied, and he had prepared accordingly. The compound was accessible only by one of the now abandoned logging roads. He had to give them credit for doing a reasonable job of concealment, but the technology that Barratt had commissioned was stunningly effective.

Sanchez and his men moved quietly. The denizens of the forest were unimpressed: hawks screed overhead and birdsongs filled the air; a doe and her two fawns moved farther into the woods, but several squirrels sat upright on their haunches and continued nibbling on a nutty treasure. Sanchez surmised that they had grown accustomed to the cadre moving in and out. He gave them a smiling apology for the noisy disturbance he was about to make.

Sanchez had arrived with overwhelming force. At this point, most of his troops were far enough away that he believed that the Powers

Patriots were unaware of their presence. He had deployed skirmishers to find and disable their lookouts without injuring anyone, if it all possible. The absolute last thing that Sanchez wanted was a violent confrontation. He knew that his troops would quickly seize the compound, but he wanted no bloodshed, no martyrs, and for God's sake, no dead Americans.

Now that he had neared his objective, his ruminations behind him, the calm that he had earned from decades of training narrowed his focus. He viewed the video feed from the cameras on the forward Humvees. Figures in the compound moved about doing ordinary tasks—vehicle maintenance, supply distribution—oblivious to what was to come.

It was time. His troops flanked the encampment, which backed up to a sheer cliff face, so controlling three sides was controlling the field. The only vehicles he had employed were the army's new Whisper Humvees. He advanced slightly with his. When he was within range of the compound with his loudspeakers, he stood in the Humvee, raised his mic, and spoke.

"Attention, the Powers Patriots camp."

Instantly, the placid forest creatures burst into activity, birds flapping from the trees, rodents racing for cover at this intrusion.

"This is General Sanchez of the United States Army. Pursuant to the Order of the President of the United States, and consistent with the declaration of a national emergency, you are hereby directed to place any firearms you have on the ground and step away. You in the buildings are directed to step out into the middle of the compound. You should know that you are surrounded by an overwhelming force. Any resistance will be met and terminated with extreme prejudice."

The response was just the opposite of what he had directed, and its chaos rivaled that of the fleeing animals. The alarm was heightened by Sanchez's words bouncing off the cliff face and reverberating throughout the compound, enveloping the people within the camp. Some men dove behind trucks and stacks of supplies, while others scattered toward various buildings and held their weapons at the ready. Because of the way Sanchez's soldiers had been deployed, all the men, except those inside the buildings, were exposed to one fire team or another.

General Sanchez lowered his microphone and turned to his comms officer and issued a one-word order: "Light." Instantly, the dim twilight of the compound was brightened by the array of floodlights mounted on the forward Humvees. Simultaneously, a dozen flares were fired and hung above the encampment.

Sanchez raised his microphone again: "Do not resist. Your weapons will be seized. You will not be harmed if you cooperate. Mr. Harden, confirm that you will comply."

The video showed all heads in the compound turn toward a man hunkered behind one of the trucks. He was dressed in the same camo as the other men, while his shoulders bore no insignia of office; the uniforms did not have nameplates, but this man was no stranger to Sanchez.

Quaker Harden had been on the FBI radar for years. He first came to their attention when he was among the anti-government marchers in Brazertown, chanting and spewing venom. He became a successful recruiter for the Powers Patriots and earned their leaders' approval and trust. His obsession with autocratic history and his aptitude for violence only solidified his position in the ranks. Sanchez expected that he would resist but nevertheless made the effort to convince him otherwise. Harden reached into the truck he crouched behind and pulled out his own megaphone. Then he stood.

"This is Colonel Quaker Harden of the Powers Patriots. I am the ranking officer in this compound. We have every right to be here, and I demand that you cease trespassing and withdraw immediately."

"*Mr.* Harden, what you will experience next is a demonstration only. You're not being targeted. However, you need to know what you are up against."

Sanchez spoke again to his comms man; comms passed the order along.

Four of the Whisper Humvees were equipped with mounted M134 Miniguns, which used a 338NM cartridge. Its six barrels fired one hundred rounds in one second. It had a terrifying, devastating effect. The gunners opened up, aiming high into the trees surrounding the compound and at the top of its radio communications tower. The impact was thunderous. Treetops were sliced off and fell into the compound. The top of the radio tower was sheared and collapsed with a shower of debris. Several of the men who were hiding behind vehicles immediately dropped their weapons and ran with panicked speed into the woods, where they were immediately captured by the soldiers Sanchez had placed there.

The thunder ceased. The silence was stifling, palpable, pregnant with potential violence.

Sanchez hoped for Harden to call out and submit. Instead, the next sound he heard was a muted thunk.

"Frag!" the forward troopers yelled.

Harden had fired a fragmentation grenade, likely from an old M79. Fortunately, he had not acquired a target and just fired blindly across the hood of the truck. It was still a deadly offer but, launched through the treetops and over the deployed troops, landing some two hundred meters away, it did no damage.

"Damn it! I knew it!" Sanchez shouted. "I didn't want this. That fool!" He picked up the microphone. "Harden! Harden! This will not end well. For the sake of your men, stand down now."

"My men stand with me!" Harden shouted back, even as more of them ran into the woods.

"Harden! This is your last chance. *Stand down now.*"

Sanchez eyed the livestream. Harden had reached into the back of the truck again and was fumbling with another fragmentation round. Sanchez gritted his teeth and shook his head. He wouldn't take the chance that the next round would do damage.

"Third squad. Target Harden and the truck. Suppression fire."

One of the miniguns roared. Sanchez watched the video screen. The truck was raked with blistering rounds that struck Harden, lifting him off the ground. The truck convulsed, then exploded as the gas tank ignited. Before Harden landed back on the ground, he and the truck were engulfed in riotous flames. The shrapnel of the obliterated truck blasted through the camp, taking out two more men. When the debris settled, the doors of the buildings where some of the men had hidden slowly opened, weapons were flung out, and improvised white flags appeared in the doorways. General Sanchez gave orders to secure the compound and to seize those men still standing. He ordered the medics to render aid to anyone injured.

Then Sanchez sat down heavily in his Humvee, shaking his head. He felt no sense of victory. Only one of loss.

5 HOSPITALIZED AFTER SHOOTING IN NW MIAMI-DADE

7 News
Miami

62.
JIMMY

JIMMY PULLED HIS JEEP to the curb a few hundred feet past the Dunkel residence. The retribution he had taken against the other families left him feeling deflated, impotent, sitting on a curb with his feet in the gutter. His intention had been to build up to similar action against Dunkel's parents. He knew now that that would never be enough. Not enough to satisfy his need, not enough to avenge Alice, not enough to stem his festering anger.

The rage he had unleashed outside the courtroom, that's what could soothe the constant pain. He left there that day feeling like a *man*, fighting back against the mad world that had sent Dunkel to Dawn River.

The news videos of the Dunkel house had dominated the airways for weeks after Dawn River; its image was burned into his mind. When the news had moved on to the next tragedy, he stayed behind. He had hoped that he could cast that image out of his mind, but he couldn't. That's why he was parked near 166 Foretell Road, the place that had housed the Dawn River shooter, Alfred Dunkel himself.

Hank snuggled on his blanket in the back seat, half asleep. Jimmy was reluctant to leave him at home. As much as he denied it, Hank was simply getting older, moving slower, keeping ever closer to

Jimmy, anxious when they weren't together. Jimmy turned and spoke softly to Hank: "All right, buddy, I'll be a few minutes. I put the windows down a little so the fresh air will come in, and I've parked under these trees so you can listen to the birds. I know you like that. Stay right here and be a good dog until I get back." Hank lifted his head and smiled the way that dogs do, then turned on his side and invited Jimmy to scratch his belly and under his neck. "You don't play fair," Jimmy laughed. Exiting the car, he shut the driver's door and opened the back door, reached in, and gave his best friend some lovin's. "All right, that's it. I have to go." He left the car and headed for the Dunkel house.

Jimmy walked up the sidewalk to the front door and knocked. The house appeared to be a typical center-hall colonial with a small porch. The lawn surrounding the house was in need of mowing; the siding was intact but begged for a power washing. There were no flowers on the porch, no decorations on or about the door. When no one answered, he knocked again. This time the door opened.

Before him stood a woman who looked to be in her early sixties. She wore pants and a silk blouse; the clothes hung on her, as if draping a skeleton. The blonde and gray of her hair fought for dominance; it clearly hadn't been colored or styled in some time. Her face was gaunt, her eyes sunken. Jimmy stood there in front of her. She had not said a word, so Jimmy spoke first: "Mrs. Dunkel, my name is Matthew Evers. I am here to talk about your son, Alfred."

The woman sighed and started to close the door.

"Wait," Jimmy said softly, "I'm not a reporter. I'm not law enforcement. I'm here because I think your son has been treated unfairly, and I think I can change the public's perception."

Mrs. Dunkel stopped before she closed the door completely. "Haven't you people persecuted us enough? Haven't you sucked all the information and energy out of us? I grieve for everyone that my son hurt, but how many more times can I say that?"

Now Jimmy sighed audibly, trying his best to stay in character, stopping himself from damning her for grieving those who were "hurt." He wanted to scream, "Your son killed Alice. He killed my *life*!" Instead, he calmly replied, "I can't imagine what you've gone through. I don't think anyone could, but that hasn't stopped them from attacking him and your memory of him. If I can just have a minute of your time, perhaps I can help."

The woman stared at him a moment longer, then opened the door just enough for him to step inside.

"What is it you think you can do?"

"I'm a researcher. What I do is challenge all the misinformation out there by writing and speaking and blogging about it. What happened was years ago, but his name is still mentioned when people talk about—excuse me for this—the monsters among us. Most people don't know how hard life can be—for your son, and for you. I think I can show them that he was troubled, yes, but misunderstood, that there are two sides to this story."

Mrs. Dunkel hesitated, then said, "My Alfie was a good boy, you know. He was a good son to me." She was silent for a moment, appearing to be pondering, then she opened the door to let Jimmy in. "What do you need from me?"

"I know that it's been some time," Jimmy replied, "but do you still have anything of his? A favorite CD? A sports award? Photos of him and his friends?"

"I... I...haven't changed anything in his room. People think I'm crazy for that, but it helps me hold on...to him. I haven't been able to bring myself to do it. If I keep his room ready I can pretend that someday he'll be back."

No wonder people think she's crazy, Jimmy thought.

"May I, with respect, see his room?"

"Yes… Okay…if you think it will help. Alfie really wasn't a bad boy. He was troubled, yes, like you said, like so many other young kids."

Yeah, but he wasn't a kid and most guys don't pick up a gun and start shooting. "It's upstairs."

"Is your husband home as well, Mrs. Dunkel?" Jimmy knew from his surveillance that he wasn't around, but wanted to see if she would be straight with him.

"No," she said, "after...everything...he...we're not together just now."

Jimmy followed her up a steep set of stairs. She moved slowly, achingly, as if she carried a great burden with her. She showed him to a room that was about ten by fifteen feet. In it were a single bed, a desk and chair, and stand-alone shelves with a CD player and speakers. The room was clean but needed painting. He did not see many books, and no posters hung on the walls. Instead, the walls were covered with charcoal drawings, dark and ominous and smudged: a very amateurish rendering of *The Scream*, an ocean shore with beached whales. On the desk were several framed photos of the same teenage girl, who did not appear to know that she was being photographed. Mrs. Dunkel noticed where his gaze was directed.

"That's Kathy. My Alfred kept asking her out, but she always turned him down. It was a shame. They would have made such a nice couple."

Jimmy's eyes widened slightly. How could a parent not read these warning signs?

"Mrs. Dunkel, may I have a moment to, you know, feel...experience the room and your son?" Jimmy asked.

"I… I guess that would be okay. I'll be just downstairs."

As soon as she left, Jimmy got to work. He looked for a spot that was obscured by the furniture, which was unlikely to be moved.

Reaching into his jacket pocket, he pulled out the cap and the timer and the small explosive, all of which he had pilfered from his last job after his gutter episode and just before he was let go. There was just enough room between the wall and the bookshelves to place them out of sight. He set the timer for eight hours. That would make it seven o'clock that night. He stepped gingerly downstairs and saw Mrs. Dunkel sitting in a worn plush club chair. She was kneading her hands, alternately rubbing the left with the right, then the right with the left. She looked up at him as he stepped into the room.

"Thank you, Mrs. Dunkel. That was exactly what I was looking for. You'll hear from me shortly."

"Don't you want to talk with me now, about my boy?" she asked, her voice barely above a whisper.

"That won't be necessary. I know a lot about his story and yours. Believe me, I will see that you get what you deserve."

5 INJURED IN SHOOTING NEAR PIONEER SQUARE PARK

Fox13 Seattle

63.
JIMMY

AT 6:30 THAT NIGHT, Jimmy was back, parked on the opposite side of the street and down several houses from the Dunkel residence. This was dinnertime for Mrs. Dunkel. In all the time that he had watched, he never saw her leave the house to go out to eat or run errands or take a walk in the evening.

The anonymous letters to the bank and to the hospital were retribution, but for somebody else. *This is personal, this is for me*, Jimmy thought. No matter what he had done since Dawn River, he had never been able to move on. He took that job after he lost Alice, but only for six months. He started making mistakes, getting orders wrong, lashing out at customers who called his work sloppy, even though they were right. His boss gave him a second chance, then a third, then he could give no more. Then one new job after another fell victim to his relentless ruminating. He spent his time reading one study after another that traced shooters' murderous journeys back to the mess the adults in their lives had made. He believed they were just as guilty as the shooters, just as in need of punishment.

Now he hoped for release. At least, he would finally be taking action. Not like when he stood in the concourse at Dawn River, watching those kids in front of him struggle to choose a snack, failing to tell them to just make up their damn minds. Jimmy just being tolerant and polite. All the while, Alfred Dunkel—angry, rejected, resentful, murderous Alfred Dunkel—was settling onto his perch in the rafters. Jimmy, oblivious, deliberate, taking too much time, tossing the drinks he had needlessly waited on when he heard the shots ring out. Ineffective, unprotecting, failing Jimmy.

6:35 p.m. He had planned to video what was about to happen, but that would leave a trail. Then suddenly Jen's image appeared in front of him, so real that he gasped. She had lost too, but—unable to comfort himself—he was even more unable to comfort her. Why was he seeing her now? Wouldn't she understand? Would she see that he had no choice? Wouldn't she know that he could not climb out of the deep, dank, fetid hole that Alfred Dunkel had buried him in unless he had revenge? Would she blame him for now abandoning her, leaving her to grieve all over again? Was that why her face was confronting him?

6:40 p.m. The evening air was cool, and he had left the windows partially down because Hank, lying on the back seat, loved the scents that it carried. Despite the chill, he felt flush, felt the perspiration on his forehead, wiped it with his sleeve. He heard Hank whimper and turned to check on him. There was no smile on Hank's face, no invitation to scratch his neck. Hank looked at him with sad and accusing eyes. Would Hank be grieving too? Wouldn't Jen take care of him, if Jimmy became a suspect and had to run, or would she want nothing to do with the chaos that Jimmy was about to create?

6:45 p.m. Now Hank growled, and that startled Jimmy. Hank had never growled at him before, had never accused or judged him. If Jen didn't take him, would he be abandoning Hank, failing Hank as he had failed Alice? Now Hank started to bark, standing on all fours. "Shush," Jimmy whispered. "Hank, quiet, or..." Would the cops somehow make a connection to him? If he did have to run, what happens to Hank? Could he take care of Hank, or would he watch him die too?

6:50 p.m. Hank's barking was incessant and getting louder. He growled and scratched the back seat, then stood on his hind legs and pawed the air. "My God," Jimmy said out loud. "What am I doing? What the hell am I doing? What have I been doing? Now *I'm* the killer?" Jimmy threw the driver's door open and raced down the street to the Dunkel house. He jumped to the porch and banged on the door with his fist and kept banging until Mrs. Dunkel opened it.

"Mr. Evers, what—"

Jimmy flew past her and up the stairs, knowing that she could only follow slowly behind. He burst into Alfred's room, threw himself on the floor, and grabbed the IED from behind the bookshelf.

6:57 p.m. He jabbed the timer and turned it off, then hurriedly shoved everything into his pockets. He left the room and descended the stairs slowly, catching his breath.

"Mr. Evers, I don't know what you think you're doing," Mrs. Dunkel said, standing halfway up the stairs.

Jimmy slipped past her. "Sorry, sorry," Jimmy said as he moved by her and continued to the door. "I left something here, and I had to take it back."

He walked quickly down the street, toward where he had parked, Mrs. Dunkel watching him as he did. Finally out of sight of her, he reached the car and slipped inside. He sunk into the driver's seat, still breathing rapidly, still sweating. He gathered himself enough to turn slowly and look at Hank. Hank was curled on his blanket, a canine smile and a look of satisfaction on his face.

1 KILLED, 3 OTHERS INJURED IN RIVERSIDE SHOOTING EARLY SUNDAY

Seven ABC, WKBW
BUFFALO

64.
ASQUANDON

ASQUANDON SAT AT THE confluence of two small rivers in the southeastern United States. As far as anyone could determine, "Asquandon" was a combination of Native American words meaning "river below the hills." In the early 1800s, northern Europeans moved into the area and began farming the rich black soil of the valleys. Later, the region was carved out of the Western Territories and became part of the United States. Its population of about 31,000 resided in the river valley, surrounded by low hills teeming with wildlife, backed by craggy mountains.

Its crime problems consisted mostly of burglaries and drug offenses, with perhaps one questionable death every decade. It seemed, therefore, incongruous that Asquandon had a SWAT team. More accurately, it was part of a regional SWAT team, populated by officers from Asquandon and three nearby towns in the region. But it got to call the team its own because it housed SWAT's prized possession: an EagleCat Mack A.

The EagleCat was a multi-terrain vehicle. Armor plated, firing ports, big run-flat tires, a roof hatch with a firing stand. It was every law enforcer's dream. It had been used by Asquandon in training, displays, and parades. There was literally no need for the police to have it. It had never been dispatched with serious intent, but federal grant money was available, and the mayor was motivated. It became the department's pride and joy.

William James Percy IV wanted it.

Percy had never had a problem sourcing weaponry in the past, but when Barratt started seizing all the guns, many of his sources dried up. Gun manufacturers were in turmoil: two had already closed, and others had suspended operations. Still, he had an enviable cache of small arms, grenades, and incendiaries. He knew, though, that in the coming civil war, which he intended to foment, he would be out-gunned and outnumbered. He could never match the military's might, so his plan was to pick remote targets then hit and run, use the terrain and some friendly locals to help him disappear into the forests and swamps like his hero the Swamp Fox, even expand the area of conflict. He could *really* hit and run with the EagleCat. In the constant competition among the cadres, the EagleCat would make the True Americans dominant, and he would be the likely leader of any rebellion.

After Barratt's executive order was implemented, big city departments, having the resources and the know-how, hardened their buildings, specifically including their armories. They knew that the armories would be targeted as guns started to disappear from the landscape. However, the smaller towns and cities had neither the resources nor the know-how. The federal government provided some funding and support, but it was impossible to harden every department in every municipality in every state in the country, or for the army to be everywhere at once. Some departments were thus left to fend for themselves.

Asquandon did what it could. Percy's spies had informed him that the armory inside the department headquarters building was guarded 24/7. The town took the threat of an attack to seize weapons seriously; townspeople knew to be on the lookout. But Percy's forces easily outnumbered the town's officers, and his complement of members with military training gave him a big advantage.

So it was, on an unseasonably warm early spring morning, that the True Americans, having moved into the area overnight, formed up in three different locations around Asquandon. During their recon, they had scouted the department facilities and the routes in and out, assessed the distance and likely response time of mutual aid officers from other departments in the region and the security where the EagleCat was housed. They also relied partially on human nature, anticipating that focus would wane as time passed and no threat materialized. They discovered that there were mobile phone dead spots on the roadways outside the town proper, making the likelihood of an early warning of unusual traffic by remote residents practically nil. Since Percy's forces used satellite phones, their communications were not affected.

Percy summoned one of his officers, Major Lamply.

"Status, Major?" he asked.

"All in place and ready to proceed," Lamply responded confidently. "Units are in position on the north and south roadways. We have deployed here in the trees above the town. It's a *go*, sir."

Percy was on the crest of one of the hills with a good view of the police compound. He took a moment to marvel at how far he had come. His brazen attack on Second Home had elevated his profile, and money from supporters poured in. After Second Home, he continued to pick soft targets to keep up the momentum.

"Keep the hammer down," he commanded his people.

This is different, Percy thought. *There's an armed, trained, equipped force down there.* But this was also, he figured, the right next step. His goal wasn't just family revenge. He didn't only want to harass the government that had denigrated and damned his people; he wanted to burn it all down.

Turning to Lamply he said, "Give the order to commence Operation EagleCat." Lamply relayed the order through his sat phone.

Immediately, the forces who had hidden on either side of the town moved out. Each of five identical white Toyota pickups with rooftop .50-caliber machine guns raced toward downtown and the police buildings. They wanted it to look like Middle Eastern terrorists had driven out of the cable news screens and into Asquandon. The squads were dressed in military fatigues, but had black scarfs covering their faces. *Allah Akbar* was on magnetic signs attached to the truck doors.

Shortly before the trucks moved in, phone calls had been made to each of the police departments in the regional towns. One call reported a three-car accident; another reported a man walking down the middle of the street with a shotgun—not unusual in this part of the state—but he was said to be drunk and firing at cars on either side of the road. The third call consisted of someone desperately screaming that his child had just been kidnapped. None of the calls were legitimate; all were made by the True Americans. Each had the intended effect: the neighboring departments that could have provided mutual aid to Asquandon dispatched their units in the opposite direction of Percy's target.

Within minutes, Percy could hear the roar of his truck engines. He raised his tactical binoculars and peered down at the police buildings. He still saw no activity, no indication that they knew what was about to happen.

The convoy raced into the compound, which consisted of a headquarters building, a motor pool barn, and a large canopied area covering squad cars and emergency vehicles. The trucks charged into the paved area separating the headquarters from the motor pool, tires squealing and True American members shouting. The headquarters' side door flew open, and two officers ran out. They were quickly chased back inside by a fusillade from one of the truck-mounted .50-caliber guns stitching a line above the door.

Two of the trucks raced to the motor pool. Others arrayed themselves in a sort of picket line around the headquarters. Percy fingered a mic that was remotely connected to a speaker on one of the trucks.

"Attention, Asquandon Police Department. We are Allah's Messengers. You are surrounded and outnumbered. Lay down your weapons and exit the building single file with your hands above your heads."

As he expected, his order was met with silence, then with rifle shots from behind the parapet that ran along the perimeter of the headquarters roof. The cadre responded with withering fire from the mounted .50s, raking a line across the parapet, sending an explosion of pulverized gray concrete crashing into the compound, the police retreating back into the building.

Just as well, thought Percy. A police officer bloodbath would not help their cause.

"We're not here to kill cops," he had cautioned his members. "We're here to get the 'Cat and send a message to Barratt."

"We're monitoring the radio traffic," Lamply reported. They've called the other SWAT team towns. They've called the governor's office for the National Guard. They're claiming that they're under attack by terrorists."

"Perfect. Nobody from the other towns will be here sooner than thirty minutes. The guard will take even longer. Order the trucks to proceed with Phase Two."

Lamply relayed the order. The trucks in the compound opened fire on the squad cars, decimating anything that could follow them. Two of the vehicles burst into flames, tires exploded, lightbars lit, sirens blared then moaned to quiet. Everything died. The two trucks that had raced to the motor pool immediately strafed the building's doors, obliterating them in a shower of freshly painted wood and suppressing anybody who was unlucky enough to be inside.

Several raiders exited the trucks and ran into the building. Two mechanics in overalls lay on their backs in bloody pools, dark red mixing with the oil and debris on the motor pool floor.

Sergeant Duo approached the EagleCat's driver-side door, opened it, and leapt inside.

"Amazing," he mumbled. "The keys are in it." Duo fingered his mic and reported to Lamply. "I'm in the EagleCat," he said, "preparing to exit the motor pool. Two civilian casualties."

"No cops?" asked Lamply.

"No."

"Good enough. Proceed," Lamply said.

Duo fired up the EagleCat. The engine thundered, reverberating through the motor pool, blocking out the sounds of the other trucks and the sporadic firing, a mechanized volcanic eruption. Duo mashed the accelerator, and the EagleCat smashed across the ruined doors and out into the compound. Following the pre-ordered plans for the departure, the trucks circled the compound and raced out to the roadway. They separated and headed off into the different directions from which they had approached. The EagleCat sped to the south, drove quickly through the open doors of a waiting trailer pulled by a Volvo tractor, and disappeared.

"Withdraw," Percy ordered. Lampley lifted his right hand into the air and circled his index finger. The cadre members who had deployed on the hillside collected their equipment and made their way down to ATVs, Percy and Lamply joining them, then they raced down the hill. The entire operation had taken fewer than fifteen minutes.

As they sped toward the rendezvous point, Percy beamed. He would shortly announce that he was responsible for the attack.

"Hey, Barratt!" he said. He laughed as he gave the sky a middle finger salute.

5 TEENS SHOT AT MANSFIELD HOTEL OVERNIGHT

WTDN 2 News
Dayton, Ohio

65.
BARRATT

PRESIDENT BARRATT AND BOBBY were alone in the Oval Office. They went back a long time, had become each other's confidants, but more than that, they had become brothers. As brothers sometimes do, they were prone to disagreements. Before Dawn River, they argued about Barratt's Phillies and Bobby's Orioles and who had the better team, about which of their college co-eds was better looking, and ironically about why anyone would get involved in politics and who in their right mind would *want* to be president. Now, their "discussions" were about foreign policy, tax reform, the midterms, and, most of all, guns. They had just left their daily strategy meeting with the army and were scheduled to meet with the FBI in an hour. Barratt was tired of the jurisdictional bickering between the military commanders, the FBI, and all the other agencies. And was astonished, was unbelieving that none of them had been able to run that bastard Percy to ground.

Seated at the Resolute Desk, Barratt leaned forward and rested his head in his hands. It had been another arduous day. Bobby sat across from him in one of the high-back chairs, crossing and uncrossing his legs, tightening his tie. They had each become adept at knowing what the other one was thinking; could sense it, feel it.

Here it comes, thought Barratt.

"Mr. President," Bobby said, "you know I've supported you in everything that you've done. I've been there for you—I'm proud of that—and I always will be."

Barratt watched Bobby's shoulders hunch, his lips purse, as he stood and walked behind his chair, rested his hands on the chair back, and lowered his head. He took an audible breath, raised his eyes, and continued.

"Mr. President," Bobby continued, "I know how important this is. I know why you're doing this, and I'm on board. But...could you... we...lose control of this? Could it take on a life of its own?"

Barratt looked at his friend. It was a fear that he shared. But...

"Bobby, we've talked this to death. We've tried to find a middle ground, and every damn time Grammar and her people in the Senate and those sycophants in the House, the gun lobby, the GRU, they all aligned against us."

"I hear you. But…you...the truth is...you're going to start a war."

"We're already at war. People are dying every day. People are getting shot every day. Cadres are planning attacks, procuring arms, recruiting fighters. If that's not a war, what is it?"

"But this is turning into another *Civil War*. Soldiers confronting US citizens, the military fighting the people, *our* people, the American people, cadres launching attacks."

"Tell me another way, Bobby." Barratt stood now as well, shoving his chair behind him with the back of his legs, sending it banging into the credenza. "This violence is entrenched. People have become inured to it, taking it for granted that nobody can do anything about it."

Barratt started pacing behind the desk. There was intensity but no anger in their "discussion." Barratt relied on it, wanted it, needed this. It made him feel that he was not alone in this fight. In public, he showed a poker face and calm demeanor, but those still waters ran deep. And if he didn't talk it out with *somebody*, he thought, he could go mad. Talking about it with someone who didn't have a competing agenda was a relief. Bobby was a safe port in an increasingly tempestuous storm.

"But *we, we* can do something about it," said Barratt. He stopped pacing and stood behind the desk. "We are in a unique position that few people have in their lifetimes. We actually have the power to change lives for the better, and we can't waste this chance."

Barratt pulled his chair toward him and sat back down.

"Why do you think I'm here?" he asked, his voice soft.

"Mr. President, I know the agenda and I know you worked your tail off to get here. You—"

"No, that's not what I'm asking," Barratt interrupted. "Why do you think *I'm* here? There's no earthly reason why I should have been able to waltz through all this chaos and wind up in the White House. I wasn't known, I wasn't rich, I had no political favors to collect. I get shot in the back and now *I'm* the fucking *president*?"

Barratt really was hoping that someone could give him an answer. He'd been asking the question of himself ever since he won a city council seat: Why me?

Barratt paused, looked down at the desk. "Resolute." It had become his mantra. He had been chosen by...life? God? Fate? There were times when he couldn't even explain it to himself, but this had to be his purpose, right? Perhaps, he thought, his mantra should be "Resigned." Resigned to what he was...destined?...to do. Dawn River started something. Barratt pictured it: A pebble slips from a mountaintop, bumps into a larger stone, which collides with a boulder, and then *landslide*! And you're caught in it, part of the scree, part of the avalanche, hurtling, powerless to stop it, but not wanting to stop it, wanting to ride its force, blasting away all obstacles, to get to the bottom, stand and look back and see a fresh new mountain, with the promise of new growth, and you say out loud: "It was worth the ride."

"This is a war, you're right. This is a war against the Old West, against rich railroad people shooting buffalo out of the railroad coach windows until the buffalo almost disappear. This is a war against the racist, greedy mentality that committed genocide against Native Americans, a war against the make-believe Christians who preach that their churchmen should man up and grab a gun. For God's sake! Against homegrown terrorists—*terrorists*—spreading paralyzing fear.

"I hate this, if you want to know the truth, but I might be the first person who can do something about it. Not because I'm smarter, not because I'm braver, but because I don't care as much about myself as all those other guys. I don't care if I get reelected.

"But I will tell you this: I don't want to see one more video of a ten-year-old kid walking out of a convenience store with a candy bar and a smile...and getting gunned down in the street."

MAN WHO HOSTED PARTY WHERE 8 WERE SHOT FACES FEDERAL CHARGE

Fox2Now

St. Louis

66.
LUCY

NO JACKIE O. First Lady Lucy Barratt was not alive when Jacqueline Bouvier Kennedy was in the White House in the early 1960s, but when Elijah Barratt was running for president, she educated herself about some of the women who would be her predecessors and was intrigued by Jackie Kennedy.

Jackie was still revered by the public. Elegant, cultured, beautiful, enthusiastically redecorating the White House and presiding over holiday galas. She was raised in New York City, the Hamptons, Washington, DC, and Newport, Rhode Island. A daughter of a wealthy family, she comported herself as a lady would, a product—and perhaps a prisoner—of her times. Lucy acknowledged those qualities and forgave her for her passivity, occasional reticence, and behind-closed-door tolerance of her husband's infidelity, but these were aspects that she would never emulate. What Lucy *did* admire was that Jackie always seemed to be calm and in control. That, Lucy had long ago vowed, she would always be.

Lucy McPhee, now Barratt, was no child of privilege. She grew up dirt-road-poor in the Southwest, in a worn-down two-bedroom house with an overgrown yard. Born to not one but two alcoholic parents; either could have been the poster child for codependency. To eight-year-old Lucy and her four-year-old sister, Brandy, their parents' screaming jags were terrifying, their threats to each other with guns and knives chilling.

When the battles started, she would shepherd her sister into the small walk-in pantry off the kitchen and shut its door. There, she kept an old red blanket and two worn patterned sofa cushions that she had rescued from the neighbors' trash. To distract her sister, she would teach Brandy how to read the names of the few cans and boxes of food on the pantry shelves: cornflakes, SpaghettiOs, instant mashed potatoes. She would tell her made-up stories of the lives they would lead, full of parties and pretty dresses and lots of sweet desserts. Pulling her sister close, she would distract herself by protecting Brandy. They would huddle on the cushions and under the blanket and hopefully fall asleep, staying there until morning.

When they then ventured into the kitchen and through the front room, they would frequently find their parents passed out, sometimes curled up together, empty beer cans scattered on the floor, half-smoked cigarettes overflowing the coffee table ashtray. Their parents would awaken oblivious to the chaos they had caused the night before, and of the nightmares that would chase their daughters through a forest of emotions throughout their lives.

Lucy would get Brandy and her something to eat, then washed up and out the door, heading for the neighbor's backyard or the swings in the park down the street, pretending to be like all the other kids, the ones with their new shoes and the latest toys, but knowing that they were looked on sometimes with pity, sometimes with disgust. They envied those kids their parents, who smiled and encouraged and cheered. Lucy left that world when she turned eighteen. She tried to help Brandy follow her out, but Brandy kept looking for the fantasy father she had longed for in every man she met. Unfortunately, she only found versions of the original. She married two of them, and now lived in the adult equivalent of their childhood pathos.

There were certain parameters Lucy observed that, in her mind, kept the pantry door shut and her parents locked away: Never drink; alcohol made you vulnerable. Never let them see you cry; that meant that someone had control over *you*. She would never tolerate disrespect by the cable news pundits or Elijah's political enemies, and she wouldn't play by their rules. Nor would she respond to their arrogance and self-importance in kind. That wasn't who she was, and she would not let anyone goad her into being such.

When Barratt was elected, her First Lady Rule #1 was: I'm In Control. She had t-shirts made for her staff with that mantra. They came in light blue and red-and-white and pink-and-navy, but the script was always hard black block letters. She had fought too hard to surrender who she was. Elijah's background received most of the scrutiny, as it should; her story was treated rather perfunctorily by most of the press, but she carried the scars of it every day.

Lucy found her way into community college, parlayed dean's list semesters and graduation honors into a scholarship at the state university, ultimately becoming a licensed social worker, a natural outgrowth of her protective nature. She met Elijah at a domestic violence conference they both attended, he to help understand his matrimonial clients, she to address the attendees about victims' emotional injuries. For Elijah, enraptured by this confident, gorgeous woman challenging the audience from the podium, it was love at first sight. For Lucy, protecting herself meant taking things slowly. Their first date was lunch in a crowded restaurant, their second a long walk in a downtown park on a busy Saturday. He finally won her over, but it was still three months before she would go back to his place.

No Jackie O. She didn't need to be. Lucy was elegant in her own way. A statuesque five foot nine, toned from yoga and Pilates, chiseled cheekbones and eyes that changed color from green to brown to hazel. She declined to be dressed by the popular designers, but she always turned heads when she was by Elijah's side, even though her favorite accessory was a thrift store Louis Vuitton bag that she had scored for $10.

Lucy readied herself for most days at the vanity in her bedroom, applying a subtle pink lipstick and just a touch of makeup. She was charmingly unaware of her beauty, but otherwise certain of who she was. She had become a writer of some renown in her profession, and these days wrote empathetic poetry that she submitted to publications using a pseudonym so no one would be influenced by her husband's status. She would be true to herself; her life experience had earned her no less. First Lady Rule #2: Never tell Elijah only what he wanted to hear when he sought her advice, and never let his aides tell her what to say on the campaign trail, but rather tell them all exactly what she thought.

She was Lucy McPhee Barratt. She had fought tough battles and won. She made her own damn rules.

And now small-minded men with giant egos were attacking her husband. *I have another rule*, Lucy vowed: *You mess with my man, you mess with me.*

14 DEAD, 21 INJURED IN SAN BERNARDINO MASS SHOOTING; 2 SUSPECTS KILLED

SUN projects
CALIFORNIA

67.
BARRATT

PRESIDENT ELIJAH BARRATT SAT in the small dining room near the Oval Office, Bobby and Lucy sitting on either side of him. He had gradually changed the room to more accurately reflect his personality: the large-screen TV, a small refrigerator, fewer staid photos of ancient men, and more sports memorabilia. The Chase Utley signed program from the Phillies' 2008 World Series, a Hank Aaron bat, a silly little trophy he had won almost thirty years ago in a night golf tournament. The TV was tuned to the sport he respected least: the blood sport of congressional politics.

There had been no official notice of the day's agenda, but there had been enough leaks to sink the *Queen Mary*. The House of Representatives was going to consider a proposal to impeach Elijah Barratt, president of the United States.

Barratt chatted continuously, a defense mechanism he sometimes used to ward off anxiety.

"And you know," he said to Lucy and Bobby, "the first time I was in the chamber, I was surprised by how cramped it really was. Yeah, it's about 13,000 square feet, but when all 435 members are in there, they only have a space of five by six feet to themselves, not much."

"Probably why they're always so pissed off," murmured Bobby, eliciting a laugh from Lucy and the president.

“And how do they fit all those huge egos in at the same time?” asked Lucy.

Another laugh, but this a nervous one.

Barratt’s voice ran down as the proceeding’s start time approached. Silence enveloped them as they stared at the screen. The Speaker of the House gaveled the body to order.

“And so it begins,” whispered Barratt.

AT LEAST 3 KILLED IN SATURDAY MORNING SHOOTINGS IN ATLANTA

Atlanta Journal-Constitution

68.
BARRATT

IN THE HOUSE CHAMBER, Representative Harlen Largessy rose to his feet. Some of the less deferential wags in the House joked that Largessy had presided over the first House session in 1789.

"That guy is ancient," Bobby murmured.

Barratt shook his head and smiled. Largessy had indeed been re-elected to two-year terms a staggering twenty-four times and had been serving in the House for almost fifty years. As an accommodation to his age and limited mobility, he was always saved a seat on the aisle, since seats weren't assigned in the House. The Chamber was packed and the upper-level gallery filled as he stepped awkwardly out of his row of seats and ambled toward the microphone.

Barratt had seen photos of Largessy from when he was first elected. He came to Congress with his dark black hair always cut just so, his suits finely tailored. He always had a pocket square and frequently a flower in his lapel. The pocket square and the flower were still a part of his ensemble, but now his still thick hair was all white. His suit hung straight down off his shoulders, with very little muscle to fill it out. He clutched his three-legged cane, a rare concession to his age, finally convinced by his aides that it was less embarrassing to use it than it would be to stumble and fall in the chamber.

Stopping in the aisle, he stood unsteadily and looked to his right. Seated there was Senator Grammar, who rose and offered him his arm.

"What the hell?" shouted Bobby. "What is she doing in the House chamber? She can't do that! She'll be part of the jury in the Senate!"

Barratt was caught off guard, but not totally surprised. "You knew she was going to insinuate herself into this somehow, and this is kind of creative, but that was some phony-looking choreography we just saw."

"The speaker should remove her," said Bobby.

"Not gonna happen," said Lucy. "Guy doesn't have the balls he was born with."

"Lucy!" said Barratt, in mock reproach. "Such language from the first lady."

Largessy, leaning on Grammar, made his way to the podium and faced the chamber.

"Damn," said Bobby, "I'll bet she's figured out a way to speak and become the face of this whole thing. She'll be the story."

"My friends and colleagues," Largessy started. Barratt thought he was feigning weariness and making his voice weak. "I rise to address you today on a matter of grave national concern." He paused and scanned his audience, then heaved a theatrical sigh. "But my voice is not strong enough to do this moment justice. I will ask my good friend"—he turned and handed his prepared speech to Grammar, standing next to him—"to assist me."

Barratt's supporters shot to their feet and yelled at the speaker. "Point of order! Point of order!" The Speaker rapped his gavel, but they continued. "She's not a member of the House! And she's got a conflict. She's a senator. She shouldn't even be here!"

Grammar's people stood and cheered for her. The speaker banged and banged his gavel. The noise in the chamber bounced off the ceiling and walls, a cacophony of chaos.

"A member is entitled to have assistance when needed for health reasons," said the Speaker, "and she will be reading the representative's words, not her own. Proceed, Senator."

Grammar smiled and stepped to the mic. She turned to Largessy and touched his arm. "It is a privilege to assist you, Representative," she said, then turned back to the chamber and began to read.

"I…" Grammar nodded to Largessy. "I rise to ask you to impeach the American president, something I had hoped over my long tenure that I would never have to say."

Yeah, thought Barratt, *Largessy said that every time*. He had been in Congress for five impeachment proceedings, remarkably four in just a ten-year span, but he was never one to let the facts get in the way of a dramatic pronouncement.

"President Elijah Barratt," Grammar continued, "has usurped the authority of this body and the will of the American people. He has decided that he and he alone should govern our nation. His misuse of his emergency power by the issuance of his damnable executive order is a violation not only of the Constitution but also of the separation of powers that is the foundation of our Republic."

It became clear to Barratt just how brazen this was going to be. Ordinarily, an impeachment hearing in the House of Representatives was preceded by an investigation and report from the appropriate House committee. But such an investigation was not actually required.

"My God," said Barratt in a low voice, speaking to himself more than anyone else, "they're going to skip the investigation, probably vote by acclimation, and not even give me a chance to defend myself."

Grammar was speaking with a deliberate cadence. "It takes a particular kind of arrogance, of hubris, to think that he—and he alone—knows what's best for all the rest of us." She increased her volume and slowly hammered each word, a roller coaster car climbing to the top of the first hill.

Barratt wondered what exact histrionics his opponents in the House would perform to support an impeachment. The Constitution established only three bases for impeachment: treason, bribery, and other high crimes and misdemeanors. But Barratt was a Federalist Papers geek, and he knew that Largessy was too. He bet they both knew that there was a loophole there. Sure enough, he heard Grammar jump through it.

"The brilliant Alexander Hamilton, it was as if he was speaking directly to us across the years. He opined that an 'impeachable offense was one consisting of the misconduct of public men...the abuse...of some public trust...injuries done to the society itself.'"

As he sat there, Barratt pictured millions of Americans hearing him vilified. No matter how much he believed he was saving the country, that the country was hearing him described as incompetent pierced his heart. He felt his ears getting hotter and hotter, as if they could burst into flames, his involuntary response to rejection. Lucy saw how red they were and reached over and took his hand in hers. Clutching it, he turned to her with a painful grimace. The House was doing exactly what he'd anticipated it would, but it was still humiliating. His "peers" were trying to throw him out of office. Could there be any greater act of rejection?

"The people elected *us* to make these decisions," said Grammar. She had reached the apex of the first hill and was now steering the car, flying down the rails. "President Barratt has declared himself a dictator," she shouted. "Could there be a greater injury to society, a greater abuse?"

Grammar raced to the top of the next hill and simultaneously to the crescendo. "In the face of such a betrayal," she read, "there can be only one response: Cry 'No!' and throw him out!"

Two-thirds of the House chamber stood and roared, chanting "NO!"—the word reverberating through the room. With a flourish,

Grammar handed the written list of Barratt's alleged offenses to the House clerk.

In short order, after other House members took the opportunity to preen for the cameras, the House would vote, and President Elijah Barratt would be impeached.

"Buckle up," he said to Lucy and Bobby. "It's going to be a rough ride."

SEVEN PEOPLE SHOT OUTSIDE OF A MEMPHIS NIGHTCLUB

Action News 5
Memphis, TN

69.
BARRATT

BARRATT WAS GLIDING THROUGH the water, one powerful stroke after another. The water rippled over his torso, a nearly silent aquatic massage, the sense of near weightlessness creating a Zen-like state.

Franklin Roosevelt, who had contracted poliomyelitis, had an indoor pool built at the White House and swam for therapy, but Richard Nixon had it covered over as part of a press briefing room. Fortunately for Barratt, former college athlete Gerald Ford built an outdoor pool on the South Lawn in 1975.

Barratt's contribution was to have a dome constructed and the pool heated so it could be used year-round. As presidents before him had done, construction was funded by private donations. Barratt deemed it money well spent. Most people buy a t-shirt at a concert; Barratt brought home souvenir pain that made the lifting and Pilates he used to do now undoable. Swimming was a godsend. He used the pool most often at twilight. He would have the overhead lights dimmed and the underwater lights illuminated. It created a separate world, sound muted, distractions at bay, a momentary escape from the unrelenting rigors of his job.

Lucy sat by the pool, a book in her hands and a towel draped around her shoulders. Barratt and she had taken to coveting any time they could be together, even just near each other. When he finished his swim and rose out of the pool, he knew that she would use the towel to gently dry his back and down his arms, then wrap him in the towel and embrace him from behind, the tenderness soothing.

Eight more laps to make his mile. The pool was only fifty feet long, which meant he had to swim 106 lengths to reach his goal. The repetitive movement let him lose himself in the effort. He reached his arms out as far as he could, made the subtle twist that helped him move through the resistance of the water, in his mind as sleek as a dolphin. He reached the edge of the pool and turned. Now one more lap. *Finish strong*, he said to himself. He stretched and kicked and pulled, and pushed himself through the last length. He touched the wall, stood up, removed his goggles and earplugs, and bent in the shallow end, hands on knees, breathing hard but steady.

As he did his post-swim cool-down, his ability to block out the daily crises—the typical threat from Iran, the blustering by North Korea, the ambiguous message from India, the hyperbole of the radicals in the House—was weakening. He turned away from the wall and stepped toward the deep end, stopping when the water was mid-chest high. This was when the ruminating sometimes began. In the early days of his presidency, it could be about upcoming meetings, public relations gaffes, maverick aides. These days it was always about The Plan.

He had conjured endgames from the very beginning, but as the poet said, the best-laid plans of mice and men often go awry. He had been cautiously optimistic that, with the might of the US military a constant presence during the early days of enforcement, those resisting The Plan's implementation would see the reality: This was going to happen. He did not delude himself that everyone would embrace what was being accomplished, not in this generation, but eventually. He believed in his heart and soul that he was saving the country from unending violence and constant division. But every day brought reports of new, bloody confrontations. Every death haunted him, whether it be of a private citizen violently resisting the surrender of his weapons, of the doomed defenders of a cadre compound, and especially those of police officers and soldiers.

Was he up against something so big and strong and pervasive as to be unconquerable? Was man—and he had never allowed this thought to completely form in his mind before but now it had to be faced—was man inherently violent? Was it the nature of man to covet? To perceive a threat where none existed? To act out of need for revenge after perceived humiliation?

Cain slew Abel. Prehistoric tribes battled for food and mates and a coveted cave through the millennia. Was that just a part of a never-ending conflict? And who was he to think that he could reverse history? What could possibly explain the Roman conquerors? The crusaders? Genghis Khan? It continued into and through modern times: Mussolini, Franco, Hitler, Stalin, Idi Amin, the British and Belgian and French and American colonizers, the genocide of Native Americans.

Barratt had lived his life believing that there was dignity in every man and woman. He looked for and always believed that he would find it when he searched hard enough. But now, when he looked at the historical sociopaths and the obstinate supremacists, he grieved inwardly. Where was the dignity now?

He breathed deeply in and out. He moved his open palms in the water, left then right, pushing the water around his body, emulating one of his favorite tai chi moves, surrounding himself with positive energy, then he raised his arms above his head, brought his fingers to almost touching as he flattened his palms, and pushed the bad energy down and away.

If he could not find the dignity in every man, he would call on the dignity of those who did express it. He would call on his own dignity, and that of his family and that of the people closest to him. He would win this fight.

And then this thought crashed unbidden into his troubled mind: or die a dignified death trying to.

SHOOTINGS IN NEWTOWN, CT 20 OF THE VICTIMS WERE CHILDREN, ONE OF THE DEADLIEST SCHOOL SHOOTINGS IN U.S. HISTORY

NPR

70.
STANLEY KNIGHT

STANLEY KNIGHT HUNG THREE MORE squirrel pelts on one of the wooden crosses he had planted in the field behind his house. There were now dozens of them, along with raccoon and rabbit skins nailed by their tails, swaying in the breeze like macabre battle flags, portending the violence to come. He had stood before them, his hands clasped behind him, a soldier observing with pride his grisly badges. But he knew from the rigorous training he had put himself through that shooting small game and boar and deer, however difficult, was not the real thing. He needed a different kind of target.

He had timed and logged the magnetometer flyovers, and the helicopter engines were not always baffled. Living as he did in such a remote area, he could hear their approach from miles away. He noted that, as the weeks passed, the flights became more predictable, and the military fell into a routine. He could retrieve his Steyr sniper rifle from its water tower hiding place in the interludes and hone his skills. Now he had to hone his nerve.

He walked cross-country to his sniper nest, atop a hillock at a remove from the interstate. The hay bale in front of him was camouflaged with ferns and lichens and small branches that exactly matched the vegetation surrounding it, its edges chopped so that it was no longer a square mass, but rather was at one with the hillside. His rifle rested in the concave swale he had hacked into the bale. It lay in perfect balance, pointing north along the roadway, the spearhead of his arsenal, his avenging angel. He made sure that it didn't protrude beyond his nest.

Stanley appeared to be part of the vegetation itself, clad in a ghillie suit adorned with the same grasses that covered the ground around him, cut that morning so they wouldn't wilt. He had used camouflage paint on his hands and face and neck. A do-rag was fitted just right to hide his forehead and ears and prevent any reflection. Settling cross-legged behind his weapon, he double-checked that the nest held no food, no smokes, nothing that could be detectable from a distance or that he could inadvertently leave behind. A CamelBak water pouch was his only reservoir for hydration. He had practiced holding this position for hours on his hunts and worked his legs tirelessly so that he could spring up and withdraw immediately after a hit.

Several cars passed on the highway below, ranged at eight hundred meters. He let a pickup go by and then a cube truck, all unsuspecting survivors. He angled his tactical binoculars along the freeway and spotted a suitable target, a semi. What luck—a piggyback, a tandem. Returning the binos to their case, he settled behind the rifle scope. Winds were calm. The only sniper gear that Knight did not have was a ballistics computer program. He envied those who did, but he was counting on his constant training and being attuned to the elements to enable him to hit his target.

He gently laid his finger on the Steyr's trigger. The scope was already sighted in. This was the real thing. This would test his nerve. This would make him worthy of his mission.

The broad windshield of the semi-truck cab approached his firing point. Traveling at 2,700 feet per second, the round he fired would reach its target in just over one second, an eyeblink. Exhaling, he stopped breathing. The truck traveled steadily. The firing point presented. He caressed, then squeezed the trigger.

Panning the rifle along the truck's path, he watched through the scope as the windshield exploded. In the same instant, the driver's head erupted with a blood-red plume. The truck careened, drifted, then jackknifed. The cab, first trailer, and second trailer became one concussive mass of screaming, screeching metal, then the trailers humped up into the air and belched their loads along the highway, spewing pallets of eggs and canned beans, launching bottled water that exploded on impact, smearing the road.

Stanley Knight packed up his gear.

He was ready.

1 WOMAN, 5 MEN INJURED IN GERMANTOWN SHOOTING POLICE SAY

FOX 29

Philadelphia

71.
ARIEL

FOUR BIG RALLIES IN THE last twelve months, twice that many appearances on cable news shows. Always surrounded by aides and supporters and people who wanted something from her. Ariel was exhausted. Her friends told her that she needed alone time, some peace and quiet. She scoffed at their suggestion that she take a few days off. Then they told her about a large forest preserve some distance south of the city. *Remote, uncrowded, the animals won't even recognize you*, they joked. Ariel had never been there before—it wasn't her thing, she countered—but online it looked like a place she could escape to, maybe hide in, for a day. She promised them that she would block news feeds and mute her phone.

GPS took her to the preserve, but it did a poor job of locating the parking area and the trailhead. She stopped and asked a man and woman, each with hiking poles, walking on the side of the country road, for help, and they gave her directions. She was relieved that they showed no sign of recognizing her.

She found the trailhead they had recommended and pulled into the hard-packed parking area, a little unsettled that there was only one other vehicle there. Grabbing her fanny pack, she exited the car—and stood still. There was a slight rustle in the treetops, the soft breeze whispering in the dark green foliage. Birdsongs filtered out of the forest, but then a yip, more like a yowl, reached her ears. *A coyote?* she wondered. She had never seen a coyote; had not even heard one in the wild. Didn't they eat small dogs and chase down children? She turned 180 degrees to check out the tree line. She always carried mace and a whistle in her fanny pack. Would these be of any use if she came face-to-face with a coyote in the woods? *What good would a whistle be*, she wondered, *with no one to hear it?* Ariel had become used to being surrounded by hundreds of people at the rallies, and several aides and a few hangers-on between appearances. She had even gotten used to the vulgar emails and tweets from those who didn't like what she was doing.

But now she was completely alone for the first time in years; it didn't feel like she thought it would. She moved closer to the presumed safety of her car, then stopped and scolded herself.

"Come on, Ariel," she spoke out loud. "That's the reluctant old Ariel, not who I am anymore. Patty calls me 'New Ariel.' This is what New Ariel needs, right?"

She beeped her car locked and headed for the only opening into the trees, which was flanked by two wooden message boards. When she reached the boards, she eyed the trail maps posted there. *I can do this*, she thought. *If I just follow some white arrows, I should be okay.* She set off.

The trail widened, then narrowed, then widened again. Her first steps were tentative, and she was startled by each rustle in the underbrush, each thud of a fallen walnut or acorn. Gradually, she became enamored with the delicate ferns and the blue and pink and black mushrooms sheltered by the trees. Slowly, her shoulders released their tension, and her step became more confident. *What a different world this is*, she mused. She hadn't expected to be so relaxed, so comforted by the stillness and isolation; she hadn't seen another hiker since she had entered the woods. She moved smoothly now, stopping often to finger some tiny white flowers or oddly textured bark.

She became subtly aware of something gnawing at her, then glanced at her watch and saw that she had been walking for over an hour and was famished. There were some granola bars and a bottle of water in her fanny pack. She looked for a place to stop and sit down.

Ariel laughed at herself as she realized she was looking for a park bench or maybe a picnic table.

"Not out here, girl," she said aloud.

After several minutes, she saw the beginning of a clearing to her right. She walked into it and stopped abruptly, struck by the beauty of the vista that she beheld. Beyond the cliff that marked the end of the clearing, the ground swept down to a quickly running stream, then climbed up the other side and into the trees. The stream was white water dancing over smooth gray rocks; wildflowers painted the far side yellow and blue.

"Wow," she said softly, reverently. She walked further into the clearing and stood in admiration. "This is stunning."

"Who are you talking to?" a voice asked.

Ariel jumped, shuffled backward, and awkwardly fell on her butt. She looked to the bushes and trees that marked one end of the clearing, maybe twenty feet away. She saw a man, probably a few years older than she, sitting on the hard-packed ground, his arms wrapped around his knees.

"Whoa!" she said. "I didn't know there was anybody here. You startled me."

He made no apology, made no offer to help her up. He simply turned away from her and gazed out beyond the cliff face. As she rose clumsily, she looked more closely at the man. He was rather lean, handsome in a rugged way, but his shoulders were slumped, his clothing somewhat rumpled, his hair needed a trim, his face was expressionless. He looked, she thought, to be the saddest person she had ever seen.

"I said," she repeated, "you startled me."

"I heard you the first time."

"Well, you might have said something, or maybe helped me up."

"Nothing much to say. And you look like you could get up on your own."

Before Dawn River, Ariel would have turned and walked away, but now she was a different animal. Having shared her story with so many, she felt compelled to know the backstory of everyone she came across.

"This is quite a spot," she said, altering her approach.

Silence in return.

"Do you come here often?" She laughed. "God, that was lame. Sorry."

A smile fought its way to the edges of the man's mouth but was quickly swallowed.

She moved several feet closer, surprised that she felt no threat from this sad stranger.

"Do you mind if I sit here too?" she said while she was in the process of seating herself on the ground.

The man looked in her direction.

"It looks like you already have."

"It's just so peaceful here," Ariel said.

"It used to be."

"Okay," Ariel surrendered. "I can take a hint."

"No," the man said so quickly that he seemed to have surprised himself. "I didn't mean that. It's just... It's... I do come here a lot... But now I come here alone."

Sad and hurting, Ariel thought.

"I didn't mean to make you uncomfortable."

"You didn't. I've been uncomfortable for a while. But this," he said as he extended one hand and waved it along the line of the horizon, "this helps."

Ariel didn't know how to respond, but she broke the silence when she saw what appeared to be a flat, smooth square stone with words etched into it to the left of the seated man.

"What's that next to you?" she asked.

The man unclasped his knees and leaned back, propping himself up with his arms out behind him. He positioned one hand to partially cover the stone.

Ariel leaned in to get a better look and said, "There's some writing on it." Getting onto her knees, she crawled forward to read it.

The man moved slightly away from her.

On the stone she read:

THIS IS HANK'S SPOT
I RESCUED HIM, HE RESCUED ME

"I wonder who Hank was?" Ariel asked.

The man repositioned himself so that he now sat on his haunches in front of the stone. Leaning forward, he delicately brushed some sand and loose grass from it. Then he settled back and raised his eyes and peered toward the woods and the trail that led into the clearing. There was a rustling in the undergrowth, then two squirrels burst out chasing each other up the trail but incongruously came to an abrupt halt and stared at the man. He heard the screech of one of the hawks who rested in the trees before continuing its hunt in the valley.

"Hank was...well, he was more than a dog. He was my best friend. He lived a great life, a long life. I wanted him to live forever."

Ariel turned to him.

"I'm so sorry," she said. The woods music continued, while the two of them sat silently for several minutes. "I... I know what it's like to grieve. It can be hard to talk about it, but it can help. I know that too."

The man moved his gaze away from the trail and looked closely at her for the first time, his eyes squinted in concentration. "Wait a minute, I know you," he said. "You're the girl that has all those rallies."

TWO MORE SUSPECTS CHARGED IN CONNECTION WITH COATESVILLE SCHOOL BUS SHOOTING

CBS News
Philadelphia

72.
ARIEL

"YEAH," THE MAN CONTINUED, "you're the one who does all those rallies. I keep seeing you outside Dawn River."

Ariel frowned. Now it was her turn to gaze off into the woods.

"I was kinda hoping I could be anonymous for a day. In fact, I was hoping to be totally alone."

The man smiled at her.

"Hey, you're the one that started talking to me, or maybe started talking to the trees." They both laughed lightly. "Besides," he continued, "I think just about everybody knows who you are by now."

A breeze continued to riffle the treetops, but dark clouds that had floated up from the south gave way to clearer skies. Ariel and the man shifted to assume cross-legged positions, facing each other. The man's visage took on a serious mien.

"Why do you do it?" he blurted.

"What?" Ariel said. She had heard him clearly but hesitated to respond. She didn't know this man. *He may be harmless*, she thought, but she was pretty sure she didn't want him dissecting her life.

"Why do you do it?"

"It needs to be done. It's out of control. Children, babies, seniors. People watching a movie. People riding on the subway. Their lives could all be ended tomorrow."

"That doesn't answer the question."

"Well, that's my answer."

"That's *an* answer, not your answer."

Ariel stood abruptly, her reticence overcome. He had pushed her far enough.

"Look, my sister was shot, okay? She's in a wheelchair."

The man rose as well. "I know, we all know, and that's terrible. But that's her. You. Is it making a difference? *You*. Why do *you* do it?"

"Why the hell do you care so much?" she said, her voice rising.

"Because I need to know. I...*need* to know. Please. Tell me."

"Because I couldn't save her! Because I'm the big sister. I was there. I couldn't help!" Ariel turned away from him. "I was there," she repeated in a soft voice. "And I couldn't save her."

Silence separated them until the man spoke.

"I was there that night too." His voice was barely audible, catching in his throat. "I was there. I was buyin' some fuckin' popcorn, and the woman I was going to marry was shot and died at Dawn River."

Ariel turned back, her face contorted in pain, stunned by the confluence, two Dawn River sufferers stumbling upon each other. Without another word they moved tentatively toward each other, hesitated, then guided, magnetized, by their shared pain, they reached for each other and embraced, delicately at first, then desperately, neither seeking affection, just a moment of comfort. They remained entwined for several minutes, then slowly separated.

"I...I'm sorry," the man said softly as he stepped back. "I don't why I did that. It's just that I've been so...hurt, so alone. Then here you are, and you've been through this, and that's just crazy."

"Sometimes I feel the same way," Ariel said.

"But you're doing something, you're moving on."

Ariel shook her head, started to speak, stopped, started again.

"I don't know if this helps. Moving hurts too, but it would be worse if I *wasn't* moving." She exhaled deeply and formed a humorless grin. "Only thing is, now, I'm afraid to stop."

"I don't know if I *can* move," the man said. "I feel like I'm buried, like I'm already in a grave. Like I can't dig my way out." He paused and looked away from her. "Maybe I don't want to. I haven't handled it well. I've done some...things. I don't know who I'd be if I did climb out." He looked back. "And, damn, how the hell did we crash into each other way out here?"

They stood facing each other, a slight distance between them. Neither knew what to say, how to stand, what to do with their arms, their hands.

Silence grew, until the man said: "I... I have some trail mix, some apples and some Snickers. Would you like some?"

Ariel grabbed the lifeline he had thrown. "I'm actually pretty hungry. Introspection is hard work, isn't it?"

"So is hiking," the man responded. "You put the two together and it's appetite critical mass."

They moved toward a level spot near the clearing edge. The man knelt and brushed away some small stones and some fallen leaves.

Ariel undid the clasp of her fanny pack and zipped it open.

"I've got some dried apricots and cashews in here."

"Hey, we're talkin' fine dining now," the man laughed.

He grabbed his day pack as they settled onto the ground. Pulling out a small canvas bag filled with his snacks and some paper towels, he spread everything out between them. Ariel contributed what she had. They simultaneously retrieved water bottles and unscrewed the caps. They smiled at each other and clicked the bottles together in a toast.

"Here's to healing," Ariel said, "however it comes."

They started to share what they had; neither spoke. Ariel looked out past the cliff edge, to the hardwood canopy on the other side. A morning mist had lingered over the stream but started to dissipate as she watched, exposing both sides of the valley.

"I can see why you come here," said Ariel.

The man didn't reply but gazed over the valley.

"Will you tell me your story?" asked Ariel.

"I... I'm... I don't know if I'm ready to go there."

"Then just tell me your name."

He hesitated a moment, then said, "I'm Jimmy."

"Hi, Jimmy. I'm Ariel." They exchanged an exaggerated handshake and laughed together. "At least tell me about Hank," she asked.

Jimmy took a long draw from his water bottle, glanced down at the ground, looked at Ariel for a moment, then back across the valley.

"The shelter said that Hank was a mutt," Jimmy laughed, "but he wasn't to me. We rescued him when he was just a pup. It was love at first sight for me and him. He was the most handsome dog you ever saw. Light brown hair, those half-floppy ears, a bushy tail, and a constant grin. He lived longer than a dog is supposed to, then time just came and gently took him. I held him in my arms as he slipped away."

Ariel smiled. "Do you know what mix he was?"

Jimmy smiled. "Who knows?" he said. "I think he had a little bit of everything in him. All the good stuff."

Jimmy's smile receded.

"When Alice...my...fiancée...died, Hank wouldn't leave my side." He turned and looked at Ariel and his smile returned. "You know how animals can tell? How they seem to know what you're feeling? How you're hurting?" He turned away again. "I was a mess," he said. "That dog saved my life." Jimmy lowered his head, lifted one hand, and rubbed his chin. "Alice gone. Now Hank's gone." Jimmy sighed. "I'm a mess again."

Ariel waited a respectful moment, then reached and placed her hand on Jimmy's shoulder.

"Come with me to one of the rallies," she said. Jimmy didn't respond. Ariel withdrew her hand but continued. "A lot of people tell me it's been cathartic for them. So many of them have been where you...and I...have been."

Jimmy pursed his lips.

"I don't think that's for me," he said. "I don't... I don't share these feelings with a lot of people." He tilted his head and glanced her way, a sly smile showing on his face. "I'm not sure why I'm sharing with you. Maybe because you invaded Hank's forest."

Ariel smiled back. "Think about it. Hey, I can get you a good seat. I bet I can even get you backstage to meet the so-called star of the show, such as she is. Here." She pulled out her phone. "I'll send you my number. What's yours?"

Jimmy didn't respond for a beat, then told her.

"Good," she said as she texted him. "Now we know how to get in touch with each other."

Jimmy just nodded in reply. He realized that this was the first time he had wanted to exchange phone numbers with a woman since the night of Dawn River.

OKLAHOMA SEX OFFENDER FATALLY SHOT 6, THEN KILLED SELF, OFFICIAL SAYS

KSL.com
Utah

73.
BARRATT

"**MR. PRESIDENT, THANK YOU** for taking the time to see me."

Attorney General Robert Seaford did not know Barratt on a personal level, but they respected each other professionally. Seaford's resume was impeccable: years of service in the US Attorney's Office in his home state of Iowa, then a stint in the Eastern District, a stepping stone for an important job in the Justice Department. He had been recommended highly when Barratt was filling out the cabinet and was said to be considered favorably by both sides of the Senate aisle. His nomination was well received, and consent came quickly.

Seaford was close in age to Barratt, but looked years older. Barratt was known among DC insiders as committed to his mile swims in the White House pool, and a reluctant but disciplined weightlifter, albeit with light weights. He suffered lingering limitations from Dawn River, but he fought against those limitations every day. Seaford was just the opposite. His pallid face and sagging jowls were partnered with his generous girth. Lawyers on the other side of him in criminal cases made the mistake of transferring that image to his legal acumen. They soon learned that he had extraordinary stamina when it came to researching and presenting his case and was a barracuda in the courtroom. He had served the country well during Barratt's term, and they were rarely on opposite sides of an issue.

Seaford sat now in the Oval Office, across the desk from the president. It was only the third time he had been there, and he couldn't help but take it in again: the massive Resolute Desk, the bust of Jefferson, the facing couches where so many crises had been argued and challenged and ultimately resolved. He sat uncomfortably on one of those couches now, the president sitting directly across. Seaford had brought one of those crises to the president's office today, and for one of the rare times in his career he was anxious about the opinion he was about to present.

"I'm happy to give you a few minutes," said Barratt. "You haven't pushed for access, and I appreciate that. You and I both know that you don't represent me personally, so these meetings should be few and far between. I am somewhat surprised, though, that you are by yourself today." Barratt smiled. "Don't you Justice guys usually travel in pairs?"

Seaford did not return the smile. Instead, he tried to swallow, his throat dry, his mouth a desert.

"I felt that what I need to discuss was better done with just the two of us." He paused. Barratt spread his hands and nodded for Seaford to proceed.

Seaford had gone face to face with organized crime, had prosecuted gangs, had successfully pursued dirty judges. Known as a straight arrow, courageous, acting ethically in every circumstance. He didn't flinch, but was very much aware that what he was about to tell the president was something that would be difficult for Barratt to hear.

"Mr. President, my staff and I have looked at this from every angle conceivable, inside out and upside down. And we have reached a unanimous conclusion: There is no basis to defend your executive order declaring the national emergency. We expect the plaintiffs to win at the trial level and at every stage up to and including the Supreme Court. I'm reluctant to send Justice Department attorneys into court to make an argument that is not supported by the law." He paused, then, at the risk, he thought, of pontificating, he added: "My oath is to the Constitution. I can't keep that oath if I misrepresent to the court."

Barratt had tented his fingers and leaned back on the couch, listening intently. He moved forward, tilted his head slightly, and leveled his eyes at Seaford. Barratt had anticipated some pushback from Justice and had a response prepared if it came to this. The next step was crucial, and he had no intention of letting one of Seaford's reluctant deputy AGs drop the ball. He was the quarterback, and he was the one who was prepared to carry the ball across the line.

"I'm going to solve your problem, Mr. Attorney General. I'm going to let you off the hook. I'm going to appear pro se."

Seaford's mouth dropped to his knees. He jutted forward and started to speak but was so stunned by what Barratt had said that amazement temporarily blocked his words.

"You..." he finally eked out, "you're going to...my God, you're going to represent *yourself*?"

"I am." Barratt let a smile form on his face. "I'm a member of the DC bar. I've been admitted to practice before the lower courts and the Supreme Court. I'm a named defendant. I have the right to represent myself and that's exactly what I'm going to do."

Seaford's reaction was why the word *flummoxed* was created. He stuttered and swallowed and stumbled as he reacted. "Mr. President, no...you...no president has ever done that. What you would be doing is unheard of."

"People have been telling me that a lot lately," said Barratt.

PAIR SOUGHT AFTER SEVEN SHOT DURING NC MOOSE LODGE CHRISTMAS PARTY

17 News

Raleigh-Durham-Fayetteville

74.
BARRATT

ELIJAH BARRATT HAD BEEN impeached by the House of Representatives and was facing trial in the United States Senate. Then, five states filed suit, *not* against the US government, but against Barratt *individually.* He was delighted that they had.

Most cases come before the United States Supreme Court in the form of appeals from lower courts. But Barratt knew that the Supreme Court had *original* jurisdiction in very limited areas of controversy, meaning that such cases don't have to work their way through the lower courts but instead would start at the Supreme Court itself. Those areas included the one President Barratt was depending on: certain actions by a state against a citizen of another state.

The five states were the ones most vociferously opposed to The Plan. Their claim was that *his* actions constituted an insurrection, and as such he should be barred from any public office. The Supreme Court immediately exercised its original jurisdiction and took the case for itself. That meant that any trial would be in front of the court. And *that* meant that it would be presided over by Chief Justice Chandler Bosworth and a court with a majority of Justices placed there by Barratt. He had assiduously refrained from contact with any of them, and vowed to never nominate a rubber-stamp jurist, but he knew that they would be sensitive to his argument. Each of them, in some way, had been touched by gun violence.

The constant media coverage of the impeachment and the pending Senate trial increased to a fever pitch when Bosworth set a hearing date for preliminary arguments just two weeks later. Barratt's persecutors were apoplectic, complaining that that was much too fast and instead that the court should enjoin (stop) Barratt from proceeding while they prepared. Bosworth chastised them, telling them that since *they* brought the case, they should be ready to go.

"Original jurisdiction," Barratt mused. Almost sounded religious to him. Not a virgin birth, but he *was* the father of The Plan. Or maybe he was forever married to the violence of Dawn River, for better or worse, in sickness and in health, with so many deaths parting so many. He had been nurturing the concept since The Plan had come to him, in that early morning epiphany, and he had been feeding and protecting his yet-to-be fully born child. Now those states and the Congress were trying to still its birth. "Original jurisdiction." Perhaps original jurisdiction was the midwife he needed to keep his infant plan alive.

As he contemplated the hearing date rushing toward him, Barratt's uncharacteristically self-important declaration to his advisors that he would represent himself in front of the Supreme Court quickly ran into his better judgment. Since the moment that he had made that pronouncement, the old legal axiom that "an attorney who represents himself has a fool for a client" ran on a constant loop in his mind. Not only had he not been a trial attorney for some time, but the perception of hubris if he stood before the Supreme Court would make it even more about him and less about The Plan. With the preliminary hearing date looming, he started having those recurring "work dreams" that had haunted his sleep when he was practicing: he dreamed that he couldn't find the courtroom; that if he did, he had forgotten his files; that if he tried to speak to the judge his voice went mute.

He awoke one morning having lost the battle with the sheets and the bedspread and covered with perspiration. He showered and dressed and was in the Oval Office by 5:30 a.m., anxious to busy himself and stop the ruminating.

When Bobby walked into the office, Barratt was relieved that he could focus on the day's work, but Bobby looked at him questioningly.

"Three people showed up at security this morning, said that they were from something called the Dependable Return Advisors and that you would want to see them. I told security to send them on their way, but they refused to leave. I'm not sure whether to have them arrested or go find out myself why they're so insistent, especially before 6:00 a.m. Any idea who they are?"

Barratt was unsure which three people were at the gate, but he was comforted by their surprise appearance.

"Bring them up to the small dining room," he instructed Bobby. "Have the kitchen bring us some fruit and breakfast stuff and lots of coffee."

"Really?" asked Bobby, but the look on Barratt's face gave him his answer. He turned and left the office.

Twenty minutes later, Barratt sat across the table from Roland Turret, Anna Appleton, and an attorney whom Barratt recognized as Michael Raphael, all of them connected to the Dependable Return Advisors, aka the Dawn River Associates.

"It's been a long time, Mr. President," Turret said, "but I remember the day you first knocked on my door as if it was yesterday."

Barratt's wounds ached, as they frequently did in the early morning. He thought about what Turret must go through when he pinned up his right sleeve, looked in the mirror and prepared for the day, his right arm ripped off by Alfred Dunkel's fusillade. Barratt formed a knowing smile, once again struck by how Dawn River was the impetus for his painful but imperative journey, this time creating the fellowship of fate among all the victims, men and women whose paths would never have otherwise crossed, now connected forever.

"We've necessarily kept our distance, Mr. Turret, but you all know how much I appreciate what you've been doing."

"It's nothing compared to what you've been going through. That's why we're here. This is not about campaigning. This isn't about votes. This is about the plan you convinced us was the way this country had to go, and you've been doing all the heavy lifting. DRA feels that we are approaching critical mass—that this is the inflection point.

"We don't know if you have already chosen legal counsel, but we brought Mr. Raphael with us, and he's prepared to represent you before the Supreme Court. DRA will take care of his fees."

"I'm familiar with Mr. Raphael by reputation," said Barratt, receiving Raphael's nod in response.

"Then you know," said Turret, "that Michael is one of the most experienced and accomplished attorneys in the country. He's appeared before the Supreme Court as much or more than anyone. More importantly, he always wins."

Raphael spoke for the first time since the introductions, evidencing a slight Mountain West accent: "Not always. Nobody wins every time, but I do succeed more than most." Raphael picked up the discussion from there. "Mr. President, I've followed these proceedings carefully, not just because I have a litigator's curiosity, but because if the opportunity arose, I wanted to be there, on your side."

Barratt gazed at the contradiction that was Michael Raphael. Bespoke dark suit, French cuffs with gold cufflinks, buttoned-up dress shirt, but with a bolo tie, carefully trimmed short beard but hair falling loosely over the back collar of his jacket. Idiosyncratic

Michael Raphael was a legend, an "Old Master," a pun he encouraged. Community college and state university education, graduate studies at Oxford, law degree from Yale. Whether or not he meant his eclectic appearance to be disarming or it was just who he naturally was, when he took a case, all eyes were on him. And despite his probably false modesty, Barratt was not aware of any important case that he had lost.

"Thank you, Mr. Raphael. You don't know this, but at one point I had planned to represent myself."

Raphael barked a laugh, then caught himself. "You're...serious?"

"Yeah, I was, but I got over it. Welcome aboard, Mr. Raphael."

Barratt sat back in his chair with his hands in front of him, one fist covered by the other hand. There was no guarantee that the Supreme Court would decide in his favor, no guarantee that the Senate wouldn't proceed with its trial even if the court did. If The Plan had any chance of succeeding, it had to break through these obstacles, and Raphael was one more advantage that he welcomed.

The White House staff brought in coffeepots with regular and decaf, baskets of breakfast rolls, bagels and spreads, boiled eggs, fruit, and an array of juices. The room went quiet when they entered, but Barratt broke the silence as soon as they had left. He looked directly at Raphael.

"Some guidelines. Going forward, I'm Eli, you're Michael. You put everything else you have on hold. You can move in here if you want. We go at this 24/7. Starting now."

COMPLETE COVERAGE: 10 KILLED, 3 WOUNDED IN MASS SHOOTING AT BUFFALO SUPERMARKET

The Buffalo News

75.
JIMMY

JIMMY RECALLED HOW DISMISSIVE he had been the first time he passed Ariel's Dawn River rallies. Meeting her had completely changed his mind.

He had been to three of her rallies since they met in the woods. Now he knew her to be smart, articulate, charming, and forceful all at the same time. After each rally he attended, he waited until her supporters and those who disagreed with her, all of whom had lined up in front of her podium, were finished. He saw her treat all of them with respect. He made sure that he was always the last one in line.

She always greeted him with a smile and lightly touched his arm. He wondered if she felt the same thrill that he did when she did so. Twice they went out for coffee, once with three of her aides. Once just the two of them, when they both confessed their love for pancakes and eggs at any time of day and happily indulged.

Six weeks after they first met, he sat in his house with his cell phone in his hand. His mouth was dry, and his knee wouldn't stop bouncing. He started to call Ariel, then stopped. Started, and stopped again. He got up and walked around the house, going over what he would say if he called and she answered the phone, and how he would probably panic and not be able to leave a message if he got voicemail.

Or worse, blurt out something inane and then have to call back and try to fix it.

"Geez," he asked himself, "what am I, back in high school?"

The first time he had ever asked a girl out, he worried over what he would say for days, then finally called; when her mother answered the phone, he immediately hung up.

He plopped down in the living room chair again. He instinctively reached to scratch Hank behind the ears but reached only air, then chided himself: "Man, I wish Hank was here to calm me down."

Then, with an almost involuntary twitch, he jabbed her contact number, then sat on his non-phone hand so he couldn't disconnect. The phone rang four times, then went to voicemail. He froze.

Then he completely panicked when the voicemail message cut off and Ariel said, "Jimmy? Hi!"

He was mute until he blurted, "Ariel, would you like to go to dinner with me?"

"Jimmy, are you asking me on a date?"

He could picture her smile, and some of his tension released.

"Yes... Yeah, I actually am. I'm a little out of practice. I feel like a damn teenager."

"I think you're just hoping you won't get rejected." Ariel laughed out loud.

"Hey, I'm living on the edge here. I just walked around the house for an hour trying to think of something charming and witty to say and then forgot everything I planned. Please, don't make it any harder on me."

"Okay, I'm going to ease your mind. I, Ariel, would love to go to dinner with you, Jimmy. It's a—what's it called? Oh yeah, it's a *date*!"

"Thank God! I was about to pass out."

Then they both laughed and talked for the next hour.

They met at Au Bord de la Riviere, a French restaurant with a river view. Jimmy arrived first and asked for a table on the open deck. It was a pleasant, late spring night with a slight chill. The tower space heaters provided just enough warmth to make it comfortable, and strings of soft lighting contributed to the ambience. When Ariel arrived and was shown to the table, Jimmy stood to greet her.

"You're a romantic," Ariel said. "It suits you."

She sat. They both started speaking at the same time, smiled, and Jimmy motioned for Ariel to go first. They talked about their childhood, about the pets they had when they were little kids, about Ariel's first kitten, and about Hank. When the waiter arrived, they confessed that they had not yet looked at the menu and asked for a few more minutes.

They laughed about their first high school crushes. Ariel thought that her Spanish teacher was the most gorgeous man she had ever seen; Jimmy admitted that every boy in junior high was sure that their history teacher was a movie star.

They talked about their favorite food, the foods they hated, their families' Christmas and Easter traditions. When the waiter returned, they sheepishly told him they hadn't yet decided, then rushed through selections. After dinner, they lingered over coffee, Jimmy's chocolate cake and Ariel's bread pudding, until they saw the maître d' eyeing them as if he needed their table.

"I guess we should go," said Ariel. "Now listen, you better call me again."

"Oh, I will," said Jimmy.

On his way home, Jimmy realized that they had not once mentioned Dawn River.

Jimmy called the next day.

Several weeks later, after dinner at Au Bord de la Riviere, which had become "their place," they sat at an overlook nearby, moonlight gracing the river in front of them as they made out in Jimmy's jeep like two infatuated teens.

“You know,” said Ariel, “I think we’re going steady.”

“I believe we are,” said Jimmy. “I guess I’m going to have to get you a friendship ring.”

FOUR SHOT ON ST. CLAUDE AVE.; 11 SHOT IN NEW ORLEANS SINCE FRIDAY NIGHT

nola.com

Louisiana

76.
STATE CAPITAL

THE IMPOSING STATE CAPITAL BUILDING was neoclassical in design. Neoclassical was frequently chosen as the architectural style of government buildings in the United States because it called to mind the history of Greco-Roman participatory democracies. Its literal crowning glory was a copper dome that reflected the morning sun onto the stairs leading to the building's entrance, designed to warm and welcome all who brought their business there.

Amos Turner was not there to marvel at the building or the domed ceiling. The dignity of the venue might inspire awe in others, moving visitors to whisper to one another, the slapping of their steps on the marble floor the only audible sound in the rotunda. To Turner, it was one more representation of the government's self-aggrandizement, taxing people to build monuments to itself and the insufferable bureaucrats who conspired behind closed doors.

Sixty, overweight, pocked-marked face, short stature, Turner did not immediately inspire confidence or respect. But he recognized that his was a commanding presence when he aggressively espoused a two-issue platform: get government off our backs and leave our guns alone. It was a popular message in his rural county, hit hard by the recession. He parlayed his rhetoric and the zealousness of a true believer into a term as a county commissioner, then one in the state assembly, where he expected to overturn water restrictions and even the already weak state gun laws.

"You can all go to hell!" was the ending of his farewell remarks in the assembly. His anger had exhausted his constituents, and he embarrassed them when the bank foreclosed on his feed store and he was found to have run the inherited shop into the ground. He was censured by the assembly and lost his bid for reelection. To Turner, it was one more story of villainous overreach, and he was the victim. Then, when Barratt announced that he was taking the guns away, Turner climbed his soapbox again and was revered as a prophet. When William James Percy IV reached out to him, Turner eagerly threw in with him, knowing that Percy was better funded, was better armed, and had a higher profile.

Turner knew the history of the capitol building: destroyed once by fire, then rebuilt in the late 1800s. Tiles from the floors of the original building—blues and reds and greens and browns—were used to create imposing mosaics on the walls of the rotunda. The mosaics depicted the state's farming history, indigenous tribes, and several of the founding fathers. They even displayed a mountainous backdrop fronted by a lush valley.

"Bullshit," Turner called it. "Anybody seen any mountains around here?" He had been speaking to flatland farmers who laughed along with him, then cheered when he called it one more government lie.

The capitol building was the pride of the state, deluged during the academic year by school tours and in the summers by tourists from around the region. When fully open, it housed some four hundred employees, including the governor's staff and the offices of the state's departments. It was a powerful symbol of American governance.

That's why it was also a perfect target for the Defenders of the Way.

Barratt's address to the nation energized Turner and attracted similarly resentful anti-government men and women from the region to his side. He formed the Defenders of the Way, now essentially a de facto subsidiary of Percy's True Americans, and whose mission he described as fighting back against government overreach. Barratt's intention to take his guns away was the impetus that pushed him from angry speeches and talk radio appearances to aggressive action. With Percy's enthusiastic support, Turner had a plan for the state capitol building that would, he believed, send the appropriate message.

His second-in-command had originally proposed to act on July 4, with all the attendant symbolism they would be able to claim, but someone finally recognized that the governmental buildings would be closed. Someone else complained that the early celebrations of independence were modeled on the British celebrations of the king's birthday, the exact wrong kind of symbolism. Turner decided that a day in November, the month in 1776 when the Declaration of Independence was actually delivered to King George, was the right time to act. Thus, on a crisp November morning, the Defenders of the Way made their statement.

Their surveillance had revealed that the building opened at 7:00 a.m., but most workers did not start their day until eight o'clock. The Governor rarely was in the capitol before 9:00 a.m., but his ambitious lieutenant governor, a darling of the media, was typically one of the early arrivals, along with mid-managers and the sheriff's officers who provided security. The Defenders decided on an early morning attack when many of the staff were still using their first cup of caffeine to wake up. Their scrutiny also disclosed that the ornate main entrance and the building's rear entrance were the only ones with metal detectors and armed personnel.

There were also three supposed-to-be-always-locked side entrances, which basically acted as shortcuts for employees leaving the building. Their other use, Turner learned, was for smokers to prop open a door and expel their smoke, thus avoiding the dank smokers' enclosure outside the rear entrance.

A buxom blonde, whom the Defenders had code-named "Mamie," was the habitual violator, using the north side door. It was mostly obscured by the holly trees that lined that entrance. Mamie stood there this morning. Turner watched as she used her left foot to prop the door open and poked her head out just enough to exhale.

The Defenders knew that she never could start the day without one last smoke. And, instead of securing the door before she returned to her desk, she always blocked the door open with a small rock that she kept to the side of the doorway. They also knew that the two guards who had the front entrance duty Wednesday through Friday were the most sleepy-eyed and easily distracted.

The Defenders attacked on a Thursday.

They had slowly infiltrated the area surrounding the building in the very early morning, and lingered unseen. Now, two of Turner's best approached Mamie's door. They stepped gingerly. They weren't wearing their typical combat fatigues, no equipment belts, no holstered sidearms. Instead, one wore a dark suit and a dress shirt with the collar unbuttoned. His muscled upper body struggled against the restrictions of this different type of uniform. The other, rail thin, wore black jeans and a conservative sweater. They did not expect to be seen as employees but, if seen at all, would look like nervous visitors arriving well before their appointment times.

Once in the building, they moved confidently, having studied a schematic of the layout. They walked at a normal pace past several shuffling workers and toward the front entrance. As anticipated, they saw one sheriff's officer seated at the side of the metal detector, holding a partially eaten egg sandwich in one hand and lifting a steaming cup of coffee in the other. The second officer was nearby, laughing at something on his cell phone. Both had their backs toward the Defenders. The two cadre members moved stealthily toward the officers, quickening their pace, each holding a tactical knife that they had removed from an ankle sheath. When they were within five feet, the seated officer felt their presence and half turned in his chair.

"Hey," he said, seemingly unconcerned. "Where did you guys—" He stopped abruptly as he saw the two long-bladed knives. "Hey!" he now shouted as he rose from his seat, dropping the sandwich and spilling the coffee. "Mike!" he yelled to the other officer. Mike turned and reached for his sidearm. Neither was fast enough. Without a word, each of the Defenders stepped in tight and sunk a knife up to the hilt in an officer's neck, covering his mouth with their offhand as they did so, then lowered the officers to the floor.

Then they stepped to the front entrance doors and opened them, as ten more casually dressed but heavily armed men materialized out of the decorative shrubbery along the building's side and entered the capitol, Turner in the lead. Simultaneously, several more entered through Mamie's door. It was the first time that Turner had been back since he had stomped out of the assembly chamber on his last day. He had returned to settle the score. Many of the officials who had been in the capitol when he was in the assembly were gone, but, to Turner's way of thinking, anyone there was fair game.

The Defenders barraged through the rotunda, unaffected by the solemnity. They proceeded as they had rehearsed. Three teams dispersed. They each had a destination: one to the Records Office, one to the attorney general's rooms, another to Environmental Protection. Turner marched his own team up the elegant stairway that led to the second-floor administrative offices. When he reached the landing, he fingered his mic and spoke one word: "Go."

That's when the shooting started.

Early arrivals poured out of second-floor offices at the sound of the chaos. Most who saw the armed men approaching turned and ran for the far exit stairs. Some, in their confusion, ran toward the gunfire. None of them survived.

Turner strode to the lieutenant governor's office and pushed open the door. He marched past a secretary, cowering in the footwell of a desk, and reached a locked inner office. After trying the handle, he stepped back, raised one foot, and smashed it against the door. The jamb shattered and the door was flung open. The lieutenant governor was standing behind his desk, frantically fumbling with a set of keys as he tried to unlock a side desk drawer. Finally, he ripped it open and pulled out a small, short-barreled revolver, but dropped it when Turner fired a dozen rounds into the room's ceiling.

"I am Commandant Amos M. Turner of the Defenders of the Way and a supporter of William James Percy," Turner announced. "This state has defiled the Second Amendment. We real Americans will not tolerate that. You are part of the price that must be paid for this abomination."

The lieutenant governor, eyes wide, frozen in place, raised his hands and extended them, palms out. "Wait," he cried. "Wait, I—"

Whatever else he might have said never made it past his lips. Turner had levelled his AK-15 and emptied the rest of the clip, shattering the photos and diplomas on the back wall, the mementos on the credenza, and the man standing behind the desk.

Turner exited the room, his men following behind. As he descended the stairs, the other teams were entering the rotunda, each announcing that they had accomplished their part of the attack. They moved toward the exit doors as Turner sprayed a fresh clip along the rotunda walls, decimating the mosaics, and fired a volley into the domed ceiling, heavy chunks of plaster crashing onto the previously pristine floor. Before he went through a side door to join his men and melt into the surrounding compound and alleyways, he placed a large white envelope on top of the debris on the floor.

It was addressed simply to "Barratt."

EIGHT SHOT, INJURED AT CARIBBEAN CARNIVAL PARADE IN DORCHESTER

WBUR
Boston

77.
BARRATT

BARRATT WAS IN A SMALL conference room where he, General Samson, FBI Director Morgan, Homeland Security Director Perez, Health and Human Services Director D'Agostino, and their chiefs of staff were reviewing the latest developments.

Barratt read Turner's message out loud: "William James Percy for president. And why wait for an election?"

"This kind of loyalty is always difficult to fathom," said Perez. "History is full of dynamic despots who have cult followings, but, I mean, Percy is the biggest psychopath of them all. They're all murderers, but what he did at Second Home was sick. And now he has all these acolytes? Still hard to believe."

"What I want to know," said Barratt, "is why the mag squads haven't found their camps. Aren't the magnetometers doing their job, or are these cadres finding some way to avoid detection? General?"

"Mr. President, you're correct that the mags are excellent. But we're getting reports that there are some materials that can act as shields, or at least make it more difficult for the mags to do their thing. We're working on it. There's some thought that ceramic coverings are one of the problems. I have DARPA working on a solution, but it could take some time."

"Time is something we don't have enough of, General. And Mr. Morgan, how could the FBI not know where Percy is? He or his followers pop up all over the country—there has to be a trail. What are you doing?"

"Mr. President, we think we've been close several times. We've arrested several of his henchmen—I refuse to call them soldiers—but they won't give him up. And we've had no luck infiltrating. We think he has compounds in remote areas that are the devil to access and has a small but insane percentage of the public that helps hide him and his munitions.

"But he's getting bolder, and from what we hear even more arrogant. We think he's going to try something even bigger, and that means he'll have to come out in the open. That's when we get him."

"Gentleman, this is not good enough. We have the most powerful military and the most sophisticated intelligence operation in the world. And right under our noses Percy's supply chain is working too well. I've read the reports that there's some indication he's supplying some of these other groups, and they're relying on him to lead the way."

"And that means—" Bobby started to say.

Barratt finished the thought. "Yeah, we cut off the head of the snake and the body dies. Find this guy, and put the bastard out of business."

SECOND TEEN SUSPECT ARRESTED IN MINNEAPOLIS "NUDIELAND" MASS SHOOTING THAT KILLED 1, INJURED 6

Minnesota Star Tribune

78.
CHANDLER BOSWORTH

CHANDLER BOSWORTH STOOD at the windows of his 27th-floor office. His law firm occupied the top four floors and owned the building, together with the buildings that housed the firm's offices in New York, Chicago, Houston, Los Angeles, and DC, and facilities in London, Berlin, and Paris.

Through the windows, he looked over the city's high-rises and the waterfront beyond. He had now practiced for over thirty years. When his father, Franklin Bosworth, had the building constructed, its twenty floors were the most permitted by the city; it dominated the skyline then and still did today. The view then was just of warehouses and wholesale produce venues and cheap motels. Now he surveyed upscale steak houses, Omni and Hilton hotels, and headquarters for national insurance companies.

There was also a celebrated waterfront park filled with amenities, including four manicured ball fields with uniformed teams playing in the sunny late afternoon. When he stood here as a ten-year-old, there was one sandlot used by a bunch of ragtag kids. When his father brought him to the office on some Saturday mornings, he would stand at the same windows, wondering what it would be like to join those kids, just walk down and say, "Can I play?"

His father would turn him from the window and point him to the table set up in the corner of the office. "Let's get that homework done," his father would direct.

Those Saturday mornings were one of the few occasions when he had time alone with the senior Bosworth, and a hand on his shoulder if his father checked his work was a rare intimacy. He craved the attention, but when it came so infrequently, he learned to live without.

There followed boarding school, where he was allowed to participate in sports: fencing, tennis, certainly not football or a pick-up basketball game. Those sports were too rife with injuries and unsavory influence. Better not to depend on a team for victory; better to depend on yourself. He followed the script. Went to the same university as his father; went to the same law school.

His one experiment with rebellion came when he fell madly in love with Michelle, an ebullient hippie, all tie-dye and headscarves and Equal Pay protests. Their differences were the attraction. When she convinced him to smoke his first joint, he didn't want to and he didn't like it, but it filled him with an intoxicating sense of independence, doing something his father would never approve of. But when she wanted them to leave the university and head to San Francisco, he panicked. He lost his courage at the thought of being the object of his father's disdain, even disgust, the thought of never proving that he was as good as his father wanted him to be. Michelle went west; he never saw her again.

He turned from his office window and moved to his desk. He appreciated the view, but for him it was more about validation than aesthetics. He had taken the firm from the one office his father had opened and expanded it nationally, then internationally. The desk was uncluttered, but did hold photos of his two children, Charles and Sandra. He glanced at their pictures now. Once he surrendered to the path that his father had chosen for him, he married the right woman and had the expected number of children. He loved them in his own way, he supposed, but his career had become his obsession. Birthdays were missed if he had to travel for business; he attended their graduations but frequently with his cell phone to his ear. When his son came out as gay, he was relieved that he was unlikely to have grandchildren, since his daughter had struggled to conceive. He would be expected to cuddle and dote on a grandchild, but that just wasn't on his agenda.

Then his eyes moved to the photo of the one grandchild he did have, and he gently picked it up. When his daughter turned forty, she miraculously became pregnant by IVF and presented the family with Tanya, a healthy baby girl. When mother and daughter came home from the hospital, Chandler made what he thought would be a perfunctory visit.

Then his daughter placed the infant in his arms. His breath stopped, he felt lightheaded, his stomach jumped. *What is this?* he thought. This perfect, little, helpless thing he held, with perfect fingers and perfect toes and a face in which he insisted he saw himself. Years of lost intimacy suddenly smothered him with regret; he literally flushed and shook as his lost opportunity to share in the lives of his own young children accosted him. As he held his granddaughter in his arms, Chandler's heart melted, flowed down his chest, and enveloped this tiny being. He never owned his heart again.

Poppi Chandler and Tanya became best friends. He replaced business flights to the coasts with Zoom calls so he could make Tanya's birthdays, surprising his daughter by arranging for ponies and clowns and the moon bounce. Insisting that Tanya accompany him and Mom-Mom on trips to the national parks, sometimes with her parents but without them was okay too. He discovered he didn't have to work sixteen-hour days. He had more important things to do.

He replaced Tanya's photo on the desk, his eyes moist, his lips quivering. He still lost himself in her, but now he was limited to memories.

He laughed at the saying that memories fade with time; his images of her and his joy at spoiling her never really left him. All these years after she was taken from him at Dawn River, he still sunk into melancholy whenever he lingered too long in her memory's embrace.

He was at the same desk when Elijah Barratt reached out to him after Dawn River. Against his nature, he agreed to meet, and he recalled how they went straight to deep inside, touching places they had been trying to bury, opening up to a partner in grief. And when Barratt described his audacious, stunning, impossible plan, Chandler had realized that it was the perfect response to Dawn River.

The phone on his desk buzzed and his secretary told him that his eleven o'clock client was in the conference room. Chandler rose from his chair and moved toward his office door. He would never be whole again without Tanya, but he had survived the years since Dawn River by nurturing the plan Barratt had planted within him.

And now, at long last, it was time to act.

POLICE: 9 INJURED, SUSPECT DEAD AFTER SPLASH PAD SHOOTING IN ROCHESTER HILLS

Detroit Free Press

79.
BARRATT

BARRATT KNEW THE COMPOSITION of the Supreme Court could determine the success or failure of The Plan. He had inherited a Supreme Court with a five-four conservative majority.

But, thought Barratt, his immediate predecessor, President Evelyn Bostic, had made a strategic mistake. When an opening occurred during her term, she had appointed her mentor, seventy-eight-year-old staunch conservative and gun rights champion Joseph Nichols, as the chief justice and the swing vote. The word was that she did so despite his advanced age and frail health, mostly to honor him and enhance his legacy. Apparently, she was so confident of winning a second term that, if Nichols passed, she figured to appoint a like-minded successor.

Not so fast, Barratt mused. *He* resided in the Oval Office when Justice Nichols passed away. While he didn't celebrate the death of a respected jurist, he saw it as one more "too much to be a coincidence" sign that he was on the right track. Taking advantage of the circumstances, he appointed Chandler Bosworth as the new Chief Justice and changed the direction of the court.

Barratt had been before the Supreme Court twice. The first time was when he was admitted to practice there, a purely ceremonial act. Barratt and Lucy had taken the train to Union Station and walked to the Supreme Court Building during a perfectly crisp fall morning.

He had worn a long black wool coat and a blue scarf against the chill. Lucy's coat was red, and her bright blue tam was cocked rakishly to one side. He had never felt so cosmopolitan, striding through the most important city in the world, actually being a part of it in some small way.

Barratt later sat in the courtroom for the swearing-in, with about ninety other attorneys, eligible simply because they had practiced for five years. He kept a photo of Lucy and him standing on the courthouse steps after the proceeding, placing it on the credenza in the Oval Office. As the years passed, he would gaze at it from time to time and see an impossibly young, naive, happy couple, totally unaware of the burden that he would one day bear.

Excited to be a part of that tradition, Barratt had learned as much as he could about the Supreme Court Building. He knew that it had been designed by architect Cass Gilbert, famous for being one of the first to conceive of skyscrapers, designing the Woolworth Building and various state capitols. He noticed that the structures he designed were massive and dignified and decorated with a multitude of sculptured images. Not surprisingly, then, the courtroom itself was large, some eighty feet by ninety feet, with a ceiling forty feet high. Coupled with the dramatically elevated mahogany justices' bench and the heavy oaken entry doors, the effect caused him to feel the intended gravitas. Barratt left that day feeling proud but rather insignificant, dwarfed by the grandeur and the history of Supreme Court decisions that had changed life in America.

The second time, some years later, he represented minority homeowners resisting a city's exercise of eminent domain. He was no longer overwhelmed. He took time to appreciate the friezes that adorned the building: King John sealing the Magna Carta and Lord Coke barring King James from sitting as a judge. *Talk about making an impression*, thought Barratt. That day he was relaxed, felt that he belonged there, and confident that his argument was solid, and he expected the justices to agree.

He was quickly disabused of that idea.

"Mr. Barratt, doesn't the city have the right to act for the benefit of the entire populace?"

"Yes, your honor, but it must act rationally, reasonably. Here, the facility doesn't have to be sited in this historic minority neighborhood."

"But hasn't the city shown the need for the recycling facility? Isn't that a rational exercise of its power? Wouldn't any location cause complaints by those who live nearby?"

Then the questions came fast and furiously. Barratt knew that whichever attorney the justices targeted was in trouble, and he was in their sights. He left with his face reddened and his ego bruised. And feeling even more insignificant.

That was then.

He was a different man now. He had been through too much to be intimidated anymore. He would come before the court as the leader of a co-equal branch of the government, destined to make history himself. He was alternately mesmerized by and practically nonbelieving of how Dawn River was the impetus for changes that affected the entire country. He would never have thought of running for president if that tragedy had not compelled him to do so, but here he improbably was. And *he* was the one who had turned the court toward a different judicial philosophy.

As he prepared for the showdown before the Supreme Court, he had been attacked by some in the media and accused of being an authoritarian: "Radical Renegade," "A Stalin, an Orbán," "Demented Demon," "Someone Help This Man!" They tripped over themselves trying to come up with the most creative appellation.

He vigorously defended himself against the accusations, but in recent quiet moments he wondered. He *was* leaving Congress behind and pressing forward. They didn't have the guts to act, he rationalized, but he did. They refused to recognize the urgency; so many screechy Neros fiddling while the country descended into anarchy.

Still, he sometimes asked himself: *What comes after?* What precedent will he have set? Could he protect democracy and still save the nation, or was it an "either/or"? If so, how could he—how could anyone—choose? And who the hell was *he* to make that choice for four hundred million people? How could he proceed with a clear conscience and do what he knew needed to be done?

What kept him on course when these questions started insisting on answers were the bloodied images of the victims, collapsed on the steps of their homes, slumped over tables at outdoor cafés, splayed on a nightclub floor like so many used napkins or spilled cups, tiny bodies under tiny tables, like little dolls with eyes sewn shut forever.

SHOOTING OF PALESTINIAN COLLEGE STUDENTS CAME AMID SPIKE IN GUN VIOLENCE

Burlington Free Press

80.
BARRATT

THE NINE JUSTICES of the Supreme Court of the United States peered down from their high bench at the front of the courtroom. Even though the first Chief Justice, John Jay, had indulged his sense of style by wearing a robe with red and white piping on the sleeves and Ruth Bader Ginsburg fancied lace collars, historically the justices had worn all-black robes for over two hundred years. The height at which they sat, and the somber black attire, made for an imposing appearance, dark and foreboding.

President Elijah Barratt sat at the defendant's table with Raphael. Joseph Howard was at the plaintiff's table. He was lead counsel for the five states that had filed suit against Barratt individually and as president of the United States. Two of the states' attorneys general and three of Howard's junior partners sat with him. Arrayed behind him were eight other plaintiffs' attorneys, all attired in severe dark suits, starched white shirts, and red or blue or yellow power ties.

"Well," Barratt whispered to Raphael, "they certainly have us outnumbered."

Raphael responded with a smirk.

Bobby, Lucy, and Gabrielle sat in the audience behind Barratt. He had advised his other aides and supporters *not* to attend. He wanted the image of the proceeding to be that of the Lone Ranger facing down the bad guys, the solitary hero standing his ground.

Both sides had submitted their briefs to the court and were now present for oral argument on Barratt's motion to dismiss the case. The states insisted that the Posse Comitatus Act, which limits the president's authority to use the military domestically, prevented Barratt from deploying the armed forces to enforce his policy. Raphael and Barratt had briefed his response, countering that the Insurrection Act empowered the president to direct the military to suppress civil disorder, insurrection, or rebellion. He further argued that the states individually were unable to deal with the violence and thus caused the deprivation of their citizens' civil rights.

Barratt was used to being the advocate, the one who argued in front of the judges. He was not used to sitting silently while someone spoke for him, as his plan—*The Plan*—was challenged, he was maligned, and his future very much hung in the balance. This was the first time that *he* was the defendant, the one whose fate was about to be decided. *This is different,* he thought. *I don't like it.*

Barratt had seen the look of confidence on Howard's face when they had walked into the courtroom and shook hands before taking their seats. He understood his sense of assurance; precedent was certainly on his side. But Barratt's own sense of confidence was buoyed by the way the Justices were handling the oral argument.

Consistent with the court's protocol, each party was allotted a half-hour to make its argument. The court had exercised its original jurisdiction. Ordinarily, it would have appointed a "Special Master" to develop the facts and submit a report before hearing oral argument, but the court in this case, given the extraordinary urgency and important consequences involved, had accepted lengthy affidavits instead.

Howard, speaking on behalf of the plaintiffs, went first. He was tall, lean, and silver-haired, articulate and patrician. Barratt knew that

Howard had appeared before the Supreme Court many times and generally had the respect of the justices, who usually allowed him to speak without interruption for the first ten minutes of his argument. This time, however, they started to pepper him with questions almost as soon as he started speaking. Howard looked taken aback; Barratt was almost as surprised. He knew it was not a good sign for the states.

"Mr. Howard," said Justice Blessing, "the five states you represent have the five highest per-capita murder rates in the country. Doesn't that show that they are unable to protect the rights of their citizens, and isn't that inability an exception to the Posse Comitatus Act?"

"Your Honor," Howard responded, "these states have not had a realistic opportunity to demonstrate their ability to control the situation. Nothing has shown that they can't do so."

"This is not a new development," Justice Blessing countered. "These states have had this dubious distinction for years. Two of them have had more mass shootings over the last decade than twenty other states combined."

Barratt could feel the justices' badgering raise the tension even more. He didn't feel sorry for Howard, but he did feel empathy; he had been there.

Justice Norelli joined in. "Whether your clients can't or won't control the situation is a difference without a distinction," he said. "This didn't start with the president's announcement. Indeed, the United States argues that the policy announced only became necessary because of the states' failures."

"Your Honors," said Howard, "many states are in a situation similar to my clients'. Our system permits—indeed, encourages—the states to pursue various strategies specific to their own different situations."

Barratt knew that Howard, struggling to turn the tide, had opened himself up. He turned and looked at Bobby, who slightly raised his eyebrows, sending a "this is really happening" signal. Barratt was careful not to make any facial expression in reply and directed his gaze back to the argument.

"Mr. Howard," the chief justice intoned. The other justices turned and looked at Chandler Bosworth. He typically did not question the attorneys until the other justices had all had their opportunities. The chief justice paused for a beat, then restarted. "Mr. Howard," he said, "you are making the government's case for it. If so many states are dealing with the same problem, and none of them are having any success, then clearly it is a national problem requiring a federal response, since the states are unable or unwilling to find a solution."

Barratt's respect for Chandler Bosworth had only grown over the years. In another time and place, Barratt thought, they could have been good friends. Their respect for the law, their love for their families, their humble recognition that people who can make a difference should—they had much in common. But he had assiduously eschewed any close personal relationship. Barratt believed this day would come, and he was not about to create a friendship that could lead to questions about Bosworth's integrity.

Barratt watched the back-and-forth between Howard and the court continue through Howard's allotted time. He was sensing that the sweat and tears, the angst and anxiety, the suffering and survival, the determination and the commitment that had consumed his life since the night of Dawn River had brought his work to fruition. It was his turn now to make his argument.

Barratt felt the huge courtroom shrinking. The almost unbearable weight of what he was doing suddenly pressed down on his shoulders, a lead-lined vest pinning him to his seat. He was in a cave, no one else was there, tons of earth loomed above him. Despite how well it was going, anything could still happen. Would the cave roof hold, or would it come crashing down, burying him alive? Raphael's voice jolted him back to the courtroom.

"Mr. Chief Justice, distinguished justices," Raphael began, "if it please the court, the states have just admitted that the circumstances of this case are *exactly* the basis for military intervention. The Insurrection Act contemplates it and the need to protect the people compels it." He reviewed the statistics contained in their brief; the affidavits of law enforcement officials around the country describing their unsuccessful efforts to tame this whirlwind of violence; the economists' and the sociologists' affidavits describing the debilitating impact that the violence had had in cities and towns all over the country.

Howard looked crestfallen as few questions were directed at Raphael. Then, somewhat anticlimactically, the hearing was over. The chief justice promised an expedited review and decision. The justices rose as one, the audience and litigants doing the same. The courtroom was deathly quiet, Barratt thinking that Howard must see it as a massive, threatening dark wave about to consume him.

Barratt felt that he was riding its crest.

Chief Justice Bosworth had promised a quick decision. One week after the hearing, the court announced its five-to-four decision: the case against Elijah Barratt, individually and as president, and against the United States, was dismissed. This being the imprimatur of the highest court in the land, there was no appeal.

The Plan had survived. It was now full go.

3 TEEN GIRLS SHOT, ONE KILLED, AFTER FIGHT BREAKS OUT AT PARTY IN COLORADO PARK

CBS News

81.
SANCTUARY STATE

THEY HAD RISEN BEFORE DAWN and loaded onto school buses, into RVs and carpools, onto rented public transit buses. The vehicles were emblazoned with all manner of signs, but with a consistent theme: our lives are more important than your guns. They left so early because they had a four-hour ride. They were heading into one of those so-called "sanctuary states," states that had vowed not to enforce the new gun rules.

Ariel had called on them to join her, and they did.

A group of high school students occupied the back of one of the buses. Their parents sat up front. Other transport carried ex-military, retirees, and parents with children as young as five years old. The mood was upbeat. Teachers joked with their students; students were curious and excited to see their teachers out of the classroom, dressed in casual clothes. The adults on one bus brought their guitars and jammed a country/folk theme. The teens on another bus rapped a raucous favorite song. The occasional horn toot from a passing vehicle elicited hoots and cheers and enthusiastic waves.

As they crossed the state line, the adults became more subdued. Each bus carried a volunteer attorney to counsel and defend in case any arrests were threatened or made, even though the proper permits had been obtained. They also carried volunteer EMTs, just in case.

The more somber mood eventually settled onto the younger protesters. When the group was within forty minutes of their destination, the buses went silent, except for the low murmurings from the bowed heads of the leaders. They were some of what were expected to be hundreds of buses headed for Patriots Park, in the middle of downtown, in the largest city in this sanctuary state. As they drove closer to the park, they saw more and more buses feeding in from other roadways, a kaleidoscope of orange and blue and silver.

Patriots Park encompassed over sixty acres. It included two small lakes with paddle boat rentals, playgrounds, outdoor exercise trails, and various picnic areas. On a Sunday such as this, it would have been crowded with happy families and boisterous children, the smell of charcoal fires wafting over the fields. But today, in anticipation of what was to come, the park was practically empty. That is, until people started to disembark from the buses. Directed by volunteer patrols, the vehicles unloaded their passengers near the park's amphitheater, then moved on to allow the next bus to do the same, a process that took over three hours.

The protesters streamed in, jockeying for a good spot. The park amphitheater could hold only a tiny portion of the people, and now the rest spread out onto the surrounding grasses, near the video screens set up there. The speakers' podium at the front of the amphitheater was populated by representatives of many of the anti-gun activist groups. They included survivors of gun violence, mourners of lost family members, officials from schools that had been attacked, staff from businesses that had been attacked, owners of nightclubs that had been attacked.

The police were present everywhere, and it was reported that the National Guard was on standby.

As the noon start of the presentation neared, much of the chaotic scene started to settle. Even the vendors selling *Trust the Plan* t-shirts (they had boxes of t-shirts with messages like *You'll Only Take My Gun*

From My Cold, Dead Hands back in their vans, waiting for a different rally) paused for a moment.

Ariel's eyes roamed the crowd as she waited for people to spread throughout the venue. Her eyes rested on a girl of about thirteen wearing a Patty hat, all pink and sequined, one of the ones that Ariel had designed and sold to support her work. And almost like the one that Patty had worn to the Dawn River concert, and Ariel had worn when she addressed Patty's homeroom class.

Ariel smiled at the girl with the Patty hat, received a smile and wave in return, then looked over the rest of the huge rally crowd. She saw more pink hats, worn by women of all ages, some worn by men.

The buses had emptied.

It was time to begin.

82.
SANCTUARY STATE

ARIEL LEFT THE CIRCLE OF PEOPLE on the speakers' platform and approached the microphone as the others took their seats. She paused and, while there were murmured conversations throughout the crowd, the people seated in the amphitheater and most of the rest of the crowd gave her their attention.

"We are here today to mourn for our friends and families who have been lost to gun violence," she started. "We are here to give our empathy to the survivors. We are here to celebrate those who are working tirelessly against this plague." Her voice was measured and steady. Then it rose in intensity and volume when she said: "And we are here today to make sure that President Elijah Barratt's Plan succeeds!" The crowd cheered and whistled.

One speaker after another echoed her talking points and rallied the crowd, damning the sanctuary state they were standing in, challenging it to change its laws and protect its people. The crowd needed very little urging. Their energy was contagious. They periodically broke into chants: "No more guns, no more killing"; "Let children live."

An hour into the rally, there was a murmuring on the edges of the crowd. It spread throughout the assemblage and stopped the current speaker in mid-sentence. People now started looking toward the perimeter of the crowd. Police officers ringed that perimeter, but beyond them the rallygoers could see another line. That line was made up of men in camouflage clothing, pistols holstered on their sides, long guns resting in their arms. They had no insignias, no logos, no markings of any kind. The police officers knew that no other permit had been issued for a protest or rally or march. But at this point the police were heavily outnumbered, at least three to one.

The speaker tried to resume his remarks. The men in camouflage had made no advance, shouted no epithets, displayed no signs. The speaker faltered just the same.

Ariel strode to the podium, put her arm around the speaker's shoulder, and gently moved him away from the microphone.

"This is what we are fighting against!" she shouted as she pointed a steady finger at the gunned-up counter-protesters. "They are here because they know we are right and we are strong and they are wrong. We will not be intimidated!"

Despite her conviction, there was palpable tension in the crowd and in some of the younger patrolmen. One of the officers posted on the perimeter spoke in a stage whisper to one of the men in camouflage: "Dale, what are you doing here?"

His partner, positioned next to him, looked at him with surprise. "Mark! Do you know this guy?"

Mark responded: "He…uh…I…I knew him in high school."

His partner grabbed him by the shoulders and turned him away. "Mark, man, stay away from these guys. These are bad dudes."

Then, in an orchestrated manner, as if a silent signal had been passed, the men in camouflage, none of whom had yet spoken, gripped their rifles by the barrels and began to rhythmically smack the butt ends on the ground. Not exactly the Celtic war trumpet or the Germanic war cry, but it had the same elemental effect as those ancient tactics. The sound was concussive and deafening. The rallygoers started to withdraw further into the center of the park. The police officers were becoming disoriented. The waves of sound angrily washed over them, battering their chests and ears. But the advantage of those in camouflage would be short-lived.

This was Colonel Sharp's region, and his was one of the largest territories to patrol. However, using dynamic positioning, he had staged his squads at locations that allowed them to quickly descend on trouble spots, and he had anticipated that this would be one. No individual squad was large enough by itself to control a large crowd, but massed together several of them would be intimidating. Sharp had several of his men undercover in the park and they had radioed him the status. While the rhythmic stomping continued, the cavalry was on its way.

Soon, the cacophony of the beating rifle butts suddenly had competition: the roar of the deuce-and-a-half transports, Humvees, and battle jeeps. The olive-colored vehicles raced to stops along the line of anonymously uniformed men; Sharp's troops deployed immediately. They set up in a line around the counter-protesters. The anti-rally group was now literally between a rock and a hard place: they were inside a cordon with the police on one side and the US troops on the other. Sharp thumbed his mic and spoke to headquarters: "Inform the General that we have reached the rally and we have them surrounded, squeezed between the police line and us. But...they are armed. Repeat, they are armed."

General Pappas responded himself: "Say again, Colonel."

"General, they are armed. AKs, sidearms…I don't see any bigger weapons, but they're all carrying something."

"We knew that this region wasn't completely cleared, but where the hell have they been keeping all of the armament? Tell me, Colonel, what is your assessment?"

"General, we can neutralize them, that's certain. But with the officers on the other side and the civilian protesters beyond, there will be significant casualties. Still, we do have them right here."

There was a pause on the General's end. He knew that every person there was a potential spark that could ignite a deadly firefight. Any shouted threat, any mistaken movement, any pointed gun could set it off. His orders were to seize the arms, but with as little loss of life as possible.

"Colonel Sharp, do they realize their disadvantage and predicament?"

"No doubt, General. They're looking around at each other, waiting for someone to get them out of this. They weren't counting on us being here this quickly."

"Okay. Colonel, here's what I want you to do. Order them to disperse. Tell them they do not have a permit and are in violation of the ordinance. Say 'ordinance,' not 'law.'"

"What about the weapons?"

"Don't mention them. Don't refer to the executive orders. I'm betting they'll be eager to take the opportunity to withdraw. The protesters won't like it, but I don't want a civilian bloodbath. And this is what else you're going to do. Direct the detectives to follow at a distance and find out where they reassemble. They are not to engage. Tell them to send us the coordinates. The strike team will be assembled from here. After they leave, you withdraw but stay close by."

Each of the squads had four plainclothes detectives attached, always positioned discreetly away from the center of the conflict. They were each mounted on a Whisper ATV, ready to track whoever they needed to track, and quietly, on road or off.

Colonel Sharp did as ordered. He switched to the mounted loudspeakers and addressed the intruders: "I am Colonel Sharp, the officer in charge of this region. I hereby inform you that you are in violation of the city ordinance controlling protest gatherings. You do not have a permit for an assembly or the use of this park for that purpose. You are directed"—he purposely avoided saying "ordered"—"to vacate this area."

No one moved. Not the militia, not the police, the soldiers, or the people in the rally. The squirrels, which had taken to the high trees and had been screeching at the protesters, went silent. The geese in the nearby pond stopped honking. The silence was heavy, palpable. Every living thing had tensed, preparing for fight or flight.

One minute passed, then two.

Sharp engaged the sound system again: “I repeat, you are directed to disperse.” He hesitated, realizing that he had to move beyond this stalemate. He continued: “You have three minutes to comply.”

Another minute passed. Then the man who appeared to be leading the group squinted his eyes, as if a sudden realization had occurred to him.

Nothing was said about surrendering weapons, he thought. They could walk away, keeping everything that they had brought with them. No harm, no foul. They weren’t going to win any fight that was started here, with his men surrounded. He nodded to the men on either side of him, and they passed the nod along. Slowly, one man moved toward one of the openings that Sharp’s troops had left. Two more followed, then three, then groups until they were all leaving the field. After passing the army line, the groups diverged down various side streets, simply walking away.

Sharp exhaled. The bloodbath had been avoided. He feared that a civil war was all but inevitable, but it wouldn’t start today, and he wouldn’t be the one who started it.

His moment of comfort was short-lived.

83.
SANCTUARY STATE

THE SANCTUARY STATE PROTESTERS were at first relieved. Then they saw that the armed men were strolling away, still carrying all their firearms.

"Hey!" Ariel shouted into the podium mic. "Wait! They still have their rifles! They still have their pistols! You're supposed to take them from them! Come on!"

Sharp did not respond. He was not about to say anything about what was now an ongoing interdiction operation. He raised his arm and circled his index finger in the air. His forces began their withdrawal.

"What's going on?" Ariel rarely lost her composure, but she was livid. "Come back here!" But Sharp only keyed his shoulder mic and reported the status to headquarters.

From their positions away from the crowd, the Whisper ATVs silently moved out. Lead Detective Lloyd hand-signaled the other three riders. They each headed down one of the side roads that the group had taken. The Whisper ATVs were perfect for this type of surveillance: low-profile, baffled to the point of being almost silent running. Each ATV was equipped with state-of-the-art GPS, a satellite phone, and a rifle sheath holding a semi-automatic weapon. They had run-flat tires and spotting and flood lights, in addition to headlights, which could tilt low-level to allow the driver to see but not be seen from distance. Although each could carry a driver and a rider, they were all singled now.

Lloyd followed at a discreet distance. The group he was following was about a half mile from the park when he saw them load into the ubiquitous small Toyota pickups, these painted black. He still saw no insignias, no logos, nothing that provided identification.

They moved out rapidly and Lloyd accelerated to keep pace. He anticipated—hoped—that his group would join up with the others and that he could track them all to whatever compound they were using. He drove out of the city and now past houses, scattered farms, and finally heavily wooded low hills. Since there was no other traffic on the road, he dropped back a little. He was confident he had not been spotted, but, he thought, better safe than very sorry.

Then the trucks slowed to a stop. Two men exited the lead truck and moved what he could now see was a gate covered with branches and shrubs that completely camouflaged it. They lifted it on a hinge and turned it out of the way to reveal a single-track vehicle path heading into the trees. They got back into the truck and headed into the woods. The last truck went in, but no one stopped to close the gate. Why not? Then engine noise got his attention. It came from behind him and in front of him further south. He whipped his vehicle off the road and into the woods as deep as he could quickly get. And just in time.

Two lines of the pickups approached, one from the north behind him and one from the south. He dismounted the ATV and stood behind a large pine tree. The pickups met at the entrance to the trees and drove through until they were all in, two men from the last truck closing the gate behind them. Unless you knew that the gate was there, realized Lloyd, you would never see it.

Minutes later, the other three ATVs silently swept into the area. Lloyd clicked his mic and told his men to stay put, then exited the trees and joined them.

"I'm going to follow them on foot," he advised. "Find some cover in these trees. Anybody goes in, let me know. Anybody comes out, trail them, and let me know your positions. And, hey, there's a mess of them. Make sure that one of them has closed that gate"—he pointed it out to them—"before you take off. There could be more than one group heading out. Stay alert. Go." Lloyd turned and walked back into the woods as the other detectives maneuvered their vehicles away.

He reached his Whisper and removed the binoculars. He had his sidearm and his tactical knife, but he left the rifle behind. The trees were thick here; it would be hard enough to maneuver without trying to have his long gun at the ready. Besides, his orders were to find and report, not engage. He headed out.

The grade up was steeper than it had looked from the roadway, and the going was tough. Keeping the vehicle path to his right, he could just see enough of it to use it as a guide and pushed upward for five minutes, ten. He heard birdsong and squirrels screeching, leaves rustling with small animals. No engine noises, no camp noises. The sun was still high in the sky. It could have been a peaceful walk in the woods, except for what he figured he would find deep in the forest. He continued climbing, now fifteen minutes in. He crested the hill.

He heard the camp before he saw it: faint voices, equipment banging as it was moved, vehicles being repositioned. The view was limited by the pine trees and their full branches. He moved cautiously down the hill toward the sounds. Finally, he reached a spot where he figured he couldn't be seen from the camp, but he could peer around and through the branches and get a good view. "Damn," he whispered to himself. "That's pretty fuckin' big."

Down in a clearing at the foot of the hill, surrounded on all sides by other tree-covered hills, was the camp. It spread out for hundreds of feet in every direction. What appeared to be the center included one very large Quonset hut and several smaller buildings. There were men in camo everywhere, like buzzing worker bees, only these bees carried long guns. Lloyd could see more pickups; many had weapons mounted on them, belts of high-caliber rounds trailing into ammo boxes. Alongside the small trucks were several jeeps and at least three large trucks; one looked to be a half-track, and that blew his mind. *I guess you could buy anything at a government auction*, he thought, *or at least until Barratt did his thing.*

Then he noticed a somewhat curious operation. The trucks and the jeeps were not being positioned in the compound's yard. Instead, everything was being driven into the big Quonset hut. Curious because, no matter how they positioned the vehicles inside, it would take much longer to load up and get moving then if the vehicles were arrayed in the clearing. Then, even more curious, individual members of the group were walking in and out of the Quonset hut or the smaller buildings. They went in carrying their rifles and packing their side-arms. They came out without them. *What the hell?* Lloyd thought. If these guys wanted those guns in a hurry, there would be chaos inside those buildings.

But wait… In one of his briefings there had been some thought that the groups resisting The Plan had found a way to possibly evade the Super Mags. Supposedly, a thick ceramic covering could make it difficult for a Super Mag to identify what was underneath. Could that be what was going on here? A ceramic roof layer that the Mags couldn't penetrate. He reminded himself that his orders were to observe and report. He removed his GPS from a pocket and checked the location, then he sent the coordinates to HQ. Time to get out of here.

"Going somewhere, asshole?" The voice came from behind him.

Shit, never heard him, Lloyd mouthed silently.

"Stand up, jerk-wad," the voice said.

Some vocabulary, Lloyd thought.

"Now turn around. . .*slowly*...and face me." Lloyd complied. "What the fuck are you doing here?"

84.
SANCTUARY STATE

LLOYD LOOKED UP AT A GIANT. The guy who stood before him had to be six five, maybe three hundred pounds. He wore the same type of fatigues as the men at the rally. His fit snug across a ripped body, muscles bulging under the fabric. He had a bristly thick black beard. In his right hand he held a Glock 17.

"Hey man, I just seen all them trucks driving around and I just got curious. Don't mean nothin'."

"Yeah, you know what curiosity did to the cat, right?"

"Come on, bro, I'm nobody. Just looking around."

"Yeah, with a Glock on your hip and a tac knife strapped to your leg."

Uh-oh, thought Lloyd. *That good old boy shtick and bad grammar didn't fool him.*

The giant moved closer, now no more than two feet away, and pointed the Glock directly at Lloyd's head. There was no tension in the giant's face, no agitation. This was a confident guy, Lloyd thought, hopefully too confident. "Hands up, pardner."

Lloyd took a settling breath, then his training kicked in. He suddenly tilted his head far to the right and simultaneously flashed his right arm out and under the attacker's gun wrist, smashed it up and grabbed the gun barrel with his left hand and yanked it away. Now the gun was in his hand.

But not for long. Hulkman was now above him on the slope. When he yanked the gun, the guy pitched forward and crashed into Lloyd, and they both went to the ground, the gun flying out of Lloyd's hand, farther down the hill. Lloyd rolled as quickly as he could so that this human tree trunk didn't land full on him. He scrabbled onto his hands and knees. The other guy was surprisingly agile and was quickly on his knees as well. Not three feet separated them. The attacker clasped his hands together and raised them high, intent on smashing them into Lloyd's head. With his bulk, it could have been a killing blow. Instinctively, Lloyd shot his right fist straight out with everything he had behind it. Given their height differences, he punched him square in the balls. The guy loosed his hands and fell straight back.

Lloyd got to his feet, but somehow so did his attacker. He tried to catch his breath as he murmured: "What is this guy made of? He should be clutching his nuts and howling."

Tree Trunk grabbed Lloyd in a bear hug and squeezed, but Lloyd had managed to raise his right arm just before the guy encircled him. The guy squeezed harder, and Lloyd struggled to breathe. Just before he thought that he was going to pass out, Lloyd lowered his right hand and thumbed the big guy's left eye, pushing as hard as he could. This was no TV or movie fight. This was real life or death. There were no rules.

Tree Trunk grunted and let loose and put both hands over his damaged eye. Lloyd fell onto his back and gasped for air. "You fucker," Tree Trunk growled, and came back after him. Now he was enraged. The guy staggered, half-blind, then stumbled over a tree root and started a slow-motion fall directly onto the grounded Lloyd. Just before the guy crashed, Lloyd drew his tac knife, gripped it in both hands, and thrust it up. Tree Trunk fell forward and came down. Amazingly, the knife was perfectly placed so that Tree Trunk's neck fell square on it, the force driving the knife completely through his neck with the point end sticking out the back. He grunted, spasmed, and was dead.

Lloyd lay on his back, with what felt like a thousand pounds of mountain man pressing down on him. He inhaled as deeply as he could. He did not want to be the guy who won this fight but was crushed to death by the loser. Exhausted as he was, he knew that there was no way that he could bench-press this dead weight off of him. Instead, he pushed up as hard as he could and created a little space. Then he wriggled and slid and worked his way sideways out from under, finally, after several minutes, freeing himself.

Now for the really hard part. If there was one sentry, he expected there to be more. Rolling onto his stomach, he got to his knees, then stood up. He didn't want to leave the body here to be discovered by a comrade. Sitting his butt on the ground and digging his heels in, he grabbed one of the guy's ankles in each hand and started to inch toward the crest of the hill. *Thank God*, he thought as he reached it. *Now I'll be going downhill.*

He figured that once he put some space between himself and the ridge he could summon two of the other detectives. One would help him drag the dead man; one would obscure the rut being made in the undergrowth. Ten feet, twenty. He thought about moving the guy sideways and trying to roll him down the hill, but all the trees made that impossible. Thirty feet. The slope was a little steeper here; he was building up some momentum. Finally, he figured that he was far enough away. He radioed to his men for help.

That's when, in the distance, he heard the unmistakable *whump* of AH-64 Apache helicopters. He knew these beasts from his time in the army and in combat. Each Apache was armed with sixteen hellfire missiles, seventy-six 2.75-inch rockets, and 1230mm chain-gun rounds. Those guys down in the clearing thought they were hot shit at the rally; wait until they get a look at this. If Apaches hovering over the compound doesn't convince them to surrender their arms, nothing will.

Two of the detectives who had responded to Lloyd's call now helped him finish moving his assailant down the hill and covering up their trail. Then Lloyd's face formed a wry smile as he thought: In a few minutes, nobody down there is going to be worried about one missing guy.

85.
SANCTUARY STATE

LLOYD NOW HEARD ANOTHER SOUND: motorized equipment, lots of it. From both directions on the roadway, armored troop carriers and Humvees with mounted weaponry approached. He ran into the road and directed them to the entrance through the trees and toward the compound. The lead vehicle simply ran over the gate and kept going, the other vehicles following.

Then came Lieutenant General Pappas himself, in his personal Humvee.

Lloyd directed his men to standby in the woods near the roadway and to alert him if any more militiamen drove up. Then he turned, grabbed his long gun this time from his Whisper, and traipsed up the hill again toward his last vantage point. He would not be a part of whatever confrontation might be about to take place, but he could be a spotter, and he needed to let the troops know where he saw the equipment enter the Quonset hut.

While the detective was huffing up the slope, he thumbed his mic and reached Colonel Sharp.

"Colonel," said Lloyd between gasps.

"Lloyd, where are you?"

"I'm in the woods near the compound."

"No need for you to be there. We've got this."

"Are you here, too?"

"Just turning in."

"Colonel, I saw where they moved their equipment, where they housed the trucks and where they stowed their guns. General Pappas needs to know that. And I can get back to my viewpoint and spot."

Sharp hesitated a moment, then responded. "Okay," he said, "I'll report to the General. When you get to your lookout let me know. But do not engage. I repeat, do not engage."

"Trust me, I have no intention to," Lloyd said and clicked off.

Lloyd wiggled up closer to the apex of the slope. He lifted his binoculars and trained them on the compound. It was alive with activity. They must have had spotters and some idea of what was coming. Add the sound of the Apaches and the agitation was understandable.

Men were running out of one hut and into another. Some of them had their uniform blouses unbuttoned, some wore caps, and others were bareheaded. A few were armed but most were empty-handed. One was barefoot. Despite the spotters, they had obviously been taken by surprise. Still, they looked like they all knew where to go. They must've been assigned to different buildings with whatever responsibilities they had there in case something like this happened. Lloyd did not see anyone leaving the wider compound area. Everyone was heading for cover.

Lloyd clicked his mic and reached out to Colonel Sharp.

"Colonel, the compound was full of men, but they've all run into the buildings, most of them into that big Quonset."

"How many?" Sharp asked.

"This is not a hard count, but based on what I saw at the rally and the activity when those guys came back and joined the others, there could be as many as 350 down there."

"All right, where are they positioned?"

"There are five buildings that I can see. The largest Quonset hut is where the equipment is being stored—trucks, jeeps with mounted machine guns, some ATVs. I'm calling that Hut 1. It's right in the middle. There are three smaller buildings to the south. Some look like they got weapons from Hut 1 and then deployed to the other buildings.

"Who's left in the compound?"

"No more than ten out in the open," Lloyd responded.

"Detective, hold your position. Let me know if anything changes." With that Sharp clicked off.

Moments later, Sharp clicked back to Lloyd.

"Detective," Sharp said, "we are positioned east and west of the compound. The Apaches will cover the flanks. General Pappas is here and is going to call out to whoever is in charge down there. No one knows what the response will be. We can expect these guys to be unpredictable. Let me know if you see anything move in response to what the general says. Do you have any view of the backs of the buildings?"

"None."

"All right, we'll put eyes on the back. Stand by."

The next sound that Lloyd heard was the commanding voice of General Pappas. Lloyd had been in briefings with Pappas on numerous occasions. As the head of the detectives, he needed to coordinate with all the officers. He knew that Pappas had a cool head. He was battle-hardened, coming through Ukraine and Iran and Belarus. He was an imposing figure. Tall, fit, dark-complected, clean-shaven, square-jawed. Whoever was in charge down in the compound would not be able to see the general, but his voice was as powerful as his image. Somewhere between a tenor and a baritone, it was clear but weighty at the same time. Pappas addressed the compound.

"Attention, the compound! I am General Pappas, commander of Region Four. I want to address the person in charge."

Down in the compound, nothing moved. All doors to the huts remained shut.

"This can be resolved without engagement, but only if you respond," Pappas added.

Lloyd kept his binoculars trained on the compound, slowly scanning from one hut to the next. He had finally been able to slow his breathing after his earlier ordeal and his climb back up the slope. Despite that, he could feel the perspiration forming on his forehead and above his lips.

Moments ticked by. Lloyd's muscles involuntarily contracted, and he tried to flex while holding his position. He had to keep telling himself to breathe. If the militia did not answer, he knew that Pappas wouldn't send his men into the compound to try to dislodge the cadre and risk who knew how many casualties. Instead, he would give a final warning and then unleash a hellish fire.

Another moment passed.

In the compound, one half of the door to Hut 1 pushed open. Out stepped a tall lean man. Lloyd focused his binoculars on him. He wore camouflage similar to those who had been at the rally. His hatless head was covered with a shock of white hair, rustling in the breeze that rippled through the compound. He looked to be in his mid-fifties.

The man took several steps forward and, using a megaphone, announced himself: "I am William James Percy the Fourth, commander of the True Americans. You are trespassing on private property. You are hereby directed to leave immediately."

"Holy shit!" Lloyd mouthed. "William James fucking Percy himself! We've hit the mother lode."

General Pappas responded quickly.

"We meet at last, *Mr.* Percy. We've been chasing you all over the country. You've committed more treasonous offenses than I can count. And you're in violation of about fifty other laws. You know and I know that I am here to seize those weapons, and I will do so. I would prefer to do it peacefully. And you must know that we've eliminated most of your allies. Simply put, you're next."

Percy remained standing outside of Hut 1, appearing unintimidated.

"My allies were patriots and gave their lives for a just cause."

Percy took several steps backward toward the double doors. "Those so-called laws are denying us our God-given rights. I repeat my demand that you withdraw."

Pappas had had enough.

"I will not continue this prattle," he said. "You have three minutes to lay down your weapons and for you and all of your men to submit to the army's jurisdiction."

Simultaneously with Pappas finishing, two Apaches rose up from either end of the compound. *That'll do it*, thought Lloyd. Percy turned and stepped resolutely back into the large Hut 1. The Apaches maintained their position.

The seconds clicked by. Lloyd knew that most of these confrontations in other regions ended with surrender and seizure. While he may have sometimes struck a cavalier attitude to tamp down his anxiety and be able to function in these explosive situations, he prayed that this would end the same way. He believed fully in what he had committed himself to, but the irony of so many people losing their lives as The Plan was enforced was not lost on him.

"Come on now, Percy," he mouthed, "give it up."

The doors to Hut 1 were opened slightly to admit Percy. As soon as he disappeared, both doors were thrown wide. Two men raced out, dropped to one knee, each shouldering a missile launcher.

"My God," said Lloyd. "Who knew they had those?"

Each man targeted one of the Apaches. The launchers looked to Lloyd to be MANPADS, available all over the world on the black market. They launched heat-seeking missiles that acquired targets by detecting the heat of an engine. Lloyd knew the Apaches had the Black Hole infrared suppression system. It dissipated the heat of the copter's exhaust to confuse the missiles. But no system is perfect. Floyd held his breath.

The MANPADS launched. One missile missed wildly, but the other one clipped the tail rotor of the second chopper. The Apache veered and wavered, and the pilot appeared to be trying to find a landing spot, but the woods were so dense nothing was available. The Apache went into a yawl as the pilot lost control and dove toward the compound. Lloyd gasped as it flipped and hit and exploded.

A cheer went up from inside the hut, and then the EagleCat that Percy had stolen in Asquandon rolled out. The gunner manning the Cat .50-caliber prepared to open fire, but Pappas was faster. He had ordered the second Apache to engage. It fired two hydra rockets at the Cat and obliterated it, shrapnel ripping through the compound.

"I didn't want this," Pappas said, "I didn't want this." He shook his head. "Percy, you arrogant bastard, you just killed your men."

Then he ordered the assault.

The remaining Apache swung around and lined up with the hut doors. The machine guns mounted on the Humvees opened fire. The Apache launched a Hellfire missile through the hut doors. A millisecond later a gigantic explosion blew all four hut walls out, followed by a series of concussions as the munitions housed inside were triggered by the Hellfire.

Pappas watched the leveling of the hut without any outward emotion, then exhaled the breath he didn't know he was holding. He gazed in awe and anger at the debris that littered the compound—not only pieces of the ceramic-covered walls and chunks of unrecognizable metal, but human body parts, severed arms and legs, and one decapitated head still spinning across the campground.

"Goddamn you, Percy," he mouthed. "So many lives."

Pappas now ordered his troops forward to secure the rest of the buildings, but first, as they descended from the tree line, he used the mic again.

"Anyone still in the buildings, leave your weapons and exit with your hands up. No one else needs to die."

The doors of the remaining buildings opened and a line of clearly shocked men, their arms raised, walked into the middle of the camp. They eyed the crumbled remains of the ceramic hut, then were ordered to their knees and zip-tied by US soldiers.

Pappas sat down heavily in his Humvee. Fires burned in the camp, painting shadow men on the ground behind the flames. Pappas wondered if the shadows were of his men and the prisoners or of the ghosts of the dead.

He didn't know if he could still tell the difference.

86.
BARRATT

BARRATT AND BOBBY WERE in the Oval Office, debriefing on the Percy battle. Barratt had already met with General Pappas and others. That meeting dealt with the difficult details, the handling of the arrests, and the detention of the surviving cadre members. Barratt had been complimentary of the military, but stoic. Sitting with Bobby was more real.

"This is huge," Barratt said. "It looks like the other cadres, or what's left of them, are slinking away. Now we need to keep the process going."

"Yeah," said Bobby, then: "God, it's been a tough road."

"Tough is an understatement," Barratt said. "You know I've been lying awake at night for months, seeing all those victims. Now...now I'm seeing all those dead bodies from the Percy camp and all the rest. My bedroom is so crowded there's hardly room for me."

"Eli, Percy, and Turner and the rest of them made their choices."

"I know, I know," said Barratt.

Rising from the desk, he turned to the window, looking outside for comfort, for distraction. All he saw were ghosts on the lawn and in the trees staring back at him with accusing eyes and bloody faces. He knew when he started this that there would be a price he would have to pay. It was coming due.

"All right, Bobby, let's go down to the conference room. I want to talk about our next step."

The short walk through the hallway took longer than usual, Barratt's stride lacking its typical confidence, the oppressive burden he carried growing heavier every day.

The Pacific Northwest is generally considered to include the states of Oregon, Washington, and Idaho. The region is part of the Ring of Fire, where the plates under the Earth's crust have created dramatic natural beauty but also threaten dangerous disruptions like volcanoes and earthquakes. It's a land of sparkling blue-water lakes and imposing mountains, teeming with wildlife and old-growth forest. It has been home to numerous native populations for thousands of years. It is now home to some fifteen million people and includes some of the fastest-growing cities in the country.

When Elijah Barratt was elected president, it was also home to one of the most notorious cadres in the country. Despite its population growth, the still expansive wilderness and some friendly local governments provided cover for such groups as they trained and organized.

Barratt decided that it would be a good place to bring the Safe America Tour. He had been holding rallies and giving speeches around the country, explaining The Plan, giving the justification, reporting the stunning decrease in civilian death and injury. His orders were certainly not universally popular, but more and more supported his actions as they saw the progress. His approval rating was now, amazingly, over 60 percent.

Barratt had convened a meeting in the small dining room located steps away from the Oval Office. Previously, the room had a small round dining table, relatively modest appointments, and a tiny TV.

Barratt was glad to see when he took office that one of his predecessors had upgraded it. It now included a rectangular table seating eight, more modern decor, and a huge television. He had always preferred to work at a table, where he could spread out his organized yellow pads and tablets and align his favorite pens. He only reluctantly used the facing couches in the Oval Office, being more comfortable with a solid front.

He sat with his back to the room's two floor-to-ceiling windows and prepared for the objections. Besides Bobby, the meeting included the head of his Secret Service detail, the director of Homeland Security, and the director of the FBI.

Barratt opened the meeting. "You have all been advised that I am continuing the Safe America Tour. The next leg includes a rally in the Pacific Northwest. I understand that there are some misgivings about that idea. I want your candid input."

Bobby didn't hesitate. "It's Gunland. It's the Wild West. You're not going to be winning hearts and minds out there after you've taken away their guns."

"You're being melodramatic," said the president. "The organized attacks have all but ended, the threats have reduced, and the polls show more and more people see The Plan as a good thing. And even if you're right, that shouldn't stop us from bringing the message to them. At this point they've only had a skewed view of why we're doing this."

"Mr. President, these people are unpersuadable. They really do believe that it's their God-given right to stroll the streets with AK-15s over their shoulders and pistols on their hips. There's nothing you can do there that is going to change their minds."

"Bobby, I'm asking people to do something that they are genuinely afraid to do. I'm asking them to help me take the guns away. Many of them are fearful, with good reason, that they might still be caught up in a violent response."

Barratt rose from his chair and stood behind it, doing backbends and side bends to loosen his muscles. Dawn River lingered not only in his mind, but also in his body.

"Some see this as confirmation of their worst fears and feel compelled to resist," continued Barratt. "I need to persuade everyone else that The Plan could save their lives, save their children. I can't barricade myself in the White House and expect them to believe us."

Barratt turned and stepped to one of the undraped windows. He would have loved to open a window and feel the fresh breeze, but they were bulletproof for a reason and had to stay shut. Standing with his hands clasped behind his back, he looked out over the Rose Garden, with its manicured lawn. All his life, he had been comforted by green. The green of the lawn that ran down to the water when the family vacationed on Lake Placid, the green of the common area in college where he tossed the football around, where some professors held class under the oak trees, where couples lay next to each other on the lawns, pretending to study. He sighed. Those days, full of promise and devoid of chaos, were long gone.

He turned back to the room.

Now, in this moment, the moment that had chosen him all those years ago at Dawn River, green meant *go*. Keep going. Keep moving forward.

"How can I ask them to join us, to be strong, if I don't show them that strength in their president, show them that I'm not afraid?"

The head of his Secret Service detail was exasperated.

"Mr. President, the scenario you're proposing is a very dangerous one. We can move the site for your speech to the open field as was discussed, and that lets us take most of the structures out of play. We can bring Marine One in from the east and go straight to the site, but we can't control that entire section of the state. You've seen the death threats that have been made since this started. We've taken all of them from that area seriously. Some of them have clearly come from people who are incapable of following through, but we haven't been able to clear every one. Those we must consider legitimate."

Barratt had retaken his seat. He looked at everyone in turn, coming to rest on the Secret Service agent.

"I don't wish to take unnecessary risks, but I can't be controlled by the threats. We get them every day. I would sit here paralyzed…" Barratt regretted his wording immediately. When he first awoke in the hospital after Dawn River, he feared that was exactly what he was. "I can't let my administration be stymied every time there's a threat." Barratt laid his hands flat on the table, moving them forward and back and feeling its solid strength. "Andy, I've trusted you since the day you were assigned to me before the election. I trust you now to keep the first lady and me safe."

"The first lady! Sir, you don't mean…sir, you're not saying…"

"Lucy is coming with me, and so is Gabrielle," said Barratt. "It was their idea. They're as invested in this as I am." Barratt paused and lowered his eyes. "What happened at the concert still haunts all of us," he said in a soft voice. "They want to show the country how crucial this is to our survival as a democracy."

Barratt heard Bobby huffing and trying to contain himself until he just couldn't. "Mr. President, please, sir, this will excite your enemies even more."

Barratt rose from his seat again, this time signaling that the meeting was over.

"Gentlemen," he said, "you have the itinerary, and you will make this happen. And you should know that Ariel—you all know who she is—and her partner Jimmy will be in the first row of the audience."

MAN, 22, ARRESTED IN CHRISTMAS NIGHT SHOOTING THAT KILLED 1, INJURED 3 IN BOYNTON

The Palm Beach Post

87.
CONVERGENCE

TWO WEEKS LATER, Barratt looked at the crowd before him. The crisp October morning had given way to a warmer afternoon, an unseasonably soft breeze coming off the surrounding mountains. He had directed that the stage be situated with the mountains as a backdrop. The open grassy plain where the platform was located and the elegance of the azure sky and snowcapped purple mountains were calming to him, protective. *Purple mountains majesty*, he thought.

Later, the crowd would be estimated at over thirty thousand. The great majority of them, Barratt could see, were there to support him. Cordoned off were various protest groups, yelling and waving signs, but their voices were drowned out by the crowd chanting Barratt's name and "U-S-A!" Barratt turned to Lucy and Gabby and Bobby where they sat on the stage, smiled, and raised his eyebrows as if to say, *See, I told you we had friends out here.* Barratt knew that his party's leaders had bussed in supporters from the wider region, but he also knew that many of them would not have traveled here unless they were believers.

The Secret Service had called in the police and the National Guard from the local area for increased security. Everyone in the crowd had gone through metal detectors and body scans and were barred from bringing backpacks or bags in with them. Barratt stood behind a wide, tall transparent bulletproof shield.

Despite this, Andy Parke, the head of the president's security detail, was practically apoplectic. He had argued for an enclosed venue with a capacity under one thousand where all ingress, egress, angles, and back areas could be controlled. He had continually complained to the chief of staff that, instead, here they were in the middle of some endless rolling plain, impossible to patrol completely. His team had secured a mile-wide radius around the stage, but the plains were seemingly endless. At a building venue, he could post rooftop marksmen, limit the number of people, take away any line of attack.

"What do we have instead of a secure auditorium?" he rhetorically asked Bobby. "A bunch of bucket trucks borrowed from the White Mountain Utility Company, with sharpshooters trying to keep their balance up there."

"It's what the boss wanted, Andy," Bobby said. "You don't win that kind of argument with him."

"Bobby, honest to God, if I didn't know better—or *hope* better—I'd wonder if the man had a death wish."

"Not him. He's always saying he has too much more work to do to even slow down, let alone kick the bucket," said Bobby. "Pun intended," he added, as he tossed his head up toward the sharpshooters, but there was no humor in his voice.

Barratt looked at the teleprompter set in the podium. He was scheduled to begin speaking in a few minutes, but the crowd had not quite settled.

"Let's get this moving," he said to himself. He tugged his cuffs and stopped himself from looking at his watch. Under his seemingly calm demeanor, he still fought the demons, the doubts, not about the rightness of The Plan but what he had done to implement it. Was he protecting the country or subjecting it to the domineering autocrat some accused him of being? Was he sacrificing the democracy or saving it?

At least the weather is perfect, thought Barratt.

At least the weather is perfect, thought Stanley Knight.

Once again, he had been able to time the retrieval of his sniper rifle to the gaps in the helicopters' flyovers, avoiding the enhanced magnetometers. He had also constructed a ceramic carrying case for the rifle in an effort to avoid detection. The sniper nest he had constructed four days earlier, after the president's visit was announced, was so perfectly created that no one could detect it. He lay inside the depression he had burrowed out, under the gray-green sagebrush cover he had constructed, clad in desert camouflage suited to the light brown grasses spread across the plain. His face was painted with a blend of olive, green, and black camo cream, his flop hat covered with some of the dry grasses. Used a tube to prevent barrel and scope glare. Raising the nest cover just enough to confirm his line of sight, he peered across the endless plan toward the stage. He knew that wind speed, humidity, and time of day would affect his trajectory. He had accounted for the impact of gravity, what snipers refer to as "bullet drop." He had considered the Coriolis effect: bullets fired in the southern hemisphere tended to drift to the left, while bullets fired in the northern hemisphere, where he was, tended to drift to the right.

Barratt looked again at the people before him: all ages, Black, White, Latino, Asian, Middle Eastern. Some in jeans and tan Carhartt jackets, others in dark coats and ties, Sikhs in white turbans, many men wearing cowboy hats, many women wearing a gray or black hajib, younger people in the latest urban style. He felt at times overwhelmed by the ecumenical support from different faiths and cultures. This could, he thought, turn out to be exactly what he hoped for, public affirmation that had grown as the murder rate and total shootings dropped and dropped again after the firearm ban was implemented.

Despite his preparation, Stanley Knight regretted that he never could afford all the equipment that he wanted for a shot like this. But he also believed in the righteousness of what he was about to do, the perceived patriotic duty that he would discharge, and the thanks that he would receive. Others might think him arrogant, thought Knight, especially because his nest was 1,900 yards from the president's podium, a prodigious distance for the best snipers. "Best snipers. That's me now," Stanley Knight said to himself.

And how could this not work? he mused. Was it coincidence that his one remaining obstacle had been finding the perfect opportunity, and now Barratt had come to his own backyard? No, he answered himself, this convergence was meant to be.

He established his tripod, finished sighting in, factored the wind speed and the humidity. And waited.

Barratt waited as more people settled and started to quiet. He had eschewed an introduction, wanting the connection with those gathered before him to be personal and immediate. In a moment he would address the crowd.

Stanley Knight lay perfectly still, as he had trained himself to do. He formed a satisfied smile. All those years, he thought, of being the butt of jokes, being the fall guy for pranks, being blamed by his old man for everything that went wrong in that miserable bastard's life. All of his anger had led him to this, had led him here, exactly where he was supposed to be.

As he looked over the gathering before him, Barratt made eye contact with Ariel and Jimmy, seated in a VIP section near the stage. *Kismet*, he thought. The Dawn River tragedy was the impetus for his life's work and—despite its tragic nature—for Ariel and Jimmy to become a part of this existential movement, and a part of each other's lives. Thousands, no *millions*, of people's lives had been changed for the better because of the ban, their hope for their country restored. This convergence of minds and bodies on this broad, placid plain, he knew now, was his destiny.

"Just give me a clean target," murmured Knight, his finger ready beside the trigger. He was flush with thoughts of how he would be celebrated for reclaiming his country's freedoms. With Barratt gone, The Plan would fall apart.

As Ariel and Jimmy smiled and waved, Barratt felt compelled to move at least a little closer to them. He stepped to his right and toward the edge of the stage, leaving the protection of the bulletproof shield. He raised his hand to wave at them as Agent Parke rushed to move him back behind the podium. Barratt paused at the end of the stage and with a grin nodded several times toward the two remarkable young people he had come to know so well. He spread his arms wide as if to hug them.

Stanley Knight squeezed the trigger.

TWO BROTHERS WITH LONG CRIMINAL HISTORIES KILLED AMID STANDOFF WITH CLARKSVILLE POLICE, FOUR OFFICERS AND HOSTAGE INJURED

ClarksvilleNow.com

Clarksville, Tennessee

88.
LUCY AND ELI

LUCY SAT ALONE IN THE anteroom of the Capitol rotunda. She wore azure, Elijah's favorite color, and asked Gabrielle and Bobby, Ariel and Jimmy, and any mourners who could, to follow suit. Not black, not dark, but elegant and bright, the color of a clear and hopeful sky. Although the casket would be closed for the viewing, she insisted it remain open now, as she sat with her husband. Within the hour, the coffin would be moved into the rotunda, where Elijah would lie in state with thousands expected to pass by.

She rested her hands on Elijah's as she leaned in, trying to smile at him but simultaneously weeping. "Oh, Eli," she said, "this is too soon. I'm not ready."

Standing, she stretched against the stiffness in her neck and legs. Her nights since the assassination had been long and sleepless. She craved rest but dared not close her eyes; when she did, she saw the horrific scene play out in her mind over and over again.

She sat back down and rested her elbows on the edge of the casket and her face in her hands. There was a light knock at the anteroom door. It opened, and Bobby stepped halfway through.

"Lucy, they need to take Eli in."

Lucy freed her face from her hands and nodded okay as Bobby left. She reached for her clutch and opened it. She removed a photo of the two of them, wrapped in soft white towels, giggling, squeezed somehow together on a single chaise by the White House pool, caught in mid-laugh when Gabrielle took their photo. Lucy placed the photo in Elijah's hands. On the back she had written: *Lucy loves Eli.*

A moment later the funeral director tapped on the door and walked into the anteroom with his assistant. Before he could speak, Lucy nodded to him and stepped reluctantly back from the coffin. He bowed his head in silent response and approached. He and the assistant reached up and pulled the coffin lid closed. It thunked as it shut, the sound echoing through the room. Lucy shuddered as it did. Then he turned the six levers to secure the lid in place. Each one snapped as it locked in, Lucy startled each time, the retorts like a slap. The director signaled his assistant, and Lucy's friend, lover, husband, the father of her child, her partner in life, was wheeled away.

Elijah's viewing was scheduled to last one day, ending at 9:00 p.m., but as the end time approached there were still hundreds of people in line outside. Lucy insisted that the doors would not be closed on them. She acknowledged each mourner with a nod or a reflexive smile.

Around midnight, a striking figure in a tight-fitting blue suit, hair pulled back into a ponytail, wearing sunglasses, appeared in line. Lucy looked quizzical, wondering who the person was, until Gabrielle, standing by her side, whispered to her: "That's Dani Blue."

A sea of azure flowed through the rotunda, hats, dresses, blazers, scarves. As the hours passed, Lucy and Gabrielle surrendered to fatigue and sat in chairs flanking the Lincoln catafalque, the black-draped support on which Lincoln's coffin had rested and where Elijah's now lay.

At 1:00 a.m., when the last person had passed through, Lucy and Gabrielle made their way back to the White House and collapsed on Lucy's bed. They held each other wordlessly and gradually, gratefully, fell asleep.

Six months later, former Vice President Meredith Jackson, now President Jackson, stood before a joint session of Congress. The reaction to President Barratt's death was immediate and profound. An attack on Barratt had been threatened constantly after the president's executive orders. It had been specifically called for by right-wing podcasters and cadre leaders, and subtly by cable provocateurs, yet his death was still a shock—the suddenness, foreclosing goodbyes, in front of his family, in front of the world.

His assassination was, in a horribly ironic way, thought Jackson, the most effective step in Barratt's long journey to deal with gun violence in the United States.

Jackson paused and looked out over the audience. Members of the House and Senate. Lucy, Gabrielle, Jimmy, and Ariel were seated in the Senate chamber well. The balcony was peopled with many of the survivors of the Dawn River Massacre, as it had become known, and others whose lives were inexorably changed by its aftermath. Roland Turret, Anna Appleton, and several other members of the Dawn River Associates. Magnus Raphael, the attorney who represented Barratt before the Supreme Court, wept when he heard the news of Barratt's death. Always so confident and assertive, he sat quietly, a mask of persistent sadness covering his face.

Jackson had invited many of those connected to Dawn River because she recognized that it was the singular impetus that had propelled Barratt on his quest. But, she thought, he was no Don Quixote, tilting at windmills. No, he had found real evil and gave his life fighting it.

She started her address with condolences to Lucy and Gabrielle. She recounted Barratt's indefatigable commitment and inexhaustible energy. Then she continued her remarks: "Consistent with my agreement with Congress, I have executed a series of executive orders canceling the national state of emergency, the declaration of martial law, and the implementation of The Plan. And I am humbled today to be signing the President Elijah Barratt Firearms Reform Act. It is a monumental accomplishment. I believe he would be proud."

She paused. This wasn't everything he wanted, she thought, but it was so much more than anyone else ever thought possible. As she signed multiple copies of the legislation, she marveled at what the bipartisan efforts had produced: banning sales of automatic weapons to civilians, requiring universal background checks, fingerprint locks, and a litany of provisions that had always previously died in committee.

When she finished signing, the audience mostly stood and applauded. There was no cheering. It was all in all a somber occasion.

Senator Grammar did not join in with the applause. She remained in her seat; her face was stern and resentful. Her plans to be the next president, in her mind almost guaranteed when Barratt had announced his gun seizure plan, had again been upended.

Jackson stepped back from the podium and summoned Lucy and Gabrielle to the dais. She hugged both of them in turn and handed each one a signed copy of the new legislation and ceremonial pens.

"This is epic," she said to Lucy, taking her hand. "What President Barratt did made a difference and saved lives."

ONE DEPUTY DEAD, 6 WOUNDED IN DOUGLAS COUNTY APARTMENT COMPLEX SHOOTING

FOX31
Denver

89.
THE END

"MEET ME ON THE OTHER SIDE," was the cryptic message Ariel had left on Jimmy's nightstand when she slipped out of their bed and quietly left the house. She stood now in the denser woods on the far side of the stream from the clearing, on the eastern slope of the valley. A light spring rain had fallen overnight, scenting the woods with the clean, fresh smell that always left her feeling that something good was coming. The purple and the white rhododendrons were still full of blooms; the ash and the birch formed a backdrop for the wildflowers. Ariel gazed down the valley to the footbridge that crossed the stream to the north, then looked back toward the clearing on the other side. She could see it easily, but standing in the trees she was intentionally hidden.

Then Jimmy came into view across the valley. Although he would have to backtrack to the trail to reach the path down to the footbridge, he stopped in the clearing, knelt by Hank's marker, and tenderly brushed away the maple spinners that had fallen there. He stood and looked across the valley. Ariel smiled with the knowledge that he couldn't see her.

Jimmy returned to the trail and moved north until he came upon the steep down path that led to the footbridge, then started across. Ariel loved watching him move, his lithe, athletic body showing the confidence he had regained since they had first met, loved seeing the remnants of the boy he must have been before Dawn River, seeing the man she wanted to be with now.

Ariel had crossed to the eastern side several times, reveling in the solitude, happening across the dilapidated old cabin she stood near now. She found comfort in the remains of someone's long-ago home, something that had survived.

She could see that Jimmy had crossed the bridge and noticed the blazes she had left for him, small spots of pink, his least favorite color, her most favorite, and a source of ribbing between them. Ariel popped out of the trees as Jimmy stepped into the clearing in front of the cabin. He seemed momentarily startled, but then his smile erased his look of surprise. They kissed lightly as she took his hand and spread her other hand wide to show him what she had prepared: doubled-up blankets spread on the ground, with lunch and wine placed at one end. As Jimmy was admiring the setup, a plaintive whining and a little yip sounded from behind the cabin.

"What the heck is that?" Jimmy asked.

"Wait here," said Ariel, as she disappeared behind the remains of the building. She returned with a yipping, barking little pup on a leash.

"He's a rescue," Ariel said, "so he fits right in with us. They didn't know his breed; I think there's some retriever in there, but it's just a guess." A slight wind rustled the treetops and caused some loose leaves to dance around her feet. "I know that no one can ever take Hank's place, but this little guy, well...life goes on, right?" She held the leash out toward Jimmy. "Are you okay that I did this?"

Jimmy ignored the leash. Instead, he dropped to his knees and scooped the little dog into his arms, getting puppy kisses at the same time that his eyes were tearing up.

"Yeah, babe, it's okay."

All three of them had lunch, then the puppy curled up on the pad that Ariel had brought for him and placed away from the blanket that she and Jimmy lay on. Hank Two, the name that Jimmy had immediately given him, was soon softly snoring.

Ariel's smiling look was returned by Jimmy as they wordlessly moved into each other and made tender, slow love on the blankets. Afterward, they lay in each other's arms.

"I was ready to accept that I would never be happy again," whispered Jimmy. "Then I met a Disney princess named Ariel."

They laughed together, then Ariel went quiet for a beat before she said, "I was so consumed by my mission after Dawn River that I thought I could never be present for a lover, a mate. Now I am."

They slipped into sleep and stayed there until they were awakened by Hank Two's whining and scratching. They gathered everything up, put it in the duffel that Ariel had brought, hoisted it, and tied it off in one of the trees, away from scavengers. The three of them started to walk farther east, but Ariel turned and took a long look back across the valley, to the clearing, to Hank's place. It seemed to her to be so far away. They started to move again, the stream behind them, Two loosed from his leash and prancing ahead.

They trekked up the hillside. Ariel was loving the peaceful look on Jimmy's face, so different from the sad look she saw when they first met. She knew that this was not the end of their journey. There were other streams to cross, other hills to ascend, other valleys to explore.

About two thousand miles away, deep in the woods of Northern Idaho, ten men sat around a campfire. The uniforms they wore had no insignia of rank and some were threadbare. Their dialogue was loud and angry, but their intention was clear.

They were plotting how to rearm the cadres.

ACKNOWLEDGMENTS

THIS IS MY FIRST NOVEL. I was surprised at just how complex the process was but even more amazed at the support and encouragement that flows from the local writing community. A big thank you to all of the writers in the workshops I've attended, those in the novel writers discussion groups and frankly all of the members of the Rehoboth Beach Writers Guild. Special thanks to my beta readers, Stella Marie Alden and Walt Curran.

A very special thanks to Maribeth Fischer, the founder and executive director of the Writers Guild, critiquer extraordinaire, cheerleader and friend.

And most of all, thank you to my wife, Cheryl, for her constant support, encouragement, and advice. And to Willow. I wouldn't be here without her.

ABOUT THE AUTHOR

S.J. LEONE served as an Assistant County Prosecutor and then started the full-time legal department for his home county. He won convictions for sexual assault, armed robbery, and murder. He is a member of the Rehoboth Beach Writers Guild and a frequent participant in workshops and discussion groups. He lives and writes in Delaware with his wife, Cheryl, and their calico tabby Willow.

www.ingramcontent.com/pod-product-compliance
Lightning Source LLC
Chambersburg PA
CBHW050610110726
47899CB00001B/57
* 9 7 8 1 6 3 3 3 7 9 5 9 6 *